Alastair's Dilemma

by
Michele A. Fabiano

KCM PUBLISHING
A DIVISION OF KCM DIGITAL MEDIA, LLC

CREDITS

Alastair's Dilemma by Michele A. Fabiano

ISBN-13: 978-1-955620-13-0
ebook ISBN: 978-1-955620-14-7

First Edition

Publisher: Michael Fabiano
KCM Publishing
www.kcmpublishing.com

This book is dedicated to

Pastor Marcia Stanford

For her deep understanding of faith...
And putting it all in perspective with her passionate and
unique delivery...

Acknowledgements

I have my mother to thank for her contribution about the saints and my catholic upbringing. This section originated from growing up and listening to her praying to many of the thousands of saints when she was in need of assistance. When I talk to her on the phone she will suggest I pray to Saint Anthony or some other saint depending on my current situation of need at the time.

Now married, the tradition continues, as I tell my husband to pray to Saint Anthony when *he* is looking for something, which is typically daily! Just recently I told him to tell his friend to get a Saint Joseph statue to help sell their home.

The incredulous grin that spreads across his face is followed by, "Are you serious?"

Ignoring him, I continue with the instructions, finishing with, "and it must be buried upside down. Call my mother if you think I'm joking."

Naturally this evokes a host of conversations and dialogue about religion, but it's all good. I just find it ironic how such little things become woven into a much larger tapestry…

As always, I am eternally grateful to my friend Laura Coffey, who shares my love for reading and is always wondering what I'm going to write next. She takes the time to read, edit, suggest, and lend support on my writing journey. After the first edit we agreed something was missing, and days later on my drive to work Alastair was born. During lunch I quickly scripted a few paragraphs. Later that evening, I turned on the computer and began to *re-write the entire manuscript.* I am filled with gratitude for our friendship, laughter, and that our paths crossed. Again, just more threads of the tapestry…

Deepest, deepest, deepest gratitude to Pastor Marcia Stanford, who never really realized the impact she has had on me. Her vibrant and funny personality was such a welcome addition to the team! Her door is always open for a question about faith, religion, God, or anything. She *always* has something insightful to help make sense of the challenges of the day or life. Pastor Marcia is also good at putting life in perspective. Like the time she easily answered my question, which I'm sure many of us ask at times, "Why is this happening?"

"Michele, God tests and stretches you with difficult stuff… or things happen because he wants to get your attention…"

Observing from a distance, as I move about the building and deal with the behind the scenes life of facilities management, I can't help but take notice of the bits and pieces of her conversations as I hurry by, on my way to some building issue, or listen to her voice resonating from the lecture hall – sometimes it's just a word, phrase or a sentence – and I realize, God is listening and just gave me the answer.

One day, during my long drive to work, I prayed to God to point me in the right direction as I struggled with a situation. A construction detour took me right by a church and in big letters there was Pastor Marcia Stanford's name on the marquee. I thought to myself as I passed the church, God has a sense of humor as he was telling me there is someone in my own building – go and seek her out! More threads of the tapestry…

Many thanks to Kate Goldner, former colleague from the IT department, who stopped by my office to fix my computer one afternoon and we inadvertently began talking about writing. We were discussing my book, *The Agony Continues. Michelangelo's Search for Art in 20th NYC* - in which Michelangelo asks St. Peter for a vacation, so he can see the art of the 20th century. Intrigued, Kate answered, "I see Heaven as this hierarchy and once wrote a paper on it…"

Stunned, my jaw dropped and mouth fell open in disbelief as she spoke her thoughts. *I had just typed those very words moments earlier*. Before she stopped by, I had been sitting in the café during lunch doing some editing and had just asked God for a sign if I was headed in the right direction since I was *re-writing* the entire manuscript. As any writer knows, it's an ambitious undertaking.

I had been questioning my intentions during this massive re-write and took Kate's comment as a sign. I went home and forged ahead. Many thanks to Kate, for having the *courage* to move on and for thinking about the possibilities above! More threads of the tapestry...

The same night, I received a text from NFL football player Tim Tebow. My husband looked at me narrowly and wanted to know *why* and *how* he has my number and what I was doing talking to him? I explained I had signed up for his devotions and messages about faith, which are sent via text. Part of it read, "…we have tremendous purpose in this life…God created you for a reason and has a plan for your life…there is purpose in why…"

Sometimes the message has to be repeated in order for it to be received. Again, just more threads of the tapestry...

There are many people that have come in and out of my life that have continued to impact me on my writing journey. I am and will continually be eternally thankful to Bill Jarnigan, my silent muse of encouragement. You make me work harder with every chapter, paragraph, phrase, misspelled word, and sentence, the struggle is real - you taught me more than you will ever know. To that I am forever grateful and truly blessed! Again, more threads…

Unfortunately Bill passed during the writing of this novel. I hope he has his wings and is proudly looking down on all those he touched throughout his life.

I am eternally grateful to fellow artist, reader, and colleague, Diana Scotti. I am honored and humbled for your feedback and to have my books added and *catalogued* to your *massive* collection! Many, many thanks for your support! Keep reading!

Special thanks to my friend, 'HVAC Professor' Mike Dymond, whose continued love of learning is an inspiration! I hope others who cross your path realize what you have to offer. Every conversation and lesson has not been wasted. Now just finish the book so we can laugh more!

To my colleague Pam Walker, a huge, bright shining star, who radiates strong convictions of faith, hope and love! Occasionally, popping in her office, she never asks why I'm questioning, but is quick to have the right words about faith, or the trials of life – I smile and just put up my hand and say, "I got it, message received." Again, more threads… Also, many, many, many *THANKS*, for the laughter, understanding the *insanity*, your *love of reading,* and for *taking a leap of faith* and reading, *You're Not A F*ucking Bachelor Anymore.* This was huge! I can't say it enough; thanks for laughing with me!

Many thanks for all those who participated and provided feedback on the cover selection. I love the process and am always amazed at how a group of people can see different things. Special thanks to fellow readers, Eva Dawson, Theresa Hart, Laura Deal, Brooke Chappell, Joe Rosasco, Sharon Hoffman, Teresa Fassel, and Pam Walker – I am filled with gratitude for your comments and weighing in on the project.

Special thanks to Ryan Fitzgerald, colleague and IT extraordinaire, who patiently explained the consequences of outdated operating systems and why my twelve-year-old computer crashed. He offered support and suggestions for a new purchase. Without him, my manuscript would be lost in the 'mysterious cloud.'

To Wayne - artist, writer, poet, master of words, creative genius - and for your unwavering inspiration of faith of which, I'm continually astounded. You taught me more than you will ever know.

As always, deepest gratitude to KCM Publishing and staff! To editors, copy editors, cover artists, and layout designers on this journey. I am always amazed at the process and blessed to be part of the trip!

Much thanks to my husband, Joe, who spent too much time in the Apple store, while I attempted to pick out a new computer! He has also become one of the best beta readers! Not his typical genre of reading, I knew he wasn't sure as he started reading. I smiled when I found him engrossed in the pages, trying to figure it out. I appreciate your patience and encouragement! Thank you for our conversations about religion, listening to me read chapters, and answering questionings about an idea or your thoughts about a character I was developing.

When I enter the room and say, "So I was thinking…" he politely smiles and presses the mute button on the television remote and patiently listens. Eternal gratitude for supporting my writing, putting up with the frustrations, notes, mess in the house, paper, printing, computer issues, editing and the insurmountable *time* it takes and, who also, is still waiting for me to make enough money so he can get a Ford-F150!

I told him he'd be better off *praying* about it! LOL! ☺

Contents

Introduction

READING! READING! READING! READING! READING! READING!

Next to learning how to talk, it's one of the many things our parents introduce us to when we first arrive into the world.

As a child my mother made sure her children had plenty of books to read. The Cat in the Hat, Green Eggs and Ham, Winnie the Pooh, the Little Engine that Could, The Tale of Peter Rabbit, Paddington Bear, Charlotte's Web, and many more crammed the shelves and bookcases in our home. We soon made a critical pilgrimage - and she introduced me to the library!

Two things happened at the library. First, I was the recipient of a library card, which was like winning a "major award!" Second we couldn't leave without an armful of books to read. As I grew older, I discovered there was so much more waiting beyond the shelves of the young adult section besides Nancy Drew, the Hardy Boys, and Harlequin romance novels!

Decades later, my girlfriend commented about *all* the books in my house. We laughed and swapped many stories regarding childhood trips to the library and our love of reading imparted by our moms. Although both avid readers, work, family and life had slowed down our reading over the years. I was currently rereading a book from my personal library when my husband joined in and wanted to know why I would reread something that I had already read.

"Why not?" we answered together; perplexed that he thought this was strange.

As she scanned the books, I stated, "Borrow what you'd like." She later returned with something she thought I'd enjoy. We both decided we should read more and the book swapping began. Our year-long reading frenzy continued into another. My mother is in on the game too. After she reads something it gets mailed to me and passed to others.

While discussing and reviewing books with one another, I began thinking about characters, and stories, with shocking endings or when you say to yourself, "I didn't see that coming at the end," *and* what *my* next story would be.

In addition to my love for art and romance, I have always been interested in time travel, angels, and signs from above. More recently, I was deeply contemplating the concept of faith too.

Faith challenges many of us daily, but lately to unprecedented levels, as the world continues to undergo severe changes - socially, politically, environmentally, technologically, financially, and medically, just to name a few! As a COVID survivor, like countless others, my faith was once again put to the test. As soon as that passed, my husband was sent on furlough - more tests of patience and faith.

Furthermore, working in a faith-based senior living community, I can't help but *not* think about God, even *more so* on a daily basis. So needless to say *faith* was lingering in my thoughts as well as the idea of guardian angels and if there is some sort of hierarchy in heaven. *God has to have some help, doesn't he?*

I also wanted to examine what happens when people are just thrown together - is it really fate, destiny, or are we all part of some bigger picture that we can't comprehend?

I don't know where the characters for this book came from or why. I began scribbling notes and the story started coming to life. The rest originated during my commute to work. As I drove further south, *'down the shore'* on the Garden State Parkway, many ideas were realized. Driving one hundred miles a day provided me plenty of time to think about what would or could happen in the next chapter.

Enjoy and have patience as you meet the characters and follow them through their thought-provoking journeys.

The more you READ,
The more you know,
The more you learn,
The more places
You'll go!

Theodor S. Geisel

Prologue

Alastair McDougal flew swiftly through the thick, bulbous clouds as he made his way toward the outskirts of the celestial kingdom. He was heading toward the Twelve Realms. He wasn't sure if he had made the correct decision, if he was traveling in the right direction, *or* what he would *say* when he arrived. Wings fully extended, he soared effortlessly through the upper dominion of Heaven as he composed speech after speech in his mind. Not one word, phase, or sentence was suitable, so he disregarded them all.

The long journey had become more like the pilgrimage to *Santiago de Compostela* or *Ste-Foy Conques* he had embarked on when he was just a young boy, sometime in the eleventh or perhaps it was in the twelfth century. It was so long ago the dates didn't matter. Only this time he was not going to see relics that offered the promise of miracles or eternal salvation.

This was by far more important. So imperative that he risked everything, including the passage through the mysterious Twelve Realms. Each area had its own challenges – the Fire Islands of Ard, Aquatic Waters of Port, Isle and Canals of Oma, The Sand Dunes of T'Ley, Hills of Obre, Plantation Forest of Leon, Rocky Terrain of Eler, Alleyways of Ney, Yellow Fields of Oye, Elements of Enly, Rain Cloud Mist of Oma, and finally, through the Sea Waters of the Murky South. One mistake and it was written that you would fall right into a subterranean or cavernous location never to return. So compelled to complete his mission, the possibility of such an inconceivable misfortune never crossed his mind.

So critical was his undertaking, he had ignored every protocol including bypassing high-ranking officials. Yes, he was heading to the very top to see the one and only.

His mind raced as he forged onward and thought about his dilemma. To his knowledge, there had never been a *catastrophe* as such during his centuries of service. Why he was assigned such a disobedient and unruly group of trainees he couldn't fathom.

Alastair trembled as shivers of fear surged through his body. He shuddered as he thought of the ramifications from the debacle that occurred on his watch. Exile, banishment, demotion, or possibly stripped of his rank – a rank that had stood steadfast in his family for generations!

As he emerged from the thick, black, seemingly endless clouds of the Sea Waters of the Murky South, he stopped, hovering mid-flight, as his arm moved to shield his eyes and adjust to the intensely blinding rays of sunlight. Quickly descending to the nearest feathery cloud, he stared, awe struck at the magnificent, and grandiose sight on the horizon. It was breathtaking! His hazel eyes followed the white tower, sparkling in the sunlight as it rose upwards through the clouds and luminous blue sky. He angled his neck sideways to see how far the building reached, but it looked immeasurable.

Alastair marveled at the miracle of the height achieved. "It's utterly remarkable," he muttered as he continued to gaze upward at the impressive structure. The only architectural wonder he could compare it with was the great cathedral building he had viewed as a boy. He could turn back but deep in his heart he knew he needed to make things right– it was the only way.

He took a deep breath and moved posthaste as he resumed flight and considered what he would say. "Maybe I should state my name first, or mayhap the reason for my journey. Perchance, I should give a detailed explanation of my error in judgment," he mumbled. Alastair breathed heavily as he maneuvered through the dense, cloudy atmosphere. He felt as if the weight of the world rested on his shoulders.

Due to the critical nature of the situation he thought it might be best to simply get straight to the point and say, "Hello God, the new group of angels in my training class escaped the impenetrable, heavenly instruction area…hacked into a computer data base and altered time… a horrifying accident will occur and now the lives of others will be transformed…and the future of the…"

"Who are you and what brings you this far into the heavenly realm?" A deep voice echoed, loudly around him, interrupting his thoughts.

Alastair's Dilemma

There isn't enough room
in your mind for both
worry and faith.
Choose wisely.

Power of Positively

Chapter 1

December 2000

Hey Sunshine,

I miss you terribly. I pray and hope every day you are doing well. I wish you could reveal your reasons for being away for so long. I understand you are unable to contact me so I will continue writing and keep you up-to-date on what is happening.

They tell me I'm foolish but only you know of my work and what it signifies. I have made such progress. I have so much to tell you; I am bursting with energy from the outcomes. I hope it brings changes in our protocols so we can help others. My new research keeps me occupied.

Oh, yes I haven't forgotten! It's that time of year. I have everything prepared, as I know this is your favorite season! All your cherished items are in place for when you return from your trip! I can already see the smile on your face.

I hope your journey is memorable. Perhaps you have made new friends and visited with old ones too? I can't wait to hear about your trip, and, more importantly, that you return happy and healthy.

I will write again tomorrow and pray that you receive my note.

All my love,

Me

Chapter 2

Hunters Glen, Montana
December 2000

The quiet night had turned out to be a disaster. The unpredictable storm had changed the lives of families, visitors, and friends within seconds. In the darkness, the emergency crews did their best. By daylight, they were still finding people.

"Unbelievable," Clint muttered, yawning, as he took a sip of the warm coffee someone had handed him. The site commander suggested they take a break before checking another section of the mountain. Signs of exhaustion and fatigue were reflected in the weary faces, evidence from working all night. "I still don't know why people decided to come out on a night like this," Clint whispered sadly as he and some of the other emergency medical personnel took their coffee and continued their search.

"It's the holidays. You know, the busiest time of the year," his partner Sam answered. "People are coming to ski, visit, and shop. Everyone is rushing around and then you have the tourists, who either didn't listen to the weather reports or read the posted danger signs - falling snow or rocks," he added, as they walked through the crash site.

"Yeah, well, those buses going to the ski resort – and the construction…they should have detoured all the traffic," Clint gestured angrily, as they walked around more crushed automobile debris looking for survivors. He squinted as he spotted some-thing gleaming in the distance. "There might be something over there," he pointed. Radios crackled and coffee was thrown away as they raced further down the embankment.

Sam did a quick survey of the area while they stabilized two more victims. "It looks like they came out of this vehicle," he pointed. "Call Franklin Memorial and tell them two more are on the way. Make sure you tag them together."

Chapter 3

Franklin Memorial Hospital
Hunters Glen, Montana
December 2000

*H*unters Glen was known for its ski resort and year-round summer attractions. The small hospital, Franklin Memorial, was not prepared to handle the chaos that had unfolded in the last twenty-four hours. Chaos. It was the only way to describe the scene as it continued to develop. Staff and emergency responders were working tirelessly around the clock tending to people as the situation unfolded.

"There's too many. Tell them to divert," the emergency room assistant shouted as he passed the nurses station. "Do it now!"

"Over here," someone called to him.

He ran down the line of bodies and began triage. "Contusions, fractures, head trauma," he yelled, as he continued examining people and calling out directions. "All head traumas, including these two, the tag says they were found together, stabilize them and stage with the team over there," he pointed. "We'll send the worst cases over to Seminole. Call ahead and let them know what's coming. We're at capacity and can't handle anymore."

Chapter 4

Her Choice
December 2000

"What do you mean I must choose?" she whispered as the fluffy clouds billowed around her. "Why?" Her head sought the male voice.

"You followed the light. You made your decision and here you are," the voice answered unemotionally.

"Who are you? Show yourself," she demanded as her eyes darted around.

The girl's facial features contorted, reflecting puzzlement and awe, as she watched a man emerged from a swirling mist. His lustrous, silver and gold robes fluttered around him. As he moved, soft pastel colors shimmered from the fabric.

"Greetings. I am Baldassare. Unfortunately you must choose," he pointed. "It's part of your journey. I don't make the rules," he countered.

"I will do nothing of the sort," she argued as she studied him. He had the longest and whitest beard. "What rules?"

"It's mandatory," Baldassare replied, as if he said this a thousand times before. "You followed the light and are required to make a choice," he pointed toward the hazy light.

"But I don't understand," she cried out. "There has to be some sort of mistake. I don't know *you* or *understand* this *choice* that you're requesting of me." She glanced down. The cloud cover was so thick she could barely see the rest of her body as it churned around her. "Furthermore, what's all this white stuff around me?" She said, exasperated, as she waved her hands through the dense substance.

Baldassare pursed his lips as she spoke and felt a bit uneasy for she was extremely lively. His eyes widened in disbelief as he suddenly realized he wasn't expecting an arrival today. He quickly waved his hands over her, and his scowl turned to utter suspicion. He immediately opened his silver-plated planner and began typing. His eyes arched, surprised, as he scanned the docket numbers and names, appearing on his screen. He cleared his throat and stated evenly, "Fortunately, it's not your time for…"

A slight shiver ran down his back as he heard the rumbling of what sounded like thunder. The immediate darkening of the thick clouds caused him to pause. He knew what it meant, yet he was a bit perplexed, as he couldn't understand how she was able to break through the gateway...something was not right… her voice brought him back to the present situation.

"What? Please explain, I still don't know what you want of me?"

Unconvinced, he double-checked the device for errors. Her name did not appear. He sucked in his breath, as he comprehended the reality – she *was* in his realm. How was it possible, he wondered. She had free will and he couldn't tell her what to do. While her path was an anomaly, he knew he could not interfere.

"Regrettably, you followed the light and must decide," his voice boomed like thunder, as he interrupted her a bit louder than necessary. "You can't stay in limbo. *Alas you must choose,*" he proclaimed irritably, for he had no clue what was transpiring.

"Well, sir, you don't have to get so angry about it!"

He hadn't meant to yell. The balance and order of time were in jeopardy. He also knew, he should not be questioning but adhere to the protocol devised centuries prior. His voice dropped an octave as he spoke. "*Midpoint stops* are not permissible in this sector. Make a selection now. It's essential to the order and stability," he indicated as he turned, raised his arms parallel, and, in one fluid motion, his fingers pointed in two different directions.

She followed his outstretched arms and didn't seem to notice that his hands had now pointed in the opposite direction of when she first arrived.

Shivers ran down her back, but she wasn't frightened. "Well, I don't understand the rush." Her head moved back and forth as she tried to decide between the light and the dark fog. As she turned to the left she held up her arms and attempted to shield her face from the extraordinary, dazzling light. There was something about the brilliant light that was intriguing. She took a few steps further.

"It's all about timing. I will remind you that you run the risk of not remembering anything if you keep moving forward," Baldassare warned. "Memory recall. It's not an easy choice."

The deep voice of Baldassare was lost as she continued moving…

Chapter 5

An Unexpected Friend

A momentary flash, and the blinding light was quickly forgotten. Her eyelids flickered as she attempted to focus, while at the same time, she turned her head and felt something wet and abrasive on her face. Attempts to push it away were futile as it returned. Forcing her eyes to fully open, she found a fluffy creature staring at her. His long tongue glided across her cheek, leaving a wet spot.

Surprised that she wasn't frightened, she laughed and said, "Who are you?"

A loud *woof, woof* was followed by a hard pouncing atop of her.

"Okay. Okay. Let me up," she smiled as she twisted her body and sat upright.

She was seated on the edge of something soft as her eyes peered at the unfamiliar space. She had no idea how to describe the contents of the room.

Woof! Woof! Woof! Woof!

"So what's next?" she said aloud as she stretched and stood. Light filtered in through various cracks, luring her toward a door. Tentatively she grabbed the handle and opened it slowly. Shielding her eyes from the unexpected, glaring brightness that hit her face, the ball of fluff ran between her legs and shot out into the brilliant rays as she held on tightly to the door to keep her balance.

"Hey, wait for me," she called after the furry beast who, was now running and jumping through endless fields of color. She closed her eyes and inhaled deeply – the wonderful smells were familiar although she couldn't place them. As far as she could see, hues and tints of color flourished. As the warm light hit her face, her mind was blank as she tried to describe what was in front of her. She shrugged and uttered, "no matter," as she continued to admire the view, before hurrying after her shaggy friend toward the magnificent spectrum of beauty.

Chapter 6

Alastair

Alastair was frantic and breathing heavily as he flew to a lower cloudbank. Searching for the individual of the unseen voice, his eyes darted back and forth, as he landed, and stood upright.

"Who is passing through one of the most sacred areas of the celestial domain?" the voice commanded again, resonating vociferously through the atmosphere.

Alastair instinctively twisted around. Only fluffy clouds, and the brilliant, blue sky were visible. Although not physically present, it was conceivable someone was watching.

Alastair thrust his shoulders back and stood straighter as he adjusted his cream-colored robes and tightened his braided, brown belt. "It is I…Alastair…Alastair McDougal…Angel Trainer of the Twelfth Order. I must speak to the Lord straight-away." Alastair stammered and trembled as he spoke.

"THE LORD!" The voice now brasher, echoed around him, bouncing off the clouds.

Alastair didn't miss the sarcasm. "Yes, *the Lord*! It's an *emergency*," he said frantically, as his head whipped around searching for somebody to appear.

"Humph. That's what they all say," the male voice reverberated loudly. "You're better off *praying* about your concern. *Furthermore,"* he snapped irritably, *"do you have a ticket? Did you make an appointment?"*

Alastair was taken aback by the questions. He had just traveled incalculable miles; survived passage through the Twelve Realms and the last thing on his mind was calling ahead. He had no idea who he would even contact to arrange a meeting. "No, I don't have an appointment," he said alarmed. "Something *terrible* occurred, and I *must* alert the Lord immediately," Alastair indicated, as he waved his hands furiously through the air. "Who are you?" he asked, feeling a bit bolder. "Show yourself."

Gruff, loud, laughter boomed through the clouds before an older man materialized and hovered before him. His round, chubby face was covered with a full beard, which was cut short and neatly groomed. Thick, white hair tapered just below his neck and was not long like most of the lower-ranking angels. "*I am Rafael, Keeper of the Twelve Realms and surrounding quadrants,*" he bellowed deeply as he floated to an upright position before landing in front of him. Alastair guessed he was approximately six feet in height as he towered over his mere five-foot, four-inch frame.

Alastair took a step backwards and tilted his head up in awe as he noticed the robust angel wore shimmering, royal blue robes tied with gold cords defining his extremely prominent status.

His large, brown eyes narrowed as he studied the intruder before speaking. "Apparently you did not hear a word I've spoken, but I will ask again just in case I have mistaken your intentions…"

Before he could finish Alastair interrupted him and nervously detailed his request, *"No, you heard me correctly, I need to see the Lord immediately. It's an emergency; there's been an incident and…"*

"*Silence!*" Roared the high-ranking angel as he adjusted the circular, wireless frames on his face.

Alastair shivered as the angel studied him.

Raphael then glanced at his bracelet and began typing the trespassers name into the device. *"I don't see your name on my list. You have no ticket or appointment; therefore, you can't proceed!"*

Astonished, Alastair's eyes widened and his mouth opened.

"As you are already aware, *any* and *all* mishaps are to be reported to *your supervisor*," he snapped, as he tapped on his device with quick, staccato-like raps. He quickly looked up and glared at Alastair as if he committed a crime. "Please return immediately and consult with your superior. Good day, sir!"

Rafael vanished quicker than he had materialized.

"Good day!" Alastair shouted infuriated. "The future of the world *and* heavenly kingdom is at stake and all you can say is *good day*," he cried, gesturing anxiously as he glanced upward at the sky.

Chapter 7

Noah
December 2000

N oah Tremonte flipped his brown hair out of his eyes and off his forehead as he pushed the broom down the hall toward the pile of trash he had accumulated. He sighed heavily as he continued to clean. He could not understand *why*, with plenty of trashcans in place throughout offices, lounges, cafeterias, and halls that people couldn't throw their garbage into the designated containers. He grumbled as he continued contemplating how technologically advanced society had become but throwing trash into a receptacle clearly labeled garbage was still problematic.

He bagged the mess and made his way to the next office. As he continued to collect the bags, one suddenly ripped and fell to the carpet. He shook his head in dismay as he cleaned up the debris. He despised his job but could hear his mother's voice telling him to be grateful for the work and the goal he was working toward. He turned up the volume on his headphones and continued to the next room.

Instead of studying for his finals, he was listening to music and reflecting on his life. "All I do is work," he muttered irritably. The frigid December air burned his cheeks as he forcefully shoved his cart outside. He once again pushed long, shaggy layers of hair off his eyes and threw on his hat. He'd overslept and his mother scolded him for not getting a haircut.

He was miserable. He wanted to quit, but the job at the hospital paid the most money and was close to campus. He heaved the trash bags into the open dumpster and wondered why he had been born into such poverty. He worked twice as hard as his classmates and his friends laughed at him because he was always working. "It's the end of the year, just call out. Come and hang with us for once," they pleaded.

Another bag followed. Many mistook him as weak due to his tall, lanky frame. While he didn't have the appearance of a body builder, nightly routines as such certainly conditioned his upper body and arm strength. Bag after bag followed. The vigor with which he threw the sacks into the air was evidence of how furious he was at God and his life's circumstances.

He had to work to pay for the school he was accepted into because he only received a small scholarship. He had great grades but because he spent his life working, he had no extracurricular activities or active philanthropy like others. In order to keep his scholarship, maintaining a high grade point average was mandatory. While he was doing well at Seminole College, he wasn't sure if he was going to continue on to the prestigious Grace General Hospital and College of Medicine, which was part of the hospital system he worked at.

He knew he was lucky to be accepted, but after all of the prep work and his grueling job, he was having second thoughts about the path to the goal he thought he wanted to achieve. It would be time-consuming and he wasn't sure he wanted to devote such a long stretch of his life to it. In addition, if his current job was a precursor of what was to come, he was getting depressed and uncertain of his future. While he had a list of reasons to give up, he also knew in his heart they were only just more excuses.

His mother had reminded him he was fortunate to receive a partial scholarship and to be grateful. "Be grateful and God will grant you more. You will see."

Noah could never understand how his mother was able to remain so positive after all that had happened to her. He fought against the wind as he returned to the loading dock. "Ugh," he sighed. The odor in the trash room and the pile of bags only reminded him of his current reality and the last thing he wanted to think about was being grateful. The crackling of his radio interrupted his thoughts.

"Noah, you're needed back in the basement."

He responded quickly and frowned as he headed to the elevator, for he knew it was going to be another depressing night.

Chapter 8

Her Discoveries

She had no idea where she was or what she should be doing; however, the days were fun and bursting with adventure! Her furry friend was quick to pounce on her as soon as the bright light arrived signaling it was time to start the day. She found it comforting to have him around. She discovered a small garden behind the dwelling. After eating the delicious treats from the garden, she and her new buddy would explore the many trails in and around the fields of color.

Today she followed him to a path that led to a large body of crystal-clear liquid. Looking up she saw the substance cascading down the rough hillside and splashing into an enormous body of more liquid at its base. She stared and was awestruck but had no idea what to call it.

She removed the material covering her feet and dipped her bare toes in. "Ahh," she moaned. "It's perfect."

Her fluffy friend had already jumped in and was splashing around. "You must be enjoying this," she called to him.

The beast shook his body and droplets splattered everywhere. *Woof. Woof.*

She smiled and joined him.

Chapter 9

Alastair

Alastair was furious. He hadn't traveled this far to be turned away. He decided the fastest way to reach the shimmering white tower was to fly. He entered his angel code into his bracelet, fluffed and extended his massive, white wings, and took flight higher into the atmosphere. The tower loomed in the distance. He hadn't been in the air fifteen minutes when a white light appeared out of nowhere and he suddenly found himself falling - as he was instantly zapped to the clouds below. "What the heck is going on," he yelled as he regained his balance and quickly looked around for his aggressor.

He noticed a large, white feather floating toward him, which promptly transformed into another angel. The bulky, muscular, male angel wasted no time in getting to the point. *"Didn't you see the sign back there? This is a No-Fly Zone! This area is restricted for flying! Walking Only! You are in violation of regulatory flight code SZ21A5226407071970 – for flying too high above the authorized atmosphere and cloud boundary requirement!"* his deep voice rumbled.

Alastair's eyebrows shot up as he gaped at the angel in disbelief. His neck and head were massive. His perfectly white teeth contrasted with his dark skin and he also spoke with a slight accent. As he enunciated each word, Alastair immediately realized he was from the southern border.

"State your name and business here," the older angel demanded.

Alastair studied the brawny angel as he immediately responded. "My name is Alastair…Alastair McDougal, of the Twelfth Order. Who are you?"

Wearing luminous robes of green, tied with a mixture of colorful cords, Alastair knew the intricately designed threads were representative of his rank and accolades. His baldhead signified he was part of an elite assemblage of angels, with an exceptional set of skills, only called upon for *extraordinary assignments.* Alastair was awe-stricken as he had never encountered or observed an angel of such status.

"I am Thelonious and responsible for Quadrant 2003, *a Quadrant that I am pleased to enlighten you, hasn't had a single mishap in centuries,*" he thundered as he began typing into his angel wristlet. "I am issuing you a citation for flying in a *No-Fly Zone,* flying in a restricted area, and for not walking. You have also violated several…"

"You can't be serious," Alastair interrupted incredulously.

Thelonious stopped typing and peered over his bifocals. "Do I look like I'm joking?"

Alastair thought lightning bolts were going to shoot out of his cold eyes the way Thelonious was scrutinizing him. "I didn't mean to…um…to…um…imply," he stammered. Alastair didn't know what to make of the sizeable angel, whose sculpted face was just as firm as the muscles on his hands and forearms, which bulged prominently. He shuddered to think what the rest of his body looked like and he didn't want to trigger his fury.

"I'm very serious," snapped the older angel. "You are in the outer limits of the celestial realm. I guess you missed the *huge sign*?"

"I was just trying to get to the Tower. I'm sorry, I didn't see it."

"Could it be because you were *flying too fast* and obviously *NOT* paying attention?" He gestured theatrically as he spoke.

"No, it was hidden behind all the clouds," Alastair argued.

"Well, Alastair," he stated sarcastically, as he continued glaring at him, "you *do* realize, *CLOUDS ARE WHAT EXISTS IN THE ATMOSPHERE OF THE HEAVENLY KINGDOM!* Perhaps this is your first time flying…"

"No, absolutely not!" Alastair interjected. "I'll have you know I received my wings in the Year of Our Lord," he stopped and scratched his goatee as he tried to recall the exact date. "Well sometime back in the twelfth century or perhaps it was the fourteenth…"

"Oh, I understand," Thelonious interrupted nodding and pointing his boney finger at him. "If it was *that long ago* then you need a *refresher course*! We do offer a class for the *aging angel population*. I'm sure you've heard of it?" He scowled. "I'll make a note on your citation that you are required to attend!"

"But, but, that's not fair…I…um…I didn't mean…" Alastair faltered and quickly stopped talking.

Thelonious seethed and his eyes darkened to almost golden. Alastair could have sworn they changed to those of an owl or bird of prey in that fleeting instant. "If you were *paying atten-tion* you *wouldn't have missed it*." His face-hardened and like a laser beam his eyes quickly examined the small-statured angel. *"What are you really doing this far beyond the realm?"*

"I'm on my way to see the Lord," Alastair answered confidently.

Chapter 10

Alastair

*T*helonious raised his eyebrows in disbelief. "Humph! I find that highly doubtful. What is your name again?" He asked in case he hadn't heard it correctly the first time.

"Alastair… Alastair McDougal of the Twelfth Order," Alastair replied nervously as he scratched his silver goatee.

"Well, Alastair, I will ask you one more time, *what are you really doing out here and why were you speeding?"*

"I told you I'm on my way to see the Lord," Alastair said exasperated.

Outraged, the angel's facial muscles coiled and his eyes narrowed like a hawk as he drew closer to Alastair. "If this is your attempt at a joke, I'm not amused," he said hotly.

Alastair winced at his frightening tone. "Seriously, I'm telling you the truth. I'm on my way to see the Lord. It's an emergency."

Thelonious continued to glare. Alastair thought the large angel's eyes were going to pop right out of his sockets. *"Do you even have an appointment?"* Thelonious probed sarcastically, as he entered something into his angel bracelet. "I don't see your name on the list," he replied looking up and back at Alastair skeptically. "If your name is not on my list, I doubt you have a ticket either?" he challenged.

Alastair stuttered, "Well…um…not exactly…but…I'm going to get one and…and well…there is a real disaster…and…and…this crisis…that I must inform the Lord of…and…it is…"

Thelonious cut him off with the wave of his hand and looked at him up and down suspiciously. "What could possibly be *so urgent* that *you* need an audience with the Almighty?"

"It's a matter of *life and death*," Alastair huffed as he tried to explain. "You see…"

"Yes, yes, now we're getting somewhere. Of course it is!" Thelonious mused as he rolled his eyes dismissively and quickly cut him off. *"It's always a matter of life and death,"* he said as he deliberately pronounced each word slowly. *"Listen, Alastair of the Twelfth Order, I suggest you pray about whatever your problem is. It would be quicker,"* he advised.

Alastair gawked in disbelief.

"I will be issuing you *another* citation for traveling *without* the proper pass. You *must* turn back." Interrupted by the beeping of his bracelet, he quickly scanned the incoming communication. Frowning and rolling his eyes, he stated, "Oh, and this alert," he pointed to the device on his wrist, "says you also *failed* to pay a toll. How could you *possibly* miss the toll and a sign?"

"I told you with all the cloud coverage and fog I just didn't see it," Alastair countered.

Thelonious ignored him. "When your fines are processed your supervisor will be notified and instruct you to complete the proper forms. If they are not received by the due date, additional penalties will be administered along with administrative fees!"

Alastair was speechless. He had never received a ticket or fine in his entire human or angel life span. He fidgeted nervously as the demerits could ruin his rank. His family would be devastated. He struggled as he decided to ignore the consequences, justifying all would be forgiven once he reached the Lord to explain.

"Can you at least tell me how one gets to the Tower," he asked pointedly.

Thelonious' nostrils flared and facial muscles twitched as he tried to suppress his fury. While it happened in seconds, Alastair was positive he saw the golden eyes again. He flinched as Thelonious spoke. *"Have you not heard a word I said? This is a No-Fly Zone. Walking Only! You are not even credentialed to be in this area. You have violated signs, were speeding, are traveling without a proper ticket, failed to pay a toll, and have no appointment – that's six, did you hear me SIX CITATIONS – and if you receive four more, I'll be forced to take you to the holding area. And just so you know, the High Judge of the Elder Court is on holiday so you will have to wait to see him. You must turn back now. You will never make it to the tower,"* he snapped irritably.

I'll figure it out. Alastair silently thought to himself.

Thelonious let out a hearty laugh as he heard his thoughts. "Really? I doubt it; besides, there is construction and detours in this sector. In addition, the cloud and atmosphere coverage are *much* denser on this side of the realm. You already overlooked one sign, I'm confident you will miss all the rest."

Alastair cringed.

"Furthermore, if you *did* make it, you have *no formal invitation or pass*. You know the rules, Alastair, or mayhap you have forgotten them. If that's so, then it's a shame," he pointed angrily. "As I already suggested, you would be better off *saying a prayer*," he said sternly. "I recommend you turn and go back before you find yourself in *more trouble* than you are already in," he reminded him and swiftly departed.

Chapter 11

Hey Sunshine,

I'm sorry I am late with this letter. I have been terribly busy these past few weeks. We have some remarkable new and demanding cases, which I am excited to tell you all about. I know you will be interested. I have been recording the details so you can review upon your return! I spend my nights writing and transcribing data.

I hope you are traveling and seeing the world. I was wondering if you are ready to come home yet? The snow is falling and the scenery is picturesque. The snow-covered mountains are absolutely stunning. I was thinking of going skiing to our favorite mountain but don't have time right now. I really wanted to wait for you so we can travel together.

Please keep track of what you are doing. I am excited to hear about your trip when you return.

All my love,

Me

Chapter 12

Her New Reality

The days were glorious as she and her furry companion continued to walk around. But something was missing. She looked every day but had no idea what she was searching for. While everything around her seemed familiar, she was having difficulty processing it all.

She desperately wanted to identify every item she saw, but for some reason could not. She didn't know what to make of any of the objects she touched. Some were rough while others were smooth. To make matters worse she soon discovered something that absolutely frightened her.

When it first happened she was in the field far from the dwelling. Suddenly the bright light was extinguished and she was forced to spend the night where she was. She was thankful her furry friend stayed by her side for comfort. When the darkness came, she couldn't see and was terrified. She made sure it would never happen again.

Chapter 13

Alastair

Alastair had been walking for miles as he headed toward the tower. Its proximity was deceiving. It looked closer than it appeared. Every instance, which he thought he was getting nearer, it faded further, swallowed by the dense clouds.

"Is there anyone out there? Is anyone listening?" Alastair called out loudly. His face twisted with anguish as he again shouted, "Time has been altered, someone is going to die and it's all my fault. I don't know if I'll be able to live with myself," he grumbled as he continued with desperate gestures and pleas. "I really need to get to the tower to see the Lord; it's a matter of life and death!"

Chapter 14

Noah's Assignment

Noah was irritable and worked quickly. Four months ago, at the end of August, someone had quit and he had been assigned to work in the basement. What a way to start his last semester. He still wasn't accustomed to the strange odor and cold temperatures. He had asked his boss for a transfer but was told that due to short staffing he was where he was needed. It was now December and he was *still* working in the basement and he loathed the assignment, which made him question his career choice more than ever. Not only was the work nauseating, but also it triggered more anxiety - anxiety about his job, and uncertainty regarding his future. He wasn't sure about anything anymore.

He made the mistake of complaining to his mother at dinner one evening. She smiled and reminded him of God's plan and to look for the good in what he was doing or to think how he would benefit from the experience.

There was nothing beneficial about it. Instead he found it eerie. It was so quiet he felt like he was being watched. He kept looking over his shoulder, which caused him to work faster.

"God, if you are listening I'm asking that you please… please find favor with me and transfer me to another part of the building!" He whispered one evening.

The hall sconce unexpectedly flickered as he passed by with his cleaning cart. Startled, he flinched as he checked the fixture and tightened the teardrop-shaped incandescent bulb and thought his mother was right – he wouldn't be so spooked if he hadn't watched so many horror movies.

Chapter 15

Another Unexpected Arrival –
His Choice

"What are you doing here?" A deep voice echoed through the clouds.

The young man blinked a few times as he took in his surroundings. It was all white. He was actually standing on what appeared to be cotton or so he thought. He stepped lightly to ensure he was not going to fall before walking toward what he thought was a person. The billowy fluff came up to his knees and swirled about his torso.

"I'll ask you again," the loud male voice bellowed, "Why are you here?" Too many strange occurrences in his sector had him on alert. He had already scanned him from the distance and knew who he was.

The man stopped moving as the voice boomed around him. "Someone is calling and needs help. I followed her voice, saw the light, and came. She needs aid!"

"You must return. You do not belong here; it is not your time," the voice resonated. A loud crack boomed through the atmosphere the minute the words exited his mouth. The angel cringed knowing he once again had said too much.

"Now see here, someone is in trouble," he argued as he spun around looking for the individual. He squinted as he tried to see through the swirling fluff.

"You are in the wrong place and will be required to make a choice."

"A choice?"

"That is correct," the concealed voice echoed.

"Why must I choose?" he whispered, as the fluffy clouds churned about.

"It is required," the male voice replied slowly, *"for some reason you followed the light."* His irritation was apparent, as the words became louder while he spoke.

"I don't understand?" The young man continued walking around. "Who are you? Show yourself."

An older man materialized instantly. Wrinkles were visible on his forehead and eyes. His long beard and hair were as white as the clouds and blended in so much that the young intruder was unable to tell the length.

"Who are you?"

"I am known as Baldassare, and you," he pointed, "decided to enter my quadrant," he said bluntly.

While the young man scratched his head and tried to make sense of his surroundings, Baldassare scrutinized the trespasser. This conversation was highly irregular, so he continued with his usual speech. "You must return. You do not belong here. I highly suggest you return." *He was exasperated and not certain what was happening. The recent occurrences were surprisingly unusual, and he was feeling unsettled.*

The young man studied the leathery-faced, philosopher-like figure who appeared out of the thickest fog he had ever encountered. His silver and gold cloak sparkled with strange combinations of iridescent pastel-like colors as he moved about. "Where am I?" he demanded.

Baldassare ignored the question as he glided through the clouds. "Once again, I have no arrivals scheduled," he muttered as he double-checked his silver-plated planner for the third time for confirmation. "I am not sure *how* you made it through, but you need to return now! Midpoint stops are not permissible in this sector!"

The senior angel was *extremely* confused and was convinced something inexplicable was occurring in the heavenly realm. This was the second time in a month that someone had broken through the concealed gateway without his knowledge. Following the light is serious business. It's a rare occurrence and reserved for those selected to deal with tests, life situations, or death. One's name *MUST* be on the list. There are reasons for this.

He shuddered, as he thought about the potential disturbance of the balance and order of the heavenly and earthly realm – a fusion of innumerable doctrines, guiding principles, and philosophies – extremely vulnerable if disturbed. A fluctuation or instability of any sort could be catastrophic.

The ancient angel took a deep breath and closed his eyes and, like a butterfly taking flight, his arms rose gracefully and horizontal with the cloud plane. Long index fingers indicated the direction of the brilliant light while the other hand pointed toward the dark fog. You must choose now," he said calmly.

The young man advanced forward. "She needs help. Now tell me which way to go." The vapor grew thicker as the ancient man floated around him. "She needs my help," he pleaded before a terrible pain shot through his head. He shook his head as if to clear the throbbing. "She's calling me," he said anxiously. "How can you be so cruel? Do something."

Running his hands through his long beard the old man thought about the peculiar situation, similar to the one that had occurred recently. This was certainly not in the manual. He had already had a few mishaps and was not looking to be sent elsewhere. He thought perhaps *he* was being tested. He knew his role was not to question but to provide guidance for any anomalies. He also knew the trespasser had free will. "If that is your choice, then you are almost there, continue to follow the bright light," he pointed. "Although I warn you – if you proceed, you are in danger of not remembering or may be unable to return. So choose wisely."

Chapter 16

Alastair

Alastair was numb as he watched the scene unfold. "This is dreadful," he exclaimed. "The danger is clearly escalating. I *must* get to the Lord to correct this abysmal blunder," he moaned. He covered his angel bracelet with the sleeve of his cloak, as he could not watch what was transpiring. "Even *I* don't know *how* this is possible," he muttered, his voice trembling with alarm.

There was nothing but heavy clouds and a fine mist as he continued walking toward the giant tower growing from a sea of white. Occasionally he stopped and gazed at the giant edifice hoping he could somehow now calculate its proximity. To make matters worse a virtually impenetrable fog had rolled in slowing his pace. The dense clouds were an anomaly to him as he was much higher up in the atmosphere.

After what seemed like an eternity, he shook his head nervously as he recalled the warning from Thelonious. "Ugh. I bet I missed one of the detour signs because I wasn't paying attention," he rationalized. Alastair stood paralyzed with fear as his thoughts wandered. *What if I did take a wrong turn? What if the distance to the tower is so deceiving that I will never be able to reach it in time? If I can't get to the Tower, then how am I going to alert God? Heaven and the earthly realm are in danger of unanticipated occurrences...once the ancient database was activated and time was altered, nobody would be aware of the changes.* "I must get to the Lord," he cried out in despair.

"Does anyone see what is happening," he shouted. "Why isn't someone listening to me? Hello? Can you hear me? Every fiber of my being is filled with anxiety - anxiety I have never suffered from previously. It is urgent that I speak to someone to correct the mistake. The celestial realm is in danger as is life on earth; people are suffering. I am going to collapse from the weight of the agony I carry and…and…this situation…it's escalating by the second…I must get to the Lord," he lamented. Alastair threw up his hands frustrated at the lack of communication as he continued carrying on about his troubles.

Days passed and soon, the thick fog began to dissipate. He eventually emerged into a small clearing. It was somewhat surreal. Surrounded by fluffy clouds, and the brilliant blue sky, there stood an old wooded post that looked as if it had been planted right in the middle of the cloud covering. Attached to the top, was a sign with the words *Information* carved into the worn wood. "I have nothing to lose," he said as he took off in the direction of the arrow.

Chapter 17

The Announcement

The temperature had changed and the material was sticking to her body. She wiped the moisture off her face as she headed toward the cool liquid. It was always perfect. She welcomed the refreshing, crystal clear phenomena and shed the apparel covering her body and walked in. She had no words to describe the liquid. It was so unblemished she could see everything. She continuously marveled at the colorful schools of life that quickly passed by. Her fuzzy companion frolicked far in the distance before returning to the shore to rest in the warmth.

So mesmerized by the beauty of her surroundings, she didn't realize her furry friend was communicating with her.

"What?" she called, as she floated peacefully with her eyes closed.

Woof. Woof. Woof. Woof.

"What? What now?" She slowly opened her eyes, squinting as she angled her face toward the noise. As she focused on the sound, her eyes widened and she gasped in disbelief. Standing nearby was another of her kind. Her hands automatically flew to her private parts as she struggled to shield herself. She quickly sunk down into the cool liquid in a final attempt to conceal her body.

Chapter 18

Alastair

"*Do you see what I see?*" Alastair bellowed as he continued pacing through the clouds. "*Another strange occurrence. It's simply forbidden.*" Alastair yelled. He had been forced to watch, as his angel bracelet would not shut down. He knew his angel wristlet didn't lie. It stopped and started on its own accord, which was abnormal.

Alastair followed the arrow and found himself on another cloud path. A few more old signs littered the footpath and he breathed a sigh of relief that he was heading in what he hoped was the right direction. He was sweating profusely as his anxiety level had risen beyond what he had ever experienced before. "I should never have left that group alone…what if my father finds out…our family name will be tarnished," he muttered.

He could feel the thick wrinkles as he rubbed his forehead thinking he had aged more. Then there is old Elias, the angel trainer who has *never* made a mistake. His record was perfect. "I will surely become fodder for *gossip* in the entire celestial realm. The angel leaders will mock me and…my family…they will cast me out…I will be disgraced…the worries I now have are unimaginable…not to mention what has started to happen above and below."

Alastair stewed as he continued walking and rambling about his troubles. He eventually threw his arms up in the air, gestured furiously and blurted, "Doesn't anybody hear me? This is a crisis of the utmost magnitude! If not addressed immediately, the consequences could be exponentially magnified; why…it might even be the end of the universe," he lamented.

Chapter 19

You Called

"Who are you and what do you want?" she called out hesitantly.

He froze. It was the familiar voice. "I heard you calling me," he shouted.

"I didn't call you," she countered cautiously.

His brows furrowed as he thought about it. He was sure he had heard her cries. "Perhaps I'm mistaken. I think I'm lost. Can you help me?" he yelled.

She was somewhat frightened as she noticed he was very tall; however, his voice was soothing, and his face was not threatening. She suddenly remembered her nakedness and became agitated as she sank further into the cool liquid. She wasn't about to walk out minus anything covering her. It just didn't seem like the right thing to do.

"You must leave at once!"

"Leave? Where do you think I'm going to go if I'm lost?" He chuckled knowing her dilemma. "I see your fear," he pointed to the pile of clothing at the water's edge. The blue top, white skirt, and undergarments were scattered about. "I promise I won't look. I'll walk far over there," he gestured. "I'll turn my back for you."

She quickly swam to the edge and grabbed and pulled the material over her wet body. She noticed he was kneeling and making friends with her fuzzy companion. "Who are you?" she called out.

"Can I turn around?"

"Yes," she answered a bit timidly when she was finally dressed.

He slowly turned and walked toward her. Her clothing clung to her damp body and her long, dark hair was strewn about. He smiled as he took in her appearance. Tall, but not quite his height, her frame was delicate. Big, brown eyes and the brightest smile filled her oval face. "Hello," he said a bit shyly.

Her breath caught in her throat as she gazed at him and her heart was racing. Up close he was even better to look at. She couldn't take her eyes off of him. He was as flawless as her surroundings. His eyes matched perfectly to what she saw when she looked high above her every day. They were arresting. White material covered the top of him and his bottom half was partially covered in something that was the same color as the tall things that grew from the ground. The fluff on his head matched the soft, uneven ground she currently stood on. As she continued to study him, she felt as if she'd seen him before. She repeated her questions, "Who are you? Where did you come from?"

He couldn't stop looking at her. Up close she made him feel funny. His mouth was dry and he was having difficulty answering her questions. Her dark hair was long and wavy and cascaded down her back. He was sure he had seen those eyes before but where? "Your eyes are as dark as your hair but I can't seem to put into words what I'm thinking."

She flipped her wet hair over her shoulders and gazed at the person standing before her. He looked confused. "Who are you? How long have you been here?" She shouted a bit too loud in case he didn't understand her.

He had no answers. He didn't know himself. His eyes narrowed as he quickly cocked his head to one side before straightening it as he tried to make sense of the situation.

She noted the dark circles around his eyes before he spoke.

"I'm not sure? I think I'm lost," he sighed. "But if it helps I feel as if I have seen you somewhere before. I just can't remember where. Your voice is also recognizable. I am *positive* you called for me. Do you need help?"

"Do *I* look like *I* need help? I'm perfectly fine."

The more she spoke the more he was sure he was right. "I heard you *call* for me. I'm positive," he answered.

"Impossible," she answered confidently. "Why would I call for someone I don't even know?"

He shrugged and nodded. She made a good point.

Chapter 20

Alastair

Alastair continued following directional arrows and veered off to the left down another cloud path. He thought about flying but was already in enough trouble and didn't need more citations. His angel bracelet tracked that he had walked over twenty miles when he finally reached a white, wooden post. Carved into another wooden sign, attached to the top were the words - *Information and Communication Assistance*. The arrow pointed in one direction. Alastair sighed heavily as he entered the dense concentrated clouds mumbling about the insanity of his journey, where the Lord was, and why he was making things so difficult for him.

As Alastair emerged from the dense cloudbanks, he noticed a strange apparatus in the center and walked slowly toward it to get a closer look. Constructed from some sturdy, shiny material unfamiliar to him with blue coloring on the top it looked as if someone had punched it over and over from all the dents in the sides and surface. As he looked further and examined the text, he muttered, "Evidently it requires coins, which I do not possess," he said annoyed. Squinting, he bent closer to make out the rest of the writing and read, "Recycled from 1986." Alastair scratched his head wondering why something from the year of our lord nineteen hundred and eighty-six would be necessary in the celestial realm, so high in the atmosphere in the middle of nowhere!

He picked up the ancient handset and was surprised when a female voice said, "Hello, you have reached customer service for the *High Office of the Lord*. Due to high call volume we're unable to take your call at this time. Waiting times may vary. We apologize in advance for any inconvenience. Please remember all offices are closed during the holiday so we may reflect, rejoice, and enjoy fellowship accordingly. This includes all celebrations of the saints, and any new additional holidays that have been added. Please feel free to access our website for a list of scheduled holidays at www.theheavenlykingdomofthelord.org for more information."

Alastair winced as his eyes widened in astonishment. "This must be some sort of prank," he murmured suspiciously as the monotone voice continued.

"If you wish to stay on the line and would like to wait for one of our alternate representatives to assist you, press one. If you'd like to leave a call back number enter the identification number of your angel device, press two and your call will be answered in the order that it was received. Press three if you need to speak to a representative from the Order of Saint Francis to assist with lost pets. Press four if you need to speak to a representative from the Order of Saint Christopher for travel directions…"

"Ah ha," Alastair smiled as he immediately punched the number four button on the device.

"You have reached the office of travel, guidelines, maps, and services. This includes celestial travel for old and new routes, current cloud coverage, areas under construction, alternate routes due to construction or renovations, updates on current construction in all wards and districts and all *new* and upcoming routes planned. If you are lost please consult the map for your destination. Maps can be requested during business hours and will be sent to your angel device after your order is processed. Due to heavy call volume and a stoppage in the workforce for the holiday we're only accepting scheduled calls at this time. Please book an appointment at the nearest office or with your supervisor. To return to the main menu, please press one."

Alastair sighed heavily as his anxiety was mounting. He irritably pressed the number one button.

The female voice resumed speaking. "Please press five if you need to speak to a representative from the Order of Saint Anthony for lost items. Press six for the Order of Saint Raphael if you are ill, need medical assistance, or have a mental health concern. Press seven for the Orders of Saint Thomas More, Saint Ivo of Kermartin, Saint Catherine of Alexandra, or Saint Genesius of Rome if you are seeking legal counsel. Press eight for the Orders of Saint Augustine of Hippo or Saint Patrick if you are planning a festival in your district and need information on permits and registration. If you need assistance with lingering addiction issues press nine for the Orders of Saint Maximilian Kolbe or Saint Augustine of Hippo. For issues with angel wings, angel device repair or replacements, press ten. To contest a ticket received for speeding, flying in a no-fly zone, disorderly flying, or any other violation involving flight, press eleven. Press twelve for the technology department for interference concerns in your region. Press thirteen for a complete list of all the Orders that will best serve your needs and you will be directed to the appropriate number. Press fourteen for the Order of Saint Michael who will assist you if you need..."

Alastair was numb. His frustration was intensifying from his inability to cope with the technology – a technology created to allow life to advance with ease and swiftness. He removed the receiver from his ear and gawked at the horrendous device as the soft, monotone female voice continued listing the respective saints and the Orders they represented. He knew there were thousands of saints and if he listened to the choice list in its entirety, he could be standing there for centuries. And that was just saints, what if there were more options. He rubbed his left temple as his facial muscles contorted. "This can't be happening," he shouted.

Suddenly a thought occurred to him. It was something he heard from a new angel in a training class that had passed through earlier in the twentieth century. He smiled and began hitting the button marked zero thinking he'd reach the operator directly. He did this multiple times and listened. Moments later a male voice said, "Please key in your angel code number."

Alastair smiled triumphantly, as he quickly entered his code and waited.

"Finally," Alastair muttered cheerfully when another female voice came on the line and said, "Hello."

"Hello," Alastair yelled excitedly.

"Hello, your angel code has revealed that your extended warranty on your angel wings has expired. If you would like to purchase a new warranty, please press one. If you would like to renew your current warranty, please press two. If you would like to add additional coverage on your existing policy, please press three. To receive information regarding your eligibility on upgrading to a newer model, please press four. If you would like to hear more selections, please press five. To return to the main menu…"

Alastair hung up the device in disgust. He ran his finger through his white hair, looked up and yelled, *"How is it possible that I'm in Heaven and I can't even speak or contact the Lord? A tragedy that could obliterate us has occurred! Doesn't anybody hear me?"*

Chapter 21

Alastair

Disappointed, Alastair left the *Information Center* and continued toward the tower. He had lost track of time and had no idea how long he'd been traveling. He felt as if he'd been walking in circles and eventually started his tirade again. *"Don't you see what is happening? Time has been altered... someone is going to die...it's a mistake and it's all my fault,"* he repeated solemnly. *"Please...I beg you...you must make an exception,"* he shouted as he looked upward toward the atmosphere.

Alastair was so desperate that he had been yelling about his situation intermittently with the hopes that someone would answer his pleas for help. He hugged his robes tightly around him and began pacing through the thick cloud cover that had drifted in once again.

"You must hear what I have to say," he shouted again. *"There has been a terrible error...time and lives will be changed...it should never have happened and it's my fault,"* he said dramatically as he continued his rant.

Startled by a strange sequence of unfamiliar beeps he glanced at his angel bracelet. It read, standby for incoming message. He grinned excitedly hoping someone had heard him. His smile immediately turned into a scowl as he silently read the note reminding him of the urgent need to upgrade his warranty on his angel wings. Alastair was incensed. "An advertisement," he shrieked. "This is absolutely preposterous! And to think I never even knew there was a warranty on my wings!"

Chapter 22

Hey Sunshine,

I am having a really bad day and I prayed to God for help but I fear he is not listening. I am a bit discouraged with today's results.

I don't want to bore you with the details, but sometimes I just can't comprehend how this happened. I know you would understand my pain. I feel as if I failed again.

It's been so long and I miss you tremendously. I anxiously await your homecoming. Thanksgiving has passed and Christmas will not be the same without you if you don't come home soon.

All my love,

Me

Chapter 23

Alastair

"Alastair tapped on the device attached to his wrist and watched as the events played out. "This can't be happening," he cried out. "Why isn't anyone listening to me? I *must* get to the Lord," he begged. "A terrible calamity is occurring. The entire situation is escalating to insurmountable proportions!"

He winced as he heard the familiar beeping sequence and shouted furiously, "Is this necessary?" he shouted angrily. He was sick of the messages regarding the angel warranty for his wings. It was annoying and no matter what he did or how many buttons he pushed it would not disappear. To make matters worse he had to listen to the communication in its entirety each time it appeared. He couldn't understand how the Lord allowed this. It was infuriating and his nerves were frazzled enough without the loathsome dispatch playing every fifteen minutes.

He paced rapidly as his facial muscles tightened. He had enough and decided to put an idea he had been formulating into action. If he was quick it could work. Decision made, he hid in the thickest cloud cover he could find, extended his wings, and soared upward. He must have ascended too fast as he instantaneously found himself tumbling back to the lower cloudbanks. It took a moment as he rolled about, attempting to untangle his limbs from his robes.

"Things are going from bad to worse," he mumbled as he stood up. It was the moment when he finally regained his balance and was stretching that he noticed he had another problem.

"It can't be," he screamed as his hands reached behind his shoulders. He felt like he had just lost fifty pounds. "No, I don't believe this is happening." He slowly twisted his head and looked over his right shoulder. He stood straight and yelled, "*Why? Why are you doing this to me?*"

Thoughts of why he never signed up for the extended warranty for his wings lingered as he considered his new predicament.

Chapter 24

Noah

Noah punched in and grabbed his paperwork. He had a big exam approaching and secured his headphones. He had recited his notes earlier into the computer device and then downloaded them. He would listen over and over to help him study. As he walked to the closet to get his cleaning cart he opened, the envelope he had retrieved earlier from his mailbox. In big red letters his nightly paperwork read, ASSIGNMENT CHANGE.

He pushed his hair away from his face, as he still needed a haircut, and groaned as he scanned the paper. *"The fifth floor!"* he shouted. "There has to be a mistake." He skimmed the yellow paper one more time looking for errors. "No, it can't be. Please. Please, *not* the fifth floor!"

Noah wasn't sure if he was going to say anything to his mother. When he complained to her about his move to the basement, months prior, she had scolded him and told him to find something positive about his work. Her words came back to haunt him as he suddenly realized he had sort of grown accustomed to working in the basement.

It was quiet there and nobody bothered him. He didn't really dislike it as much as he thought. After a few months, he knew the regulars and even assisted with the late-night deliveries. The sadness and depression he felt when he was first transferred eventually faded, for it had become routine. He was like a robot on autopilot, yet he still found something to complain about because some days were tougher than others.

"Isn't that the reason you took the job?" his mother had reminded him.

"Not really," he responded, annoyed. "I only work to pay for school and because I work the night shift, I make *more* money. But you *already* know this," he said as his eyes narrowed and lips twisted in disgust.

Noah's mother raised her eyebrows and glared at him. He was almost six feet tall and she had to look up at him. He favored his father with his brown hair and brown eyes. She knew the likeness bothered him, so she had removed the photographs. If he wanted to see pictures of his dad he could look through the few albums they had in the closet.

Noah knew that look and mentally prepared his mind for another lecture.

Instead his mother shrugged and said nonchalantly, "Well if this is your career path, don't you think you're in the right place?"

She had a point. He was learning things that would be useful to his future occupation. He thought about the sermon in church about gratitude. His mother frequently reminded him of it. "Be grateful for what you have and be careful what you ask God for," she would tell him when he moaned about his job.

Noah crumpled the paper and threw it in the trash. "The fifth floor?" He muttered angrily as he thrust his cart into the hall. That was the absolute *last* place he wanted to be. He was immediately sorry he had prayed for a transfer.

Chapter 25

Alastair

"**M**y wings," Alastair shouted. "Don't you think this is going a bit too far?" His hands cut through the air as he gestured in annoyance.

"Not really, but you already know the answer to that question," a male voice answered quietly before emerging from the thick cloud cover.

"Finally! Someone has heard me," Alastair exclaimed, as he rushed toward the figure. His expression of delight turned to curiosity as he approached with trepidation. As he grew closer he realized the angel's white hair was cut short and swept back on top. Short haircuts were undeniably reserved for the highest Angel Orders as he observed when he met Raphael. His clean-shaven face was smooth, unblemished, and glowed radiantly. Wearing robes of shimmering white metallic inlaid with silver threads, which would glisten even on the dreariest of days, Alastair immediately knew this was no ordinary angel.

"I am Lucius."

Alastair took a step backward as his eyes widened in awe. "Lucius, Angel of the Light and teacher?"

Lucius nodded. His green eyes were as bright as a freshly polished emerald.

Alastair was a bit shaken and immediately bowed with respect, as he was standing before one of the *most powerful angels* in the heavenly realm.

Chapter 26

Her and Him

"*I* promise I don't know you," she repeated as he continued staring at her. "I'm sorry but you must be mistaken. You're not familiar to me." Forgetting everything, she blurted, "come we must go to the dwelling. If we don't hurry, seeing will become so difficult that it's terrifying!"

He followed "Are you lost too?" he asked.

She thought about it as they walked faster. "I guess so but can't be sure."

"Are there any more like us?"

"I have seen no others until you appeared." Her pace quickened so much that she was almost jogging.

"Hey, wait for me! What is the rush?"

"I told you. What's above us," she pointed upward, "changes until it's so bad you can't see! We must hurry," she huffed, her voice strained as she moved faster.

With his long legs, his stride lengthened and he easily caught up to her. Gently touching her shoulder he said, "Hey, why don't you take my hand and hold on to your friend with the other. I'm sure he knows the way. It will be okay. I promise you." His eyes sparkled as he spoke.

Anxiety filled her, but the thought of being in the darkness frightened her more. She tentatively reached for his hand. The moment their fingers touched something happened and together they let go as if they had both received an electric shock. They stepped backwards and regarded one another. Something had gone through her, but she had no idea what. She couldn't explain it.

He was first to break the awkward silence. "Did you feel what just happened?"

She didn't know what to think. Moisture formed on the back of her neck and she grabbed her chest as if it would stop the loud thumping. She looked upward and fumbled nervously. "Come, we must hurry," she stated anxiously. They walked briskly in silence and, as predicted, darkness descended upon them.

Chapter 27

The Dwelling

As soon as the dwelling appeared she ran as if she was being chased. Her furry friend followed. The last thing he saw was her long hair fluttering behind her.

She gasped for air as she made it through the entrance, thankful that she had remembered to leave on the bright orb illuminating from above. She sighed heavily as she sat upon one of the soft, oversized items meant for relaxing and thought about the day.

She didn't know what to make of him. At first she had been a bit frightened probably because she had left all that covered her body in a pile, while she floated to enjoy the cool liquid. For some reason he had made her feel vulnerable with nothing on, yet she hadn't felt like she was in any danger. They were also both lost.

What she found strange was the sensation she experienced when their fingers touched. Something happened to her entire body that was inexplicable. In addition, she heard voices but they were jumbled. Someone was yelling but whom? She could have sworn he was there, but he didn't answer. It was too much and her head ached. She thrust her head into her hands and began massaging both sides hoping to make the pain stop. Her furry companion ran over and began licking her face and she threw her arms around him for comfort.

Chapter 28

Noah's Dilemma

N oah had been silent throughout dinner. His mother looked forward to hearing about his day, but tonight her son was lost in his own thoughts.

"Noah! This is the best time of the year – Christmas! What could possibly be wrong now?"

"Nothing really," he said quietly as he moved the food around on his plate.

"Nothing really," she mimicked. "You're acting as if you lost your best friend. I can tell there's something going on."

He pushed a few locks of hair out of his eyes and looked at his mother. "I have a new assignment at work. It starts in January," he muttered, rolling his eyes helplessly.

She peered at him over her glasses and said a bit too sarcastically, "Really?"

"Really, Mom you *don't* understand," he answered a bit too harshly.

She rose and started cleaning the table. "*Honestly,* Noah? I can't possibly imagine what could be *worse* than working in the morgue!"

Noah sighed. "I'm being sent to the *fifth floor,*" he blurted angrily.

His mother turned from the dishwasher and back to the table and erupted in laughter. The irritation in her son's voice was apparent. Hands on her hips, she smirked. This was followed by animated hand gestures and more questions. "The fifth floor… What is wrong with that I can't imagine. Is that like being sent to your room?"

"It's not funny *Mom*. You just *don't understand*."

"What, do they have *more* trash cans up there? No, let me guess; there is *more* mopping than you can handle?"

"Mom, you just don't get it…I've heard too many stories from the others. It's creepy…and…"

"Noah, I *do understand*," she interrupted. "All you do is *complain*. Poor me!

My poor life…how *hard* you have to work! You complain about your job, your life, your assignments at work, or what you don't like at school. Quite frankly, *I have had enough*!"

"Yeah, well Merry Christmas to me. It's my final semester and the *last* place I want to be is on the *fifth floor*," he snapped, as he threw his fork down to emphasize his disappointment.

His mother regarded her son critically. "Noah, when you're at work tonight I want you to take a good look around at everything you see," she gestured as her fingers drew circles in the air. "Because whether it's the first, second, tenth, basement morgue, or the fifth floor – *it's all the same*! You better start figuring out how to put everything, including *your* life, in perspective!" she finished sharply. "It's Christmas! Find something to be thankful for," she snapped, exasperated.

"But…"

"Don't interrupt me, young man! I'm surprised at you, being how book smart you are. I would have thought working in the morgue would have taught you something! I'm telling you now, my son, if you *believe* that going to school and simply choosing a career because of all the *money* you *think* you're going to make, is going to make you *happy*, then you should reconsider!"

She placed some pots in the dishwasher and turned back toward her son before continuing, "Money isn't going to buy you happiness, Noah," she pointed at him. "So you better *think* long and hard about the time you invest again and the *financial* strain you will subject yourself to. Do something that is going to make *you happy;* otherwise, you will be *miserable* for the rest of your life," she finished as she collected more dishes.

"But mom, we've been poor..."

His mother banged a pot on the stove and whipped around like a twister. Her brown eyes zeroed in on his face like a hawk.

He winced at the verbal beating he knew would follow. He should have kept his mouth shut.

"Noah, do you *ever* see me complaining? *Do I grumble about how financially challenged life has been for us? Or about how bad life is? Do I complain that we live in this apartment?"*

"No, but if Dad hadn't..."

Annoyed, she cut him off before he could finish. "Don't bring him into this," she spat. "Noah, you need to let it go. That ship sailed a long time ago. Now, as I was saying, do I *moan or carry on* about how poor I am or how bad life is?"

"No, ma'am," he whispered.

"That's right! You have a roof over your head, food, and clothes on your back, and your health! Think about what *those people* in the morgue have? What about their families? Can't you appreciate or find anything to be grateful for? You need to get your priorities straight. Perhaps your faith is lacking and you don't think you're smart enough? If that's the case maybe you should just quit school and go flip hamburgers or continue cleaning. While it would be a shame to waste that education, it doesn't matter what you choose to do – just do it because it makes *you* happy. Do it because you *want* to do it! Instead of complaining, *just figure it out*!"

Chapter 29

Hey Sunshine,

I read the notes over and over hoping that I overlooked something.

I understand you are unable to return for Christmas. I'm heartbroken. I thought I was prepared but realize that I'm not. I can't bear the thought of spending the holiday without you. I'm also disappointed Logan and Harrison will not be coming. I don't understand their reasons but have no choice to accept their decisions. I still have hope and faith that you will make it home in time.

All my love,

Me

Chapter 30

Him and Her

His eyes scanned the dwelling as he entered. The space was wide open and a dim glow of light from the dark orb above, streamed in from the multitude of windows that filled the sides. His head felt fuzzy. It was as if he couldn't think or understand what he was looking at. Although it was sparsely decorated, it was comforting, but he could not recall what he was attempting to visualize. "I think I've been somewhere similar to this before."

Surprised, she blinked as she often felt the same. "Really? So where are we?"

He continued to walk around, touching the soft items scattered about the room before sitting down. "I'm not quite sure, but the images are here," he pointed to his head. "If I concentrate, I'll see them," he tapped on his head again.

She bolted upright from where she was seated. "Yes," she responded excitedly. "I see things here too," she grabbed her head with both hands, then frowned and let her hands drop, "but they come and go. Sometimes I think so much it hurts."

Seeing the pain on her face he switched topics. "Who is your friend?"

She looked puzzled.

He got up and sat on the other side of the shaggy creature and rubbed his neck. "Who is he? What do you call him?"

"Call him?"

"Yes. You can't just say, hey you. What is his…his um…his name?"

"Name," she muttered. She repeated the word several times as if she was hearing it for the first time.

"I think I've found the answer. He is wearing something around his neck, it's buried beneath all his fur. It says Bear," he read. The tail of the shaggy beast started to wag.

"Bear," she shouted. At the sound of his name her furry friend jumped up and began licking her face and continued flapping his bushy tail.

"Well it's obvious that's his name," he chuckled.

She repeated his name. "Bear, it's a good name," she nodded approvingly.

"Do you know him? Did he arrive with you?"

She rubbed her chin and shook her head. "I don't know. If I think too hard, it aches."

He was confused. He cocked his head to one side and ran his hand through his hair. "I understand how you feel, but I promise I'll be here. Try to concentrate; it'll help."

She put her hands in her lap and laid her head in-between them.

"What do you see?" he urged.

"I see people and, um, I don't know. Ugh! It hurts *too* much. I *must* stop! What does it matter? He has a name," she stated exasperated. She was overly tired from the incoherent voices, images appearing and disappearing, and then his arrival.

There was an awkward moment of silence before she spoke again.

"I stay in there," she pointed to the room on the far left. "There is one for you over there. Come, Bear."

Chapter 31

More Names

The following day he found her outside with Bear in a lux-urious patch of greenery. He stood looking at her before he approached. He liked the way the sun was shining down on her hair and petite form as she bent over and picked at the colorful crops. He watched her lips curl into the biggest smile and couldn't help but notice how white her teeth were.

She felt his presence, looked up and beamed. "Here this is for you," she extended her hand as he walked toward her.

He examined the red ball she placed in his palm before taking a bite. "I've seen this before. I think it's called a t…ma…to? Tomato."

"How do you know that?"

He shrugged. "It tasted familiar and I see pictures in my head. Don't you see the images or hear the voices?"

She grabbed the handful of food she had picked and walked to a nearby bench.

"Did you hear me?" He asked again.

"Yes, I heard you," she answered a bit too sharply. "And I told you, it's too painful." She dismissed him with the wave of her hand. She didn't want to discuss it.

Seeing the pain in her eyes and fallen facial features, he asked, "Are you injured?"

"No, it's all the pictures in here," she said as she pointed to her head. "It hurts too much. They are all jumbled."

Her eyes and expression on her face told him he shouldn't press the issue. She offered him more of the tomatoes and other green crops and they enjoyed the small feast.

"Ok, so what do you do here?" he asked.

She shrugged. "Bear and I just roam. There is so much to see. Come and I will show you." She smiled.

"Ok, but what do I call you?"

Chapter 32

Him, Her, Bear, and a Name

"What do I call myself?" She muttered, not sure of the question. She stopped walking, turned, looked at him, and grinned. "Does it really matter?" She enjoyed gazing at him and stared a bit too long before she resumed walking.

He blinked, surprised, and once again felt this was odd. "Well, I feel it's right that we have names." He thought hard about it as he continued to follow her.

She pushed her hair behind her ear. "Is it really that important?"

"I don't know for some reason it just occurred to me that we need names too."

As she stopped and turned to face him, the light from above momentarily blinded him. He squinted and there was something in the way she moved that caused him to pause and suck in his breath. In that moment the brilliant rays showered down on her hair and face in such a way while highlighting the beauty that surrounded her – well *he* couldn't stop gazing at her radiant features.

It was one of the most beautiful images he had ever seen. She was framed perfectly with the lush landscape in full bloom behind. Suddenly his eyes lit up and he smiled. "I shall call you Lily. For some reason it fits. I have an image of you surrounded by the beautiful flowers that I see before me brightening this place. Like this one," he reached over to cradle one of the yellow blooms in his hand. "For some reason it reminds me of you."

She nodded a few times and grinned. "I like it. I think I've heard it before but can't be sure; besides, I love the smell," she added as she bent down to sniff the scent of the huge bloom. "You must have a name too! I think it's only fair," she beamed as she gazed into his eyes.

He cleared his throat nervously. "Why do you look at me like that?"

Embarrassed she quickly glanced away and ran from him.

"Hey, I'm sorry. I didn't mean to upset you. It's okay. I'll let you in on a secret," he called after her.

She stopped running and waited for him to catch up.

"I think I know how you feel. I like looking at you too," he grinned.

She breathed a sigh of relief. "I don't know why I stare. It's like I know you and I'm trying to figure it out." She reached up and gently touched his face. "Your eyes they are, um, like, what I see above us," she pointed upward.

Her gentle touch electrified his body and he felt hot. What he wore was now sticking to his skin. He sensed he needed her but didn't know why or what it meant. He swallowed and grabbed her hand. "How about we go to the liquid where we met and enjoy the day and perhaps you will think of a name for me?"

She nodded. Her face radiated with delight. Something happened when their hands connected. It made her feel warm.

They slowly walked hand in hand with Bear by their side.

Chapter 33

Hey Sunshine,

The New Year is approaching and I don't know if I can go through this again. I need your help. I wish we could talk but I understand you are too far away. Please let me know everything is going to be okay. I'm afraid and I'm not sure of anything. I need to know you still love me and that I'm doing the right thing.

All my love,

Me

Chapter 34

Alastair's Reality

"You may rise," the great angel stated to Alastair, who bowed as protocol dictated. "There is no reason for such formalities, while I'm very traditional, that is one ancient custom that is unnecessary."

Alastair noticed how his robes shimmered with every movement. He could tell the inlaid, silver thread was of the finest quality.

"Greetings once again. I am Lucius, Angel of the Light," he said officially.

Alastair breathed a sigh of relief. "Finally, I've been calling and…"

"Yes. The *entire kingdom* heard you," he interjected as he briskly unrolled a scroll-like piece of parchment. "You are causing a disturbance and it is not tolerated in this quadrant…"

Alastair cut him off. "I have important business. It's *imperative* that I see the Lord," he blurted impatiently.

"Yes, *you* and *many* other people," Lucius replied evenly. "My superior is extremely busy and doesn't like me to waste time, so I'll get right to the point." He stood straight and in a business-like fashion began reading. "*According to article one trillion, five hundred fifty billion, forty-seven million, six hundred forty-two thousand, seven hundred thirty-six 1.a.2.b.c.AA. BB.M1.2-42.9786.a.b.c.d.m.683.09.06. a.1.B.22.12.07.04.26.6*

*3A.M.2b.z.SS.1.F.116.07.07.1970.J.24.187372387205.22.64.0
4.26.63.07.07.70.05.12.358.1000.100.100.500.1.b.c20.25.214.
LX35016..."*

Alastair's hazel eyes bulged from their sockets. Incensed, he interrupted, "What are you going to read the hundreds of numbers attached to that article? Do you know how large the *Angel Code Book* has become? Nobody can keep up with it let alone remember half those rules including the updates. It's just like that *NFL Referee Rule* book I've heard people complaining about!"

Lucius nodded in agreement. "I'll summarize the pertinent parts. Failure to follow protocol…failure to report any incident that could bring and/or produce devastation or upset the balance and order of the heavenly or earthly realm…failure to report to your supervisor…leaving an assignment and failure to contain your training group…and causing a disturbance in the sacred celestial quadrant," he responded.

Alastair's leathery skin, from years of working outdoors, turned as white as his goatee, which was clearly in need of a trim

"I also understand that you have *six citations* for flying in a No-Fly Zone, including disregarding the posted signs, traveling without a ticket, and failure to pay the required toll… Would you like me to continue?"

Alastair closed his eyes in shame and couldn't imagine what his family would think, as he listened to the charges. He nodded and gestured indifferently for Lucius to resume. *How much worse could it get,* he thought, scowling.

"Paragraph 2B24785938437273 states, "Your actions are grounds for the loss of angel wings and re-evaluation of your position. Angels will be required to stand before the Council of Elders for discussion."

Alastair's jaw dropped and his mouth hung open. He was speechless. *The Council of Elders?* He closed his eyes and again wondered what his parents would say. He could see the disappointment on their faces. The shame he would bring to his family would be known throughout his entire celestial neighborhood. His head snapped up to protest but he bit his lip instead thinking perhaps he should compose his thoughts, when his gaze met the blazing eyes of Lucius.

"Sign here," Lucius said as he thrust a white, feathered pen toward him.

Chapter 35

The Statement

"That's it? I sign and you leave? Don't you even want to listen to why I came?" Alastair stood, confused.

"Oh, yes of course. My apologies. It has been a *long time* since there has been a *circumstance* as such," he said evenly. "If you would like to record a statement please do so in section B," he pointed to the parchment. "If you need more time you can log into the website; passwords will be established when you sign in. After you download the document, you will be required to create several *additional* passwords due to the *sensitivity of the statement*. Finally, you will be prompted to make a record of your account and submit it electronically."

Alastair couldn't have felt more humiliated. Life was so much easier when there was just parchment. He had no time to download anything as he found the entire process daunting; furthermore, he could barely remember his password for his angel bracelet, let alone numerous others. His mind was racing. He needed a plan. He knew without his wings he had no angel magic. He smiled and took the pen and began writing. He spoke aloud as he carefully scripted his statement and recorded,

"This new group of angels arrived in my training class. They were incorrigible. In all my thousands of years, I've never seen such an unruly assemblage of youth! They

refused to listen, disobeyed all instruction, and were pursuing of all things - something they referred to as 'the cloud.' I told them they were surrounded by clouds and to stop with their foolishness."

What sounded like hearty laughter resonated from the atmosphere above? Alastair stopped writing and looked at Lucius. "Did you say something?"

"Not at all," he smiled. "The weather deities must be arguing again. Perhaps a storm is brewing," he surmised.

Alastair could have sworn the great angels captivating, green eyes twinkled mysteriously, almost to the point of laughter. He shrugged it off and continued writing and talking aloud. *"This group was seeking something called 'video games' and then of all things demanded a mouse! I explained no rodents were allowed in this part of the celestial realm! Can you imagine? I believed there was something dreadfully wrong with the entire collection of misfits and was certain a terrible mistake was made and then…I was going to report their behavior but later decided…"*

Alastair looked up. "I need another pen; this one ran out of ink."

"Your statement is limited to a word count of exactly one hundred and twenty-five words, as indicated in the fine print, which you should have read. I'm sorry you've exceeded the limit," he said calmly. The pen and parchment flew out of Alastair's lap into the waiting hands of Lucius, who added, "Scripting irrelevant facts is not going to help your situation."

Alastair rubbed his temple in annoyance. "What am I to do now?"

"Fix the problem you created," Lucius said calmly.

"*Fix it*!" Alastair said aghast. His eyes and neck protruded as he arched forward. "How am I to do that *without* my wings? Or my angel bracelet?" Which he had just realized was now missing.

"Ah yes…I almost forgot according to article 0426196357358-56-150F of the privacy act, I am unable to comment on your unfortunate circumstances."

Alastair was astonished. "So what am I to do? Just sit around here?" he said sarcastically.

Lucius nodded as he thought about the Angel of the Twelfth Order and his predicament. "Just give me a minute," he said as he scanned the ancient document. "Ahh, here it is. Apparently you must report to the *Reflection Pond…*"

"You must be joking," Alastair interrupted, his voice exploding in disbelief.

Lucius rolled the ancient parchment, stood poised and stated quietly, "I never joke. You will have to watch the story unfold and fix your error! If not the Council of Elders will be your next stop. The Reflection Pond is down the cloud path and to the right," Lucius pointed. "You must figure out a way to solve the problem you've created."

"How much time do I have?" Alastair fidgeted nervously.

"Before the story ends."

Overwhelmed, Alastair's jaw dropped. "But, but…there isn't time…it's an emergency…"

"I'm sorry. I don't make the rules," Lucius interjected apologetically. "If you read the *Angel Code Book* you would already know that article 450000000.500000.1. 75.100.A.D.57.1000.5000 states every situation has its own timeline and is dictated by…"

"Really," Alastair interrupted, annoyed. "This could take years," he argued.

"Then I suggest you get right on it," Lucius snapped his fingers and added, "may I also remind you that this *IS A NO-FLY ZONE*." He was gone before Alastair could blink.

"Well that would be impossible since I don't have my wings," Alastair shouted, his eyes blazing. He was devastated he was left alone in what had instantly transformed into a sea of fog. He stood in the middle of the fog as it engulfed him wondering how

he arrived at this juncture? How did this happen? Why him? Why didn't anyone want to listen to him? Didn't anybody care about the emergency? Where was the Lord? Why didn't he see what was happening? Anxiety and fear surged through his body like water flowing in a creek. He felt as if he couldn't breathe and in his desperation to reach the Lord, he failed. Utterly disgusted, the entire situation looked bleak. He was broken and his world had been torn apart. The negatives outweighed the positives. His face twisted with anguish as he wanted to scream but he knew nothing would come of it.

As he headed in the direction of the Reflection Pond to contemplate his next course of action he suddenly realized there was *one positive outcome* of the entire situation; his face brightened and he took comfort in the fact that he no longer had to listen to messages regarding the purchase of an extended warranty for his wings!

Chapter 36

The Reflection Pond

Alastair had been walking in the direction Lucius had pointed. The fog hadn't lifted so he had no idea if he was even traveling on the correct route. He considered turning around and returning home, but he was so lost and without his wings or bracelet he would have a lot more explaining to do. *Why would God do this to me,* he silently wondered. "You know, Lucius," he spoke out loud, "I can't fix something if I can't *even* find my way. If you would let me go to the *Tower* instead of the *Reflection Pond,*" he emphasized, "then I would have the opportunity to see the Lord, clear up this mess, and return home then things would be back to normal, but no…"

Suddenly the heavy fog began to lift and the mist became clearer and clearer until Alastair was standing on dirt surrounded by thriving trees. As he surveyed his surroundings he noticed another wooden post, lying on the ground. He rushed toward the fallen marker, which had rotted at the base. He turned his head and read aloud each of the signs:

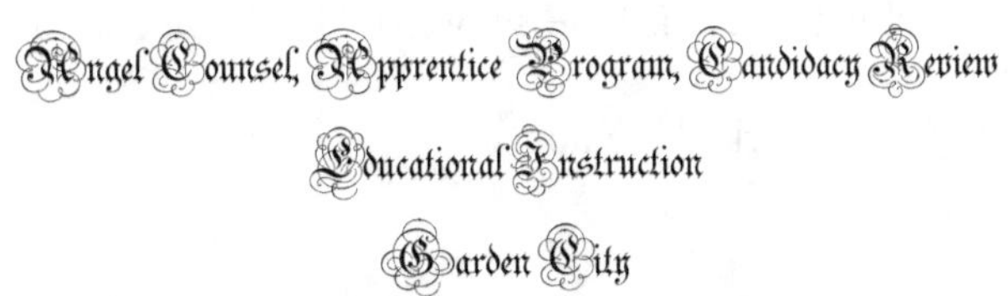

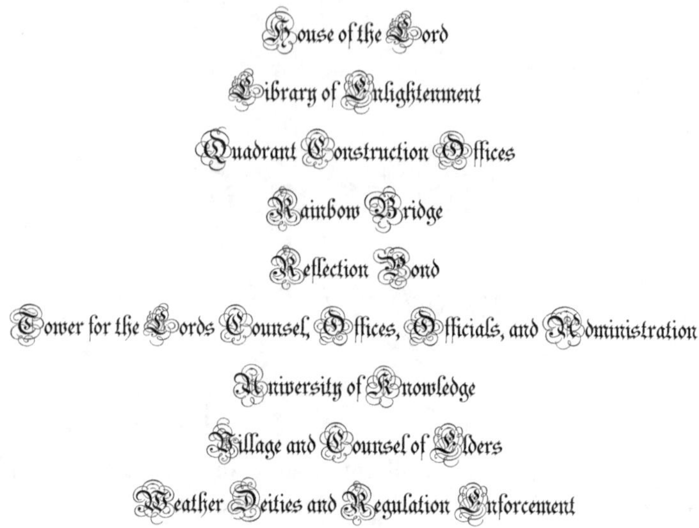

He threw up his hands in frustration. "Just great," he yelled. "Nobody notices a fallen sign? If I ever get out of this mess you better believe I'm going to report this quadrant," he shouted to the clouds above. "How do you expect me to fix something if I can't even get to where I'm going?" he taunted.

Unexpectedly, the rest of the fog evaporated and multitude of paths were revealed – some rough, others smooth, which all led into a forest of dense trees. Alastair could see fog hovering above all the pathways. As he was deciding which path he should take, a big, brown, shaggy dog came walking down the worst and rockiest of all the routes. The dog stopped in front of Alastair and shook his body from side to side, splattering him with mud and cold water. "Thank you for that," he winced as he wiped the mud and water off his face and now stained cloak. "Do you think I have time to launder this? The Lord will never see me looking like this," he scowled. "I look like a common beggar! Ugh!"

Woof, woof barked the dog.

Alastair sighed and studied the dog. "Ah, a retriever. I'm guessing you came from the Rainbow Bridge?" The dog cocked his head to one side as if questioning him.

"Have you come to help me?" he joked. "I'm lost too." Alastair bent down and reached for the tag on his collar. "Cooper," he read. "It says your name is Cooper. Is this true?"

Woof.

"Okay, I'll take that as a yes. It will be nice to have some company," he said as he began walking toward one of the paths. "Cooper let me tell you something I have had the most devastating journey and…"

Alastair had stopped moving when he realized Cooper was not at his side. He spun around when the dog began barking only to find him heading toward the muddy and rocky path.

"No, not that one," he shouted. "Come this way, it's cleaner. Look, there are no rocks, or sludge and it looks easier to navigate."

Woof, woof barked the dog as he continued through the mud and rocks.

"No, come back. Let's go this way," Alastair gestured again.

The dog twisted and pawed at the mud-covered ground as if to say he was wrong and continued at a leisurely pace, down the dirtiest and rockiest path of them all.

"Do you know how to get to the *Reflection Pond*?" he teased.

Cooper stopped and looked at him once more before resuming his pace. Not wanting to be alone, Alastair shook his head in defeat, gathered his muddy robes and followed. "What have I got to lose?"

Chapter 37

Noah
January 2001

*I*t was January seventh. The holidays and New Years had passed quietly and Noah was back at work. He pushed his broom down the hall and was thinking about the recent conversation with his mother before his thoughts were interrupted. He stopped when he heard the familiar codes called and watched as a team of people raced down the hall into a secured wing. While there was a separate entrance and elevators for families and physicians, you could still hear the commotion that something was happening. The evidence was in the sounds of the equipment from the nurse's station, beeping, the faces, the tears, and the all too familiar page to the basement, which told him what had occurred.

"It's sad. Isn't it?"

Noah jumped, startled. He had been so transfixed on the episode down the hall, he hadn't realized someone was behind him.

"Hi! I haven't seen you here before. Are you new?" she asked cheerfully.

Noah *seldom* spoke with anyone at work. He simply nodded or waved as he passed. He was too busy listening to his headphones that played his recorded notes from lectures. Most people ignored him for they thought he was strange, as he always seemed to be talking to himself when he was actually studying and repeating terms back. It didn't matter; everyone left him alone because he showed up for work and did an exceptional job. He continually received great evaluations and never had a complaint registered against him. "Umm, um," he stammered. "I was…um, just um, assigned here."

Ugh! She must think I'm an idiot. I barely got the words out.

She was stunning. Blond hair fell just below her shoulders. It was wavy and she had some of it pinned back. He couldn't stop staring into her eyes. They were as blue as the sky on a clear day. Her blue scrubs only enhanced the color. His eyes traveled to the small birthmark that rested high on her right cheek. It only enhanced her sex appeal.

She was beautiful. Her complexion was clear and her face was warm and friendly. She had a camera-friendly smile to complement her perfectly even white teeth. If she hadn't been wearing scrubs, he would have mistaken her for a fashion model. The pretty girls at school *never* talked to him, and he wouldn't even consider attempting to chat with them. He kept to himself, hung with his nerdy friends, and worked. He was speechless. He couldn't believe someone *so* gorgeous was *actually* speaking to him.

Her blue eyes sparkled and her movie star smile grew as she glanced at his name badge. "Well hello, Noah. Welcome to the fifth floor. I'm Gemma. I've been working here for some time. That's the south wing," she pointed in the direction of the disturbance. "It's the worst place on this floor."

Noah groaned. It was just what he feared.

The frightened look on his face was apparent. "I'm sorry. I didn't mean to upset you," she said calmly.

Noah noticed her voice too. She was soft-spoken but there was a confidence about her. He bet all the patients liked her.

"What I meant was, well, it's sad because after time passes most people stop coming and then, well, you saw what happens. It's restricted. Even we don't have access so don't worry so much. I work here and know everybody. I'll show you around to make it easier."

Chapter 38

Him and Lily

"*I*t's amazing," he shouted. "I've never seen anything so exquisite."

Lily had taken him on a different path through a dense growth of trees. It was not as bright but when the two of them emerged, not only was there another huge body of liquid, but countless things shooting through the air.

Lily pointed. "I don't know what they are do you?"

"They're birds and butterflies," he shouted excitedly over the noise as he easily identified the flying critters.

"Birds and butterflies," she repeated. "Why do you know so much and I have such difficulty?"

"I don't know," he frowned. "Perhaps you have to think harder."

The noise was earsplitting as the liquid fell and crashed loudly on some huge formations below. "It's remarkable," he yelled in awe, as he dropped her hand and walked toward the liquid. Bear had already run in and was splashing around.

"What do you think?"

He bent down and scooped up the liquid. "The water…it's perfect! Not too hot and not too cold."

She ran to his side. "Water? You called it water?" she shouted enthusiastically.

"I don't know," he contemplated. "The image, it just came to me. Yes, it's called water. I'm positive," he answered confidently.

Lily nodded. "It sounds right. Water," she repeated.

They both removed the coverings from their feet.

"Come, let's go in," he said eagerly. He shed all his material but his bottoms and jumped in.

Self-conscious, and when she was sure he wasn't looking, she took off her skirt then ran into the water. Her top was long enough to provide the coverage she felt was proper. They spent the day having fun, laughing, and later resting on the shore, basking in the warm light from above.

"I feel like we should be talking more," he announced.

"Talking," she muttered. "I'm not sure I understand."

"It's like what we're doing now," he pointed to his mouth.

Lily thought about it as she touched her pursed lips. "Is this talking? Well, is it necessary? What is the purpose?"

His eyes narrowed. He felt confused. "I don't really know," he answered. "I guess you have a point, but why not?"

She shrugged, as she had no response. She simply liked watching him but didn't understand why. He was nice to look at. There was something about the way the water glistened and dripped off his hard form that moved her. She couldn't describe the feelings she experienced when their bodies touched. It was as if she knew him, except there was no image of him in her head. It was strange and disconcerting.

He liked being close with her and often reached for her arm or shoulder as they enjoyed the day. He was glad the water and material separated them as he felt a confusing yearning that he was sure he had never experienced before. It was indescribable.

As the day wore on she desperately tried to recall if they knew one another but, again, nothing came to mind. What she did see were images of pictures. His body reminded her of something and she unconsciously reached out to touch his stomach.

He rose on his elbows at the jolt from her fingers as she ran them across his well-sculpted form. Her touch was electrifying. Before he could say anything she said, "I see this, I see myself examining and looking at pictures and making pictures from what I see."

He couldn't think. Nothing made sense. He was feeling frustrated and so puzzled that he couldn't express what was happening to him. The only thing he knew was that her caress was soft and he enjoyed it. "Do you see anything else?" He sighed as he lay back down.

She quickly removed her hand. She felt as if she had done something wrong. "No." She stopped thinking about the unexplainable images that filled her head and decided to enjoy the day.

"Do you think we've been here before? Don't you feel this is something we've done already?" he asked.

"Perhaps," she muttered. She didn't care to think about anything but having fun with him and Bear. She had not realized how alone she had been until now.

Chapter 39

Him and Lily

Days later, they sat together at the wooden structure near the garden trying to determine how they arrived at a place they had no idea existed. He persisted with the idea that it was necessary they speak. "Perhaps we were already here and just wandered from the other side," he offered. "Do you have any idea how long you've been living here?"

Lily was enjoying the juicy fruit as she had every day after the darkness had passed. She loved the warm light from above. She gave him the same response, as she was tired of discussing the topic. "I already told you I *just don't know!*"

"Do you think we came here at the same time? Perhaps we arrived together and were separated? Maybe if you think harder it would help. I keep telling you about the images I see, and sometimes they are clear. Like for some reason I keep seeing figures, who wear white, like the material around you," he pointed. "There are other people, but I can't see their faces. Then it all turns black."

Lily shook her head. *"I told you I don't see anything,"* she said adamantly.

There was no way she was going to tell him what she really was seeing in her head.

He eyed her suspiciously. He was getting annoyed with her because every conversation was the same and she refused to try.

The more questions he asked, the further she retreated into her own darkness. Her silence told him she didn't want to talk about it, but he did. "Lily. Please I need your help," he pleaded.

She looked up and made the mistake of staring again. His eyes were so mesmerizing. The color – it was so deep, she just loved looking at them.

"Lily! You have to try to recall something. Please! We're here together for a reason and we need to figure out why. There may be others too!"

His deep voice broke her trance and she looked down at the table and sighed heavily. Her head hurt from all the questions. For some reason she didn't want to remember. Suddenly her head shot up. He could see the sparkle in her eyes as the sides of her mouth formed into a smile. "J.T.," she blurted out.

"Huh?"

"J.T., that's your name."

He thought about it for a minute and shook his head in agreement. "J.T. I like it. Did you see an image in your head? How did it come to you?"

She nodded. "Yes. I saw an image. I heard someone call your name," she lied easily. She couldn't stand when he badgered her with questions. She didn't want to remember. She didn't want to think about anything. The truth was she had been looking down she saw the letters carved on the side of the bench.

Chapter 40

Noah and Gemma

*I*n the weeks that followed, Gemma met Noah when he arrived on the unit. In the beginning, he just cleaned rooms and she trailed behind him and talked. He wasn't accustomed to chatting with people, especially women. He barely had time for his nerdy friends let alone a girl. Not just any girl, but a gorgeous one. He soon found it easier to talk with her the more she spoke to him.

"Noah, what are you doing with those flowers? You're not going to throw them out, are you?"

Noah turned with the vase in hand. "I change the water while I'm cleaning the room to keep them fresh. People bring flowers all the time and just forget about them. This guy," he pointed toward the patient in the first bed, "he has so many floral arrangements; it's too much. I'm putting this vase and some others over here for this patient. I feel sorry for her."

Gemma smiled. "Lilies, yellow lilies…my favorite."

Noah noticed the sad look in her eyes. "Are you okay, Gemma?"

"Yes, I'm just so moved that you take the time to do this for the patients and I bet nobody notices. Always remember, Noah, women *love* flowers. You should *always* make sure they have flowers."

They eventually settled into a pattern. He cleaned while she did her rounds in each room. Each patient had a story. Gemma knew who they were, when they arrived, and what happened that brought them to the fifth floor. He watched closely as she did some treatments, adjusted computer monitors, moved patients, and massaged their limbs.

He also learned that Gemma was highly educated. She had degrees in biology and chemistry and a doctorate in neuroscience. She explained the importance of chemistry; how it related to neurology and rambled on about cutting-edge treatments involving neurotransmitters and other technical terms that were beyond Noah's comprehension. She told him she liked working the night shift as she enjoyed the quiet and was able to learn a lot more about the patients.

Noah thought what she did was fascinating. He found himself wanting to spend more time with her too. "This is interesting; do you think you can teach me more?" he asked one evening.

Gemma smiled. "Of course, I'll teach you everything I know. If you agree to help me with some of my therapies."

Noah was a bit wary. "Um, I'm not sure. I don't think I should be doing something like that. Don't you have other doctors to help you?"

"Sure, but that's why I'm assigned to this floor. If I need help I could ask; however, I see you're interested, so I'm asking you," she said as she pulled hair into a ponytail and secured it. "It's not like you're going to be performing surgery."

Noah frowned and his lips twisted.

Gemma's eyes sparkled. "Say what you really mean, Noah."

"It's sort of scary, the people," he pointed to the male and female patient.

Gemma whispered, "Just pretend they're sleeping and it's our job to get them to wake up! You look troubled, Noah. What is it?"

"It's just that they look…look um…like the people in the basement…in the morgue…and then…oh…I…I…don't know," he said frustrated as he ran his hand through his brown hair.

Gemma regarded Noah curiously. "Noah, those people in the morgue can't come back. These people we can help," she stated positively. "They have a chance."

Noah nodded. *She was right. She must think I'm foolish.* "Um…ok, but um…"

"It's okay, Noah. Say what you mean and always be honest."

"Wh…at...what…I mean," he stammered, "why at night?"

"It's the best time. The body is in a resting state and responds better. It's a study I'm working on. I'm on the verge of a huge breakthrough and technology is part of it. Yes, the treatments are done during the day. But you would be surprised what you learn just from talking and watching someone especially at night." Gemma frowned. "Perhaps you're too scared to learn something new? Perhaps you really are too afraid of them?"

The challenge hung in the air for a brief second before Noah responded confidently, "I'm absolutely not afraid! I *want* to learn, and I *will* help you!"

Her perfectly white teeth glistened as her smile widened. "Good, we'll start tonight."

Chapter 41

The Reflection Pond

"There has to be some sort of mistake," Alastair gasped in disgust when they arrived. The Reflection Pond was dark and murky. The gloomy clouds above hadn't moved and a light mist hovered over a surface of dirt and mud. To make matters worse, rocks in a variety of sizes littered the area. Ominous cloudbanks of gray hues floated like a thin veil above and around him. The dismal atmosphere combined with his plight only added to his depressed state of mind.

Alastair found a spot near the pond and sat on some flat rocks and waited. His apprehension grew as he fidgeted nervously as nothing was happening. His occasional outbursts toward the atmosphere, revealing his displeasure with the situation only increased his anxiety and fury. Nothing changed until days later.

Cooper, who had curled up by his side, raised his head and barked. Together they watched as the ripples on the water finally became still, and to his surprise, the story he previously saw on his angel bracelet was now depicted on the pond water.

Alastair was perplexed as he tried to put the pieces together. It didn't help that he arrived late and apparently had missed some parts; however, it was obvious that his group of trainees had done a lot of damage, more than he realized. The problem was he had no idea how to fix any of it.

Chapter 42

Hey Sunshine,

I feel as if I did something horrific and I'm sorry. I'm sorry I hurt you. I wish you could call me; I miss talking and laughing with you. I wish you could tell me it's going to be okay. I wish I could go back. I hope you are doing well. I beg for your forgiveness.

All my love,

Me

Chapter 43

Lily and J.T.
February 2001

*L*ily awoke to screaming. Bear was by her feet as she threw back the blanket and ran to the other room. She watched in horror as J.T. struggled, his arms punching the air, yelling, "Help me, help me," over and over again.

Franticly she knelt by his side and called his name, "J.T. wake up, what's wrong?" She pushed his hair, which had grown past his ears, away from his face. "You must wake up!" She tried to shake him, but her herculean efforts failed as she didn't possess the strength. He was too big to move. Another chorus of, "help me and get out," began.

"J.T.," she shrieked anxiously. Bear jumped up and began licking his face while he continued to yell incoherent thoughts. Lily rose and hovered over him as she was going to try to grab his arms one more time. As she reached out, her limbs became tangled with his and she landed on top of his chest.

Stunned at the warmth that penetrated her skin she lay there as the yelling slowly ended. She could feel an occasional jerk or spasm as his body began to calm down. Lily put her head on his chest and caressed his face as she attempted to relax him further. "Shh, it will be okay. Please wake up. You're going to be all right," she muttered over and over.

His arm tightened around her back and that was how they fell asleep.

Chapter 44

Noah and Gemma

"What was that all about?" Noah asked, stunned. He and Gemma heard the commotion from the other room and came quickly. He was a bit frightened by the patient's reaction. He was yelling and Noah didn't want anything to happen. "Who were those people that just left?"

"Two members of his family," Gemma muttered. "Visiting hours are over and they must have snuck in again. His family is a mess. When they visit, they argue and you've seen how he responds."

"What if he's reacting to something else?"

Gemma shrugged, as she checked and made adjustments to the computer. "That's possible too. But that family is definitely a trigger. These patients are in different levels of unconsciousness and I think they're listening to us. I believe we can bring them back only if they want to return. If the injury is too serious they may not make it. Nobody wants to live in a vegetative state. I'm working on a stimulation treatment, like I showed you. We keep the lights low, play music, show videos, or read. Did you see how he reached for her? These two need one another. Help me move the beds a bit closer," she said enthusiastically.

Noah was barely listening. Gemma had on her usual pale blue scrubs and her hair was pulled into a ponytail. The extent of her make-up regime was nothing, yet her face always looked sunny and bright. She continually smelled like fresh flowers. He was still in awe that someone so stunningly beautiful would converse with him. But tonight there was something about her that made her look so lively and pure.

"Noah," she grinned as she looked over at him, "I need your help. Or are you going to stand there staring at me all night?"

Noah could feel the blood rushing to his face and was sure his cheeks were red with embarrassment.

Chapter 45

Willow

Willow Rose Laurent was eager to start her new job. She had left her fast-paced career in a New York hospital for something different. After several interviews she was offered the position. It was temporary but could become full time if the other person didn't return from sabbatical, but she didn't care. She desperately needed a change. She gave notice, sublet her apartment, and within two months had moved.

The townhouse she rented overlooked the mountains. It was nice to wake up to clear skies and wide-open spaces, instead of tall skyscrapers and the discordant noise from the traffic and hustle-and-bustle of city life. She relished the quiet as she sat on her balcony having her morning coffee and marveled at the wildlife that wandered by on occasion.

She was eager to meet and work with the distinguished Doctor Aaron Carter. He was a neurosurgeon who was partially responsible for building a state-of-the-art research facility for the care and study of coma patients and people suffering from head trauma. Unfortunately, their meeting had been postponed. The director of human resources informed her they would continue with the orientation process and she would be meeting with Doctor Carter when he returned from his vacation in March.

Her initial reaction was disappointment. She was a bit perturbed, as it was never mentioned he was taking a vacation during her interview. If she had known, she might have looked around more before she selected her current rental. Willow shrugged it off and used the time to get settled in.

She received a warm welcome from the staff. They were glad someone was finally hired to help manage the workload. The person who had the job prior was a Doctor Christo, who left mounds of paperwork behind, so she had her work cut out for her. She was also attempting to learn anything she could about Doctor Carter from the employees when she was promptly summoned to the human resources department.

The middle-aged director, whose taut, wrinkled skin, indicated she clearly spent too much time in the sun, curtly reminded her about the privacy statement she had signed. Willow studied her as she spoke. She guessed she was in her late fifties. Her outdated make-up, coarse, reddish-black hair from bad hair coloring did little to preserve her youth. Her glory days were long gone.

The director, sensing she was not paying attention, cleared her throat, and Willow immediately stopped her profiling. "In addition, you must repeat the entire orientation competency regarding the *strict hospital gossip policy.*"

Willow's brown eyes expanded in disbelief. She had never been exposed to such stringent rules, but due to the nature of the cases and the protocols it was necessary. Privacy of the patients was the same for the staff who worked there too. Apparently Doctor Carter's personal life was off limits along with the rest of the physicians.

The staff was bound to multiple non-disclosure agreements and it seemed everyone was tight lipped about all the doctors' private business, inner workings of the center, and the patients. "Gossip will not be tolerated and it does not have a place at the Coma-Trauma Center at Grace General Hospital and College of Medicine," the leathery-skinned director snapped brusquely.

Idle gossip not only violated a host of privacy acts, but also, was disruptive and took the focus off patient care and learning. The medical college was part of the campus and gave students the opportunity to train, study, and learn. "Concentration is strictly on patient recovery, learning, and research and *not* what everyone did over the weekend or who is available to date! It's all right if people *volunteer* information, but it's *not* okay to *gossip* about it," the director sternly warned her. An image of an alligator with bifocals came to mind as the leather-skinned director glared over her glasses at her.

Willow winced and quickly apologized, claiming she was only trying to discover Doctor Carter's latest projects so she wasn't behind in her work. The cantankerous director was not fooled. "Miss Willow, you already have the credentials and that's why we hired you. There will be plenty of time to *impress* the doctor with your knowledge. I'm sure you have a lot to offer. Just take your time settling in and do your best until Doctor Carter returns. Doctor Judy Ann Mason will assist you. She is familiar with the entire program!"

Willow smiled politely and departed. She was incensed! Forty-five years old and she couldn't recall the last time she was reprimanded. It was not her intention to pry or break any policy. It wouldn't happen again. So while she waited to meet Doctor Carter she wasted no time getting acclimated. She participated in rounds, continued meeting the staff, and learning their responsibilities. The rest of her days were spent reviewing records, organizing, and making sure expected reports were in order when the doctor returned. She worked closely with Doctor Judy Ann to complete and keep up with the data charts she wanted to view daily and was ready to give a full report. She was also busy in her research lab and was excited to share her ideas.

Chapter 46

Lily and J.T.

J.T. had no recollection of last night. He awoke fully rested and content. Lily explained how he screamed and grabbed her for comfort. She apologized for falling asleep on top of him, but he didn't seem to mind.

J.T. ignored the voices and the blurred faces in his head. He was more interested in spending time with Lily. When he awoke to find her sleeping on his chest, he couldn't describe the peaceful feeling and wanted it to last forever.

They agreed to stay close to the dwelling due to J.T.'s incident. When night fell, he tried to coax Lily to come outside. He had to beg her to come. She made it as far as the porch and sat down on the stairs. He pointed to the sky and they sat staring in awe at the bright orb that shone down upon them. It was exceptionally luminous. "It's brilliant," Lily muttered.

J.T. agreed but wasn't referring to what was above. Lily was bathed in a soft glow of light as she sat with her arm around Bear, gazing quietly at the wonder above. Her long, wavy hair hung down her back. The light highlighted her curves, as his eyes wandered across her chest and torso. She reminded him of softness and innocence. Subconsciously he already knew she would never hurt him. Why he thought this, he had no idea.

Chapter 47

Dear Sunshine,

For the first time I have nothing to say. I am again angry and bitter. I miss you terribly and keep deliberating if I made a mistake? I question if I should have let you go on your journey so soon? If only we were able to speak prior...

I'm heartbroken. Please try to contact me...if possible.

All my love,

Me

Chapter 48

The Wilson Family
March 2001

"Why is she still here?" Warren Wilson demanded.

Doctor Aaron Carter jumped at the unmistakable voice. He put down the chart, made some notes, and returned it to the chart rack. His meeting with the Wilson family was not for another hour, but they had intercepted him during his morning rounds in the hall.

He turned toward the hefty man. Equal in height and stature, yet opposite in temperament. His imposing presence and loud voice commanded the attention of anyone listening. "I don't care what you want, Mr. Wilson," he said briskly as he grabbed another chart. "I explained to you back in December that a private room was not possible. Don't you remember what happened? Don't you recall the conversation we had?" He asked, as he recorded more information in the notes section. He spoke firmly but not rudely.

Warren Wilson was incensed. His red face indicated his blood pressure was on the rise. "Doctor Carter, do you think I'm foolish? Of course I remember. I recall the phone call, flying out here, and spending Christmas and New Years in *this* hospital. We *now* have an apartment in town and I'm commuting back and forth from New York. *When the hell is he going to wake up?*"

"Mr. Wilson, you need to lower your voice and relax or I'm going to put the blood pressure cuff on you and if it's too high, I *will* admit you!"

The woman next to him confirmed it when she told him to calm down. "Warren, the doctor's right. Your blood pressure, *please*, you need to relax."

Aaron didn't miss how she nervously touched the back of her neck. Her blond hair was swept back into a perfect and elegant chignon that framed her delicate face. He wondered how she ended up with this overbearing man.

"I will not be silenced," he roared, as he ignored his wife and followed the doctor moving about the long, circular counter. "I demand to know *who* this woman is and *when* my son is going to *wake up*!"

Aaron rubbed his temple and sighed heavily. "Mr. Wilson, please. It would be more appropriate if we spoke in my office during your scheduled appointment and not in the hall," he whispered.

"I don't care. I've waited for you to return from vacation and I want some answers and I want them now!" His displeasure was noted as his hands gestured swiftly through the air.

"We already discussed this, apparently they arrived together."

"*Impossible*! As I previously explained, we don't know who she is. I've never seen or heard my son mention her before!" he stated adamantly.

"Well, it's a fact. You can read it in the police and emergency response report. They were discovered together," he reiterated as he moved around the nurses' station.

"Warren, please, you need to calm down," his wife reminded him again. Her blue eyes blazed with fury. "Warren, you're making a scene. I think it's best if we come back at our scheduled appointment."

"Stella, we need answers and I've waited long enough."

His wife sighed and shook her head regretfully.

Doctor Carter leaned on the counter. "Look, Mr. Wilson, I have kids too and as much as I try to keep abreast of all their friends, I don't know everyone. I'm sure you understand. And this thing called the Internet has made parenting rather difficult. They talk to everyone and have acquaintances, networks, groups, and contacts all over. I can't keep up! Isn't it *conceivable* that he knows her from someplace? Maybe he met her during his vacation?"

The older man's lips curled in annoyance. "*It's highly unlikely!*" he barked as he pounded his fist on the counter. The nurse on the phone jumped, startled.

His irritation mounted and his eyes bulged from his sockets and his facial muscles tightened. "I know *all* his friends and *who* he associates with and…and she just doesn't look like someone who could be in his inner circle."

The doctor's eyes narrowed, displeased, as he peered at the frustrated father over his glasses for the acerbic comment, "Really, Mr. Wilson?"

"The people he was with before the accident *knew nothing* about her either! They confirmed they have no idea who she is!"

Aaron glanced toward Mr. Wilson's wife, who stood by silently as her husband continued his rant. She shook her head, and mouthed, "I'm sorry," as she once again apologized for her husbands' behavior.

He nodded and flashed her, a half-smile, silently communicating that it was okay.

"My son is getting married. Do you know who he is engaged to?"

Aaron rubbed his neck and grimaced. He hadn't slept well last night and had been feeling the effects all morning. He breathed heavily. He understood their anger. He looked the infuriated parents in the eyes. "Mr. and Mrs. Wilson you need to face facts. Unless a miracle happens your son will not be getting married anytime soon. The only thing I know to be true was he was found holding hands with her at the crash site. Maybe he was seeing someone else on the side. Isn't it feasible?"

Warren Wilson's eyes looked as if they were going to pop out of their sockets. He hesitated before exploding, "I'm telling you, doctor, I highly doubt it!" He pointed at him for emphasis. He clenched his teeth and his jaw tightened as he spoke. "I know my son and he does *not know that girl!*" he spat heatedly.

"I read the police report, Mr. Wilson. His fiancé and his friend confirmed they left the ski resort and returned to their lodgings. Your son stayed back and continued skiing with others. Perhaps he met her after," he suggested. "All we know is he left the mountain and somehow was involved in that dreadful accident. Again, it appears he *was* with her as they were discovered together holding hands," he repeated for emphasis, hoping it would help them face reality.

Chapter 49

Family Demands

Doctor Aaron Carter was silent as he watched the stunned faces of the parents. Their blue eyes and blond hair, contrasted with their pale faces. The tragedy had definitely taken its toll on the husband whose blond hair seemed to turn grayer every time he visited. He glanced at Mrs. Wilson. He could see the tears streaming down her cheeks. She was trying to hold it together. This was the part of the job he disliked. Surgeries were easier than having to speak with the families. "I didn't mean to sound disrespectful, Mrs. Wilson, but I can only tell you the facts as we know them."

She nodded, as she was too shaken to face the truth and wiped away her tears.

Aaron knew she was brokenhearted and felt bad she had to put up with this man. She wasn't as tall as her husband and Aaron guessed her to be about five-foot six. She was striking. Her complexion was clear and she was perfectly coiffed. The expensive, tailored clothing equaled money. When they first met, he assumed she was just another trophy wife and a stay-at-home mom who went to the spa daily. Appearances were deceiving as he soon learned.

"I just don't see how this happened or how he would wind up with someone like her," her husband spat angrily.

"Warren!" his wife said appalled.

"Look, Mr. Wilson, I'm going to ignore that last comment only because you're upset. None of us know who she is. For all we know she could be some rich heiress that he somehow managed to hook up with."

"*Never*. I know my son and he's not a *cheater*," he said confidently. That girl doesn't look like any rich heiress. Besides he is already marrying someone with money!"

"I wasn't aware someone with money had to have a certain look," he countered sarcastically. This family was trouble and he was visibly annoyed. The nurse handed him the chart he'd requested.

The older man's eyes darkened as he seethed. "What about the private room I asked for?" he said through clenched teeth.

"Unfortunately, since they were found together we thought it was best not to separate them, and you know we're filled to capacity. As I told you before, if a room opens up you will be the first to know, but in the interim, just do me a favor and let us do what we do best. He is in the right place and is getting the best care, including the exercising of body limbs, the administering of fluids and proper nutrients. The computer stimulation we do is state of the art and we continue with sensory studies also..."

"It sounds like a brochure for..."

"Warren," his wife interrupted angrily. "The doctor is doing everything he can. We're not moving him," she said unyieldingly as she glared at him.

He ignored her and continued, "If it's so great, then when the *hell* is he going to wake up?"

"Perhaps he's just not ready yet? The levels of unconsciousness and trauma are deeply..."

Warren whipped his hand through his receding hair and glared at him as he was barely listening. "I'll sue you and this place!" he rudely interjected.

Aaron shook his head, sighed heavily, and looked him in the eyes. "Do you know what the most difficult thing about my career choice is? People like you. Go right ahead. Do what you want. But it's not going to help you, your family, your son, or anyone else who needs our services now *or* in the future. All the money in the world isn't going to change *any* of the circumstances. This is the *best* place for people in his condition to be."

The blood drained from Warren Wilson's face. He wasn't ready to face the reality. "It's all that other facilities fault! That hospital isn't equipped to set a broken arm," he stated bitterly. "I'll sue them too!"

The doctor rubbed his temples and raised his eyebrows. "Really, Mr. Wilson? I told you before, you're lucky they arrived when they did; otherwise, they wouldn't have made it."

"I should move him back to New York."

Alastair watched in horror as the scene played out. He twisted nervously and exhaled, as he hadn't realized he was holding his breath. "Humph, that would have killed him," he muttered as he continued observing. Cooper lifted his paw and put it on his leg as if in agreement. Alastair glanced at the dog and said, "Doesn't he see how dire the situation is? This is all my fault and I can't do a thing about it!" he shouted gloomily at the water as he grabbed his robes and pulled them forcefully around him. Brows furrowed and eyes blazing, he stared angrily at the pond and then toward the dark atmosphere above. "How could you let this happen?" he shouted.

Cooper whined, stretched, and put his head between his paws and closed his eyes.

Chapter 50

The Facts

Doctor Carter removed his glasses and rubbed his eyes. "Mr. Wilson, you're an attorney so let's talk your language and examine the *facts*, which we have discussed on numerous occasions. Traveling could kill him right now. I wouldn't advise it. He has broken bones, some brain swelling, punctured…"

"He is my son; he is *strong* and he can make the trip," he interrupted hotly.

His wife gasped as her hand flew to her mouth. "Warren, you're not listening. Please forgive him doctor, we're just upset and not sure…" her voice trailed off as her eyes again filled with tears.

The doctor nodded empathetically. "Look, Mr. Wilson, we're *not* going to have this conversation every time you visit. You need to understand the reality of the entire situation. If that doctor hadn't stabilized them both back at Franklin Memorial they would have died! So I suggest you get it *together*."

"I want him moved!"

"Warren, you can't be serious!" his wife said boldly as she grabbed his arm.

Aaron adjusted his glasses. "Sir, I can tell you a private room isn't going to make a difference. Now, I suggest you gather your thoughts and get focused. If you're not calm you can push him further away and that will only impede the progress we've made so far. The doctor already spoke to you last week and explained there was a change. I reviewed the chart and notes and I think he is starting to slip away; the scans show…"

The elder man's face paled as he cut the doctor off. "What do you mean? We took him off the breathing machine and he's breathing on his own. I thought that was a good sign."

"It is, but if he does wake up, we don't know the extent of his cognitive impairment and…"

"He's a fighter," he interjected loudly. "There is no way he would leave. He has his entire life…"

Aaron saw the tears in the man's eyes and understood the pain especially when it came to watching children suffer.

"Warren, please *STOP* and *listen* and you need to *stop shouting*!" his wife hissed. "The doctor is right; he can probably hear us!"

"It's not possible. We're in the hallway, Stella!"

"Mr. Wilson, I mean no disrespect, but your wife is correct. We spoke about this before. You and your family come here yelling and shouting all the time. It *is* conceivable he can hear you. It's *possible* you could be pushing him away. Something is changing and I need to find out what. I am going to review his chart *and* check his visitor log again. I suggest you start *limiting* guests and change *your tone* when you enter his room. He is not responding as he did prior. Something happened. But this constant quarreling is not helping *him* or *anyone*!"

"Come, Warren, he's right. I'm begging you to stop." Stella grabbed his arm and steered him away from his proximity to the room. "I can't let you see him like this. You're too upset," she whispered. "Let's go and get some coffee before we go in. We will see you shortly, doctor," she said firmly and then told her husband exactly what was going to happen when they returned.

"I'm sorry, Stella," he sighed heavily, as he sniffed and wiped the tears from the corners of his eyes. He didn't know what he'd do without his wife. He knew she was just as heartbroken as he was.

Chapter 51

Alastair

"**A**lastair, you're wearing a path in the clouds and they are getting discolored. You need to focus and get a hold of yourself. Zachariah will be *incensed* when he sees what you have done. It will take him months to revive them and return them to their resplendent shimmer," a voice stated calmly.

Alastair stopped pacing through the swirl of clouds that had floated in earlier and quickly looked around. "I have no time for games, Lucius. Where are you? Show yourself."

Woof, woof barked Cooper who was standing at the water's edge.

Alastair heard the loud rippling of the water and quickly returned to the edge of the Reflection Pond. The water instantaneously became still and the image of Lucius appeared in the center.

Alastair was exasperated. "There is a tragedy unfolding and all you can think about is cloud beautification?"

"Alastair, you understand changes in the celestial kingdom can affect life in the earthly realm too. I think you have done enough damage already. I'm sure you don't want to be the cause of a monsoon, terrible storm, or other weather disaster?"

Alastair sat on a flattened cloud and rubbed his temple. "No, you are right," he answered gloomily.

"Your reckless actions could be the cause of more trouble. You need to pay attention," Lucius said adamantly. "By the way, who is your new friend?"

"He was wandering around, probably from the Rainbow Bridge or animal kingdom. He's keeping me company."

"Well, as I was saying you need to focus on the issue."

Alastair apologized. His face was etched with pain as he spoke. "It's disturbing to see the sadness of the family and everyone involved. It's really troubling me, and knowing that I am the cause only makes me feel worse. The guilt is starting to eat me alive."

"Again, you need to concentrate," Lucius stated firmly.

"May I ask why you are so interested?"

"You're in my quadrant," Lucius answered calmly.

"Then you can fix things?" Alastair subtly suggested. "Then life could return to normal."

"Unfortunately, that's not how things work and you know it, Alastair, of the Twelfth Order." His brows arched, "It seems as if you have forgotten your training?"

The last thing Alastair wanted to talk about was his rank or training. "Then we're all doomed. I see no way out."

Cooper whined.

"Well, if that's your response, I must report to my superiors at once."

"Humph. For someone that's not going to help, you seem concerned," Alastair questioned again.

Lucius smiled mischievously. "As I already stated, this is my quadrant. Things are normally quiet and extremely calm at this end of the realm. It's been centuries since we have had…"

"Just great," Alastair interrupted. "I'm sure the entire heavenly kingdom is snickering at my expense. I bet the chief angels are wagering…"

"*Surely you jest as you know gambling is forbidden*," Lucius interrupted sharply. "I must depart. You must think harder, Alastair. Pay attention."

"I am," Alastair whispered. "But the Lord isn't listening. And if he's not listening, then we're doomed."

Chapter 52

Noah and Gemma

It was mid-March, and Noah worked quickly at night just so he could spend more time with Gemma and help her with rounds. She was easy to talk to and he loved looking at her eyes. He often dreamed about her soft blond hair that curled and framed her face so perfectly. Each time he looked at the sky he thought of her blue eyes. He often gazed at her too long. He wanted to ask her out on a date but something always got in the way. After her shift, she always had more work to do at the hospital, reports to write, meetings or seminars to attend. He admired how hard she worked.

He tagged along with her as she checked on patients. They conversed about everything while they worked. He told her about growing up in poverty and how hard his life had been. "I was born and raised in Seminole. My mom and I live in the apartment complex…on the other end of town. You know where the freight train passes?" he asked a bit embarrassed.

Gemma shook her head. "No, I'm not sure where that is."

He shrugged uncaring.

"I went to school back east before coming out here. But I've lived in an apartment before. It's not that bad," she added.

"Apparently we had a house once, but I don't remember it," he stated gloomily.

"So how can you be bitter about something you don't even recall?" Gemma questioned as she massaged a patient's arm.

He never thought about it like that and he didn't have an answer.

"Noah," Gemma said softly as she looked him in the eyes, "have you ever really thought about *why* you're so angry?"

Noah stared at Gemma for the fifth time that night. Her blue eyes were so mesmerizing. He was thinking what it would be like to kiss her soft lips. He still couldn't get over the fact that she spoke to him and *cared* about what he thought.

"Noah?"

"My father took off when I was little and left us penniless when he ran off with a younger woman. My mother and I had to move into an apartment when she discovered he sold the house and pocketed all the money. I don't know how my mother did it, but she worked many jobs to make ends meet. The joke was on him as she learned of his death years later," he stated bitterly.

"Then why the anger?"

Noah stopped wiping the counter and looked at Gemma sadly. "He took *everything* from my mother and left her *alone* to raise me."

"Unfortunately, you can't control what people do," she said as she moved about and adjusted some settings on the computer. "Your mother did what she had to do in order to survive and make a life for you. From the looks of it, she did a pretty good job. *It's what you do next that counts*. She did what she could to ensure she could take care of you and give you the best. I don't see a homeless person before me, but a smart intelligent man! You can thank *your* mother for that," she flashed him her model-like smile.

Noah was stunned. In just a few sentences she had summarized his life and made him see and think differently. "You always have a way of putting things in perspective."

Gemma smiled. "I just don't know why you are always talking about dropping out of school or not continuing your education? So why don't you tell me the *real* reason."

Noah was taken aback but more surprised so he gave her an honest answer. "I think it's just an excuse. I'm only in it for the money. I want so much to help my mom. I'm mad at my father and what he did to her. She sacrificed everything for him and then he left us. Sometimes I get really angry when I think about it. My friends all live in these nice homes, go on vacations, and buy what they want…I um, well…I work all the time," he stated angrily as he thrust a bag of trash into his cart.

Gemma cocked her head to one side. "Is where you live that important? It's only a location on a map. Who cares? Besides if you had a big home, think of all the *extra* outdoor work you would have to do, mowing the lawn, watering the grass, shoveling snow, keeping up with the garden, and then there is the interior chores and repairing all the things that break down. Those fancy, extravagant, mansions you see *cost money to buy and maintain.* They really don't mean a thing if they are not filled with the love of families."

Noah scratched his face. "I have enough chores in our two-bedroom apartment to keep me busy."

Gemma walked across the room and put her hand on his arm.

Noah's breath caught in his throat at her soft touch. Her face and smile were so beautiful.

"Noah, it's inconsequential. Forget about it all and focus on *your life*. There is so much more for you after you graduate and enter the next level of the program. I can assure you; you're going to love it! Being a doctor is about *helping others and saving lives*. You can make money at many jobs. If you choose *this* profession, do it for the *right* reasons. Don't let someone else's mistakes dictate *your* choices in life!"

Noah was stunned. She really knew him and how to get to the root of everything. He nodded his head and smiled buoyantly. "You're right about everything, Gemma. Don't worry, I'm not going to drop out of school."

Gemma laughed and said, "I guess it's a bit late for that now since you'll be done with finals in another month and you've been accepted to the medical college."

Noah brushed his hair off his forehead with his fingers. "I felt like I was at a crossroads. I wasn't sure what I wanted until I met you. All the things you've shown me have opened my eyes. I thought working here at the hospital was just a means to get me somewhere so I could eventually make *more* money. I was blinded by my goal to study in a profession that was profitable so I wouldn't have to be poor anymore. I never thought about the *people who are sick and really need help*. I have been so resentful about my life circumstances that I didn't see what was right in front of me."

Gemma's eyes brightened as she smiled jubilantly. "If you go through life bitter, it will eat you alive and you will miss out on so many great experiences. Remember, you can't control the actions of others or what someone *did* in the past. Just learn or understand the lesson and do your best not to repeat the mistake!"

"I know you're right, but sometimes it's just so hard. I feel like my mother and I spend all our time working."

"You have to put the time in for the reward. Nobody said it was going to be easy."

Noah nodded. "You're right. My bitterness had taken hold of my ability to see clearly. I guess I have some work to do."

Noah noticed how radiant her complexion became every time she flashed her infectious smile. "Now that's the spirit! *Just remember, always be honest, and it will take you far.* It wasn't easy-going for me. I had to study and work hard. But once I decided what I wanted to do, it became easier and I fell in love with medicine and helping others." She made some notes on a small pad she removed from her pocket.

Noah stuffed the mop into his cart as they headed toward the next room and listened to her talk about the massage technique she used. He loved what he was doing *now*, but he still wasn't sure if it was because he liked working with Gemma or valued the idea of becoming a doctor. He knew he would have to figure it out soon.

As the weeks progressed Gemma continued to encourage Noah to find what he was passionate about when it came to medicine. Together, they visited every patient. She taught Noah how to talk to them, the signs to look for especially anomalies that occurred at night that went unnoticed. He took notes and went to the library to research more. He suddenly discovered a new direction and focus that motivated him. At the same time he was falling hard for Gemma. One of these days he was going to get up the nerve to tell her how he really felt about her and perhaps ask her out.

Chapter 53

Willow and Doctor Aaron Carter

"**G**ood morning, doctor. Here are your reports from last night," Willow stated as she handed the file to Doctor Carter. "I also brought you a cup of fresh coffee."

Aaron looked up and removed his glasses. He ran his fingers through his hair, a mix of brown and blond, now slightly peppered with gray. His children pointed out the gray strands and suggested he think about dying it. "I'm only fifty years old," he responded. He cringed at the thought of his hair turning gray so early.

He was glad to be back at work. His new assistant was not only intelligent but also very attractive. The wavy chestnut-colored hair flowed down her back like a Greek goddess. He had never seen such beautiful hair. He noticed the many different ways she wore it as well. Due to personal circumstances, his involvement in the hiring process was cut short. He had only met her a few weeks ago and already knew he was going to like working with her. While he was on vacation, she had reorganized the lab, files, and current research. He appreciated how she was able to get him up-to-date on patient reports while he was out.

The day before he had stopped by human resources to review her file again, for he had been too preoccupied with his personal life to remember everything clearly. She was forty-five and had a doctorate in both chemistry and neuroscience. She also ran a research lab back in New York. She had written some impressive papers and was *extremely* qualified to run the neuroscience lab as well.

She was definitely going to be an asset to their team. He also felt guilty because he liked spending time with her. They had an easy rapport and she was upbeat about everything. But what stood out in his mind at that very moment was that nobody had *ever* brought him coffee before.

As Willow handed him the cup, she was thinking about the day they first met. The first thing she noticed about him was the color of his eyes. Nobody but models in magazine advertisements had eyes that blue she thought as she stared at him a bit too long. A chill ran through her when she looked at his face and was once again drawn back to his eyes – they were like magnets forcing her to make eye contact. She was having difficulty speaking to him without smiling so much. She was so nervous that she stumbled over her greeting and rambled on about the weather, the hospital elevators and something about more directional signage needed in one of the wings. She believed she came off sounding somewhat scatterbrained.

The gold ring on his left hand indicated he was married. She immediately thought about her ex-husband and how it didn't stop him. Her stomach twisted in knots as she tried not to think about the turmoil she endured the past year.

She noticed how the female population endlessly flirted with Doctor Carter. She didn't understand until she overheard staff talking in the cafe that he was a widower. It was the same old story – someone was continually looking to marry a rich physician. Getting involved with a doctor was *not* on her radar.

She had already been reprimanded about gossiping. Besides she was too busy to be bothered with stories about someone else's life. She also vowed she was not going to talk about her past. This was going to be a fresh start for her.

She actually liked working with Doctor Carter and his team. He was not demanding like some of the others she'd worked for in the past. It was hard to find someone decent to collaborate with. She also relished that she was more involved with the patients. This enabled her to see just how much of the team's research was applied.

"Thank you, Willow. I really appreciate the coffee. You can call me Aaron."

"Thank you, but I like to keep it professional; it sets a good example for the students," she smiled

He was doing his best to keep it professional but couldn't help but notice her beauty. She wore little make-up, which made her face look fresh. Her disposition was always sunny and pleasant. Her clothing was stylish and not overtly sexy. It was the first time in a long time that he actually took notice of another female.

"Is everything all right, sir?"

He quickly realized he had been gazing at her a bit too long. "Sorry. I was composing my thoughts," he gestured to the file he'd been reviewing. I keep looking at these reports, and since January there have been some irregular patterns that are repeated, especially at night. You or someone else didn't by chance change the frequencies on the computer while I was on vacation?"

"I would *never* do something like that unless you or another doctor approved it. But I will check with the other staff."

The doctor shook his head. Something was bothering him. "I want all the equipment checked too. It looks like the formula was changed."

"If it makes you feel any better I noticed the irregular patterns too…"

"But someone would have authorized the change in protocols to record at that high of a frequency," he interjected. "It's not something I would recommend."

"Is there someone else who would?"

Doctor Carter leaned back in his chair and sighed heavily as he rubbed his forehead. He had a strange, distant, and sad look in his eyes.

"Doctor Carter?"

"No," he answered abruptly.

Willow shrugged. "Perhaps it's a multitude of brain waves acting up or just body reflexes. We're monitoring for any eye and body movements. The vitals are stable, and physical therapy continues." She paused. Her eyebrows furrowed, "You don't think that crazy family is sneaking in here at night, and causing a disturbance of some sort, do you?"

Doctor Carter leaned forward and reached for his coffee.

Willow caught a glimpse of his wide shoulders and biceps that stretched his lab coat and quickly averted her eyes.

"You must be referring to the parents, his best friend, and the fiancé. Yes, they have been caught before, and I thought we put a stop to all night visits. That family just doesn't listen though," the doctor muttered, clearly annoyed. "We can have security review the tapes to see who comes in and out and at what hours and then compare them to who visits during the day. That may help us."

"Could there be something else happening?" she asked.

He tapped on the file with his pen. "What is most perplexing is that the female patient has not had one visitor and the male has an entire parade, yet they both have the same test results," he said, as he scanned the pages of information. "I can't explain the data," the doctor answered. He couldn't help but notice Willow's perfectly white teeth as her jaw dropped and eyes widened upon hearing this.

"Really?" she said stunned. Willow took another sip of her coffee. She thought for sure the doctor would have an answer.

He nodded slowly to confirm it was true. "This is the first time I've encountered a case like this. Two patients progressing together and one we know nothing about."

Willow scratched her head as she digested the information. She then leaned forward in her chair and offered her theory. "It's strange. It's as if they really are progressing together, but how is it happening?" she questioned. "The stimulation is done during the day. We're monitoring the vitals, watching for eye movements, continuing with the muscle therapy, rotating the bodies to prevent bedsores. We talk, read, show pictures and nothing, but at night the brain scans are much more active. So, I think they really *do know one another*."

Doctor Carter was just as puzzled. "Well, they did arrive together. They could be listening to us too. They are sharing a room together."

Willow was captivated. She loved a good romance story. "Perhaps they really are *secret* lovers and *communicating*," she smiled seductively. "Or is it that she is just hearing his family so that's why they are responding at the same pace," she added excitedly. She leaned back and smiled thoughtfully, "however, I still like the idea that they do know *one* another."

He folded his hands and frowned. "Interesting concepts, however, the family still contends they *don't* know one another and continuously requests a private room for their son."

"Yes, I know. While you were on vacation it was the first question out of the father's mouth every visit. They will pay anything for a private room," Willow added as she continued to fill him in on the family's shenanigans. "Can't you do something about them?"

"While the hospital would benefit from their money, it is difficult. We haven't had such an intense group of people here in a while. It's unfortunate for the family and the patients."

Doctor Carter closed the file as he rolled his eyes. He wasn't concerned with hospital politics and did his best to avoid the board of directors. "The family should be more concerned if he is going to survive. Head trauma is so tricky. It's like trying to unlock a piece of a puzzle. I studied the charts, graphs, and the results and keep looking for clues. Something is going on. Let's re-examine the entire case. We'll start with the basics. Call security and request times and dates when people visit. They should be able to get you a report. I'll review the notes and some of the protocols. Therapy is tricky too. What one person responds to another may not. It just depends on the injury. Perhaps we need to make some changes in the computer stimulation applications.

We can also review the monitors and all the data and see if we can zero in on more precise commonalities. And don't forget I want that equipment checked."

"What if they really are lovers and are causing the monitors to change. Perhaps they really are trying to communicate with us," she smiled alluringly.

Eyebrows arched he grinned, "Then it would be a first for science," he stated with great skepticism. He was momentarily interrupted by a call. "That's fantastic," he grinned and hung up.

"Anything wrong?"

He shook his head. "Some charts went missing and they were found in the science lab. Nobody seems to know how they got from the nurses' station to the lab."

"Charts are moved all the time, perhaps someone was studying them?" she offered. "This is a research hospital."

"Mmm. Not sure. This is the second time charts from the two patients in room 524 have been misplaced," he said steadily.

"It's like I said, they're communicating with one another," she grinned.

"Willow," he said exasperated and looked at his watch. "I have to meet with the team to prepare for another surgery. Why don't you come back after three and we can look over the charts a bit more," he suggested.

"It's a dreadful mistake," Alastair yelled at the Reflection Pond. "Can't you see that?" At that moment small ripples gently cascaded across the water. Alastair looked around. No breeze blew through the motionless air. It was still shadowy and a heavy, unmoving mist hovered above the area. "They shouldn't be there… if they die I will have blood on my hands," he wailed toward the clouds above. "Why are you letting this continue? The additional apprehension I am suffering is cruel and unjust. I will be a silent assassin of innocent people and never forgive myself…"

Chapter 54

Lily and J.T.

*L*ily sighed. She was so content. She loved lying in the soft, smooth substance by the water. Sand and water are what J.T. had called them. It was so calming.

"J.T.," she called. "I was wondering if you hear sounds in your head?"

His eyes were closed and he was relaxed. "I was trying to recall the faces I see, but they are blurred. I keep hearing yelling and I don't like it. I often see two others together. They whisper and are worried. Afterward, the noisy people enter, I want them all to leave but for some reason I can't tell them to get out. What do you see?"

Lily closed her eyes again. "It's all jumbled and I feel like, I don't want to listen. It's just a waste of time. I love what *we* are doing – it's so much *better*!"

J.T. mumbled in agreement. He treasured his days with Lily, but he was on edge. Something was troubling him and the voices in his head were getting louder and stronger daily. As each day passed, the faces were becoming sharper. He said nothing, for he didn't want to frighten Lily.

Chapter 55

Dear Sunshine,

I was thinking about the journey you have been on. There is much to say but then I sometimes think...what does it matter...yet it still consumes me...filling my head with old conversations...

I know you are unable to write. I remember what you said to me two years ago but...well, I guess I can't talk about it just yet.

I want to tell you about Willow, only I don't feel it's appropriate. But then again she really is a big help. She also brought me coffee and I like spending time talking to her... only because she shares my passion for the program. So why do I feel guilty?

All my love,

Me

Chapter 56

Lily and J.T.
April 2001

J.T. and Lily walked to a place beyond the field they had never traveled to before hoping to find others like them. Bear followed them everywhere they went. Like Lily, J.T. wanted to look at all he saw. Together they admired the beautiful landscapes and places they uncovered. Water, rock formations, flowers, forests – everything they discovered was familiar but new. They quizzed one another as they each tried to recall the names of objects. Lily hated the game only because she had difficulty recollecting names. J.T. was getting much better at it and it unsettled her.

J.T. also insisted they keep walking. She didn't like to venture too far due to the darkness that came later. When it was dark and the bright orb above was at its brightest, she would come out. But when she couldn't see in front of her, she was terrified. J.T. convinced her she was safe and wouldn't let anything happen.

When night came and they were further from the dwelling, he would find a place to shelter under a tree, rock outcropping, or they would simply lie on the cool earth next to one another. Together they would look at the beauty of the bright illuminations that twinkled in the darkness above. He would wrap his arm around her and pull her close to soothe her fear. She felt safe.

One evening, when the temperature dropped and before it became totally dark, he started gathering debris from the ground around him.

"What are you up to?"

"I'm going to get us warm. It'll be okay."

Lily was perplexed. She didn't know what he was doing but it seemed interesting. She watched, uncertain what was going to happen, as he made a pile in a circle of hard stone and started rubbing some of the pieces of debris together.

And true to his word, before night fell, a hot light began to rise from his ring of stones. Lily watched in awe as the colorful hues slowly moved, providing light and warmth. "How did you know how to do this?"

J.T. shook his head. "It's something I saw in my head. I did it before. I was with somebody else – we were doing this together."

J.T. stopped talking. Lily had an odd look on her face and she suddenly began edging away from the hot light, as it grew bigger. She started back toward the cave they had sought shelter in earlier, but suddenly remembered it was dark there too.

"Lily? Are you okay?" She stopped walking and turned. Her eyes were transfixed on the hot circle.

"I don't know. I feel strange. I can't explain it," her voice trembled. Something was wrong but Lily wasn't sure what was happening. Beads of moisture were forming on her neck and forehead. She put her hand on her chest and could hear a loud thumping. She was afraid but not sure why. She didn't want to admit something was not right. She felt as if she couldn't breathe. "Tell me more about what you see," she prodded so she didn't have to discuss her new fear. "I'll just stay over here." Lily shuddered as she kept her distance.

J.T. continued to see more and more images in his head than she did. His memories were perplexing and intimidating. It was as if he knew what he was talking about but it was all foggy for her. Yet at the same time he seemed to be searching for something.

"Are *you* feeling okay, J.T.?" she asked timidly.

"I'm not sure. I told you I feel like I need to figure something out about myself and I can't. I see visions of those like us but they are blurry. An older gentleman is very angry and always yelling at someone in a strange garment. The woman, I think I know. She is gentle, kind and tells him to stop. 'Red Lips' comes and goes and smells funny."

Lily laughed. "How so?"

J.T.'s eyebrows furrowed and he frowned as he thought really hard about how to describe it. Then he started laughing. "Lily, when the darkness disappears, what do you *notice* around you?"

"Beauty."

"Exactly," he agreed. "It's like what I see in my head," he gestured. "I see lots of flowers. There are flowers; lots and lots of different types of beautiful flowers. They fill the space I see. Then there is 'Red Lips,' she smells like a strange combination of too many of the blooms combined. My mother wears it too. It comes in a bottle and she sprays it on and it is a scent that smells really nice, but 'Red Lips,' well hers is strong and potent and for some reason I don't like it and…"

"J.T.," Lily interrupted anxiously. "Are you listening to yourself? Did you hear what you just said? You are remembering something. *You said, flowers, mother, it comes in a bottle and is sprayed on,"* she rambled.

J.T. stopped speaking. The images and words were coming to him. "Lily, I see people like us, they are my…my…my family. I have a *family* and they are *calling* me."

A family – what is that? What does it mean?

"What do they want?"

"They want me to come someplace. The trouble is I'm not sure *where* they want me to go," he finished. He shook his head as if he could make the images appear again.

Lily felt his frustration and confusion as he tried to put the pieces together.

"Lily, I was wondering if you know *any* of the people I speak about? Perhaps we need to look for them?"

Lily rubbed her forehead and shook her head. "I'm sorry J.T., I wish I could help you but I can't. I don't even know who you are. How can you expect me to know what's in your head?" She had momentarily forgotten about her fear until J.T. began moving around.

He strode to the side and adjusted his creation so it was centered.

As if in a trance, Lily watched in horror as the light danced and grew higher. Tremors of some sort made her body shake as her breathing quickened.

J.T. moved to grab more wood from his pile and as he walked toward the blaze he tripped. In that split second Lily screamed out, "Nooooo!"

J.T. caught himself before he fell, but Lily sprung forward. She wrapped her arms tightly around his waist and was pulling him away from the fire.

"Lily, stop! Stop! It's okay! What are you doing? Let go of me!"

Her grip tightened and they toppled backward to the ground.

He untangled himself from her and grabbed hold of her torso and called her name, "Lily. Lily. What happened? What's wrong?"

Her eyes fluttered open and she quickly scrambled out of his grip and away from the flames.

He inched forward and clutched her shoulders, wrapped her tightly in his arms, and called out her name. "Lily, what is wrong? It's okay. It's okay," he whispered in a soothing voice.

"Lucius, I know you can hear me," Alastair called. "This ubiquitous torture is unnecessary. I hope you're satisfied watching these poor souls suffer as well as myself. I'm filled with anguish. I understand I did wrong, but this is uncalled for." He rose and began pacing. "How do you expect me to fix this? How can I

possibly do anything when I'm sitting in these dark, infested, murky waters," he gestured angrily at his surroundings.

"Perhaps you have some magic," he shouted to Cooper, who was sitting on the cool stone. Coopers ears went back as he watched Alastair.

"There is nothing in the Angel Code book about situations like this," Alastair muttered crossly, as he made another lap around the pond wondering how much time he actually had to fix the problem. He shuddered as potential doomsday scenarios flashed through his head. He wondered if the Lord knew where he was or if he even knew time was altered.

Chapter 57

Lily and J.T.

*L*ily held J.T. tightly and cried while he assured her everything was going to be okay. She sobbed more. "I saw those flames," she pointed to his fire pit. "They were so bad that I couldn't escape. That's why I don't like to think or see the images. It hurts too bad."

He drew her closer.

"And that," she pointed to the warm blaze. "Please make it stop. Get rid of it!" Her eyes were filled with fear and her delicate face had turned white.

J.T. was alarmed, as he didn't know what the problem was. She kept staring as the flames danced higher and continued crying. J.T. picked her up and walked further away from the heat. He wrapped her in his arms as she continued sobbing uncontrollably. "Shh. Shh," he whispered as he rubbed her back. He was not sure what to make of the situation. "If I put it out it will be dark and then you'll be terrified. Let it burn. You don't have to look at it. Just close your eyes," he suggested.

Lily buried her face between his arm and shoulder and clung to his body, trembling as she wept. She was exhausted and J.T. was grateful when she finally fell asleep.

Alastair felt bad. "Cooper, do you see what is happening?" The dog raised his head, opened his eyes, and his tail wagged for a few seconds. Alastair had been conversing with the dog, as he had nobody to talk to and was beginning to feel the effects of being so isolated.

"I've aged one thousand years as I watch. They seem like nice people and it's unfortunate they are caught up in my mess," he mumbled. "They are going to die because of me and I have no angel magic to help," he sighed exasperated. "Sitting here watching isn't going to help them. It's imperative that I find a way out of this dreadful place," he stated aloud. Cooper rolled on his side, stretched, and breathed heavily.

Alastair's mind was racing and suddenly his lips curled and a smile formed on his face. "That's it," he shouted enthusiastically. "I need a plan."

Chapter 58

Willow and Doctor Aaron Carter

"**I** have the security reports," Willow announced as she entered his office, putting the file he requested and a cup of fresh coffee on his desk. Once seated in the leather chair in front of the mammoth executive desk, she said, "You were right, the only visitors were the family. The girlfriend comes with another male. I think he's works in the law firm too. They usually come after hours, in the evenings, but don't stay long. They don't converse much either, only stare at him. In the beginning they visited more, but their trips have dwindled." She was getting annoyed. His back was to her and he was shuffling through papers on the credenza behind his desk. "Doctor Carter? Aaron? Are you listening to me?"

He turned, nodded, then picked up his phone and dialed the nurse's station. "I don't have those files." He paused and listened to the poor nurse on the other end. "Then make everyone start signing out the charts," he stated tersely. The receiver hit the base a bit too hard and Willow winced. "I'm sorry, Willow. Some charts are missing again and yesterday's lab reports were again found in the science lab," perplexed, he rubbed his head. "We never had issues like this before on this floor."

"Perhaps the med students don't understand the process or importance for charts, lab results, and their placement," she laughed.

Aaron chuckled.

"Coffee," she pointed.

"Thanks," he grinned and sat down. "I did hear what you were saying before. Over time visitation starts dwindling." He adjusted his glasses and took a sip of the coffee. "As time passes, and people get over the initial shock, they realize life has to go on. They just can't sit around and wait any longer. Don't get me wrong, some families are here all the time, but others, well you see what happens." He continued to flip through the pages of the latest notes from the file she brought.

"I guess it's something like going through a grieving process."

The doctor leaned back in his chair. He still hadn't been sleeping well and was once again feeling the effects. He rubbed his forehead and temples hoping to prevent his oncoming head-ache. "Exactly! In this case, it's a grieving process of stages. First, the unfortunate incident that brought the person here. Second, is the unknown. If the patient does wake up there is the discovery process for the extent of the injuries – including cognitive assessments and the help they may require, and finally if they pass. It's the *unknown* that takes a toll on the human emotions."

Willow nodded understanding.

"I really want to thank you again for the coffee. I really needed it today."

He looks tired. Probably up late with one of those young nurses I hear are after him. Why do I even care she thought? It was hard not to look at him directly for he was so handsome. She could feel the blood rushing to her face and hoped he didn't notice.

"No problem," she muttered politely.

She wears no rings on her fingers. I wonder if she's married. I never bothered to look at that part of her application. Why did they send me someone so attractive? Every time I'm with her, I start feeling guilty.

"The only other people who go in and out of the room at night are the staff," Willow continued as she anticipated his next questions.

"Are you positive?"

"I knew you'd ask, so I double checked."

"What about the equipment? The settings were changed again," he snapped irritably. "Do you think something malfunctioned?"

"I can change it or have it checked *again,* but if you are implying that someone is tampering with it, I doubt it. Who would do such a thing? But now that we're on the subject, perhaps it's not a bad idea? Maybe we could try something *different*. I have some ideas. I was thinking if we make some changes. Doctor Cristo, who was here prior, left some notes and…"

"Absolutely not!" he snapped incredulously, as he rudely interrupted her. "The design was already implemented and proven. We will *not* be making any variations to the protocols…"

Willow's eyes grew like saucers and she drew back in disbelief at the sharp tone of his voice as he spoke.

The doctor stopped himself knowing he was out of line when he saw her facial expressions change from shock to utter disappointment all within seconds. "Never mind! It's not important," he spat as he quickly handed her the file.

An uncomfortable silence followed as his sharp words hung in the space between them and resonated in her brain. Stunned at his response and irate tone, she barely recognized her own voice, which was strained as she spoke. "I'm sorry, I didn't mean to recommend…"

Willow immediately stopped talking and changed her statement. "I take it back. I'm *not* sorry I suggested it," she retorted defiantly, as her posture stiffened and she sat straighter. "I left New York for a better place and to work together as a team. If I'm not going to have a say in the research or protocols, then perhaps I made a mistake in taking this job. I will not be *silenced* or sit on the sidelines!" She grabbed her file and stormed out of his office.

Aaron wasn't sure what surprised him more – her willingness to stand up to him, her honesty, or her abrupt departure.

Chapter 59

Noah and Gemma

True to her word Gemma had taken Noah under her wing and helped him get better acquainted with the fifth floor. He had grown accustomed to the noises and different sounds from the computer monitors. He knew the names of the patients and often stayed late. He and Gemma read and talked to each of them.

Gemma also knew the doctors, when their rounds were completed, and who was due for treatment. She made sure she and Noah were alone when they met with the sick. "Shouldn't we have the help of a doctor?" Noah questioned one evening.

"Normally I would but they are very busy, especially tonight. Someone isn't doing too well in the south wing."

Noah thought nothing of it since he was learning and absorbing so much. She taught him massage and magnetic therapies. Then she showed him how to observe eye and body movements and what they might reveal. She talked about the importance of sensory touching, rotating the body, monitoring the vitals and fluids. She also told him about her high-frequency brain study and how it worked. One night they looked at brain scanning taking place on the monitor and what it could disclose. "More importantly, you must *always talk* to everyone," she emphasized.

Noah nodded understanding.

"Don't ever think they can't hear, because no matter what level of their unconsciousness, they *could* be listening. *Don't ever forget that*," she reminded him.

At home, his mother was getting suspicious and started questioning him about his peculiar hours. She was worried something was interfering with his studies.

"This is your last semester, Noah. You *need* to make it count to keep that scholarship money. I know it's not a lot, but every bit helps."

"Mom, it's April and I only have one exam left. I'm doing extra credit and working on a project," he lied easily. Well, it wasn't exactly a lie. He was working on a project. He secretly referred to it as the "Gemma Project."

His mother didn't believe one word of it, especially when he was offered to switch to days. She happened to be home when she intercepted the phone call from his supervisor, who wanted to offer the day position to Noah for the summer.

"I just don't want to mess up my sleep," he claimed when she questioned him.

She found it odd that he was spending *more* time at a job he had complained so much about. She was concerned he was sacrificing his career and for what, she wasn't certain. In the weeks that followed, he left her speechless when he announced he would be taking a summer prep course! Perhaps it was a sign that he was becoming serious about medical school after all, she remarked to her best friend one evening at the cafe.

Noah knew the real truth – it was Gemma. He was forming a genuine bond with her. He *never* had a close female friend before and he found he couldn't wait to see her. He was also learning a great deal and felt energized. That's when he decided to take one of the recommended summer classes before he started the next chapter of his career. He'd also have something more to talk to Gemma about. For the first time, he was excited about his life.

Chapter 60

Alastair

Alastair was deep in thought as he paced frantically around the Reflection Pond. "I didn't realize it was *this* bad," he shouted anxiously as he had watched more of the story unfold. His stomach was a ball of knots, and if he wasn't afflicted with an ulcer he was certain he had one now.

"I just can't believe this is happening," he said as he looked over at Cooper who was sitting and watching him. "You have it easy," he said as he gestured toward the dog. "Not a thing to worry about. But me, I'm a nervous wreck. My heart bleeds with sorrow. The last time I felt such anxiety, I was carving an arch for a cathedral. The master carver demanded we find a way to make it larger!" He gestured madly. "Of all the preposterous suggestions…ugh…you're not even listening to me," he shouted at Cooper who, he noticed, had closed his eyes.

"If I can't find a way to remedy this and someone finds out what I have done…I shudder to think of my punishment. If I could just go back in time…"

"Well, you can't," a familiar voice called.

Alastair stopped pacing and looked toward the center of the pond but did not see Lucius. He looked around and jumped nervously when Lucius suddenly appeared next to him.

"Why must you sneak up on me like that?" Alastair demanded, as he jumped backward and clutched his chest. "I have enough on my mind and my nerves, what I have left are on the precipice of coiling around my soul..."

Lucius laughed heartedly. "Alastair, you must stop with the theatrics. I must say you missed your calling, as I find your dramatics humorous. Have you always been so nervous and anxious?"

"Humph! I'm glad you find my state of mind amusing," he answered annoyed. "I was a craftsman. We were always worried if we were building the cathedral *too* high or if it was going to fall. My nerves were calmer when I reached heaven *until this* unfortunate mishap," his voice trailed off.

"Come, let's sit over there," Lucius pointed to a cluster of stones.

Once seated, the powerful angel adjusted his stunning, metallic-colored robes of white. Alastair sighed dejectedly. Next to Lucius, his once vivid, cream-colored robes were filthy. His goatee had grown and was becoming an unkempt beard. He was once again reminded that he looked like a vagrant.

"Alastair, I must ask, what made you disobey protocol?"

"The enormity of the situation," he immediately replied.

"Mmmm. You have been one of the chief angel trainers; I wonder, did you not think about requesting help?"

"Yes, but by the time the problem would have been reported, and reached the top supervisor, it would have been *too* late," Alastair answered exasperated. "Procedures have changed so much, just like the group that was assigned to me. They should not have been sent to me," he pointed angrily. "I fear a mistake was made."

"Really," Lucius frowned. "So now you're questioning the type of people you are charged with teaching and implying the Lord made an error? Surly an angel of the Twelfth Order would understand how to handle any situation."

"No...that's not what I meant," Alastair said nervously, as he ran his hands through his white hair. It was long and hung down his back, secured with the regulation clasp.

"Then what did you mean?"

Alastair was silent as he tried to compose his thoughts.

Lucius furrowed his brows and nodded. When no answer was immediately forthcoming he said, "So your impatience caused you to act so impetuously – sort of like those in your training group?"

"No!" Alastair exclaimed taken aback. "It was easier and quicker if I handled the situation alone. I was concerned for all of humanity above and below," he stated with grave concern.

"Yet you feel the Lord made an error in judgment?"

Alastair sucked in his breath, as he finally understood the gravity of what he'd said. The words were stuck in his throat as he tried to correct his thoughts. His face muscles scrunched as panic set in. He had just accused God of making a mistake. How much worse could it possibly get?

Alastair cleared his throat to speak, but Lucius shook his head and held up his hand indicating he'd heard enough. He then folded his hands and slowly rose. "My superior will want to hear of this development," he said sadly. "In the meantime, I will leave you to think about how you are going to remedy the situation as you watch more of the events unfold. Oh, and by the way, it has been brought to my attention that you neglected to tell me some of the facts."

Alastair bowed his head in shame.

Chapter 61

Dear Sunshine,

I work harder than ever just to get through the day without having to think about how much I miss you. My pain is so deep I work and ruminate over how you are doing. I go home wondering if you are okay. I think about life, the incident, and what she must think…then my thoughts return to what if…

Sometimes it hurts so bad I don't know what to do…

I'm still mad and can't get past my fury. I'm so angry that I yelled at my assistant Willow. I didn't intend on shouting at her, it just happened.

You would like her. She is bright, has advanced degrees, and wears nice clothes. I don't know why I said that but for some odd reason, I just notice her clothing. She is extremely intelligent and I find myself looking for her during the day and I feel bad that I am doing it. I justify my actions by telling myself it's pleasant to talk to someone who is interested in my work. I'm relishing our conversations and she's supportive of my research. She also brings me coffee.

I wish you were here. I wish I didn't have to speculate.

All my love,

Me

Chapter 62

Lily and J.T.
May 2001

J.T. was resting on his back with his eyes closed and was thinking about the passage of time. He, Lily, and Bear developed a routine. They ate what he recalled were fruits and vegetables from the garden behind the dwelling and continued to walk around day in and day out. Bear had a bowl of water that was always full. "What do you think he's eating?" Lily asked one morning as she watched Bear take off.

J.T. shrugged. "It looks like he survives off the environment." They occasionally saw him licking his paws or returning with a fish in his mouth. Together they'd laugh at his antics.

J.T. sat up staring out into the distance as he continued to ponder his concerns regarding time, and it dawned on him that he had no idea how long he'd been with Lily. It was frustrating that he couldn't recall. He was overly anxious and didn't know why. Something was also happening to his body that he could not explain. His attachment to Lily was growing in a way that made no sense to him. He wanted to be with her, yet he was always on the verge of feeling that he should be leaving. Where he would go, he had no idea.

While his confusion and anxiety were mounting, there was also always something new to see. Today they climbed another hill and sat enjoying the warm light from above. Bear lay by

Lily's feet as she quietly slept. Her eyes were closed and she looked so peaceful. Her face was fresh and natural as opposed to the image of 'Red Lips,' who wore a lot of color on her face. Her lips were always bright; bright as the color of the crops Lily picked. 'Red Lips' was speaking to him, but he couldn't make out what she was saying or what she required. She was often arguing with others and it made J.T. feel bad.

"What are you thinking about?" Lily whispered as she began to stir. His vacant expression hadn't gone unnoticed.

He smiled. She always knew when something was on his mind.

Lily was worried. She recognized the grief-stricken look again and immediately knew he was remembering. "I saw 'Red Lips' again, and the voices, they keep calling me. I see visions of people like us. Don't you see it too?" he asked. His voice was filled with anguish and his face paled.

She shook her head. "No, J.T., I don't see any of that."

"Lily, it's getting worse every day. I know you don't want to discuss it...but…it's um…like I feel I need to go to them, but I don't want to leave you here."

Lily rolled over to face him. Not only had his facial hair grown but the rest of the hair on his head too. It hung unruly down his neck. He was propped on his elbow looking pensive and sad. "I don't want you to leave! I can't imagine my life without you here! Why would you leave? How would you even get to them?" she cried out.

He saw the fear in her eyes and pulled her close. He loved her scent and simply just holding her. "To be honest, sometimes I feel as if I'm slipping away, but I keep coming back to you. But lately something else is happening. I can't describe it, and I don't want to lose you!"

J.T. felt strange jolts throughout his body at different times during the day and night. He dreamed of people shouting for him to come home. He had no idea what it meant or where home was. The visions were getting more vivid. He was so frustrated and confused that he wanted to scream. He didn't tell Lily, as he didn't want to upset her.

Lily's heart was racing. She treasured being wrapped in his arms. It was safe and comforting. Ever since the night with the blazing circle of light, she discovered relief nestled in his body's strength. She sought him out any chance she could get. When they were like this she felt as if she needed something else from him but wasn't sure what it was. "You will never lose me J.T. We will always be together."

J.T. hugged her tightly. When they hugged or touched, something always happened to his body. He felt a hunger that he couldn't describe. He felt he needed her in a way that he didn't understand. He felt as hot as the fire he had built that one evening. The way his body was reacting and the images he saw in his head were so perplexing. As the images grew stronger, he needed to convince Lily to stop being so panicked. He wanted her to remember. For some reason he felt it was essential but had doubts that she would.

Chapter 63

Lily and J.T.

J.T. quickly untangled himself from her arms. "I'm going to the water. I need to cool off."

"Okay, I'll come with you."

"No!" he stated abruptly. "I need to go alone." Before she could utter another word and change his mind, he took off running as fast as he could away from her.

She watched and instantly felt horrible. She was terribly confused and didn't understand. Tears slowly fell from her eyes. She didn't know what it meant or what was happening to them. They did everything together. This was the first time he journeyed without her.

"Why did you leave me?" she whispered. "Bear, come here," she called. More tears flowed down her cheeks and she wiped them away. Her head was pounding as unfamiliar images came and went. She had no idea what they meant. She didn't want to. The only thing she knew was that she didn't want to lose J.T. Suddenly, the tears poured like a damn that had burst. She sobbed so hard her chest hurt. Bear lay by her side and nuzzled between her arm and face. He licked the tears as they fell.

Chapter 64

Willow and Doctor Aaron Carter

"*I* came to apologize," Doctor Carter said as he peeked around the door of her office.

Willow looked up from her computer and grinned warmly. She noticed his hair was combed and slicked back. "You can come in; I'm not going to bite you."

Doctor Carter entered with two fresh cups of coffee and some cinnamon scones.

"They smell great. Please sit."

"I brought it black; just the way you like it."

Her eyes sparkled as she raised her eyebrows, "Observant, aren't we?"

He shrugged. "Habit of my profession. We constantly study, watch, and look for the slightest changes." Doctor Carter shifted a bit in the chair. He was nervous and wasn't sure why. Perhaps it was the yellow blouse she wore that emphasized the color of her brown eyes. "Look, I, um, I came to apologize about the other day. I didn't mean to disregard your ideas; it's just that I have other personal stuff going on and have been under a lot of stress lately…then there was the missing files…the equipment…and well, it doesn't matter, I should *not* have snapped at you and I am sorry. You were hired so we could work together and I deeply apologize for my actions. If it happens again, yell back at me."

Willow didn't understand why he was always on her mind. It bothered her and she didn't like it. She didn't like that she thought about him at odd times. She noticed him talking with families and staff and did her best to walk the other way. If he was going to act like a child she was going to ignore him. He was now looking like a lost puppy dog. She'd been here before she recalled, as images of New York flashed through her head. She was going to give him a piece of her mind until she made the mistake of looking at his face and into those blue eyes. She smiled. It was a smile of forgiveness.

She took a bite of the scone. "These are delicious. Where did you get them?"

"One of the local coffee shops downtown." There was a brief minute of silence and he was wondering if he had made the wrong decision to come to her office. She had been avoiding him and it was his own fault. For some inexplicable reason he found he *needed* to see her. He watched her from afar as she interacted with the staff and students. She was like a breath of fresh air. Beautiful, intelligent, and she had a great personality. Everyone loved her. She had numerous viewpoints on treatment procedures and he had to figure out how to justify his actions – but he couldn't seem to get the words out.

He rubbed his temples. His heart was pounding fast as he was so tense.

"Thank you for the apology. I was just hoping to share some treatment proposals with you. I hope you apologized to the rest of the staff you barked at. By the way I checked the equipment and had it swapped; however, the computer department said there is nothing faulty with it."

Aaron was relieved she forgave him. He nodded, "Yes, they sent me a rather terse memorandum assuring me the million-dollar equipment the hospital has invested in is functioning appropriately. They added a security code to the program that only I can access."

"Perhaps the patients are getting up and changing the dials," Willow laughed as she continued, "can you imagine the possibilities? Now that I think about it, I could have sworn I saw the guy in 522 reading one of the charts! That's it – the patients are getting up and taking their charts from the nurses' station!" She giggled more.

He chuckled and gave her a half smile. "I think you watch too many movies!"

"Someday we will have the answers, but right now I have some time to listen to *your ideas* if you'd like to discuss them?"

Chapter 65

Alastair

Like a child, Alastair resumed plotting his escape. His robes fluttered behind him as he paced nervously around the pond. He thought he could fly straight up but had forgotten he had no wings. After Lucius' last visit, he wasn't sure how much time he had left. For the past few days, he had silently been engaging in his own recognizance.

The small, enclosed area was surrounded by the cloud path with layers of dirt and mud, of which, he could barely see through the dirty, drab, gray clouds. Rocks of varying sizes, some large enough to sit on or small pebbles, littered the surface. Mist hovered above and below the dense clouds. The dismal sight only added to his intensely, depressed state of mind.

Interestingly, he noted, the various paths projected into the unknown as he walked around. His pace quickened and his eyes darted back and forth surreptitiously, and when he felt the moment was right, like a jackrabbit, he scurried on to one of the footpaths.

"Ahh," he screamed in agony. The moment his foot touched the path, excruciating currents from an unseen force field surged through his body and propelled him back into the pond area within seconds. He landed with a loud thud on his back in front of Cooper, who was sitting upright.

Cooper leaned over and licked his face as he lay on the ground in shock.

"A booby trap," he said with contempt as he slowly rose on his elbows. "I could have been seriously disfigured. Of all the low down, despicable tricks…I'm at my breaking point…the regulator for time was dialed back to the threat of impending doom…I need to see the Lord," he shouted fiercely.

At that moment the area darkened ominously. The clouds turned from gray to shades of black. Thunder resounded in the distance. The only light was from the lightning bolts that flashed angrily above the atmosphere. Alastair collapsed back on the ground and closed his eyes in defeat as the slight drizzle began. He pulled his hood over his face before silently expressing regret for his latest action, before the deluge of water pelted his body as if someone was casting stones at him. At least his robes would get clean he thought.

Chapter 66

Noah

Noah breezed through his last exam and met his mother for lunch at their favorite cafe downtown. They ordered burgers and sweet tea. "You know we've been coming here since it opened," his mother remarked. "I just love the views of the mountains."

"I know it's one of my number one spots too." *He was thinking about asking Gemma here for lunch.*

His mother interrupted his thoughts. "Are you glad school is over?"

"I am; however, I'll be happy to move on," he said as he took another bite from his burger.

She raised her eyebrows in surprise. "Really, and have you decided what you want to do?"

"Okay, Mom, don't think I don't understand what you're asking. But yes, I thought about what you said when I was complaining about working on the fifth floor, and I put it all in perspective and have continued to think about it since."

"And?" *She silently prayed her son was on the right path.*

"I put an application in to work with the trash company and at the hamburger place in the mall. They both offer good starting salaries and benefits," he said casually as he continued eating his fries.

His mother's face turned white. Her stomach churned into a ball of knots and her throat constricted. She could hear her heart pounding against her chest as she stared, incredulously, at her son. "I'm not sure I heard you correctly," she managed to mutter.

When he looked up, he shrugged, "Well, it was kind of what I was thinking and a few..."

It was at that moment, when he looked up, she saw the familiar glow in his eyes. "You're joking!" she shouted, as she interrupted him.

Noah couldn't contain himself as he burst into a fit of hilarity. "You should have seen the look on your face, Mom."

His mother grabbed her chest. "I'm too old for a prank as such. My heart is beating so hard it's going to jump right out of my chest. I have to make an appointment with the cardiologist now. The blood just drained from the top of my head to my toes," she gestured elaborately. "What's wrong with you?" She laughed as she tried to catch her breath. Moments later she reached over and swatted him playfully on the arm. "Tell me what you've decided," she demanded as they continued laughing.

"Well, I believe I've figured out what I want to do with my life."

Chapter 67

Hey Sunshine,

It is difficult to describe the level of pain I feel daily. It's so bad that I'm unable to discuss it. I work hard to forget, but when I have one minute of down time my anger starts again. There are also all the reminders and then I work harder. When I'm alone at night, the pain starts again. The ache is so raw that sometimes I feel it's eating right through my own flesh. Then I regress and start thinking and deliberating over the choices I had to make.

Adding to my agony is Willow. Don't misunderstand me she is not a problem. Willow is sharp and open to new research and ideas. She wants to make some changes, but I'm not ready to go there yet. However, I do enjoy listening to her viewpoints and we have developed a habit of sharing coffee and having lunch together.

I find myself looking forward to this every day. I do feel very guilty about it and am not sure if I'm doing the right thing. Guilt is like a terrible illness that one doesn't recover from. It is really starting to consume my thoughts to the point that I don't know what to do. I wish you were here.

All my love,

Me

Chapter 68

Lily and J.T.
June 2001

.T. was exhausted. When he arrived at the water he stripped naked and swam as far as he could to relieve the fire that burned deep within his body. He was so tired he slept on the fine sand by the water before he returned to the dwelling the following day. He found her underneath a tree by the vegetable garden crying.

He felt his throat constricting. He didn't want to see her like this. He saw images of people like this in his head too, and it made him sad.

He ran to her and knelt down beside her. "Lily, are you ok? What's wrong?"

She gasped and wiped the liquid off her red, tear-stained face. "I don't know. When you left so quickly, I felt, like, I don't know…empty inside. It was as if you weren't coming back. When you didn't return, I wasn't sure what to think."

"Lily, I promise I will never leave you. I'm just trying to tell you that something is happening and I keep seeing more images day after day. I'm frustrated because I know they are important and perhaps if you try to remember it will help. I don't know why we're here, or for how long? Nevertheless, I believe the images are the key. We need to talk."

"Talk about what J.T.? We're here with Bear. It's so beautiful and relaxing. What is there to talk about?"

"I want to know *what* you are seeing, in here," he pointed to her head.

"I can't. It hurts too much," she gasped as she clutched her head.

J.T. pushed the hair away from her face and wiped the tears. "It's going to be okay, I promise," he whispered, as he scooped her up in his arms and carried her into the dwelling.

Chapter 69

Alastair's Consequence

Alastair shook his head back and forth. "They're going to die because of me," he muttered sadly. "Cooper, I'm at a loss of how to deal with the situation. I wish you could help me."

Cooper, sitting upright, responded by barking. *Woof. Woof.*

Alastair sighed heavily as he stood and looked at the dog. "Unfortunately I don't understand. Perhaps you can give me a hint," he said jokingly.

"Alastair," a familiar voice called.

Startled, Alastair looked around and suddenly the face of Lucius appeared in the Reflection Pond.

"Lucius, you gave me a fright," he said as he walked closer to the water. "I don't know how much more I can take…my nerves are withering and the tightness in my chest is gnawing at me like a beaver chewing on a log…"

"Focus, Alastair," Lucius bellowed. His words reverberated off the small wooded area that was surrounded by clouds.

Alastair began pacing. "I can't help it; I've always been like this…well, not always…there was a time when I was carving stone in the stone yard and…"

"*ALASTAIR,*" Lucius interrupted, "do you have any idea what is going to occur if you don't do something? And look what you've done to the cloud cover again. I will *not* be responsible for the bad weather Zachariah will surely send your way!"

"Yes, yes, I know. I'm still drying out from the thunderstorm that was cast upon me," he spat annoyed. "Look my beard is still wet," he said as he took hold of the long hair and twisted it. Water puddled at his feet.

"I think we can agree that you brought that on yourself," Lucius stated unflinchingly.

The last thing Alastair wanted to discuss was his attempted escape. He was humiliated with his feeble efforts at scheming. It wasn't his nature but he was desperate and only hoped his mother hadn't heard about it. He shuddered as he thought about her disappointment.

Alastair stopped pacing and took a deep breath and rubbed his temples. "The situation is so hopeless, if I can get down to the earthly realm then…"

"Really? After all you have already done? Do you actually think that is going to happen?" he asked sarcastically. "Besides, you've lost your wings…you know the rules."

"Thanks for reminding me," Alastair responded gloomily as he sat down on a cloudbank.

"Alastair, why do you think I have such an immense group of support to assist up here?"

"I understand, but the situation I experienced is so extraordinary that I felt…"

"What makes your situation different than someone else's? What you are saying is you did not *trust*…"

"No. No. It's nothing like that," Alastair countered. He was deeply troubled.

Lucius nodded. "After much observation, I believe you have *lost your way*! I have decided to escalate the reevaluation of your status and position," he stated decisively.

Alastair's jaw dropped. He was speechless.

"Perhaps you will have some answers as the story continues to develop. But may I remind you *time is running out,* and you need to repair the damage you have created. I am submitting reassessment paperwork for you today," he stated sharply.

Alastair could not voice his questions as Lucius instantaneously disappeared. Another torrential downpour immediately followed. Miserable, Alastair pulled his hood over his head, realizing he was already soaked. Cooper had already sought shelter somewhere under some of the larger rocks leaving Alastair drenched and alone with his thoughts as he waited for the rain to subside.

Chapter 70

Noah and Gemma

The monitor beeped in succession. The chirping was routine so Noah ignored the noise and continued emptying the trash cans. He was just about finished and was on his way to find Gemma. He had something important to discuss with her. "I heard the beeping from the next room," Gemma exclaimed as she entered.

Noah's face brightened instantly. He was head over heels in love with her and didn't know when or how to tell her.

"Noah, look," she pointed toward the bed. His hand flew to his face in disbelief as he watched eyelids flutter followed by tears.

"Gemma, did you change the computer program again? How did you bypass the security codes on that equipment?"

Gemma checked the monitors and made some quick notes. Her eyes were filled with joy and excitement. She grinned as if she had a secret. Noah recognized the look on her face, and her enthusiasm became his. It was as if she had discovered a cure for the common cold. "The doctor told me the code during our last meeting," she said quickly. "Noah, do you remember the stuff about shock waves and my high frequency brain study I was telling you about?" She said anxiously as she moved around the patient. Before he could answer she looked at Noah and whispered, "I found a flaw in my formula, made some modifications, and implemented it again. Look at what's happening," she pointed to the patient's face. "Come help me. I think I know what we can do."

Chapter 71

Willow and Doctor Aaron Carter

"Is it necessary to move him to another room doctor?"

"I'm sorry, Willow, it can't be helped. The family is complaining to the board and they have agreed to donate an *excessively* large sum of money to the hospital if we comply. It was inevitable," he said with resignation.

"But there is activity on his chart. What about the girl?"

Aaron shook his head in frustration as he threw a file on his desk before interrupting her. "That's another thing; her chart went missing again."

She frowned. "I thought you implemented a sign out system." His face was always clean-shaven, but today he had light stubble giving him a somewhat, rugged appearance. She found it sexy.

"I did," he shouted. "One day I found the file in my office, and I'm telling you Willow, I never took it out," he said exasperated.

"Perhaps someone left it there."

"Willow, my office is a secured area. Then, it went missing again and was found."

"Well at least they're not disappearing. Where was it this time?" she asked smirking.

"Last week, I was stuck in the elevator. I've never been trapped in an elevator before, and when the technician got the car going it let us out on the floor below. The head nurse saw me and thrust the chart into my hand and had the nerve to tell me to make sure we keep track of our files. I asked her where it was found and would you believe she told me it was in the lab where they do blood draws."

"Perhaps you or someone left it there by accident." She concluded. "Why are you really upset?"

Aaron took a deep breath, sat down, and shook his head. "I don't know it's a lot of things. We've never had missing files on this floor ever, and then the Wilson family is driving me crazy." He took off his glasses and rubbed his eyes with both hands. "Perhaps I'm just overworked and the board is adamant that we move the patient in 524." He paused and held her gaze then quickly looked away. He reached for the water bottle on his desk to take a sip. There were other things but he didn't want to admit what he was really thinking. Instead he said, "it's just… there are too many strange things happening…and that Wilson family…"

"Can't you find some medical reason to convince them it's not the best thing to do?" She interrupted.

He shook his head. "I don't like it either but apparently the family is part of a powerful law firm in New York. They did an extensive investigation and it seems they believe their son and the girl *did not* meet while skiing or *anywhere* else while he was on vacation. The friends *insist* they were *always together* and *never separated* the entire trip. The best friend said it was impossible," he gestured helplessly.

"That's absurd. None of us even know who she is. So how can they investigate? Besides, he could have met her someplace else. Perhaps they met in town on a shopping trip, or in one of the bars or eateries. We still don't know what happened while he stayed behind to ski and the others departed the night of the accident."

Aaron laughed cheerfully. "Willow, he was out here with friends and his fiancé. Do you think he was having a fling in town while his fiancé was skiing?"

"Well, you never know. People do crazy things when they want, even a burning love affair," Willow giggled. "It's the plot for a torrid love story and he wouldn't be the first," she smiled seductively.

He fidgeted nervously. His stomach was in knots as he looked at her soft lips. He quickly shook his head to clear his mind from his X-rated thoughts. "A hopeless romantic, are you?"

"Yes, we've already discussed this," she stated proudly.

"I thought you were kidding."

She pressed her lips together wondering about his strong arms or who was the lucky woman that he held at night, or… she quickly looked up, hating that her thoughts had wandered. "Nothing wrong with a little romance or a good passionate romance novel," she grinned. "Perhaps I can speak with the family?"

He stood up, yawned, and reached for his lab coat. "Willow, I'm telling you there is no reasoning with them and hospital politics are now involved. It's out of our hands. I need you to assist with the preparations for the move," he said firmly.

She again took notice of his large arms as he twisted into the white coat and her thoughts wandered to his fitness routine.

"Willow, are you listening to me?"

"I still say it's a mistake. I think he knows her."

He looked surprised. "We've already discussed this. Why can't you let it go?"

The muscles on her face twisted as she shook her head. "I know it's ambiguous, but the labs and charts show they are improving together. I just find it interesting and worth more study," she indicated. "I don't know. It's just a gut feeling or instinct…"

"Really? When did intuition become the cure over science and medical facts? Until you can provide some scientific evidence we must move him!"

Chapter 72

Lily and J.T.

J.T. carried her to the room she slept in and laid her gently on the bed. His body snuggled next to her as he wrapped his arms tightly around her waist. "Lily, I don't want you to cry anymore."

"I'm sorry but for some reason I just feel strange. I need you." Lily nestled closer to him. She was getting warm. It was more like her insides were boiling again and felt hot like the blazing circle J.T. had constructed. There was something pulling at her. She felt an aching she was positive she had never experienced before. She wanted and needed something she couldn't explain and knew he was the only one who could provide it. She was frustrated and confused. His hand was gently rubbing her back. He was whispering that things were going to be okay. The more he caressed her the more she wanted him. Her body tingled and trembled. She craved more than his touch but couldn't comprehend what she desired. "I love being with you this way."

J.T. felt his entire body stirring in a way he couldn't describe. It was as if they were connected by some powerful force but for some reason he felt as if he couldn't have more. His fingers lightly traced circles on her arm and shoulder before he hugged her tightly.

She sighed and turned toward him. "Please. I love this and being with you," she said again.

His head shot up and he looked around the room in a panic.

"J.T. what is wrong? Is it the voices again?"

J.T. whispered, "Yes." He sighed heavily. He closed his eyes tightly and pressed on his temples hard as if the action would stop the noise. The voices were louder and the faces were becoming clearer. "I love being with you too! But something is happening. I can feel it. People are calling for me. It's the ones I keep telling you about. They are nice and want to help. I feel like I'm moving back and forth. I'm floating and I can't focus. They are telling me to come quickly. They need me. It's like I have to go."

Lily reached up and gently touched his face. "You can't leave me," she whispered. "I don't understand," she sobbed. "How can you possibly go when you don't even know how you got here?"

J.T. cradled her face in his hands and looked into her eyes. "I'm telling you, Lily, whatever transpires I need you to *promise* me you will start to remember. Something is tugging at me. I need you to listen to your head and look at the images that appear. You must try," he pleaded. "I'm positive we're connected to them. Will you *promise* me you will come and find me no matter what it takes?" he implored.

Lily gasped and her eyes widened with alarm. She put her hands on his face. "J.T. please don't talk like this. It's terrifying!"

"The energy is here. I'm telling you, Lily, I feel a strange sensation that I can't explain." He nuzzled her neck, inhaling her scent. He wanted to remember everything he could about her. He could feel he was slipping away. "Lily, swear to me," he pleaded. *"Promise me you will try to remember. Promise me you will find me!"*

Lily looked deep into his eyes, which were so blue and hypnotic. She was feverish with desire, a yearning she couldn't define. Then something happened that neither had expected. Their lips touched and ignited the fire that burned in their bodies. The kiss intensified leaving them breathless. They didn't want it to end. Their bodies tingled and yearned for something so intense they couldn't fathom. They clung to one another as if their lives depended on it. They shouted for each other but could no longer hear their voices as the words became lost in a muffle of beeps.

Chapter 73

Noah

Noah was glad that school was finally over. He completed his four-year degree and was ready to move on. His mother made such a fuss at the graduation ceremony one would have thought she was writing a photo essay with all the photographs she took. "Doesn't he look good with his nice hair cut?" she asked his friends.

Noah blushed. "Mom, enough with the photos," he smiled after he and his buddies posed for another picture."

"Just documenting this momentous occasion for your children someday," she said as her brown eyes sparkled with pride.

His friends and their parents joked and laughed with him about his new haircut, future children, and other funny stories from school. His mother promised to make a small photo album for everyone. Later in the week, they would all come over for some good home cooked Italian food. Noah hoped his mother would find a nice man and settle down. In her early forties, she was attractive. Her olive skin and clear complexion was always glowing. She claimed it was from not wearing makeup. Her brown hair was styled in a messy, layered cut, which fell below her shoulders. He didn't know how she stayed so thin with all the food she cooked. His friends often teased him about dating his mother. "Not going to happen," he'd respond all too seriously.

After the graduation ceremony, she insisted they go out for dinner. But today it wasn't school or graduation that was on his mind.

Noah decided he was going to tell Gemma how he really felt. He had been considering and planning it all week.

They worked so well together and then the other night… well, he couldn't stop thinking about it. It was a miracle! Gemma assured him it was a technique she had performed on many occasions. Some combination of magnetic therapy, neurons, tissue connections, and a computer program she developed to spark brain response. He was a bit frightened by it and when he arrived at work the following evening and saw the empty bed, he thought at first the patient had died. He soon discovered he had just been moved to a private room in a location he had no access to.

Disappointed Gemma hadn't met him like she normally did, he worked quickly hoping she'd appear. He breathed a sigh of relief when she finally surfaced at the end of his shift.

"Noah," she called.

Noah spun around as he closed the closet door and grinned. "Gemma, where have you been? I need to talk to you. Did you hear about that guy?"

She nodded excitedly. Even with the reduced lighting, as was the energy-saving procedure at night, Noah noticed her blond hair glistened. It was as if the sun was shining down on her, in the middle of the dimmed hall. He longed to reach out and run his hands through her hair and give her a hug.

"Noah, come. I need you to do something for me." She led him to one of the private conference rooms and Gemma explained her technique in detail and had Noah take extensive notes with instructions. She was focused and serious as she asked him to record other information pertinent to her discovery. She told him she would need to refer to the journal later and asked him to keep it in a safe place.

Noah found the entire process odd. "Gemma, why didn't you just write all this down earlier?" he asked.

"Noah, sometimes I like to talk out loud, it helps when I'm trying to figure something out; besides, I thought this would be good for you too. You are only adding to our existing notes."

He shrugged in agreement and continued. After he was finished writing he looked at her and she gave him her biggest and brightest smile ever and held his gaze. Her blue eyes were hypnotic. She then said, "Noah, I believe you're going to be a great doctor one day." She quickly broke contact, pulled her hair back and told him she was needed elsewhere. Everything happened so quickly that he never had the chance to ask her out. He berated himself for the many missed opportunities and his own nervousness.

Determined, he stopped by the hospital early in the afternoon the following day. He had a bouquet of Gemma's favorite flowers, lilies, and was going to formerly ask her out. He checked all the stations and she was nowhere to be found. Finally he asked the head nurse, who was getting suspicious. "Can I help you, young man?" she asked sternly.

"Have you seen Gemma?"

The nurse looked at him strangely.

Noah didn't recognize her but then again he didn't really know many staff on the day shift.

"I'm sorry. She is no longer with us."

"You mean she just left. Just like that," he said a bit shocked.

"I'm sorry. People come and go. It happens."

"What do you mean it happens? People don't just leave. They say goodbye. Do you know where she went?"

The nurse didn't know what to say. He was clearly agitated and she thought about calling security, but he looked so heart broken. She felt bad, except she wasn't about to violate the hospitals privacy policy.

"I'm sorry she no longer works here. That's all I can tell you."

Noah felt the blood drain from his face as he tried to process the information. His mouth went dry.

"Did she transfer?"

"Yes, as a matter of fact she did," the nurse stated.

Noah's stomach lurched and his body shook. "Young man, are you all right? Do I need to call security?"

Noah gulped. He wasn't looking for trouble. "No, ma'am." He sighed heavily, left the flowers on the counter, and departed feeling distraught.

The nurse picked up the beautiful yellow lilies and put them in water. She would distribute them to the patient's rooms.

Chapter 74

Doctor Aaron Carter

Aaron was stunned when he received the news. His paced quickened as he raced across the hospital with excitement. The staff was in the process of getting the patient ready for his move to a private room when an issue with the air conditioning caused the transfer to be delayed a day. Then a miracle occurred. He was sure the family was going to find some way to blame him or the hospital for not relocating their son sooner.

"He's awake. A bit groggy but give him time. We need to find out how his body will function. Don't be surprise if he can't talk. I'm going to see him now. You should come immediately," he stated clearly into the telephone.

The family was on their way. The minute they were told their son was transferring to a private room, they dropped everything and made preparations to fly to Montana. They would arrive tomorrow, so he didn't have much time.

"Hello, how are you feeling today? I'm Doctor Aaron Carter," he said smiling, as he took hold of his hand. "Squeeze my hand if you understand me?" Aaron smiled when he felt the strong grip. "Good. I'm going to look at your eyes with my light," he said as he flashed the small light within his view to avoid frightening him. "Then you are going to get a full examination so we can find out how you are doing."

"L…," he whispered. "I…y…," he choked out again. Then added, "He…lp me…f…," his voice trailed off.

Doctor Carter made notes. He could barely make out what the patient was attempting to vocalize. His vitals were stable and he gave the nursing staff some instructions.

The doctor watched as the patient's eyes opened and closed. "Turn the lights down a bit," the doctor motioned to the nurse.

"Li.." he whispered again.

Doctor Carter squeezed the man's hands and smiled as he instantly responded. "I'm not sure who or what that means; however, we'll talk about it later. You can rest now," he said as his patient shut his eyes. "Is he snoring doctor?" The nurse questioned.

"It sounds like he is," the doctor said as if it were a normal occurrence.

He dialed security and gave them some new parameters. "I want dates and times of everyone that was in that room and I want to know how long they stayed. I think we missed something very important. I'm going to my office and will return when the family arrives."

Once settled behind his desk, he was on the phone with another department when Willow appeared. He anxiously gestured for her to enter. "I came as soon as I heard," she huffed as he hung up the phone. She was out of breath as she had raced from her research lab to the other side of the building. She dropped a box on his desk that she had been carrying.

Wisps of her hair had fallen from the twisted bun she had secured with a large clip on the back of her head. She looked cute and alluring all at the same time. Uncomfortable with his thoughts, he quickly looked away. "Yes, it's true," he told Willow excitedly. "I need you to start running some tests immediately. I also want to examine all the labs from last week as well. I would like to chart them on a graph too."

She quickly made notes as he spoke and turned to leave.

"Willow, what about your box?"

"I'm sorry. I almost forgot. I found it in one of the closets in the research lab. It belongs to Doctor Cristo but your name is on the box too. Someone wanted you to have it. I tried to organize the files. There are a lot of logs that I would like to review with you. I think this is noteworthy information that we should discuss and perhaps implement..."

"You should *not* have been looking through *it. Just leave it,*" he said tersely, as he cut her off.

Willow could tell he was irritated just from his tone. "I'm sorry. It had your name on it and I thought..."

His eyes grew dark as he interrupted her. "*Absolutely not*! You had *no* right to go through this! Just leave it and start the tests," he spat angrily as he waved her away.

Willow turned and walked out without saying another word. She wasn't going to reply. She had absolutely no idea what had set him off this time.

Chapter 75

The Miracle

"**G**ood morning again. I'm so glad to see you. We're just going to take some vitals and I'm going to have a look in your eyes again. Can you tell me your name?"

He was silent for a moment as he tried to focus. It was all blurry. The sounds and figures moving about were all blending together. He felt light touches on his body.

"Son," the voice repeated, "can you tell me your name?"

"Ja…ck..son," he whispered softly. "May…I…have so…e…wa…ter?"

Doctor Carter smiled. "Well, Jackson, it's a pleasure to meet you." He squeezed his hand and nodded to the nurse that it was okay, and she poured him water and brought the straw to his mouth. To everyone's surprise, he raised his hand slowly toward the cup and said, "I can…do…it…myself."

Doctor Carter's eyebrows arched in shock. While the motion was a bit slow, it was enough for him to take notice. He smiled and said confidently, "Jackson we'll have you up on your feet in no time. I bet you're anxious to get moving. In fact, your recovery is going to start today!"

Recovery? "Wh…at ha…ppened? Wh…ere am I?" He spoke slowly but his voice was a bit louder than before.

"You're at Grace General Hospital and College of Medicine. It's one of the largest medical schools and teaching hospitals in the country. Located in Seminole, Montana. You have been in the trauma-coma annex. You had an accident that left you in a coma for six months."

Jackson blinked as the room came more in focus. Images of flowers, medical equipment, and people moving about became sharper.

Six months? Impossible. That had to be some type of cruel joke. The man in the white coat was talking to more people.

His heart started racing and a cacophony of beeping from the monitors he was hooked to echoed repeatedly through the room. Nurses around him reacted immediately checking and recording information. He barely heard what the doctor said to the people in the room. At the mention of the word sedative, the machines began sounding again.

No. No sedative.

"No, pl...ease," Jackson called out. He did not understand why the doctor looked so content as he waved his staff to stop moving about.

"Okay. No sedatives for now."

"Why are you so...hap...py?" he blurted.

"I'm smiling because your mind is reacting to our dialogue and I'm positive you're going to be okay!" He said as he flashed a light and checked Jackson's eyes again. "How many fingers do you see?"

"Two," Jackson blinked as he slowly spoke the words.

"Are you having trouble focusing?"

Jackson nodded.

"That should clear up in no time. I know all of this is confusing, so I want you to take a deep breath and try not to worry about anything right now. Hopefully your memory will return and everything will become clearer. Jackson, I like to be as honest as I can with all my patients. We've been taking good care of you and with some hard work and therapy I believe you're going to make a full recovery."

"I've been...in a coma?" he whispered.

"Yes, you were in an accident," he nodded. "Do you recall anything about the incident?"

Accident? I don't understand.

Jackson's face paled. His facial muscles twitched nervously as he tried to make sense of it all.

The doctor smiled. "You're awake and we'll talk more later! Right now we must focus on your recovery."

Accident. I don't understand. Six months? Impossible.

The doctor looked at his watch and asked the nurse to record some additional vitals before turning back toward Jackson. He wanted to keep it simple and professional, as he didn't want Jackson to see how worried he was about the upcoming visit. "In about two minutes a group of people will be entering this room. They are *your* family and have been waiting to see you. They can be *very* demanding," he grinned as he said it. "If it becomes *too* much I need you to do this," he demonstrated as he raised his thumb. "Once you give me the sign, I'll ask them to leave. Can you raise your thumb for me?"

Jackson slowly repeated the gesture and the doctor nodded. "I'll be right over by the window," he pointed. "I'll be watching for your signal."

Suddenly the door burst open and people piled into the room.

The doctor was livid as he rubbed his forehead and silently cringed. He normally would never allow this many people in the room for someone just waking up from this type of trauma, but the father had insisted and once again, threatened to sue the hospital.

They were in various states of emotion. Showering Jackson with hugs and kisses. The mother, the overbearing father, siblings, the beautiful fiancé, and his best friend, it was too much. They were all talking at once.

It took less than five minutes before Jackson glanced toward the window and gave the signal.

Doctor Carter threw up his hands clearly irritated. "Enough everyone. It's too much for one day. I will call later on and arrange to meet with Mr. and Mrs. Wilson with an update on his condition."

"What!" the elder Wilson shrieked. "We just arrived. This is ludicrous!"

"Mr. Wilson, it's *too much* for him. There are *too* many people. You can visit again later. Out, out; you need to leave," he pointed toward the door. "He needs rest or he could have a relapse."

Upon hearing the word relapse, Mrs. Wilson's head shot up and her face turned white. "Come, everyone, the doctor is right," she readily agreed. "We can return later," she smiled happily. She was ecstatic her son was awake and didn't want to do anything to cause a setback. She quickly herded everyone out of the room and could be heard issuing directions to the rest of the family in the hall.

Aaron chuckled as he overheard her explain exactly how visitation was going to work. She was firm and didn't care who heard her. She then told her husband she had enough from him…and to save his loud banter for the courtroom. She cut him off more than once while she communicated instructions for her son's recovery.

Aaron was grateful she stepped in. He had forgotten she was an attorney too, and from her tone of voice, he realized not one of them would challenge her. As their voices faded, he called his staff and immediately had them transport Jackson to another examination room. He'd meet with the family later as he had promised.

Alastair didn't realize he'd been holding his breath as he watched the events develop. He sighed heavily with worry but was happy he had witnessed some progress. He sensed there was more to come and muttered, "Perhaps everything is going to work out. He turned toward Cooper and said excitedly, "If that is the case, my friend, I'll be able to return home and get my wings and angel bracelet back."

Cooper's tail wagged noisily as it hit the ground.

"If it all works out then I don't even need to see the Lord and everything can return to normal." He folded his hands and sat up straight with a renewed sense of hope.

Chapter 76

Dear Sunshine,

I did it again – I got angry at Willow. She was just trying to help, unfortunately, when I realized what the box contained, it took me back to another time. The anger is so raw that it's painful. I thought I could manage – evidently I was wrong. My outbursts are uncalled for. I don't know how to apologize. I'm anxious, as I'm not certain she will forgive me. Not that it really matters or does it? What happened to me? When is my pain going to end?

Some days I feel like I'm going to explode and all the pain will be released and I will be free. Deep down, I know the reality; facing it is just another layer that I struggle with and then my thoughts drift back to Willow…

It's just…it's just that she is smart and has countless ideas. I can't bring myself to explain why I can't listen to them. I feel cheated but can't tell her that – it's too terrifying.

The other problem is that Willow is so beautiful that, sometimes I don't know what to say. She always smells like fresh flowers. Her hair – it's long with a soft wave - like she just came off the beach. I don't think I've ever noticed hair so beautiful. Her face and hands are so soft I can tell she takes care of herself.

I overheard her and the nurses talking about moisturizers, lotions, and creams one day. I smiled as I passed by their table in the cafeteria. I just nodded and kept walking because I didn't know what to say to them. It all sounds so ridiculous, doesn't it? Forgive me if I'm repeating myself...I think it comes with the guilt I feel.

Every day I deliberate and reflect on life. My mind wanders and I wonder what you are doing? I go back and forth between anger and then I just think about all the, 'what if scenarios'...and eventually, the pain starts all over again...

Despite the fact that a miracle occurred today, I am still left wondering...

All my love,

Me

Chapter 77

Lily
July 2001

*L*ily awoke and Bear was snuggled at her feet. There was an inexplicable silence in the room and she immediately understood J.T. was gone. She could feel it. She started crying. Bear was at her side immediately. She clung to his furry body for fear he would disappear at any minute too. "It just can't be," she sobbed over and over, until she had no tears left. She cried out his name, "J.T., please come back. I need you," before falling asleep.

Lily slept deeply and when she finally stirred, she wasn't sure how much time had passed. She had stayed in the dwelling and had no desire to rise until she felt Bear licking her face. Her body felt heavy and she ached all over.

She thought about the recent events. Something had happened. J.T. told her he was leaving and she didn't believe him. Where he went and how he left, she wasn't sure. She became more confused as she tried to recall what transpired. Her mind was blank. She was positive she had never felt the emptiness that existed inside her now. While she wasn't in physical pain, she felt like she was.

When she finally decided to venture outside she and Bear continued to roam around, but it wasn't the same. Everything was different without J.T.

She called for him late into the night as she lay in the dwelling. The tears came daily. She was intensely apprehensive and jumped at every sound. As time passed she also felt herself growing weaker. She lacked the energy to go on.

One morning she sat at the outdoor table tracing his initials on the bench and realized many of the vegetables in the garden had stopped growing.

The other thing she observed was how quiet it was without J.T. It was a strange silence that made her overly anxious. She kept thinking he'd return and checked all the spots where they had spent time together. Other days she just strolled with Bear or stayed at the dwelling, as she felt too lethargic to move.

She eventually made another trip to where J.T. first appeared, where she sat by the water and had relaxed with him so many times. Suddenly, she recalled the final words he had spoken. She promised him she would try to remember, no matter how excruciating it was. It was at that moment she knew what she had to do.

Chapter 78

Noah

Noah was so distraught he called out sick for his shift. His mother demanded to know what was bothering him when she came home early one afternoon and discovered he had called out for the entire week.

"I met this girl…"

"Stop. I've heard enough. What? Did she break your heart? When are you going to learn that life is *not perfect*? You need to understand *how* to deal with disappointment! People are *not* flawless! Relationships will come and go, and many will be challenging too. Countless individuals that pass through *your* life are going to have a profound impact on you. Some will be acquaintances, and some will remain friends. Some may inspire you. Others, who you think are friends, may disappoint you. The sooner you comprehend this and learn how to deal with the *trials* you will face, the better you will be!"

"But we were so close and she just…she just *departed* without saying goodbye or giving me an explanation!" he pleaded.

His mother sighed heavily. "Noah, perhaps she had a reason to leave so quickly. Maybe she tried to call. You don't know. Now this girl must have made some sort of impression on you for you to *call out of work for an entire week*! Perhaps you should focus on the good and not the bad. Then think about the consequences of not learning to *deal* with life's problems.

Not showing up is *never* an option! No matter what obstacles life throws at you, you must *always* show up! God *always* has a plan."

Noah winced as the door slammed behind her. He never understood how his mother had become such a strong woman. She had been through a lot, but her steady belief in her faith always kept her going. She never gave up. She had continued to put herself through school and worked in an x-ray lab before becoming an MRI technician. In her spare time, she liked working in the local coffee shop – only because she enjoyed it, not because she had to. She *never* complained about anything.

He knew his mother was right. While he was sad over Gemma's disappearance, he returned to work the following day. He continued to visit with the patients. While he was still unable to see the male patient, formerly of room 524, who subsequently was moved to a private room in a secluded area of the hospital, he continued to visit with the female patient who remained.

He left flowers, talked to her, and described how depressed he was about Gemma. One night he reiterated the entire story and all the regrets he had. He held her hand and couldn't stop the tears as they flowed from his eyes. "I wish you would come back. You're the only one who knows about Gemma."

A single tear fell from the corner of her eye as he spoke.

Noah blinked in amazement. He could feel his heart beating against his chest, as he was not sure what he should do or if he ought to tell someone. Too many questions would be asked, so he quickly decided against it; instead he grabbed a tissue and gently wiped her face. "I *know* you hear me," he whispered in her ear. "You need to come back. Gemma said you can't leave and I believe her."

School would be starting soon and Noah knew he would be pressed for time. He developed a real affinity for the female patient in 524, especially after he witnessed the tear. He always made sure he spent extra time with her. He continued to talk with her daily and massaged her arms and limbs after he completed his trash rounds at night.

One evening, while he was arranging the bright yellow lilies in the vase in her room, he noticed she looked different. He moved to her bedside, sat in the chair next to her, and as if in a trance, gazed upon her face. For a minute he could have sworn she looked like his Gemma, so peaceful and angelic. He shook his head as he quickly realized her hair and face didn't even match. He felt remorseful because nobody came to visit her. So he leaned over and gave her a quick kiss on the forehead and then did something he hadn't done in a long time. He took her hand in his, squeezed it, bowed his head, and prayed for her.

Alastair's head snapped to attention as he watched the scene. "Oh no," he muttered solemnly as he realized his error. Lucius was right. He had become too self-absorbed and wasn't paying attention. He had been too busy complaining and dwelling on the incident with the trainees that he not only lost his focus but purpose as well. Why, he wasn't fit to even be an Angel trainer or a member of the Twelfth Order.

Alastair also knew his epiphany came with obstacles and consequences. He realized getting his angel wings and bracelet returned was not going to be easy as he adjusted his filthy robes and made himself comfortable on a gray cloudbank. An image of the damaged controller flashed in his head and he knew time was his real enemy. He sighed deeply, greatly troubled as he felt the weight of his blunder. Raphael and Thelonious had also reminded him of the solution and he hadn't been listening. There was only one answer and it had been in front of him the entire time – PRAYER.

Chapter 79

Jackson and Doctor Aaron Carter

ackson was restless and tired. He had already completed a month of physical therapy and, according to the doctors was progressing at a rapid pace. He had no desire to sit still. When he wasn't in therapy, he met with Doctor Carter and other physicians daily. His strength was returning rapidly and his speech and motor skills were improving. He had every test imaginable and they all reflected that he was proceeding toward a complete recovery. There was one problem. Something was troubling him, only he couldn't figure it out. He felt agitated and everything bothered him. The doctor told him it was anxiety and he needed to relax.

His family continued to visit and fuss over him, which disturbed him immensely as he wanted to be independent. Then there was her. Apparently he had a fiancé – the beautiful Saviella Bernet. They had both gone to Harvard and she had become one of the most sought-after entertainment lawyers in the field. Like Jackson, she too entered the family business and was employed at her father's law firm.

Jackson's father continued to fill in the blanks as he recovered. "When you and Saviella set the date for your wedding, we'll be merging and creating one of the largest, and most powerful law firms in New York."

Jackson had a headache and the last thing he wanted to discuss was Saviella or mergers and acquisitions. Her last visit had left him emotionally exhausted. She ran her hands through his two-toned, blond-brown hair, which had grown past his ears, and she insinuated he needed a haircut and shave. His facial hair had grown so much that she said he looked like a caveman. Saviella also wanted to bring him healthier food and costly clothing to wear. He was more comfortable in his sweatpants, hospital scrubs, and the occasional pair of jeans. She fussed over him and was worried about his health. Something bothered him about her, which was odd because she was so stunningly beautiful. When she came to visit, she looked out of place in her perfectly tailored clothing and expensive jewelry. He made the mistake of telling her she wore too much make-up and her lips were too red. She pouted and stormed out of the room. His father chased after her and assured her that his son would be back to himself in no time.

To add to his agitation, he was fatigued and felt emotionally drained after therapy. Doctor Carter questioned him like he was on trial. His answers were the same. No, he didn't remember anything about the night that brought him to the hospital. His family told him he was skiing, which he couldn't recall. Yes, he knew his name, where he went to school, and that he was a lawyer. No, he didn't remember anything that happened while he was sleeping. No, he didn't want to talk about Saviella, their wedding, or his family. No, he didn't know anyone named Li.

"No to all of it doctor," he hollered exasperatedly, as his hand slashed through the air and he shook his head in annoyance. "I keep telling you it's like a black hole! Saviella told me I needed a haircut as did my mother and I didn't even understand what it meant!"

"I think getting a haircut is the least of your problems," he gestured to Jackson's long hair and explained. "Perhaps shaving will make you feel better," he demonstrated as he pointed to his face.

"Well then, I'm not cutting my hair or shaving," he said adamantly.

The doctor laughed. "That's okay. When you're ready you will do it, but because *you* want too, not because someone asked or told you to do it. Is there anything you want to talk about today?"

Jackson rubbed the hair on his chin. "Nothing! For the first time in my life I feel as if I have absolutely nothing to say!" He promptly got up and limped out of the room.

Later in the afternoon, Jackson apologized to Doctor Carter when he ran into him outside.

"I hope you're enjoying the fresh air," Aaron said. "Do you mind if I sit down?"

Jackson gestured for him to sit. "It's really beautiful here. I like the peace and solitude. I like to come and clear my head. I'm sorry I got angry before. I'm just *so irritated* and I don't *even* know why!"

Aaron nodded in agreement. "I understand how you feel. It's frustrating when you only have fragments of your life to look at. It will all come together. Your recovery is amazing thus far."

Jackson smirked, "Yes, I understand I'm a miracle. I hear talk of it all over the hospital."

The doctor smiled and turned to Jackson. "Well, you're extremely lucky. Think of all the people who don't recover and the alternatives for the ones that wake up so cognitively impaired… let's just say you are *very* fortunate. I know it's difficult as you try to put the pieces together daily. You just need to give yourself *time to recover*," he said as he stretched his back.

Jackson nodded in agreement. "What are you doing outside? Did my family send you looking for me?" He laughed.

Aaron smiled. "No. Like you, I came for some fresh air. Sometimes just walking around and enjoying the mountain scenery helps put things in perspective."

"Sounds like you're trying to sort through something too. Perhaps I can help. Since I have no memory I may be able to provide a fresh viewpoint," he stated as he tried to add some lightheartedness to the conversation.

Aaron didn't give his suggestion a second thought as he sighed deeply and loosened his tie. "I got mad at someone who didn't deserve it and don't know how to apologize."

"Well, that's pretty simple; just start with the basics. How about, I'm sorry," Jackson said as his face brightened and he was grinning from ear to ear.

Chapter 80

Willow

Willow was studying the notes from the security tapes. Unfortunately not all the dates requested were included in the package. Again, it was just the staff who had entered patient rooms. She scratched her head in disbelief. "Something isn't right, I just know it," she muttered.

She dialed the number for the head of security and it went directly to the answering machine. "Hi Roberto. This is Willow on the fifth floor. I read the reports you sent and some of the dates are missing. I would like to discuss and perhaps view some of those tapes. Please contact me and let me know when you have some time to meet." She left her extension with the best times to call.

Chapter 81

Willow and Doctor Aaron Carter

Doctor Carter made his way to the research labs. It had been awhile since he was on this side of the building. He took a deep breath and walked quickly down the familiar halls, nodding and smiling to surprised staff as he passed. It was a secured area but he had the necessary credentials to enter.

"Have you found anything interesting?" Willow was in the midst of studying blood samples and making notes when she heard the familiar voice and looked up. Her jaw dropped and her eyes widened, as she was stunned to see him dressed so formally. Although her boss was turning out to be a bit erratic at times, she liked the job and decided she wasn't going to question his mood swings. She worked hard and did her best to keep her distance.

Her eyes did a quick scan. She didn't know if it was simply habit from her research abilities or a female trait as she studied him for a moment too long. He was dressed in a suit jacket and crisp blue shirt, not his usual scrubs. The shirt complemented and highlighted the color of his blue eyes more than ever. He was undeniably handsome. She quickly turned her head for fear he would see the grin on her face and sparkle in her eyes. She was not someone who could hide her emotions easily.

"Well," he said after a brief pause. "I came to formally apologize for my behavior."

Willow turned back toward him and smiled warmly. "You didn't have to get dressed up for that. Apology accepted. I know we all have stuff going on."

Willow wasn't surprised she forgave him so easily. It was her nature not to hold grudges or argue. Due to the fact he was her boss, she decided not to say anything.

"True, but it's not my normal behavior and my response was inappropriate. I am just trying to work through a personal issue right now and never intended to take it out on you or any other staff members. My conduct is deplorable," he said with resignation. "I still have a lot of personal reflection to consider. So please forgive me."

Willow couldn't remember when someone actually said they were sorry and admitted they were wrong, much less twice in a few weeks. Her ex-husband, the bastard, would never consider it. Every argument was always her fault and lead to unfortunate confrontational behaviors. It was refreshing to actually have someone admit their faults. "Don't worry about it," she answered sincerely.

"I know this is a bit last minute but I am heading over to the university. A colleague of mine is giving a talk on brain studies and I thought perhaps you'd be interested.

Willow blinked. "Are you talking about the lecture scheduled with Doctor Callahan? It's sold out!"

Doctor Carter smiled as if he had a secret. "True, but I think they will make room for me," he stated as he pulled two tickets from his jacket. "Would you like to go?"

"Really?" she answered excitedly.

"Well, I am the director," he shrugged nonchalantly. "Besides Roger and I went to school together. If you'd like to meet him in person, you can join us for a bite to eat afterwards, that is, if you're not too busy."

Willow didn't have to think twice. "Absolutely!"

Chapter 82

Willow and Doctor Aaron Carter

When Doctor Roger Callahan was finished speaking, he received a round of applause. Willow was excited to meet one of the best neurosurgeons in the country. She leaned toward Aaron and said, "Thank you for asking me. This was fantastic," she smiled jubilantly. "I can't wait to ask him some more questions."

"Roger will appreciate your willingness to learn more, especially if it's about *his* work," he chuckled as he touched her lightly on the shoulder and steered her through the crowd.

They stood and waited as people departed the lecture hall before joining in the swarm of people. As they slowly moved toward the exit, Willow stopped and was intently staring off to the right.

"Willow, is there something wrong? You are holding up the line."

"That young man over there. The one with the red shirt going up the far aisle, he looks familiar. I've seen him before but can't place him."

Aaron shook his head. "I can't see him that well. He's probably a student from the school and you recognize him from the campus. After a while you get to know them all. Come on, let's go and meet the great Doctor Roger Callahan and grab something to eat."

Chapter 83

Hey Sunshine,

I think I made some progress today. I went to the research lab. You would have been proud of me. I also made it a point to apologize to Willow again. I should tell her the truth, but I just can't say the words; instead, I let my anger boil slowly, like a pot of water until it bubbles over. She is a very intelligent and classy person. I like the way she dresses too. I know I already told you this. Sorry for repeating myself; I don't know what I'm thinking. Perhaps I just notice it because everyone around me looks the same. Admitting the truth is harder; perhaps it's better not to discuss anything.

I went to see your friend Roger Callahan. I called him prior to let him know I was attending and explained the situation, which he fully understood and promised to keep quiet. I asked Willow to accompany us for pizza afterwards. It wasn't like a date, right? Since Roger and I were going to get something to eat and catch up anyway.

Willow was excited to meet Roger. He was happy to entertain her questions. I don't know why I asked her, I was very nervous, so I just blurted it out during my attempt to apologize for my rudeness. Honestly, I already had the tickets in my pocket but wasn't sure if she would accept my apology. I'm not making any sense, am I?

This is so difficult. It wasn't really a date, just two of us, going to a lecture. I still feel very guilty. I'm certain she was more interested in meeting Roger, who is much more attractive and far more noteworthy than me!

Please forgive me as I am once again repeating myself and rambling…and I don't know why. I don't know why I feel like I'm doing something wrong. I don't know what I'm doing anymore. I feel like I'm unraveling, but when I'm in surgery, I'm laser focused. How is this possible?

All my love,

Me

Chapter 84

Alastair's Confession

Alastair was sitting on a small outcropping of rocks. Cooper was lounging at his feet. He felt the cool stone as he leaned back and breathed deeply. "Hello, Lord, it is I, Alastair again. So I was thinking – if I confess and tell you what really transpired, perhaps you will return my wings and angel bracelet and then we can forget this ever happened." Alastair looked around for any sounds or movement. Not that he expected an immediate response. The only thing he saw was the dog's ears perk up and go back, almost like an antenna.

"In any event, I believe I am the victim of a dreadful error. My training group deceived me. They suggested I go to the archive library and return with *proof* regarding the existence of *'the cloud.'* In return, they *promised* they would read chapter five of the Angel Code Book. At first, I told them no. I'd be in violation of policy if I left them unattended, as they were new angels. As they continued to hassle me, I deliberated how they passed the entrance exam to even qualify for the angel-training platform!"

Alastair took a deep breath before he continued. "Suddenly one of them blurted out that *I* was *not worthy of my position* if I wasn't even aware of this information regarding the mysterious *'cloud,'* they were seeking."

Alastair grimaced as he regretfully recalled the day. "The challenge hung in the air like the heavy fog I encountered when navigating through the Twelve Realms. I admit I surrendered to the pressure and childish behavior. I then proceeded to lock them in the classroom and headed for the library to see if there was any merit to this *'cloud.'"*

Alastair adjusted his robes and glanced at Cooper for support. The dog simply wagged his tail. He looked toward the pond and continued, "The extremely young clerk conversed with an arrogance that my parents would never have allowed! When I explained her behavior was grounds for an immediate flogging, she told me she didn't care where she was and that she'd call someone named DYFS who would come and rescue her!"

Alastair nervously tried to comb the knots from his beard before he continued. "I tried to explain about life in the middle-ages and respect for authority when she said, "I don't need a history lesson, old man, and besides none of what you ramble about applies to me. Don't forget about DYFS!" She warned me as she glared at me with the most piercing stare."

Alastair shuddered as he recalled the encounter. "I had no idea what she was talking about or *who* DYFS was and was fearful he might be someone like Thelonious."

Alastair stopped talking and looked at the Reflection Pond for any signs of movement before he continued. "Sneering, she then proudly conveyed she was a 'millennial' and part of some 'Y generation!'"

"I was suspicious as it sounded like a cult of *unsuitable worship*. Anyway, she was all too happy to provide a crash course on this *'cloud,'* which basically encompassed computers – specifically their operating systems, data storage, the internet, servers, and more. The moment I heard the words *database*, out of the tech-savvy female's mouth, I immediately raced back to my group as I quickly realized our classroom was just below one of the older computer operating systems in the quadrant. While it was not operational, I was still concerned."

Anxiety mounting, Alastair rose and began pacing in front of the pond. Cooper's head moved side to side as he watched Alastair trudge back and forth. "But it was already too late, they had figured out how to hack the learning confines computerized enclosure and found their way into the secured area below. How they were able to break into the computer room, I have no idea."

His hands and fingers intertwined nervously before he continued. "When I arrived, the board lights were as colorful as a rainbow and the group of scoundrels scattered like flies. Flabbergasted, I couldn't comprehend how they managed to get it operational, but what stood out was the blue light on the outdated board. Encased in its special housing it was blinking rapidly. I gasped in horror as my eyes scanned the panel and observed the arrows spinning backwards on the ancient database. Finally understanding what was happening, I tried to stop it, but I could not. When I removed the plug, the unit shut down, but not before the dials on the indicator panel completed their final backwards revolutions."

Alastair paused and swallowed hard. He felt as if he was drowning in grief. His shoulders slumped and he massaged his temples hoping he could somehow press a rewind button and reverse time. He stopped walking and looked out across the pond at nothing in particular and could barely recognize his own voice as he continued.

"I was shaken to my core and stood paralyzed with fear as I realized they actually keyed the sequence for altering time and events. When my angel bracelet revealed the accident, I realized it was too late. I have been trying to fix my mistake. I have been watching people suffer. They don't deserve this pain due to my error. Lord, I have been desperately trying to reach you. *I feel I could better explain it all in person*, as I know you are the only one who can fix this. Why are you letting them withstand such pain? Are you listening to me at all?" He gestured; his eyes filled with regret.

Cooper let out a small whimper.

Alastair ignored the dog, as he was so deeply troubled, he felt as if he could no longer think straight. His hazel eyes were red with fatigue. He had been praying and praying for days, only nothing happened. Discouraged, he looked back toward the reflection pool and waited.

Chapter 85

Noah
August 2001

Noah placed a vase filled with fresh lilies near the window in room 524 then sat down next to the young girl. He worked quickly through his shift, as he always liked to visit with her last. He felt heartbroken that nobody came to see her and wanted to spend time with her. He only knew that fact as he overheard the nurses talking about it in the cafeteria one evening.

Like Gemma had done, he held her hand and talked to her. He rubbed her back and shoulders. Sometimes he read her stories. Today he chatted about Gemma again. He told her how he missed her and was sorry he didn't get to tell her how much he loved her. He spoke about his summer class and that he would be starting medical school soon and had submitted his two-week notice. Since he would no longer be an employee at the hospital and she was not family, he would not be allowed to visit the fifth floor. "First year medical students don't receive credentials for this floor," he said sadly.

A tear trickled down her face.

Noah jumped back. It was the second time this had occurred. "Don't cry. When you wake up, I promise it will be okay. His adrenaline raced as he thought about the possibilities. He smiled as he suddenly recalled something Gemma had told him.

Noah squeezed her hand, leaned over and kissed her on her forehead, and again prayed really hard for her before he left.

Chapter 86

Jackson and Doctor Aaron Carter

"**W**hat's wrong, Jackson? Are you feeling okay today? I understood you were looking forward to going home? By the way, I noticed you trimmed your beard," he said grinning.

"Humph," Jackson grumbled. "Only because it itched." He liked Doctor Carter and his staff. With their help, he made rapid improvements with his recovery. He had just returned from his daily walk outside. His left leg hadn't healed properly. He walked with a slight limp and utilized a cane. The doctors suggested reconstructive surgery but he wasn't interested.

He sat in deep reflection. He had grown accustomed to the clean air and absence of noise. He often felt as if he had stepped out of a painting as he admired the majestic snow-covered mountains that loomed in the distance. Breathing in the fresh air as he walked around the tranquil, crystal clear lake and gazing at the wildlife that roamed nearby was tremendously peaceful. He was sad that he was leaving and a part of him really wanted to remain longer.

His shoulders slumped as he shrugged indifferently. "It's like my father said, the quicker I get back to my life, the faster I will recuperate."

"Is this what *you* want to do? Is this what *you* believe is best?"

Jackson stood with the aid of his cane and limped over to the window. "You know, doc, I stare out these windows every day and can't get over the picturesque scenery. Although I've been here before, it's as if I'm really seeing it for the first time. I wonder how I *overlooked* all of this. I've been out west and apparently have traveled all over the world and it makes me curious as to what I *haven't* seen and *what* I have been *missing*."

"Ahh, just like a lawyer, successfully avoiding the question," he laughed.

Jackson turned and chuckled as he limped back to his chair and sat down again. "Perhaps my old attorney personality is returning. Honestly, I can't answer your question right now because I *just* don't know."

"Don't be so hard on yourself. Like I keep telling you, these things take time and patience."

"I keep hearing bits and pieces about the accident from my family but *I* can't recollect what happened. Yet I can remember some parts of my life, like going to law school, growing up, and even fragments of my relationship with Saviella. But will I *ever* remember *every memory* and *all* the details?"

"I wish I could tell you the truth, except the brain is so complex. I always tell people if they want to remember they will. Or perhaps something will trigger a memory and you *may* remember *or* you *may not*. Just take it slow and don't put so much pressure on yourself."

"It's frustrating to rely on other people to fill in the gaps *all* the time."

"Well, look at it this way. At least you have friends and family, who, as crazy as they may be, are there to help you. In addition, you have that gorgeous fiancé.

Jackson nodded in agreement.

"We have patients here without families, or who have had family members pass away while they are still incapacitated. The ones without, we must research to discover their past. I have a patient now that looks as if she just appeared from nowhere."

"Can't you post pictures on television or the computer."

"Sure, but since we don't know what was happening in their lives beforehand we try not to. What if they were running from an abusive relationship? We don't need some crazy person coming to our facility with alternative motives."

"I see your point," Jackson nodded in agreement.

Aaron opened a pad on his desk and began writing some information on the paper. "I have arranged for you to have outpatient physical therapy with a colleague of mine in New York. We can continue our sessions by phone if you'd like. It may help with your recovery. I will need you to keep notes. Write anything that is happening or you're thinking about in relation to your accident as we've discussed prior."

Jackson grinned as he stretched his leg and readjusted his position. "You just want as much material for your papers, lectures, and that book you are writing," he challenged.

Doctor Carter waved his hand through the air. "Jackson, *your* recovery is a *miracle* and I'm not going to deny it. I want to provide as many significant and relevant facts, so I can help doctors and scientists discover and/or make advances in the field to possibly find cures. My research may benefit another patient just like you. I'm not going to apologize for that," he said confidently.

Jackson took the paper from the doctor's hand, folded it, and put it in his pocket. "I'm sorry, doc. I appreciate all you've done. I know I'm lucky and I will help you. It's just that I feel so *disconnected*. I still believe there is something that I'm overlooking. Then there are those crazy dreams I have that don't make sense. It's like I've misplaced a lot of the pieces of the puzzle and I desperately need to find them before it's too late."

"We still have some more sessions before you leave. Stop being so impatient. It'll all come together. We can talk more about it later. For now just enjoy the view. Once back home, I doubt this," he gestured to the landscape before him, "is what you will be seeing when you look out your window."

Chapter 87

Jackson and Doctor Aaron Carter

A few weeks later, Jackson was in his final meeting with Doctor Carter. They had spent most of their remaining time outside or in the huge indoor solarium. It was like walking through a giant botanical garden complete with water features, fish, butterflies, and birds, but it was indoors. Jackson found it peaceful and relaxing. Today, he was admiring the waterfall as they walked through the garden.

"You know, I met a woman at a waterfall once and…"

"Hmm. This sounds like an R-rated movie. Jackson, I don't think I need to hear about your past indiscretions," he interrupted.

"No seriously, doc. It came to me in a dream…"

"I'm sure it has something to do with you and Saviella or another past relationship, and I certainly don't require the particulars. Now let's get focused. I'm going to show you a group of photos. I want you to tell me who they are when I hold them up. Don't hesitate. I need you to respond instantly and not think about it."

Jackson scowled suspiciously. "Is this another one of your games that is going to delve into my inner psyche?"

The doctor grinned. "Save the questioning for when you're in the courtroom counselor and do your best. The exercise will not work if you don't answer honestly and instantaneously."

Jackson limped to one of the benches, stretched out his leg, and he made himself comfortable. Aaron sat opposite and opened his tablet. Once he accessed the file he turned the device toward his patient and began the exercise.

Jackson answered quickly as the photos popped up. "Mother, father, Saviella, my brothers, my sister, nurse in PT, nurse that changes my dressing, head of PT, never saw her before, night nurse, transport, clearly a police officer - only I don't know him, security, cafeteria lady, nurse on 3rd shift - have no idea who she is, that's my best friend Adam, and the women from housekeeping," he answered clearly uninterested with the entire exercise.

Aaron nodded and turned off the tablet.

"Well, how did I do? Did I pass the test?"

"You passed."

Jackson frowned. "That's it? That's all I get? What am I missing?"

"Believe it or not I understand how you feel, but as I keep telling you these things take time. However, I will say, it's evident who you received 'the impatient gene' from," the doctor laughed.

Jackson smirked. "Yes, I notice how edgy my father can be at times." He then pounded his cane into the ground. "I just want so desperately *to remember* and I feel like the answer is right in front of me but I can't see it. Does that make sense? For example, I have these bizarre dreams but when I wake up I can't really remember what I was dreaming about and can recall only small images. It's frustrating, I get weary thinking and trying to figure it all out!"

"Jackson, you need to relax," he said exasperated. "There is nothing strange about your experience. This is normal for all of us. However, what I'm interested in is if you remember something pertinent to your accident. If so, you need to write it down. Keep a journal by your bed and try to record anything you remember when you wake up. Carry it with you. It may help us figure it out."

"I know. I know. You just want more research for all the books and papers you are going to be writing about," Jackson grinned as he leaned forward.

"Well naturally!" Doctor Carter laughed heartily. "Jackson, we already had this conversation the other day, but I'm going to say it *again* to make sure you really comprehend and your father doesn't sue me," he joked. "Your recovery is *amazing*. I have never witnessed anything like it. Any awakening like yours is a breakthrough for all scientists, researchers, and physicians. I'll be writing papers and giving lectures about our treatment protocols to others. Whatever I can learn may help someone else. While I don't agree that you are ready to leave just yet, I think in this case it is time."

The eyebrows and muscles on Jackson's face contorted in question. "What makes you say that?"

"Believe me, Jackson, I would not recommend this to just anyone. But you have an *incredible* support system to help you. Let's see what happens when you get back to your life and normal environment. Perhaps you'll start to recall more. You're right, sometimes the answers are in front of us, but we either don't want to see or just don't want to believe it."

Jackson smirked. "You make it sound like I'm some sort of science project."

"I just want to help you heal."

Jackson was about to ask another question and also wanted to talk more about the strange dreams he was having but instead said, "Spoken like someone who understands more than he wants to."

Aaron rose. "I have another appointment; we'll talk more before you leave."

Chapter 88

Noah and Doctor Aaron Carter

Noah stopped by the hospital to pick up his final paycheck and decided to take a trip to the fifth floor for one final visit. He wanted to say good-bye to his friend. He was stopped by security and immediately brought to the director's office. "Doctor Carter, this is the boy we found on the videos we spoke of in the reports. He is one of the night housekeepers."

Doctor Carter quickly glanced at the young man. Tall, a bit on the thin side, and in need of a haircut. He hadn't recalled seeing him around. He looked harmless. "Thank you, Roberto. That will be all. Have a seat, son."

Noah immediately sat. "Did I do something wrong, sir?" he asked as he pushed his hair off his forehead.

"Noah, is it?"

Noah nodded. "I'm sorry, sir, I don't understand. Did I do something wrong?" he repeated.

Aaron peered over his glasses and eyed him skeptically. He didn't look like someone who would cause trouble. His file was impeccable. "I understand you go to school and have been working here full time?"

"Yes, sir, that's correct. I work at night, second and third shift depending on my schedule. Is there a problem?"

"Well, that's what we're going to find out," the doctor said formally.

Noah was on edge. He could feel the perspiration dripping down the back of his neck. His shirt was already sticking to his skin. His stomach was so twisted in knots he felt like he was going to be sick.

The phone rang. "Excuse me for one minute; I need to take this call."

Noah didn't like his tone. He was getting ready to start graduate school and he didn't want anything to jeopardize his partial scholarship. His mother would be so disappointed. He glanced around the room. He'd never been in this office. The physician's and research offices were assigned to certain staff due to the sensitive nature of the materials inside. He studied the wall behind his desk and was in awe of the advanced degrees and accolades. The man was extremely accomplished.

The other shelves were filled with books and miscellaneous objects. His eyes roamed to the far left and zeroed in on some photographs resting on the end of a credenza and other bookcase. His eyes widened in disbelief and he jumped out of his chair to get a closer look.

Noah picked up a photo and stared. Bundled in ski clothes she was posing at the top of some mountain. The hood of her jacket had fallen slightly. Her face and blond hair were partially visible, ski goggles in hand and smiling brightly – he was positive it was her smile!

Doctor Carter hung up the phone to find Noah looking at photos.

"Is there something wrong, son?"

"Do you know her?" he asked anxiously, as he turned toward the doctor with the frame in his hand. "Do you know who she is? Do you know where I can find her?" he asked a bit impatiently.

"That's my daughter. She is away studying. You look too young to know her."

"But, sir…"

Aaron cut him off. "It's impossible that you would know her," he repeated. He was not willing to discuss her and was irritated Noah was touching the photos. "I would appreciate it if you would put the picture down."

Noah immediately returned the frame to the table. The annoyance in the doctor's voice was obvious. He immediately apologized. "I'm sorry. She looks familiar and reminds me of someone."

Aaron saw the forlorn look on his face. "Son, have you been to Switzerland?"

"No, sir," he said unsure where the conversation was heading.

"See, then you can't possibly have met her because *unless* you have been to Switzerland in the past eight years it would be difficult! Now please have a seat," he gestured to the chair.

Noah's mouth was dry. He really wanted to avoid any further interrogation by the doctor. He cleared his throat. "Is there something you need, sir? My mother is waiting for me. I told her I'd be home for dinner."

Aaron rubbed his forehead. He was mentally drained. His face was ashen and his voice was distant. "I understand you clean the rooms on the fifth floor. I just want to know why it takes you so long."

Noah was so nervous he could hear his heart beating against his chest. If the doctor discovered what he was really up too, his entire life could be ruined.

"Are you listening to me? Why does it take you so long to clean the rooms?" the doctor repeated.

Noah took a deep breath and answered immediately. "Just because people are incapacitated doesn't mean they shouldn't have a clean room. I take pride in what I do. It's what my mother taught me." Noah held his breath. It was true just not the absolute truth.

The phone rang again and the doctor answered. "*Yes!*" He shouted annoyed that he was once again being disturbed. "*Unbelievable!*" He exclaimed to the person on the other end as he quickly stood. "I'm on my way."

He dropped the phone into the receiver and immediately dismissed Noah for some emergency.

Chapter 89

Alastair

Alastair sat with his legs crossed as he looked into the Reflection Pond again. He had been praying and praying, yet nothing was happening. He tried a different approach and began talking. "I should have done more. I obviously failed, and for that I'm sorry. I pray you will find it in your heart to forgive me. Why don't you help them?" he shouted impatiently. The silence continued. "This should *not* have happened; it's all my fault," he said solemnly.

Alastair listened, waited, and then scowled. "Why don't you answer me? Do you hear me? These people need your help." He reached around his shoulder and felt his back. "Nothing," he muttered. His wings had yet to appear. He had a brief flashback to the ancient speaking device and momentarily thought he might not have lost his wings if he had the extended warranty.

His head rolled back and he looked toward the sky and thought about the possibilities – if he had his wings he could try to convince Lucius to give him special dispensation. Alastair huffed and shook his head in disgust.

He didn't have to look at his wrist, as he knew his angel bracelet would not be returning today. "Cooper, do you know how long I've been praying?" He gestured furiously. Cooper rolled on his back and began twisting and scratching in the dirt. "Great you don't want to listen to me either! How is it possible that I'm in the heavenly realm and I can't even get an audience with the Lord? I've been a good steward. I don't understand why he's not listening to me?" He pouted.

Cooper quickly rolled over, got up, sauntered toward the pond, and jumped in.

"Humph," Alastair grumbled. "Fine time to be taking a bath. I have a *serious crisis* here. You need to come out," he called to the dog, who was swimming around. "I might miss part of the story," he gestured passionately. "I can't see what is going on if you're creating waves."

Chapter 90

Lily

Lily was having difficulty sleeping. She was so restless that even Bear jumped off the bed, leaving her to curl up on the couch. She eventually fell into a deep slumber. Hours later her body flinched and trembled. Bear had returned and was cuddled in a ball next to her. The dog whimpered as Lily cried out, "No, no," as she tossed and turned again.

"I keep wondering why you're here?" a voice called out to her.

"I don't know. I keep trying to remember but…"

"I don't think you want to remember. Why? You're missing out on everything. If you don't start to recall, you're going to fade away."

The voice echoed loudly in her head. "Why do you care?" she whispered stubbornly.

"I care about you. I've watched over you for a while now. But you made the wrong choice and do not belong here. You have things to do and take care of."

"Who are you? I don't recall ever meeting you." She absently rubbed her head, as the echoing grew louder. She tossed back and forth as if she was trying to get away.

"Yes, you do! I come every night. Search your mind and remember. You can do it. You're my only hope. I need you to give a message to someone for me."

"I'm afraid," she answered as tears fell down her cheeks.

"Don't be. You must face your fears. Now this is what I need you to do…"

Chapter 91

Doctor Aaron Carter
September 2001

Doctor Carter breathed a sigh of relief. He missed Jackson but had already spoken with him soon after he arrived back in New York. He was still having difficulty with memory recall, but made appointments for outpatient physical therapy, which his father had astoundingly given his approval.

With the departure of Jackson's family, it was quieter. He was tired of their demands for special privileges as they stressed and pressured the hospital staff to unprecedented levels of apprehension.

Weeks later, another miracle occurred on the fifth floor. He had been so busy with two trauma patients waking up within months of each other he hadn't had time for anything else. He had welcomed the work. It took his mind off his personal life, which he cared not to discuss, even with his own therapist; instead, he threw himself into the hectic pace of seeing patients, performing surgeries, endless analysis of data, writing reports and talking with colleagues.

Willow occupied the rest of his time. Their friendship grew as they studied Jackson and the mystery girl's recovery. Willow was also involved in a clinical trial so they settled into a comfortable routine of seeing one another daily. The guilt he felt was increasing and festered in his mind like a spider spinning a web as he tried to rationalize their relationship was strictly friends, but in the back of his mind he knew the truth. The reality was there; only he didn't think he'd ever be ready to face it.

Chapter 92

Lily and Doctor Aaron Carter

"Hello, Lily, how are you feeling today?"

She smiled at the handsome doctor. "Better, I think? You and your staff have been running tests for weeks and I feel like some type of laboratory experiment."

Aaron smiled jubilantly. "Well, like I told you earlier, you have been with us since December 2000. Ten months is a long time, and we want to make sure you are well. If it's too much just let me know and I'll slow the lab work down."

"Believe me, I'm not complaining."

He did a brief examination of her eyes and took some vitals while he spoke to her. "Have you thought about your full name?"

Lily shook her head. "Sorry, doc, still working on it. If you want me to make-up something I can," she smiled brightly.

Aaron grinned; her smile was infectious and masked her sunken cheeks and dark shadows around her eyes. As he detailed more notes, they continued chatting.

"Am I going to be okay?" she asked.

"It's going to be a process and take time. Although it's only been a few weeks, I am confident you will recover. The nurse is going to come in and take some blood. I know you had physical therapy today, so if you're not too tired we can talk later. How do you feel about that?"

She shrugged. "I guess it's okay. It's not like I have some-where to be, or do I?"

"It's good to see you have a sense of humor," he laughed. "I'll see you after lunch, Lily."

Lily winced as the door closed. She was afraid to tell him the truth. She fluffed her blanket and snuggled deeply under the covers as she thought back to the week when she first woke up. The startled nurse gave her some water and then wanted to know her name. She was confused and didn't understand what was happening or where she was. As her eyes struggled to focus on her surroundings she caught sight of some pretty flowers in a vase. When the nurse asked for her name again, she simply answered the first thing that popped into her head – Lily.

Chapter 93

Jackson

Jackson was sitting in his office at the family law firm wondering if he had made the right decision to return to work. He missed the jeans and T-shirts he'd been wearing while recovering. He felt strange wearing a suit and loosened his tie. His father had insisted. It wasn't the first thing he thought he should be doing, but after a few weeks, he decided it was time. He had overheard his parents arguing one evening while they were having coffee in the family library.

"Warren, he needs time to get settled," his mother contended.

"Stella, you and I both know Jackson and I have had our differences, but he'd never want to be coddled. I'm telling you work is the best place for him right now. He's smart and strong…a phenomenal lawyer and needs to be…"

"I don't know, Warren," she interrupted tersely, "the boy has been through so much."

"Stella, he's thirty-two years old. He's *not* a boy but a man! He needs to be surrounded by people he knows. It will help him get his memory and his life back. He can start by getting a damn hair-cut and shave!"

"Well, I don't know where *you* obtained *your* medical degree from, but if this pace gets too demanding and something happens to him…"

Jackson never heard the rest of her words as his father cut her off mid-sentence and the disagreeing continued until she stormed out of the library. He wasn't one to be pampered and the next day he told his father he was getting restless and thought he should go to work.

Sitting at his desk, he tried to recall what his life was like before the accident, and his mind wandered to his current circumstances. He stretched his leg as he tried to get comfortable in his desk chair. Having a permanent limp and walking with a cane didn't bother him as much as it did his father. He went to physical therapy and there was again talk of a potential surgery, except he wasn't interested. The leg had been fractured in so many places and hadn't healed properly. He'd been in the hospital too long and it was the last place he wanted to be again. If he limped the rest of his life, he didn't care. His father still suggested he think about the operation.

As he sat doodling on a legal pad his thoughts wandered to Saviella, who helped him get settled in his penthouse, which he discovered was close to work. After the accident, she couldn't bear to stay in the penthouse without him so she moved into her own condominium. When she heard he would be coming home, she had the place completely cleaned and moved back in. The first week did not go well. He was restless as he tried to get acclimated to his space and life. Saviella was frustrated when he kept asking her where things were located and then accused him of having another girlfriend when she heard him talking in his sleep. She demanded to know with whom he was having an affair!

Jackson had no idea what she was talking about. "I've been in a coma, who the hell do you think I've been with? Perhaps I was running around the hospital in the middle of the night with one of the nurses," he snapped bitterly.

The arguing continued until Jackson explained he needed some breathing space. "I think it's best if I try to get adjusted on my own. I'm sorry, Saviella, I'm still recuperating and I have physical therapy, doctor's visits, and then my father wants me to start coming to the office *more*. It's getting to be too much. I just need to develop my own routine. I promise everything will be back to normal soon. Just give me some time," he pleaded one evening.

She stormed out of the penthouse angrily and when he called to apologize she hung up on him.

Despondent, Jackson picked up his phone and called Doctor Carter.

"Jackson! It's good to hear from you! So how is life on the East Coast?"

Jackson wasted no time and got right to the point. "Saviella is *mad* at me because I had a bad dream about someone I don't know and thinks I'm having an affair, which would be impossible since I've been in a coma. She then got pissed because I didn't let her move back in, my father is *fuming* because I refuse to cut my hair, shave, and don't want to return to work *full time,* and my mother is angry at my father for pushing me so much! That's just the cliff notes," he said exasperatedly.

Doctor Carter laughed boisterously. "Well, I guess life is returning to normal for you? That is, of course, if you like the constant chaos. How do you feel about that?"

"I'm not sure yet. I went out with some friends, which apparently we do every week."

"How did that go for you? Did you remember them and that part of your life?"

He shrugged. "Some of it. But to tell you the truth, I felt like I was on the outside looking in. I felt so disjointed."

"How so?

"It's as if something changed. For example, apparently I was the one organizing and leading. Now, although I'm physically present, I'm really not part of the group; I'm just observing them."

"Well, something *did* change. You had a terrible accident. The type of trauma you suffered is not easy," he reminded him. "You may *not* be the same and you may *think* differently about countless things. The only advice I can give you is to take it one day at a time and address your feelings because if you don't, you'll end up trying to satisfy everyone but yourself. This will only lead to anger later on. Perhaps *slow* your pace a bit. If it's not comfortable, don't do it. I take it your dreams are still the same? I saw the notes the doctor sent."

"The same and make no sense. Water, sand, trees, it's like I was on vacation, only I can't remember where I went," he laughed.

"Perhaps you don't want to remember and you're blocking it out? Give it more time. Write down anything you recall and send it to me for your chart. I may be able to help piece things together. Listen, I have another consult, surgery, and a family to meet. I'll talk to you next week. Call me if you have any immediate problems or concerns. Regards to your parents."

Chapter 94

Lily and Doctor Aaron Carter

*L*ily was waiting for Doctor Carter in the solarium. He found her sitting in her wheelchair by the pond in the far corner. Although she stood at five foot, six inches, her delicate frame looked fragile as she had lost weight and muscle mass. "You're not going to ask how I'm feeling again, are you?"

"Lily, you're always smiling." He stood leaning against the railing that separated the waterfall from a walking path and admired the flowers.

"It's just because you're so handsome," she chided. She glanced at his fingers and saw the ring. "Your wife is a lucky lady. You must go to the gym daily to have arms like that?"

Aaron paused before answering. "There was a time when I was thin and nerdy as could be. My wife was beautiful and to compete with the other guys, I started working out in the gym – I haven't stopped since. Now enough about me, let's talk about you."

She grinned. "So what's next, am I cured yet?" she joked.

He glanced at her, rolled his eyes and laughed. "I think you're fine, but we have to figure out *how* you got here. By the way, you look wonderful today. Did you do something with your hair?" He asked as he sat down next to her. Her brown hair was trimmed below her shoulders and the color was different.

Lily's face was radiant. "Willow and one of the nurses cut it. They also gave me some bangs and highlights. Do you like it?"

"I think it looks wonderful. The question is *do* you like it?"

"I do," she beamed as she ran her fingers through the soft waves. "It made me feel better."

Doctor Carter was pleased Willow had suggested it. She and some of the nurses got involved. Next week they were going to surprise her with a facial and a makeover.

He folded his hands together and said, "Okay, let's talk about your memory."

"I told you I have no recollection. I just see snow."

"I need you to tell me anything you can about yourself."

Lily frowned. "I'm not sure. I see faint images, but they're unclear. I do know that I enjoy being here. When I look out the window at the snow, I feel I've been here many times before."

"Mmmm. Perhaps you are responding to the music and photos we played during treatments to help stimulate your mind. Beautiful landscapes, seascapes, waterfalls, all help to create calming environments or maybe you like to travel and have been to places as such?"

Lily wasn't convinced. *But it was all so real, she mused.*

"Not to worry. I have many techniques to help you recall your memory. Tomorrow we'll go to the learning center."

She sighed heavily. Her brown eyes looked sad. "Do you think I'm going to walk again?" Before he could answer she added, "Doctor Carter nobody comes to see me but the staff. Does anyone know I'm here?"

He could sense the anxiety in her voice. "With lots of therapy we're going to do our best to get you walking again, but we need your help too. I already told you, as far as I know, you have no family. I know this isn't easy, but if you could remember your last name, it would help.

I can't even recall my first name, she thought.

Chapter 95

Willow and Doctor Aaron Carter

Aaron was genuinely looking forward to seeing Willow. He didn't know when it happened, but he suddenly wanted to see her daily. He hadn't felt this way in a long time and constantly deliberated if and when he should ask her to dinner or how to even approach the subject. He also thought many times about the hospital gossip policy and if it didn't work out. He'd never felt more uncertain in his life.

Willow smiled brightly the moment she saw him waving at her. She was positive something was going on between the two of them. There was a chemistry brewing that she couldn't ignore. He had many opportunities, but never asked her out. Unsure, she would second-guess herself and her emotions. *Perhaps it's just me or I could be imagining things. Or maybe it's because I'm just lonely.*

He handed her a cup of coffee, black the way she preferred and they sat in the cafeteria for a quick lunch. "You must be busy. The media and medical community are anxiously waiting for a statement on your recovery procedures, especially with Jackson's case."

"Well, they'll have a long wait. That's why the hospital has lawyers, a media department, and a board. They can handle the press for now. We can't risk violating who our patients are. What do you want to discuss today?"

"My theory."

Aaron nodded. He wasn't going to dismiss her concepts so quickly this time. "Mmm. You're still stuck on that. Well then, you and I have a lot of work to do. Let's go over your current notes."

Willow was excited that he was willing to listen to her ideas and listed the facts she accumulated. She finished with, "The two patients who arrived together have more in common. You can't ignore the data from the computer or their charts. It clearly shows them progressing together; however, I still need to figure out the rest."

He liked her confidence. Her eyes grew wide as she spoke enthusiastically about her thoughts. His mind wandered back to the task of asking her to dinner. *Perhaps he could just suggest it, or that he was stopping at the restaurant and she might like to accompany him, or maybe he should wait until after he was done with his last surgery, or maybe he could tell her he was going after work and it wouldn't have seemed so forced...he didn't even know what she liked to eat for dinner or the type of food she preferred...hell, he was too old for this...*

"Doctor Carter? Are you listening to me?" *He had that look on his face again and she knew he wasn't paying attention. It was irritating.*

"Yes, of course. You were talking about the arrival of the patients in 524."

"I told you this before, the computer shows there was a lot of activity at night, especially after midnight. I know it's inconclusive, but I feel we missed something."

"Yes, and we already discussed this and agreed we don't do anything late in the evenings, especially after midnight."

Willow took a sip of her coffee. "Perhaps they were talking to one another?"

He looked up from his note pad. "Don't be ridiculous," he stated incredulously.

"Oh, you almost smiled. I was just joking, but what if they were? What if it's possible?"

"We've already ruled out that those two didn't know one another."

"No, his family did that," she affirmed. Willow's eyes beamed with excitement as she continued speculating. "Does it matter if they knew one another? Perhaps they were getting acquainted. The subconscious mind and..."

Doctor Carter gazed candidly at her as she spoke. He was thinking about when he was going to ask her to dinner again and where he would take her. His hands were sweating and he was fidgeting. He felt as if he was back in high school when he asked his first love to the junior prom.

Willow stopped talking and snapped her fingers in front of his face. "Hello, are you *listening* to me?"

Truthfully, he hadn't heard a word she said. Like a sports highlight reel, his mind had unconsciously wandered back to high school, to his wife, college, children, and other events in his life. It was the sound of her voice that brought him back to the present - the attractive woman sitting in front of him with gorgeous brown eyes and the longest eyelashes. He was on the verge of asking her to dinner, the words were on the tip of his tongue when he abruptly changed his mind. He wasn't sure if it was from the guilt, which was like an IV flowing through his veins, or the interruption from his buzzing phone.

Chapter 96

Noah

Noah was in the library working with his study group when his mind began to drift. He fluctuated between the same topics – work, school, and Gemma. He sighed heavily as he thought about the past year. He was glad he no longer had to work overnight and enjoyed his new part-time job working in one of the biology labs. Although he received a small scholarship, which basically covered books, student loans financed the rest of his education. The part-time job just gave him some spare change for necessities. He especially liked that he was able to help other students and was able to utilize the lab at the same time for homework.

Then there was Gemma. When he started school Gemma was always on his mind so he kept to himself. He was still not over her and believed she would eventually contact him. He scanned every blond haired, smiling face in lecture halls, the library, labs, and corridors, hoping she'd appear. He wanted desperately to share what he was studying. He missed her and the way she left still hurt.

He attempted to enter her name into the computer one evening while he was at the library when it occurred to him that he didn't even know her last name. Thousands of people with the name Gemma, including physicians, populated page after page. The more he thought about it, he realized he really knew nothing about her. His stomach lurched, as it had never occurred to him to ask. He'd been so self-absorbed in his own 'poor me' life, so when she came along – it was still all about him. Dejected he closed the program as his friends had arrived for the study group.

While the course work and homework were intense, he was extremely prepared. Not just because of the subjects he took in his undergraduate program, but from his job with the environmental services team at the hospital. He knew it was just a fancy term for housekeeping or porter, but he finally understood the value of what he observed and heard in the years he had spent working on the different floors and wings. He had never comprehended until now just how much he had actually absorbed.

He smiled to himself when the pathology professor was discussing certain techniques and terms. He eagerly participated, as he knew the answers. He hated to admit to his mother the education he received in the basement morgue was not wasted. She was always right. There was a reason for everything.

He doodled in his notebook as he again thought about Gemma and tried to rationalize how he felt. Did he think about her too much? Was he obsessing over what happened? She popped in and out of his mind at the oddest times. While he hoped she was okay, he still desperately wanted to hear from her. He wondered what he would say if he ran into her on campus.

"Noah? Are you listening?" one of the guys asked. "Are you going to participate? We need to prepare for the upcoming exam."

Chapter 97

Alastair

Once again, Alastair had changed locations – moving to different rock outcroppings thinking the Lord would respond if he sat in a different spot. While he knew his thought process was absurd even for him, he was grasping at anything, even if it was relocating to a different area to get the Lord's attention.

"Hi, Lord, it's Alastair again, Angel Trainer of the Twelfth Order. After you get through with me I am sure I will be demoted. I am praying for those I see before me suffering due to my incompetence. I should have been paying more attention; perhaps I am getting *too old*. The people that I have been mandated to observe are undeserving of the misfortune and torment and desperately require my help. I don't know how to reach them. I know I already put in a request but I wouldn't ask again if it wasn't so urgent!" He pulled on his scruffy goatee before he continued.

"Perhaps you could find it in your heart to return my angel wings and bracelet to me; it would make it *easier* for me to help them. If I had my *wings*," he emphasized, "I could just fly down to the earthly realm and conceivably sprinkle some angel dust, time could be reversed, and everything could return…"

Alastair jumped as thunder rumbled loudly before he could finish his thoughts.

Cooper let out a soft, low bark.

"It was just an idea," Alastair responded. Even he couldn't believe he suggested time reversal. He wasn't God. "It's my anxiety; it's eating at my flesh," he stated to Cooper and then quickly apologized to the Lord for overstepping. He continued conversing with the dog as if he was a person only because he was lonely. Sitting in the gloomy, solitary environment made him restless. The apprehension and waiting for what was to come shook his body to his very core.

Cooper put his head on Alastair's lap while Alastair tried to figure out what he should do next.

Chapter 98

Lily and Doctor Aaron Carter
October 2001

"You look worried today, Doctor Carter."

Lily was an enigma. When she first woke up she was confused but talking slowly. Within a few weeks she was back to conversing normally. Her motor skills were improving daily and her brain scans were clear. It was as if no trauma had occurred. The only thing afflicting her was her memory or lack of it.

Aaron removed his glasses, rubbed his eyes before returning them to his face and leaned back in his leather chair. "I'm not worried, Lily, I'm perplexed."

Lily frowned. "I'm not sure I understand."

"Don't get me wrong, your physical therapy is progressing; however, I believe you are holding back mentally and I don't know why. The only thing we have learned recently is that you have a fear of the dark. The anxiety you expressed last week in the solarium was a breakthrough. I wish you could tell me more."

Lily's jaw dropped. The apprehension she displayed during their evening session was confusing and embarrassing. "I felt trapped and…I just don't know," her voice trailed off. She didn't want to discuss the incident further and quickly changed the subject. "What about the learning lab. I discovered I can paint and Willow has been working with me," she grinned.

"Yes, I heard," he said as he folded his hands together. "We did a search for anyone studying art nearby but there are no names that match. We just need to discover more of your likes and passions. You are avoiding something and we need to figure out why. This sometimes indicates some other trauma or perhaps an upsetting life event that may have occurred."

Lily was disappointed. She thought she was recuperating. "So what does it matter?"

Doctor Carter rubbed his neck as he leaned forward in his chair. He was exhausted from lack of sleep and wanted so much for Lily to get better. "I know what you're thinking. You're making physical progress; however, that's just the beginning. You need to be *mentally* healthy too. I can't let you leave here and have a breakdown. I want to try some hypnosis to see if we can learn more about your life. We'll record the session and you can see what transpires. How do you feel about that, Lily?"

Lily thought about telling the doctor her name wasn't really Lily, but what good would that do, for she didn't even know her name; besides, she felt better that at least she had a name to answer to.

Lily shrugged. "Whatever it takes doc, I'm up for it."

Chapter 99

Jackson and Saviella

Saviella was fawning all over Jackson as she attempted to fix his clothing, "Your jacket is creased and your tie is crooked," she said as she leaned toward him to assist. He was getting annoyed and quickly pulled away. "I can do it myself, Saviella. You need to let me. It's not like I lost my hands," he barked.

Tears immediately followed. "I'm sorry, but you snap at everything I do or say. I'm not sure how to act anymore."

Jackson sighed and pulled her close. "I'm sorry. I just want to be independent. You didn't do anything wrong. It's been such an adjustment getting back to my life and I didn't think it would be so demanding. I'm still fine-tuning everything. Let's just go to the restaurant and have some fun. Just tell me who we're meeting again."

The restaurant was apparently one of their favorites. Friends hugged and kissed them and said they looked stunning. Jackson watched as Saviella's svelte body glided effortlessly across the room. Her designer outfit showed off every curve, including her ample bosom. Jackson couldn't believe she was so devoted to him.

"To the perfect couple," a fellow attorney friend toasted.

The Italian food was freshly made. Expensive wine flowed from the special reserve from the restaurants wine cellar. They were with friends and colleagues and everyone seemed to be having a good time, except for Jackson.

Once again, he felt like he was on the outside looking in. It was as if he was at another table listening to conversations from people he didn't know. Elaborate vacations and trips, when and who would be joining were covered. They chatted about work related events and upcoming functions. Someone had a box for baseball and football and they were talking about plans for the season and who was going to the football games next week. Someone's private plane was flying to Philadelphia to see the Eagles play the Giants. He and Saviella were invited. Apparently, he was a big football fan, but could barely remember that part of his life.

Another person made a joke about his hair and beard, and if he was ever going to cut it. "Your father must be pissed."

"I'd say he's a bit irate, but I'll cut it when I'm ready," he said pointedly.

"It's sort of growing on me," Saviella laughed, as she played with the hair on his neck.

Then the question he had been avoiding came from his best friend Adam Chadwick. "So when is the big date? Have you figured it out yet?"

While the details were still sketchy he was told that he and Adam grew up together in a fancy, gated community in Long Island. They attended private schools from kindergarten through high school. Adam had jet-black hair opposed to Jackson's sandy blond hair and stood a few inches taller than Jackson's six-foot frame.

His mother had saved his trophies from his glory days, from which he discovered he and Adam both excelled in baseball and basketball. "You would joke that you two were easy to spot on the basketball court because of your different hair color," his mother laughed as she pointed out photos in the multitude of albums she had created. She helped him fill in the gaps about his relationship with Adam. It seemed as if they did everything together.

It was only natural they would be roommates when they attended Harvard. Harvard Law followed. Jackson's father didn't have to think twice about hiring Adam at the family law firm. They had history and there was nothing they didn't know about one another. Jackson was still trying to remember their entire friendship. For some reason it annoyed him that Adam asked him about their wedding in front of the entire group. He silently fumed as he took a sip of his wine.

"Jackson," Saviella whispered, "did you hear the question?"

"Oh, sorry. I'm sure Saviella and I will announce the new date as soon as we discuss it. But don't worry it will be some place nice and everyone will be invited." His smile was forced because planning a wedding was the *last* thing on his mind. Saviella leaned over and kissed him on the cheek. The group clapped and the laughter, conversation, and drinks continued. It was his standard answer and he knew he was going to be questioned again when he and Saviella were alone. Ironically, she had not pressed the issue. But he knew the clock was ticking and he would have to address it soon.

Adam offered to give Saviella a ride home later in the evening.

Jackson's eyes narrowed suspiciously when he heard Adam's suggestion.

Had this become a practice? He'd been so focused on his recovery that he realized he had neglected Saviella.

"She's coming back with me tonight," Jackson interjected firmly. He put his arm protectively around her shoulder and pulled her closer. He didn't know why he said it, but suddenly he knew he needed to figure out his relationship with his fiancé and he realized that spending time away from her wasn't the answer. Doctor Carter was right; he needed to take a good look at his life and Saviella was a big part of it, especially if they were going to be married.

Chapter 100

Jackson and His Father

ackson eventually returned to work full time only because he didn't want to be "coddled" as his father had put it. As the weeks passed he was able to learn the majority of the staff and quickly memorized locations of offices, the library, and file rooms. He settled into a routine. He was helping the team by writing some briefs for a few cases. He was going through a stack of files when his secretary called and informed him that his father wanted to see him in his office. He groaned, grabbed his suit jacket, and limped down the hall.

"You need something, Dad?" He held the door open and peered in. His father was sitting behind his desk and was busy navigating through stacks of paper work. Post it notes were torn from the pad and attached while his pen made brief comments. Jackson empathized with the attorney who'd be at the receiving end of all the corrections.

"Jackson, please come in and sit," he gestured.

Jackson entered, limped over and took a seat before the huge, antique, mahogany desk that once belonged to his grandfather.

"I'm wondering when you will be ready to start going back to court. The case load is piling up and I really could use your expertise..."

"Absolutely not!" He interrupted, infuriated. "We already had this conversation. I'm not up for it. I can barely get through the files on my desk. I guess you forgot that I was in a coma for six months!"

His father, loosened his tie and stood up. His eyes narrowed as he regarded his son and then he started pacing. His height, over six feet tall, wide frame, and deep voice made him someone to reckon with. "Jackson, *you* are a *Wilson* and *you* need to get control of *your* life," he gestured angrily. "I know you suffered, as your poor mother and I did, but you're lucky to be back and need to move on with your life! Feeling sorry for yourself…"

Jackson exploded. His blue eyes blazed, and like a leopard he shot up from the chair. "Are you fucking kidding me? Is that what you think I've been doing?"

"Jackson, the *language* and keep your voice down. I didn't mean to imply…"

"If you haven't noticed that's what I've been trying to do and I'm sorry I'm not moving at *your* pace, Dad," he spat angrily as he continued to fume. "I can't help it. So for once *get off my back*!"

"Get off your back? I'll get off your back when you start acting like a Wilson! Look at you," he gestured at his son. "This is a *professional law firm*, get a damn haircut and shave, you look ridiculous," he yelled.

Jackson stormed out of the office, past his mother, who was meeting her husband for lunch. She had heard the shouting match down the hall and immediately knew what transpired. She marched into her husband's office to discuss his behavior. An argument ensued the moment she entered.

"I'll be out of the office for the rest of the day," Jackson grumbled as he quickly limped by his executive assistant and headed toward the elevators.

Chapter 101

Willow and Doctor Aaron Carter

Aaron had been meeting Willow at the Mountainside Café on the campus on a regular basis. As the weeks passed, he found himself looking forward to their lunches and for the first time he made sure his schedule was clear so he was not late. "I have to say, Willow, this was a great idea. I never realized I needed to get out of the office and take a break."

Willow unwrapped her sandwich then removed the lid from her coffee cup and sipped the hot beverage. "When you're so focused on your patients and research, it helps to change your environment and just go someplace different to think and clear your mind. It's even better if you find a place where the food and coffee is good too," she grinned.

"Do you know how many times I've given lectures or attended meetings here and I've never stopped to eat? I'm always working. How did you find this place?"

She shrugged. "I like to explore. I equate it to traveling. The entire campus is so beautiful. I just started walking around to learn what the area and town has to offer. I enjoy the mountains and the abundant views. I was looking for a new lunch spot and stumbled on this new café. I think it's incredible there are so many good food choices for the medical students. It makes studying easier for them since they don't have to worry about running off campus for meals. This grilled panini is fantastic," she said before taking another bite. "You should try it next time."

Willow rested her chin in her palm while he took a phone call. She admired Doctor Carter immensely. He worked hard and was responsible for many new techniques that proved effective with trauma patients and their recovery. She was lucky to have this job. His blond hair was wind swept as they had taken a walk outside before lunch. It reminded her of that sort of unkempt style she saw in a hairstyle magazine at the beauty shop last week. She was thinking how sexy it looked.

She never grew tired looking at his blue eyes. It didn't hurt that he was in shape either. His lab coat hugged his broad shoulders, clearly defining the muscles beneath. He was very into fitness and making sure the body and mind were just as healthy. It was a way of life he lived by. She learned he was an active hiker, rode a bike, skied, and liked walking the trails in the multitude of parks nearby. She understood why the nurses flirted with him all the time, but he never even realized it or paid attention to their overtures it seemed.

Sometimes she believed there was something passing between them. The light touches of his fingers on her shoulder as he directed her toward a table or steered her toward the elevator sent chills down her spine. It was electrifying. But that was all that happened. He kept it extremely professional. She gathered she was imagining things and was probably just reacting like the rest of the females that came in contact with him.

One afternoon, one of the nurses mentioned that Doctor Carter never went to lunch with anyone but his wife and it was always in the cafeteria as he was busy working and didn't want to be too far away if he was needed.

Willow replied tersely, "We're just colleagues and that's all!" She hated that she was a bit harsh but didn't want any cruel gossip to spread. She had too much respect for him. She also didn't want to be called back to the human resources office.

He *still* wore his wedding ring and she often wondered about it and his life before his wife passed. She didn't know him well enough and wasn't going to pry. If he wanted to share he would. He was apparently very devoted to his family, an admirable quality in the medical profession. She witnessed too many affairs at her former hospital. She too eventually became one of those casualties.

"How is it going with, Lily?" she asked after his call ended.

"As you know she is walking better so her physical therapy is progressing nicely. But it's her mental condition I'm concerned about. She is having great difficulty with her memory. I am going to try something different. I can help her along but this is part of the therapy. You'll see the results soon enough."

"Why is she different from the others?"

"They had families and friends. Since she is alone we need to tread lightly. We don't know what she was doing at the time of the accident, if she was really with someone, and why she was there."

"What about the photo we sent to the police departments?"

"So far no missing person matching her description has been reported," he answered.

They talked more about his upcoming surgeries, her work in the lab, and some of the side trips she had planned for the upcoming weekends. She signed up to participate in the wellness program the hospital offered to the staff. "You should come hiking with us. It will be good to get back to nature."

"I have probably been on most of them," he laughed.

But not with me. Willow was a bit dismayed when he declined her offer to tag along on the group trip. She knew it was a bit forward of her, and he seemed too busy.

He saw the flash of disappointment on her face and looked away. He could have gone. But the moment she mentioned it, a wave of guilt washed over his skin then seeped into the pours of his skin and found its way into his blood stream. His heartbeat increased and the perspiration trickled down his back, sticking to his tailored shirt and lab coat. The tension mounted as he wrestled with his feelings. It was a hospital-organized trip.

It wasn't like a date. There would be lots of others attending. What the hell was wrong with him?

In the end he quickly changed the subject and they talked more about her projects in the lab.

Willow barely heard him. She felt as if she made a mistake in mentioning the trip and was sorry she suggested it.

Chapter 102

Alastair

" **H**i, Lord, it's me Alastair McDougal," he sighed indifferently, as he sat at the edge of the water staring out at the Reflection Pond. "You know, Angel of the Twelfth Order," he repeated for what seemed like the hundredth time. He sighed heavily, slowly rose and began pacing around the pond. "I'm saying a prayer for the people I've come to somehow care about even though I don't know them. What I do know is that they need help. I don't understand how you could let this continue for so long. Perhaps if you could convince Lucius to return my wings I could help. My enchantments are all I have to help them. I fear something big is amiss. I pray you hear my prayer."

Alastair paused and continued, "I beg of you, Lord, if you could help me put an end to this, I will be in your debt forever and do what you wish." A slight movement caught his eye and he quickly turned only to find Cooper rolling and twisting on his back as his legs danced in the air. "Humph. How can you find this amusing? Don't you see the vulnerable state I'm in? I could use some support. I sense you're laughing." He stopped and shook his head as he questioned his own sanity for conversing with the dog and expecting an answer.

Chapter 103

Jackson and Stella Wilson

"Jackson, what's wrong?" She absently ran her hands through her new multi-layered, pixie haircut, which fell to her shoulders as she regarded her son.

Jackson pushed the food around on his plate. He had been having brunch on Sundays with his mother since he returned home. They went to different places. He admired her a great deal. She was an attorney, who managed to raise three boys and a girl. Nick and Blake were the oldest and twins. He was the middle child. His younger sister, Rachel, was studying fashion. While the entire family had blond hair and blue eyes, he and his sister looked more like their mother, while the twins favored his father.

His facial muscles twisted. "I don't know anymore, Mom. Things have changed. To everyone else life is the same and just continued, but for me everything is different."

His mother studied her son. His eyes had a dark and distant look she'd never seen before. As he spoke, she realized he was in pain. She put her hand on his. "It's okay, Jackson. You've had a long year. Perhaps you're pushing yourself too hard?"

"I'm not sure. Dad is getting too demanding and I feel as if everything is shifting. Things are tolerable, but in a different way. I just can't figure out what my problem is."

"I know your father can be challenging, but he only desires the best for you. Sometimes he doesn't know exactly how to express himself," she said softly.

"Well he does an exceptional job expressing and making his point in the courtroom," Jackson spat back as he continued moving food around on his plate.

"Well, that's what he *loves* to do and he's great at it. He just wants you to be successful and enjoy what *you* do as well. You know you didn't have to go to law school."

Jackson knew what his mother was saying. "I didn't make a mistake. I love the law and wouldn't have wasted the time and money if I didn't. You know that!"

She nodded. While he was more like his father than he realized, he didn't have the roughness or toughness that came from a hard life of struggling. "I'm going to say something you're not going to want to hear. I know your father can be challenging…"

"That's an understatement," he smirked, interrupting her. He didn't know how his mother put up with his headstrong father but they seemed to make it work and did love one another.

"Jackson," she said firmly. "I know you have been through a lot. But you are thirty-two years old and have been given a special gift. You came back to us. Your father isn't going to change his ways, so stop quarreling with him. It's only fueling your anger. Be honest with yourself and don't live with regrets. The doctor said you shouldn't try to rush your recovery and that you need to be patient. What's the hurry?"

He ran his hands through his hair and scratched his neck. "I know, Mom, I'm just irritated and I want everything to be the way it was, but I can't even remember half of the way it was so I don't know what I'm trying to remember! I don't even know if what I just said made any sense at all!" He shook his head. "Why the hell did this have to happen to me?"

His mother saw a flash of sadness in her son's eyes, and again was worried. "Jackson, you know I can't answer that question. Perhaps God gave *you* a *time out*. Perhaps the path you were heading down was the wrong one?"

Jackson crumbled up his napkin and threw it on the table. "Great, first Dad and now I'm going to get a lecture about God. You know…"

"Jackson," his mother interrupted firmly. "You're fortunate to be alive, young man, and not only did *your* world change but *ours* did too! You have *no* idea what the family has been through and *yes*, your father and *I* spent many days in the hospital chapel praying for you."

Jackson's eyes widened in disbelief as she spoke. His family was not that religious and he couldn't recall the last time his father set foot in a church. He also had never thought about the stress his family had been through during his ordeal.

"It's a miracle that you survived. It's an even bigger miracle that I am able to have a conversation with you. Now I suggest you give everyone that is trying to help you some slack. You also need to wake up every day and be appreciative. Perhaps try to put things into perspective. You may not remember your life and what it was, so what! Just start making new memories with the life you have now." She put her hand on top of his again. "Be happy, Jackson, with *what* you do with your career, *who* you spend time with, and stop putting so much pressure on yourself. Remember, live without regrets."

Jackson adjusted his glasses. He knew what his mother was saying. She was extremely wise and only wanted the best for him. His face brightened. "Thanks for the pep talk, Mom."

She smiled. "By the way, I like your haircut!"

He lifted his eyebrow, smirking and said, "It's about time you noticed."

Her face brightened. "I have been sitting here busting. I didn't want to make such a big deal about it. But since we are on the subject, you're so handsome with that clean shaven face. You look like that actor, Ryan Reynolds," she laughed. "Has your father seen you yet?"

"No!"

"I don't think he is going to recognize you," she grinned.

Chapter 104

Lily and Doctor Aaron Carter
November 2001

*L*ily looked petrified. She kept staring at the photo as if she were in a trance.

"Lily, are you ok? Tell me what is wrong."

Lily's heart was racing. She could feel drops of sweat trickling down the back of her neck.

"Lily!" Aaron called again. "It's okay. You need to tell me what is happening. It's just a photo."

"Take it away!" she screamed.

"Not until you tell me why this picture is upsetting you," he said calmly.

"No..ah, Gem…ma…help me," she screamed.

Aaron's eyes widened, as Lily continued shouting for Noah and Gemma.

"Doctor Carter, do you want me to bring her back?" the technician asked calmly. Aaron, still surprised, did not immediately respond. The technician repeated the request. "Doctor Carter?"

The doctor shook his head and motioned for the technician to wait with his hand.

"Lily, who is Noah? How do you know Gemma?"

Aaron's heart was pounding and his own anxiety was building as she continued to yell.

Lily was barely listening as she continued shouting the names, "Noah and Gemma. He..lp me…I..ne…nooo…now…ack." Her words were undecipherable and sentences incoherent.

"Her pressure's rising doctor. I think it's *best* we bring her around *now*," the technician advised, his tone was harsher than his first request. "She could go into shock!"

The doctor agreed. "Let me know when she is stable," he whispered as he angrily thrust his gloves, mask, and gown in the trash. "Tell the nurse to bring the transcription immediately to my office," he snapped as he left the room. The irritation in his voice didn't go unnoticed by the team who scrambled to get Lily stabilized and back to her room and the reports completed.

Chapter 105

Jackson and Saviella

Jackson walked out of his building and was assaulted by a cacophony of horns, people yelling, rambling vehicles, and construction. The earsplitting noise from the daily hustle and bustle of the city was starting to grate on his nerves each time he departed his apartment building. His chest constricted and he felt like he was having an anxiety attack. He had stopped walking to the office because of it; instead, he'd call daily to alert the doorman who had a cab waiting for him.

Jackson fell into a pattern of working, which was challenging for he had to be apprised on the cases before evaluating them. He spent more time talking, reading, and having his executive secretary take notes. For some reason his "lawyer memory" was better than his "personal memory." The legal recollections and procedures were coming back quicker, but he still needed assistance. He decided if he worked harder, the rest of his memories would return too.

To do this, he tried to balance his grueling work schedule with his social schedule, which included getting reacquainted with Saviella and their friends. Life was starting to move faster and, for some reason, the pace was disturbing him. He often felt like he was running a marathon with work, physical therapy, doctors, and friends. Only he never made it to the finish line. It was as if he veered off the course and couldn't find his way back to the right path.

His physical relationship had resumed with Saviella too. There was no denying her beauty and intelligence. He was a lucky man to have her by his side. The problem was, he felt disjointed when they were together, which bothered him as she was so gorgeous. Sometimes he felt like he was somewhere else, but he had no idea where that "somewhere" was. While people surrounded him, he still felt a strange emptiness that he couldn't describe to the doctors.

Then there was his immediate family. His twin brothers Nick and Blake were both doctors at the cancer center. He met with them weekly and they helped him reconnect the dots. He was closer in age with his sister Rachel and spoke to her on the phone. She was always flying somewhere in Europe.

Saviella, his law colleagues, and friends were always about, yet he still felt alone. There was also a strange feeling that he was always forgetting about something or that he needed to be somewhere else, but again, he had no idea what or where that was. Saviella suspected he was having an affair, again, as she felt he wasn't focused one hundred percent on her.

"Saviella, you need to stop accusing me of this! I can assure you, it's all I can do to keep up with work and getting my life back together."

Stunningly beautiful, blond hair, and not an ounce of fat on her, she worked hard to stay in shape and take care of her appearance. Her expensive clothes and makeup were always impeccable. He was positive having an affair had never crossed his mind.

Saviella had moved back in but only stayed a few days and then spent two at her condo to give him some space. Jackson surmised it had something to do when he asked her what was for dinner one evening. They were sitting on the couch enjoying a glass of wine and the view of the city when he asked.

Saviella looked at him suspiciously. "Jackson, you must be joking. Me? Cook? Don't be absurd!"

"You don't cook at all," he said aghast. He wasn't sure why he even asked.

Saviella flipped back her thick long, layered hair and sighed heavily. "When have I ever cooked a meal?"

"If I could remember, I wouldn't be asking," he retorted irritated. "Well, why do I have such a huge kitchen?"

"It's mostly for entertaining."

"Do *I* cook at all?" he asked a bit sheepishly.

Saviella shrugged. "I have absolutely *no* idea, Jackson. We either go to the club with friends or out with our families. There's also a chef who prepares meals at both our parent's homes," she gestured. "We *had* a personal chef, but because we go out too much *you* let him go."

"So we don't eat here at all?" he asked just to make sure he heard correctly.

Saviella was exasperated. Her voice was a bit strained as she retorted, "I don't understand what this is all about? We eat out *every night*! You *love* eating out and trying new restaurants and cuisine. We keep coffee, beverages, a few snacks, and other essentials but that's it! We have *no time* for cooking *or* cleaning. We *hire* people for that. Since the penthouse was empty, I only had the cleaning service come once a month. I called them to resume when you returned. They come during the day on Mondays and Fridays. I left the information in the kitchen. Didn't you read it?"

No, I probably missed it.

He could not recall seeing it or this part of his life. It was disconcerting. His face muscles tightened as he scratched his neck. Saviella was talking again.

"Jackson, you promised we were going to try the new Thai restaurant downtown so please stop with the questions. You need to get ready. Our reservation is at 6:30 pm sharp!" She patted his thigh as she rose. Her high heels echoed through the penthouse as she made her way toward the shower, leaving Jackson to wonder if he even liked Thai cuisine.

A week later Saviella handed him a calendar for the next month. "I thought this would help you get organized and remember some of the activities we participate in."

Jackson grinned and kissed her for her thoughtfulness. His smile turned into a frown as he gaped at the color-coded schedule in disbelief. Their social agenda it seemed was just as hectic as their work schedules. They were *constantly* going somewhere. Almost every night was a night on the town for some event. There were dinners, political affairs, and philanthropic events for both families, and the respective charities they supported. In addition, there was the *A-list* events they were invited to that Saviella said they *must* attend.

He felt as if he was on a merry-go-round that he couldn't get off of because it simply would not stop. It was exhausting and he was beginning to resent the demanding calendar.

"Saviella, were our lives always this chaotic? Couldn't we just stay in for one evening and relax?"

"Don't be ridiculous," she chided. "Jackson, we went out *all* the time. You especially loved going out to meet and network with my celebrity clients. This is necessary as we establish our careers."

"Saviella, I don't see how missing *one* event is going to hurt our professions. We have been going non-stop for weeks," he argued. "I never realized it until I looked at the planner you created. I just want a night of peace and quiet," he pleaded again. "I'm still recuperating."

"Jackson, how do you think I feel? I thought I almost lost you in that terrible accident and then you made a miraculous recovery and I don't want to miss anything. Do you know what my life has been like without you?" she pouted.

Jackson sighed heavily. He knew the tears and fighting would escalate. "Okay. But I'm telling you I need some time off from the social scene. Perhaps we could plan a quiet vacation."

She clasped her hands together and leaned over and kissed him on the lips. "That's a wonderful idea! I'll call my travel agent tomorrow. We can go after the holidays," she gestured excitedly. "Now hurry and get ready. I don't want to be late. The car is picking us up at seven and we're meeting your parents at the Carlyle promptly at 7:30 pm. Remember it's a black-tie affair." She left the room before he could answer.

Jackson shook his head in disgust as he made his way into his closet to start getting ready. He had a feeling it was going to be another long night. He wondered exactly what part of the conversation Saviella actually heard.

Chapter 106

Jackson

Jackson had just hung up the phone with a client when Adam poked his head in his office. "Hey buddy, just checking in to see how you're feeling. I thought we'd grab a bite to eat after work."

"Yeah, well Saviella has me on the social circuit from hell. And my parents have some events that are a *must* attend. I don't ever remember life being so crazy!"

"Probably because you've been sleeping for six months," he chuckled as he entered and sat on the leather couch.

"Very funny," he stated dryly. He was getting tired of the sleeping jokes. They were getting a bit old.

Adam was sorry he said it and quickly apologized. "Sorry, I didn't mean anything. It's just that sometimes I don't know what you're thinking. We used to joke and laugh all the time. Now you're moody and distant. Almost like a woman. What the hell has happened to you?"

Jackson threw the pen he was holding across his desk. He didn't need another lecture on his disposition, especially from his best friend. "How would you feel if you missed six months of your life and then just like that," he snapped his fingers for emphasis, "were thrust right back into the *rat-race* and everyone expected you to go about business as if *nothing* happened? And at the same time you are trying to overcome physical limitations, recall *who* your friends are, *and* the places you've been? Sorry if I seem a bit different. I don't mean to be, Adam; I'm just trying to put the fragments of my life back together."

Adam apologized again as he loosened his tie. "I'm sorry, Jackson. I don't think any of us are thinking straight. We don't know what you *do* and *don't remember*."

"Well *that's* my problem. You and dad check on me daily. Just *stop* asking if my memory returned. It's getting annoying."

Adam shifted in his chair as he cleared his throat. "Okay. I was just trying to help."

Jackson changed the subject. "Where were you the other night? Saviella wanted you to meet one of her friends. She was really good looking. You would have liked her."

"I told Saviella I wasn't interested in meeting anyone right now so I just didn't show up."

"Saviella was pissed and blamed me for *your* absence. She and her friend departed early and I was left going home alone. You could have told us. I would have stayed home. I'm getting tired of the nightlife and need to slow down. It's really taking a toll on my recovery!"

Adam rolled his eyes. "I can't believe *you're* tired of going out!"

"Look, this isn't college anymore," Jackson retorted. "We work for my father and our positions are demanding and stressful. In addition, I'm trying to get well again. It's not like I had the flu and was out sick for a week. It's hard simply remembering *how* to do my job again."

"We just care about you."

"Yeah, well, if you care so much, stop asking me if I remember anything. If I do, I'll let you know okay."

Adam chuckled. "Point taken. Perhaps we can grab a beer after work next week?"

"Let me check my calendar," he laughed.

Chapter 107

Willow and Doctor Aaron Carter

Something was going on with Doctor Carter, and Willow had no idea what had happened. He abruptly stopped meeting for coffee or lunch. He cancelled every meeting possible. The staff said he was working late hours and *did not* want to be disturbed. He responded by email and only received calls if it was patient or family related. He told the staff he was researching something for a family, which required all of his concentration. He was cordial but distant.

Willow didn't buy any of it. Something occurred and she pulled out the calendar to see if she could pinpoint their last lunch or coffee together. She then checked his schedule to confirm what he was doing when the change happened. She circled some dates in October and November and quickly determined it all pointed back to one patient. She smirked and made her way to the nurse's station.

"Willow, what are you doing with that chart?" Aaron barked.

Willow jumped and was too stunned to respond as she turned to face Doctor Carter. Not in all her years had a doctor *ever* questioned her about why she was examining a patient's chart.

"Willow, I thought I made it clear to everyone that any new or old information needs to be discussed before charts are taken out. I need to know exactly what you are doing," he asked a bit too tersely.

"I'm sor…ry," she stammered as she quickly returned the chart to the shelf. "I just wanted to know the recent progress. You know we're doing a blood sample study…"

Aaron was barely listening. He was furious. Frowning he shook his head, interrupting, "If you have something important to tell me about your findings, send it to my office and I will look at it!" He thrust his hands in his lab coat and walked briskly toward the therapy wing.

Speechless, Willow stood with her mouth hanging open. "What the hell did you do to piss him off?" the head nurse asked as she turned and looked up from a file she was processing.

"I have no idea but believe me I'm going to find out. How dare he talk to me that way," she said eyes blazing.

"Well, don't get fired in the process," she whispered. "We like you around here. You're a great addition to the team. I'm sure they'll make you permanent soon. Don't let him fool you. He really is a nice guy."

Willow stayed in her lab and worked later than usual. After she heard the doctor had left for the evening, she returned and peeked in the chart and discovered what she had been looking for had been removed.

Chapter 108

Alastair

"*L*ook at all these people – Jackson, Lily, Doctor Carter, Willow…they're all a mess, suffering various levels of stress, frustration, sadness, confusion…my anxiety is swelling to the extent, that I feel I can no longer stomach the consequences of my error, as I watch…it's all so perplexing. *SOMEONE HAS TO BE LISTENING TO ME,*" Alastair pleaded as he walked back and forth around the reflection pond.

"Is this my punishment?" he called out. "Well, thank you for tormenting me! Why don't you just send me directly down there," he pointed to the ground. "Lucius," he yelled, enraged, "*how can I ever fix this problem without my wings!*"

The sky instantly grew darker and a light mist began swirling around the ground, eventually growing thicker over the pond. Cooper sat up began barking.

"Don't tell me it's going to rain again," Alastair moaned, as he felt light drops of moisture on his face. Cooper continued to bark as the mist whirled about, getting denser until it formed into a funnel and began spinning in circles across the surface. Panicked, Alastair took a step backward. He could barely see as Cooper continued barking. The twister instantly dissipated and out walked Lucius.

"Humph! And you call me dramatic! Really, was that necessary," Alastair said exasperated. He threw up his hands and gestured sharply. "Enough with the theatrics, I need my wings back!" he quickly demanded.

Lucius slowly walked around the pond and said softly. "Alastair, your continued pacing is wearing out the cloud coverage. Zachariah has already expressed his consternation and feels that you are not taking his efforts seriously. Furthermore…"

Alastair was frantic as he quickly chased after him. "*Is that all you can think about, the flattening of the clouds? I'm sure there are thousands of other clouds he can attend to,*" he gestured upwards. "*I implore you; I require my wings and angel bracelet.*"

Lucius raised his eyebrows, his face projecting a look of warning causing Alastair to shudder.

"Not really, the Reflection Pond is part of Zachariah's quadrant of care. Lucius adjusted his robes and took a deep breath and gazed candidly at the water as they walked. "I eternally love this pond. Countless and unseen solutions are available to those who listen. If you clear your mind and unravel your thoughts you may find the answers are right in front of you," he stated philosophically.

"Yes, and the answers that I seek are to have my wings and bracelet returned posthaste!" he spat like a petulant child.

"Alastair, do you know *why* you have an angel bracelet and wings?"

Alastair huffed impatiently as he was not in the mood for another lesson from the Angel Code Book. "The bracelet, an outcome of nineteenth century technology and pushed further with the digital revolution in the twentieth century, which I personally find loathsome, provides daily information, it allows us to process and receive information quickly. Based on the status or level we achieve, our credentials are greater. The wings enable us to fly from realm to realm. But as an Angel of the Twelfth Order, they also allow me to fly to the earthly realm as well. It is an honor to receive them after passing many trials. For some it takes decades or even centuries."

As Lucius slowly sat down on a large rock, Alastair realized how out of place the great angel looked with his shimmering robes next to his filthy garments. Lucius motioned for him to sit. "Alastair, can you give me one *good* reason *why* you should have your wings and angel bracelet returned."

"If I had my wings I could go right down to…"

Lucius held up his hand signaling for him to stop talking. He shook his head and scowled as his lips tightened before he spoke. "Unfortunately it is impossible, you didn't follow protocol and it seems as if *you* have forgotten the rule book, so I will refresh your memory. According to article four million three hundred twenty-seven thousand five hundred and four, it is *forbidden* to fly from the heavenly to the earthly realm *without* a special assignment or permission…"

"Yes, yes," Alastair interrupted irritably. "But by the time my request would have been processed, it would have been too late," he countered adamantly.

Lucius folded his hands together and placed them on his lap. "How do you know if you never took the time to ask?" he probed calmly.

Alastair's eyes widened and his face became a mask of terror. *"There was no time,"* Alastair indicated as he quickly stood up and gestured emphatically. "The situation was so dire that I thought if I could go *straight* to the Lord and explain, for it would be much quicker. I never anticipated the delays. I never thought my wings would be removed."

"Have you forgotten you received a ticket for flying in the no-fly zone, speeding, amongst other violations. As such, you have demerits against you and would not be able to fly out of the heavenly realm thus your wings would be useless…"

"You have *got* to be kidding me," Alastair interrupted, shouting. "You are one of the most powerful angels. You could fix all of this with the snap of your fingers."

Lucius nodded reflectively. "So you are asking *me* to break the rules again?"

Alastair's jaw dropped in alarm. "Well, it wouldn't really be like that. *This is an emergency.* If something happens to these people on earth I will never be able to forgive myself. *Further, the consequences in both the heavenly and earthly realm could be disastrous.* What is going to happen to them? God is going to blame *you* and he will want to know *why* you didn't come forward and explain my situation," Alastair rambled franticly.

Lucius frowned and his emerald eyes grew dark. "Mmmm. I didn't realize there is a section on *bargaining* in the Angel Code Book," his voice boomed.

Alastair closed his eyes and quivered.

"Perhaps there is a new chapter that I haven't read," he added sarcastically. "It's possible you have been a trainer *too* long and are assimilating bad habits from your training groups."

Alastair's face paled. "No, sir, that's not what I meant… and…you see…"

Lucius stood and the sky grew dark. "I fear things may be *worse* than I thought," he said cutting him off. His muscles tightened and his face was etched with deep concern as he stood and began walking. He stopped and turned back and gave Alastair a long searching look as he regarded him. "Why don't you tell me the *real reason* you didn't go and see your supervisor."

Alastair looked down at the ground in shame. His body trembled with humiliation. He took a moment as he composed his thoughts. "I was…was…um…"

He looked up and Lucius was gone. His shoulders slumped; he sank to the hard ground and gazed out at the Reflection Pond. Cooper sat quietly cleaning his paw a few feet from him.

"I was distraught. I was too embarrassed at what happened. If my family found out, they would be humiliated. I thought I could handle it alone. I panicked and just decided to go straight to the Lord to explain and plead for forgiveness," he muttered softly as he rubbed his temples with both hands.

Alastair had no idea how long he'd been staring at the murky pond before the calm water slowly undulated causing small ripples that eventually cleared, and the story continued leaving Alastair to wonder about his destiny.

Chapter 109

Doctor Aaron Carter

"*I*'m sorry, sir, but he is in court and not available. Can I help you with something?"

Aaron was desperate. "I have been trying to reach him for weeks and he hasn't returned my calls. Has he received my messages?"

The receptionist kept her composure, as was appropriate at the firm. Customer service was priority. "Yes, sir. I make sure he receives all his messages. I'm sorry he hasn't returned your call, sir, but Mr. Wilson is extremely busy. If you could give me a detailed message perhaps I can assist you?"

"Damn lawyers," Aaron muttered as he rubbed his temples.

Laura heard his comment and did her best not to laugh. "Mr. Wilson is working on an important case right now. He is also getting married and has an extremely tight schedule. I'm sure you can understand this, being a prominent doctor?"

Aaron got the message. "Just tell him I called and I could really use his assistance answering a question. He can call anytime. He has my cell phone number too."

"Humph," Alastair muttered, "so much for technological progress. At least he's not the only one attempting to get in touch with someone. "Perhaps you should pray about it," he said sarcastically, as he thought about his failed attempts at prayer. Sounds

of thunder once again reverberated in the distance. Alastair's shoulders slumped as his eyebrows furrowed. "Sorry," he muttered. "I wasn't trying to disrespect the Lord or anyone!" He rubbed his forehead in anguish and wondered how he got into this mess and how he was going to find a way out. Unmoving, he sat on the rock and didn't bother putting on his hood as the rain began to fall once again.

Chapter 110

Noah

"This is the greatest, Mom!" Noah exclaimed as he walked around the new apartment. "What made you decide to relocate now?"

"I haven't heard one complaint since you started med school, and it looks like you're not going to drop out, I thought it would make it easier if you were closer to the campus. Plus, I like being able to walk downtown. I put my name on the waiting list last year and finally received a phone call. It's unfortunate we have to move immediately, but…"

"Who cares?" he exclaimed. "It's not like we have a lot of stuff. I'll ask some of the guys at school to help."

"I hate that it has to be this weekend, Noah, but our lease is about to be renewed, I know it's Thanksgiving but we need to make a quick decision."

"Mom, we'll make this a great Thanksgiving! We can make something here or eat downtown or the school is serving meals too. Who cares; we have a lot to be thankful for!"

His mother smiled lovingly at her son and hugged him tightly.

Chapter 111

Alastair

"You know, Cooper," Alastair said to the dog as he absently rubbed his fur. "I'm impressed with Noah's mother. She is an extremely hard worker and no matter what the circumstance, she has always stayed in faith and has managed to make things work. She never complains; instead, she just keeps on praying and believing things will come together as they should.

I now recognize this is where I failed. Lucius is right. I know I lost my way and I don't know when it happened. I think it began with the different groups that are arriving. As the centuries progressed, I didn't. The world transformed and people are different and my training hasn't changed to accommodate people, when some don't even go to church anymore. You know back in the day we went to the great cathedrals for religious education…"

Cooper whined and covered his snout and eyes with his paws as he scratched his fur.

"Yes, well, I can see how this is boring you. You're right. Nobody cares about the past. I never adapted myself to the current events and people. I haven't kept up and if I did I would have been prepared to deal with that *disgraceful* class of angel trainees. Other than the introduction to technology, I can't recall a time in my life when I've been so tormented. I don't even know *how* they made it to the Angel Training Program. Well, no matter. I need to try to stop dwelling on that badly behaved group. I am beginning to see, that *I have much to resolve.*"

In that instant the clouds above parted and for the first time in a while Alastair saw a glimmer of sunlight shining down on him and Cooper.

Chapter 112

Lily and Doctor Aaron Carter

"Hi Doctor Carter," Lily said cheerfully. She was feeling much better. Physical therapy was rough in the beginning but after two months her body was acclimating. The physical therapists were excited with her progress and speedy recovery. "It's as if you were working out while you were sleeping," they often joked with her. Muscle atrophy was minimal and she was getting stronger every day.

Doctor Carter returned her smile. "Lily, you look absolutely wonderful today!"

"Why are we meeting in your office?"

"No reason. I had an unexpected conference call with a family and didn't want to rush from my office to get to the other side of the complex; besides, I knew you were having therapy down the hall. I hope you don't mind."

"Of course not. Are we going to talk about the results of my recent tests?"

Aaron pulled off his glasses and wiped them with his lens cleaner before returning them to his face. Leaning back in his chair he said, "I'm going to be very honest with you. You kept calling out some names; Noah and Gemma."

Doctor Carter watched for any reaction at the mention of the names. He was pushing her and he knew it. He had his own reasons and desperately needed to get to the bottom of this mystery. Lily tilted her head and her brows furrowed. "And?"

He leaned forward. "Well, I was hoping you could tell me *who* these people are to you or *how* you know them? It might help us solve what you were doing the night of the accident."

Lily shrugged. "I don't know, doc, perhaps they are friends or family members."

"Possibly," he muttered. "Is there anything new you recall?"

Lily pushed some strands of her hair behind her ears and shook her head. "No! I told you all I know. I see people with blank faces and places in my dreams that mean nothing to me. I just think about painting all the time."

Doctor Carter took a sip of water from the bottle on his desk. "I'd like you to paint more too but we still don't know what you were doing in Montana."

She bolted out of the chair and started pacing. "What if I *never* remember? What if I was going to marry someone and he thinks I left him, what if I was going on a job interview, what if..."

"Lily, come sit, you're making me dizzy," he motioned.

Lily plopped back down in the soft, leather chair. She turned her head and her eyes narrowed as she glanced toward the corner of the room.

Doctor Carter regarded her curiously as she slowly rose and walked toward the table.

"*Who* are these people?"

"Just family photos. Now come and sit, we have much to discuss."

The pictures fascinated Lily. "The *woman*, she is very pretty. She looks familiar. I'm sure I've met her before. Who is she?"

"She is away. I doubt you would know her."

Lily's eyes were cemented to the photo gallery. She picked up one of the frames to get a closer look. "But Doctor Carter, I'm telling you I *know her* from somewhere."

"Lily, please put the photo down," he said a bit too harshly. "It's impossible you've met. She's been out of the country for a while."

"She just reminds me of someone, but I can't remember who."

The doctor saw the tears in her eyes. "I'm sorry. I'm just out of sorts lately and I want *so* much for your *memory* to return."

"Th…the girl in the photo" she stammered, "what does she do?"

"She is a doctor of pediatric medicine. She is working in the Doctors Without Borders program. She's been traveling for many years. I doubt you would know her."

"And those handsome guys?"

"Those are my sons, Logan and Harrison."

"Brown, blond hair and blue eyes. Ve…ry good-looking – doctors also?"

He nodded.

"You didn't push them into the profession did you?"

Doctor Carter smiled proudly. "My wife playfully accused me of that until she realized they simply watched what I did growing up and wanted to help people too. Enough about me, come sit. Let's talk about what we're going to do next."

Chapter 113

Jackson
December 2001

It was the first week of December. Jackson had made it through the traditional Thanksgiving feast at his parent's home without embarrassing his family by forgetting some relative or friend who visited.

It appeared that Saviella had their social schedule planned for practically the entire year. She booked a vacation in January to an island in Greece. He told her they didn't have to travel halfway around the world for him to relax, but she insisted that he rest and rented a villa on some remote island.

Life became routine for him. The more time he spent with her, the more he was able to reconnect. What wasn't to love about her? It was like dating all over. Gradually she stayed over more and more and they agreed she would move back in permanently after they returned from their vacation. She would not sell her condominium until after they were married or maybe they'd sublet it as an investment.

He did outpatient physical therapy but still wasn't interested in surgery. Saviella and his father kept insisting, but his response was always the same, "I already spent enough time in the hospital and don't intend on wasting another minute of my life. I can live with the slight limp and walk with a cane. You'll just have to get accustomed to it!"

"Warren, stop badgering him. It's his choice," his mother argued over dinner one evening.

"I only want what's best for him," his father grumbled.

"Dad, I've been through enough. Who cares if I can't bend my leg all the way?"

"You can have reconstructive surgery. It's very innovative you know. I know this doctor and…"

"Warren," his mother said firmly. "You need to change the subject."

Jackson smiled as his mother frowned at her husband. He didn't know how his mother did it, but she managed to deal with his father's domineering personality.

His relationship with his father hadn't changed from what he could tell. His father was always pushing him to excel more. While his father was happy he had returned to work full time and looked more like a professional lawyer with his haircut and clean-shaven face, Jackson still had yet to set foot in the courtroom. He wasn't ready and continued to work behind the scenes. The firm won two big cases and everyone knew the victory was due to Jackson's diligence researching facts and litigation strategies. Before his accident he had already created quite a name for himself. He was a good corporate attorney and brought more business to the firm. His father and the partners were elated. His adroitness and how he defeated his opposing clients was what the firm remembered of him and desired. The battle to return to the courtroom lingered like a black storm cloud.

While life was moving forward, he still felt as if he was an outsider looking in. Something was bothering him so much so that it was like having a mosquito bite that wouldn't stop itching. The anxiety was mounting but he refused medication. He was still having weird dreams and would often wake up in the middle of the night in a cold sweat. Saviella asked him what the dreams were about, and he told her he had no idea. It was a blur of images. She insisted he speak to his doctor.

Jackson refused to mention the dreams to the doctor, as he wanted to decipher them on his own. He still met with the psychologist but found himself cancelling more and more appointments simply because he was too busy. He was looking through a stack of messages and muttered, "Shit," as he fingered the slips of paper. He had no intention of ignoring Doctor Carter, but his life had become so demanding, he kept putting it off. He was just about to call him when Adam entered his office.

Jackson was extremely apprehensive and irritated this morning. His chest was tight and he felt like he was having another anxiety attack but attributed it to the stress of his work and all the things that were piling up. He had no time for Adam today.

"I was just speaking with Saviella and she is going to introduce me to some model from a photo shoot of a client she is representing. Do you want to meet for drinks after work?"

Jackson forgot about the call he was making and hung up the phone.

"Adam, I understand we have known each other for a long time so don't take what I'm about to say the wrong way, but every time you and I speak, you're talking to my fiancé. Why?"

"Sorry, but you know how it is, Saviella meets a lot of people and always wants to set me up with someone, and I'm never going to turn down a hot chick."

Jackson shook his head in disgust and smirked. "Adam, when will you ever grow up?"

"You know me, divorce attorney extraordinaire. Always willing to help a woman in need. Plus, you forget when you were incapacitated Saviella didn't know what to do. I was there for her and helped her through a very difficult and challenging time. We were distraught, worried, and always on edge as we didn't know what was going to happen to you."

"I understand from others that you were not too fond of her when you first met her."

"That's because she wouldn't go out with me and chose you instead," Adam chortled as he recalled the memory. "I couldn't believe it when you introduced us. She was in one of my litigation classes and I had asked her out and she told me she was already seeing somebody. When she showed up with you that night at the restaurant, I never imagined she was the girl you had been seeing."

Jackson scratched the back of his neck. "I have no recollection of that evening. Just do me a favor and give us some space. I need time to reestablish my relationship with her and that's what we've been doing."

Adam stood up. "Sorry, Jackson. *It's not what you think.* It's like I said…and…"

Adam was in the middle of his sentence when he saw his best friend blink a few times and then grab his head. "Jackson? Jackson? Are you okay? Can you hear me?"

Jackson's eyelids fluttered as his hands rubbed the sides of his head. He barely heard his name being called. "No! No!" he screamed. His desk chair toppled over as he stood up. The blood drained from his face. His breathing was labored and his nostrils flared as he gathered himself together. His face instantly became redder with each passing second. His eyes blazed like a hawk as he came around the desk holding on for support as he zeroed in on Adam.

"Jackson," Adam called sharply, trying to get his attention, "are you okay? Do you need a doctor?"

Adam never saw Jackson make a fist or saw it coming toward his face. The only thing he heard was the cracking of his nose. Blood splattered everywhere. "*You bastard!*" Jackson screamed.

Adam didn't see the next punch to his ribs as it forced him into the wall and his six-foot frame crumbled to the floor. Jackson jumped on top of him screaming more expletives as he continued punching him in the face. Blood spewed and more bones shattered. Adam blocked and returned some blows as blood continued to spray on the expensive carpet, freshly painted walls, and glass partitions.

Someone called security and eventually Jackson was pulled off Adam.

A crowd of staff and clients had gathered in the hall area and gawked in disbelief as they watched the brawl through the glass walls. "*Jackson,*" his father hollered angrily as he pushed through the crowd. His father's eyes narrowed and were like lasers as he scanned the scene. He was mortified at the spectacle and couldn't imagine why his son and Adam were fighting like animals. "*This is a place of business and not for petty arguments. What is the meaning of this?*" he demanded.

Jackson was breathing heavily. His eyes narrowed and flashed like fire from a dragon. It took two security guards to hold him. "*Ask him,*" he yelled between breaths. "*He is the cause of my accident! Ask him how it happened. Ask him how he stole months of my life from me! Ask him!*" he roared.

His father's eye's widened in disbelief. "Let him go," he gestured to the guards.

Jackson pulled free from the guards and stormed out of the room as quickly as his limp would allow. Covered in blood he headed for the elevator but not before stopping to tell the receptionist he'd be gone for the rest of the afternoon. The last thing he heard was the deep, thunderous voice of his father shouting as he entered the elevator.

Warren Wilson was all business. "Someone call an ambulance for him," he pointed at Adam. "Then have human resources clear out his desk immediately. Tell them Adam Chadwick just resigned. This is correct, isn't it, Adam?" Warren stated harshly. While he had no idea what had happened, he knew the facts would surface later. The only thing that *was* clear – Adam was the cause or somehow connected to his son's accident. The accident that had left his son in a coma!

"*Is this true?*" he demanded in a tone of voice he used in the courtroom. "*Is it true,*" he shouted again, as his eyes filled with fury.

Adam lay on the floor his face now grotesquely contorted and body covered with blood, nodded, and raised his hand to acknowledge the statement was true.

Alastair was intrigued at the latest turn of events. While he didn't know what Adam's role in the accident was, it meant perhaps the entire incident wasn't his fault. Perchance he was mistaken and never needed to see the Lord. But then there was the altering of time and a few other miscellaneous things that he still had to work out. Alastair's mind raced as he considered the various scenarios. Nonetheless, he still felt terrible that another person was now suffering due to what occurred on his watch.

He walked toward Cooper, who was wagging his tail, and sat down as he tried to piece the story together.

Chapter 114

An Unexpected Stranger

"Doctor Carter, I know you're busy but I have a young man who has traveled from Hunters Glen to see you. He says it's very important that he speak with you," the receptionist called over the intercom. Aaron was barely listening. He was too tired to remind her of the protocol for guests and simply replied, "Send him in."

"Hi, sir, thank you for seeing me on such short notice," the bubbly voice began. "My name is Christopher Easton and I think a friend of mine is here…I've tried to call but it's difficult to get through, so I told my wife, Danella, who just had a baby, that I'd just drive up myself and check it out."

Aaron looked at the young man and rubbed the day-old stubble on his face, as he had no time to shave. He was exhausted from the grueling pace he was keeping. He didn't recognize him. Dressed simply in a turtleneck, flannel shirt, and worn jeans that had splotches of old paint on them, Aaron couldn't imagine what would bring him to the facility in Seminole. "Have a seat, Christopher. I don't want to ask *how* you even made it past security because then I'll need to launch an investigation and I'm too busy for that! So tell me *who* is it you're looking for?"

Christopher smiled. "My friend Anna…she was on her way to see me and was in that terrible accident in Hunters Glen…I thought she died but then I saw…"

Aaron's head snapped to attention and he interrupted Christopher. "Did I just hear you correctly? You said, the accident in Hunters Glen?"

"Yes, sir, he nodded. "I'm looking for Anna, Anna Sinclair. Is she here? Please tell me. We thought she died in that terrible accident and I never thought to check your facility… and the hospital in Franklin was so overwhelmed when the incident happened…and they didn't have any information…and then recently my wife was at the hospital with the baby for a checkup and saw a pamphlet for this facility…inside was a photo of an art room with some paintings…when she saw this painting she knew immediately that…"

He stopped talking, stood, and pulled a crumpled brochure from his back pocket and handed it to the doctor. "She saw that painting," he pointed to the picture, "and was positive it was Anna's work." He was animated and lively as he spoke and Aaron hung on to every word.

Aaron put his hand up to signal him to stop speaking. "Did anybody ever tell you that you talk too much?"

Christopher smiled as he sat back down and said, "Yes, my good friend Anna and my wife."

Aaron was suspicious and apprehensive. "Before we continue this conversation do you have a photo of Anna? How do I know you're not some crazy ex-husband or boyfriend?"

Christopher laughed at the absurdity of the comment, leaned forward, and reached into his back pocket for his wallet. "Well, my wife Danella, might say I'm a bit nuts sometimes but aren't we all, doc? Here, this is Anna," he thrust the photo he pulled from the worn wallet toward him. "That's the three of us at our college graduation," he stated proudly.

Doctor Carter leaned back in his chair as he stared at the picture.

Christopher was worried. If the doctor recognized her, he didn't show it. "Is it her, doc? Do you know her? Please tell me she is alive. Please tell me it's her," he whispered.

Doctor Carter removed his glasses and rubbed his chin. "Before we go further, tell me again, how do you know this Anna?"

"We went to college together and she was relocating to Montana and was going to work in our art gallery and…"

Chapter 115

Lily and Doctor Aaron Carter

*L*ily went to the observatory. It was like the solarium but Doctor Carter had a night theme programed into the ceiling and said she needed to go three times a week - at night. It was part of her therapy to help overcome her anxiety about the dark. She loved this place because of the lush greenery and plants that one would not normally see in Montana. The best feature were the giant rocks that almost reached the ceiling and the stunning waterfall that fell down upon them. Three dimensional, white, puffy clouds filled the sky during the day but at night, the design, darkened and the sky was populated with stars. The moon phases matched the current moon phases each night. The designer incorporated the exterior landscape with the interior design. So when darkness fell at night, the stars that filled the night sky were visible from the windows that surrounded the observatory. Not only was the view stunning, but further emphasized that night had arrived. A waterfall emptied into a giant pond filled with colorful koi fish. The water followed a path around the entire display. There were benches to sit on and soft music played in the background.

Lily was meeting Doctor Carter here today. He suggested she get there on her own for the appointment. She was seated near the waterfall when he arrived. He sat on the bench across from her. "How did I know I'd find you at the waterfall?" he chuckled. She was wearing jeans, a white turtleneck sweater, and sneakers. He knew Willow had gone shopping and purchased some clothing for her.

"It's my favorite spot, but you already know that. I like the other rooms, especially the art room that has views of the entire snowcapped mountains, but this area is so soothing. You know I like coming during the day but I'm enjoying the night better, thanks to you. I wish I could build something like this in my own home someday."

"Well perhaps you can paint some pictures for me and we can hang them in the complex for others to enjoy."

Lily's eyes brightened. "I would love to do that, but that's only if I discover if I'm really *talented*."

"I've seen your work, and you *are* a very gifted artist." Doctor Carter smiled. His eyes danced as he tried to contain his enthusiasm.

Lily regarded him curiously. "What? What is it? I can see it in your eyes," she laughed. "You're hiding something?"

Aaron could never fool her. For a coma patient she was very intuitive. "I have nothing to hide. I'm just happy to hear your voice and excited at your progress. Plus it's almost Christmas and I have much to be thankful for."

"Wow, then that would make it a year since the accident?"

"Yes," he nodded not sure how she was going to react.

"Well then, I have much to be thankful for as well. I'm glad that I made it through all this. I couldn't have done it without you, your staff, or this clinic. It's the best Christmas present ever!"

Aaron nodded in agreement. Just then someone rounded the corner and his pace slowed as he approached. "Excuse me," he said as he passed in front of them. "I hope I'm not interrupting, I just wanted to see the waterfall I heard about."

"No problem," Lily answered cheerfully. "I think it's one of the best features of the garden."

The young man looked her directly in the eyes and said, "I agree."

"There's another water feature if you keep following the path," she pointed. The young man thanked her and turned to walk away.

Aaron watched the interaction. "That was nice; it shows you're compassionate. You helped someone. You know, Lily…"

The peculiar look on her face made him pause mid-sentence. "Lily, are you ok?" He asked, uncertain she heard him. He watched as she stared, transfixed on the stranger. Without warning she gasped as her hands flew to her cheeks. Suddenly tears were running down her face and she shot up off the bench like a rocket and began running down the path.

"Ch…ris…Chris!" Lily shouted spiritedly.

The moment he heard his name he whipped around and ran back toward her. Lily ran and jumped in his arms. "Chris, is it really you?"

He hugged her tight. "Anna! You're alive!"

"Yes. Yes, it's me!" She was crying and laughing at the same time. Chris put her down gently and held her at arm's length. "You're alive! You're really alive!"

"Anna!" she shouted as her hand flew to her chest and she sighed heavily. "I have a real name. My name is Anna," she bawled as tears poured down her face.

The doctor smiled like a Cheshire cat as the two walked back toward him holding hands.

"I knew you were hiding something," she shouted joyfully. "I remembered someone! I remembered a part of my life," she sighed. "I remember my name," she beamed excitedly. "I heard his voice and remembered my name and him," she shouted.

Aaron made a mental note to add voice recognition to her file. "Well, why don't you two sit and *Anna,*" he said, putting extra emphasis on her name, "you can tell me all about it. You can also tell me *why* you told us your name was Lily."

Anna wiped her tears as she sat. She looked guilty. "I'm so sorry, doctor, but when I woke up the nurse was asking so many questions and wanted to know my name. I saw the vase of lilies by the window and it was the first thing that came to my mind," she said as she hugged Chris again. "I'm sorry; I just couldn't remember my name and I wanted to have a name and when I saw the vase of lilies…" she rambled.

"Well, she really didn't lie, doctor; you see her middle name *is* Lily. Anna Lily Sinclair. Lily is her grandmother's name," Chris interrupted.

Aaron nodded. "Subconscious memory recall perhaps?"

"Or could it be that I just saw some flowers and that was the first thing that came to my mind?"

Aaron wasn't convinced. *Perhaps. She could barely talk when she woke.*

Anna was so happy to see a familiar face. "Tell me everything, Chris. Help me remember everything!"

Chapter 116

Doctor Aaron Carter

"Security," the young male voice answered. "Hi, this is Doctor Carter from the fifth floor. I'm looking for Roberto?"

"I'm sorry, sir, he had a family emergency and we're not sure when he will be returning."

"I put a request in for some information. Is there someone I can speak to regarding the status? I really would appreciate an update."

The young man scribbled names and numbers the doctor provided on a piece of scrap paper. "Let me see if I can locate the file."

Aaron was annoyed as he listened to the shuffling of papers and wondered about the disorganization of the security department and safety measures at the hospital. He would be sure to bring it up at the next meeting.

"I'm sorry, sir, the only notes I see are marked pending. It looks like they're still looking for someone named Noah. He's no longer at the address listed. I don't see the rest of the file. If I find it, I'll call you."

The sigh of disappointment from the doctor did not go unnoticed. "It's the holidays, sir, most of the senior staff have taken vacation or went to visit family. I'll let the supervisor know you called and what you are looking for. I'll make sure he follows up with you."

Aaron yawned as he hung up the phone. He leaned back in his chair, closed his eyes, and massaged his temples. He was so fatigued. He felt like he was on the verge of something but pieces were still missing. It was maddening. He jumped when his cell phone rang. Smiling as he glanced at the number he muttered, "Finally."

Chapter 117

Jackson and Doctor Aaron Carter

"You must not be paying your receptionist enough money at that fancy law firm you work at. I don't think she gave you my messages. I thought you forgot all about me," the doctor laughed. "Or are you calling to invite me to your wedding? I'm still waiting for the invitation."

"No, don't blame her," Jackson chuckled. "Sorry, doc, it's all my fault. I owe you my life," he said his voice a bit strained. "I have been trying to keep it together and in the process it all unraveled."

Aaron understood. Recovering from a major accident and getting back to the life previously known was not as easy as it may seem. People often begin to think and see the world differently. There is also the support system of family and friends. The small amount of time he spent with Jackson's family was enough for him to know Jackson was probably under an enormous amount of pressure. "Well, since you missed so many sessions, I have some time to listen to you now. Tell me what's been going on."

Jackson gave him the highlights of the past few months.

Aaron's mouth dropped in utter disbelief when Jackson told him how he punched Adam.

"I'm surprised you didn't come to blows when you originally walked in on him and your fiancé."

"I don't know, doc. In that moment, I remember feeling nothing. I gawked at the two of them as if I was watching a bad porno flick. When they realized I was there, they just looked at me in absolute horror. Adam quickly separated himself and began damage control. He said, "Jackson, *it's not what you think.*"

Jackson stopped talking and took a deep breath. "I remember thinking, do they believe I'm an idiot? How insulting. Another man might have been angry, charged forward and beat Adam to death, but for some reason I recall saying they deserved one another and stormed out."

"Are you sure this is what you remembered?"

Jackson's mouth was dry and he swallowed. "Doc, when Adam uttered those words, *"it's not what you think,"* it brought me right back to that night. It was like I was there. The only problem is I don't know *what* happened after that. I probably got in my vehicle and eventually wound up in the accident."

"Jackson, just the shock of seeing them together in a compromising way, especially when you each have such a deep history together; Adam your childhood friend, who you thought you knew, and then your beautiful fiancé, who you believed you'd spend the rest of your life with. I can't imagine what you walked in on. The loyalty, trust, and plan for a future *all changed within seconds.* It's hard to work through these issues sometimes. The trauma of the accident perhaps made you block it all out but then fortunately you remembered. So you still have a lot to process and come to terms with."

"Do you think I'll ever be able to piece it all together?"

The doctor shifted in his chair. "Perhaps. It's like I've told you before, you have to give yourself a break and not try so hard. Your father would not appreciate me suggesting this, but sometimes it may help if you consider returning to where the accident happened."

Jackson grew silent. His face paled and he could feel his heart racing.

"Jackson, are you still there?"

"Sorry, doc, your recommendation is perplexing. That's the *last* place I want to visit right now. Just the thought of it has me breaking out in a cold sweat."

"Perhaps you're not ready for that. Sometimes it helps people and sometimes it doesn't. It could turn out to be a positive or negative experience. It depends on the person and the trauma suffered. You're clearly wrestling with many issues and need to clear them up first. Just work at your own pace."

Jackson scratched the back of his neck. "I don't know, doc, going to the accident scene…that's a pretty big step."

"You'll know *when* and *if* you're ready. Not to change the subject, but I find it interesting you called me on the anniversary of the accident."

"Don't read too much into it. My mother called this morning wanting to know how I was feeling. She rarely calls me at work. And then my father wanted to take me to lunch! I *never* have lunch with my father! That's when I looked at the calendar and it suddenly hit me, it's December second! I thought I could do this on my own and I thought I was doing better but…"

"You and I have discussed this before Jackson, healing and processing events take time. We all have setbacks. Have some patience," he recommended.

"That's easy for you to say when your life is so perfect."

"Jackson, I can tell you there is no such thing as perfect. Life is a journey and you're lucky if you have many people and experiences along the way. Some are good. Others may be bad. It's how we cope with them that makes the difference."

"You sound tired, doc. If I remember, the last time we spoke you were going to apologize to someone. Did you do something wrong again? Because if you did, you better make sure to ask for forgiveness," he chuckled.

Aaron burst out laughing and shook his head. "Spoken like someone who understands women."

"Obviously not," he chuckled. "But I do recall observing my father over the years. He was always in the doghouse. My mother doesn't put up with his nonsense for long. There were always flowers in our house. Buy her flowers and make things right! I'll call you after the holidays. Merry Christmas!"

"Merry Christmas to you too, Jackson." He hung up smiling as an idea suddenly occurred to him.

Chapter 118

Anna, Chris, and Doctor Aaron Carter

Chris was seated with Anna in Doctor Carter's office the following day. The doctor had accommodations set up for Chris in the family wing so he could stay and help reconnect with Anna. Anna insisted Chris be part of the meetings hoping he would trigger memories about her past.

"Tell me what you know, Chris. I want to hear everything again," Anna beamed breathlessly.

Chris shrugged, "Well, as we already discussed, your name is Anna Sinclair. We went to college on the East Coast. You and Danella studied art together, painting specifically. I majored in business and minored in photography. After Danella and I were married, we moved back to Montana where I'm originally from. You decided to stay and work in the museum on campus. When your work was consistently not chosen for even the local community shows, you eventually decided to leave to come and work in our gallery. The community here has a real art vibe and we figured there would be some great opportunities. Unfortunately you never made it."

Anna frowned. "Am I a good painter?"

Chris grinned. His brown eyes were wide open as he leaned forward and looked her right in the eyes and said, "You're one of the best, but the stuffy old museum director didn't like your designs or use of color or the subject matter…it was always something. I personally think he was jealous and trying to hold you back. So Danella and I convinced you to come stay with us. We were in shock when we heard what happened. Then when Danella saw the paintings in the brochure, she was stunned."

"Where did Danella see my work? How is it even possible?"

"Let me explain," the doctor interrupted, when he saw the confused look on Anna's face. "The hospital put out another advertisement for the trauma center. They must have photographed some of the therapy rooms. A painting you were working on was left on the easel, photographed, and included in the brochure. Why the pamphlet was in the pediatric wing I couldn't tell you, perhaps left by a visitor, but luckily Danella is so observant."

Chris nodded. He turned toward Anna who sat next to him. His hands fell to his sides. "I didn't believe her at first," he said a bit sheepishly as he shook his head with regret. His lips trembled as his facial muscles knotted, tightly, as if he was going to sob. "But she has painted with you so much that she knew your style and was *convinced you* painted that picture. She *forced* me to come up here."

The doctor watched as the two spoke and took notes. He watched her face for signs of recognition.

Anna fidgeted with her hands.

"It's okay, Anna. Ask him anything you want," Aaron urged.

"How old am I?

"Twenty-eight years young?" Chris smiled.

Anna looked up at Chris again and sighed heavily. "Do I have any family?"

Chris was afraid to answer. Wide eyed, he looked at the doctor for reassurance. Aaron nodded, and encouraged him to continue. "As we discussed previously, it's all right if you repeat things, it may take some time for Anna to remember everything at once, and there is the possibility she may *not* recall at all."

Wanting to be totally honest, Aaron turned toward Anna, whose face now displayed the troubled look he knew all too well. He leaned forward and looked directly in her eyes and added, "Anna, you need to understand and accept this. The anxiety you may feel could impair your progress."

Hands in her lap she hadn't realized how tightly she was squeezing them. Knowing she needed to hear the truth, she sighed deeply, as her lips curved into a partial smile and nodded toward Chris that it was okay to continue.

Chris immediately shook his head. "Anna, you are an only child. You were raised by your grandmother," he said tensely.

Her body slumped in the chair as her eyes filled with tears. "Is she still alive?"

Chris wasn't sure if he should answer. He looked back to the doctor for support. "It's okay. She needs to hear the truth if it's going to help her recovery," he repeated again.

Chris shifted nervously in the chair. "She passed away while you were in college."

"And my parents?" When she saw Chris hesitate, she urged him on. "Tell me, Chris, I need to know."

He breathed heavily and nodded. "Your father was a violent alcoholic and chain smoker. One evening he was fighting with your mother and left a cigarette burning and the house caught on fire. The fire department found you hiding in a closet."

Tears rolled down Anna's face as Chris spoke. She looked at the doctor. "Is this true? How can we be sure?" she cried.

Aaron handed her more tissues from the box on his desk. "It's true, Anna. Before I allowed Chris to meet you, our security team researched and verified everything Chris has told you thus far. I have information about where you grew up, copies of your birth certificate, diploma, and articles about the fire. I suggest you read them later when you feel you're ready. This is a lot to grasp in one day."

Anna's eyes blinked. Her hands flew to her head as she closed her eyes. For a minute she saw flames flash through her head. "Fire," she whispered. The color drained from her face. She saw images of her screaming. She opened her eyes and whispered, "This is why I'm afraid of fire and the dark, isn't it?"

The doctor handed her a bottle of water and nodded to confirm it. "Most likely."

"It's understandable after what happened," Chris confirmed. "Are you feeling okay?"

"It's just so hard to comprehend, but now I understand the images of flames I see over and over in my head."

"This must be the trauma that we have been trying to break through," Aaron muttered, as he scribbled more notes. "The anxiety about the dark is perhaps part of it too."

Anna had tears in her eyes. "Will I ever *not* be afraid?"

The doctor smiled and nodded. "We have some work to do, but I think we can help. That is only if *you* are willing."

Chris grabbed her hand. "It's going to be all right, Anna," he said confidently. Danella and I are just glad we found you. You have no idea what it was like for us. Your belongings and art supplies arrived. But when you didn't we began to get worried and there was no one to call. We were devastated when your name popped up in the paper as someone who died in the accident. Your rental car was discovered and…"

He took a deep breath before he could continue, "There was so much chaos at the hospital…it's a small facility and they are not accustomed to dealing with a tragedy on such an immense scale…we couldn't get information…the mountain became a grave site for bodies that were severely burned, disfigured and…"

Anna began hysterically, sobbing to the point she was gasping for air.

The doctor immediately ended the session and called for the nurse to take Anna back to her room and give her a sedative. "Okay, that's enough for today, Anna. We have a lot of time to learn more. You need to rest."

Chris started to rise but the doctor told him to stay. "We have much to discuss about her upcoming care."

Chapter 119

Alastair

Alastair had been silent as he continued watching. Cooper sat by his side swishing his tail back and forth as he spoke aloud. "I'm elated that things are turning around for everyone. I don't exactly feel bad for Adam, as his behavior was appalling; however, it's not my place to judge."

Alastair shuffled as he repositioned himself. "Cooper, we need to do the right thing." He instantly bowed his head in prayer and prayed for Adam, hopeful he would turn his life around.

He prayed that Anna would regain her memory and shed tears when he learned how she had suffered as a child. He prayed for her friends and how they agonized wondering about her.

He thought about his own life and current position as trainer of new arrivals – it wasn't a position that was just handed out when one arrived in Heaven. Numerous tests and training had to be passed before one was even considered. While he had a lot to be grateful for, he wondered if he even wanted to be an Angel Trainer? Did being a legacy get him through the program quicker? He didn't need to think too hard, as he already knew the answers.

He quickly discovered his birthright was a destiny that labeled him the moment he entered the heavenly realm. He quickly moved ahead of others through the tests and rapid train-ing – others who had to wait and work hard just to be considered for the program. The animosity he felt from many angels was not only a painful reminder of his position but caused him to shy away from the group. He kept to himself most of the time, brooding silently about his plight. His attitude changed when he later discovered Twelfth Order Trainers enabled one to train and travel as the centuries changed; whereas other trainers were restricted, to specific time periods. Twelfth Order Trainers also had greater privileges including traveling into the earthly realm to deal with certain situations.

Nonetheless, Alastair realized he had drastically drifted off course. When he had digressed, he couldn't identify the time or century when it occurred.

His mind raced through the time periods, from the fifteenth, sixteenth, seventeenth thru to the industrial age, senseless wars with other countries, the Civil Rights movement of the fifties, or the incessant protesting and unrelenting hostilities between man and other countries. Then there was that rock and roll that arrived in the sixties – he recalled being shocked that the Lord allowed it all!

He thought about the rest of the twentieth and twenty-first century – the seventies, eighties, and nineties. Perhaps it was the continued political unrest, drugs, tensions in the Mideast, in-stability and disorder in political climates everywhere, inflation and continued relentless changes in politics, media, technology, sexual identity, war, and violence that added to his failure to stay on course. He pulled at his long beard and became more agitated as he visualized his own disappointments.

"Oh Cooper," he called to the dog, "you have no idea how I have failed. You know the common thread I see as history pro-gressed is the absence of family values and religion." He shook his head as his body was heavy with grief and said out loud, "Because nobody seemed to care about religion and family, I forgot about the true meaning behind what I was *supposed* to be teaching. Instead of *teaching,* I was caught up in listening about life from the new trainees. I was too focused on irrelevant and inconsequential nonsense that I forgot the basic spiritual principles and my thinking changed. I was supposed to be training angels to help them help others but after constantly listening to how life changed so much…well it was depressing and at some point I just *stopped caring*. Not only did I stop caring, I *stopped believing*. Life became too overwhelming and I also didn't want to disappoint my family and," his voice cracked as it filled with torment.

Wiping away the tears that started to fall from the corners of his eyes, he sought out Cooper, who instinctively came to his side. "I was once a rising star but lost my footing and drifted way off course." Alastair closed his eyes tightly in agony as he wondered how he'd neglected the basics and many other things; he couldn't even say the words as he realized what he had *really* overlooked.

Then he did something he hadn't done in a long time – he apologized to God and asked for his guidance and prayed harder than ever. "I hope God finds it in his heart to forgive me, Cooper. I still have much work ahead of me and I know it's not going to be easy."

Suddenly, more of the dark, murky clouds from above parted. Alastair looked up and grinned with delight as he rose to stretch. He knew he had much more to account for, but it was a start. He truly believed he would not have to justify his actions and things would just work out.

Cooper closed his eyes and put his head between his paws as he rested in new rays of warm sunlight that were now filtering in through the clouds.

Chapter 120

Willow
Thursday December 13ᵗʰ

Willow was ready to put the brakes on the emotional roller-coaster she'd been riding. She liked her job and working for Doctor Carter but his behavior had become too erratic. She didn't know what to make of it. The mixed signal's he was sending were confusing. She wasn't heading down that road again. She was in the process of finishing some reports when the mail clerk stopped by the lab and brought her a huge bouquet of mixed flowers. She was speechless.

"Someone likes you," he said as he wheeled his cart away.

She grabbed the envelope sticking on top of the plastic protruding holder and opened it. The card read,

Dearest Willow,

Sorry. I have no excuse for my behavior. I'll be at the café at 1:00 pm, if you want to join me for coffee. I'd like to talk with you.

Your Friend

Willow was incensed. "How dare he?" she muttered. "Absolutely not! I'm not getting back on this ride just because he has a minute in his schedule."

Chapter 121

Willow
Friday December 14ᵗʰ

illow was in her office when she received another bouquet of mixed flowers the following morning. She quickly wrestled the card that was nestled in the Styrofoam holder of the flowers. It read,

Dearest Willow,

> *"Your no-show at the cafe leaves me to believe that you are either too busy or still mad at me. Not that I blame you, but I can't seem to say the right thing anymore. It's not a good ex-cuse, but I feel like I'm sailing in uncharted waters and either don't know how to navigate the ship or perhaps interpreted the map wrong? I'll be having lunch at the café at 1:30 pm. If your schedule permits, please join me and we can talk.*

Your Friend

Willow stared at the card. She didn't know what to think. It was clear they shared a connection. She debated the positives and negatives. A chill ran down her back when images of the emotional merry-go-round she'd been on filled her head. The negatives outweighed the positives. She wasn't sure if this is what she wanted but had the weekend to think about it.

Chapter 122

Willow
Monday December 17th

When the third bouquet of mixed flowers arrived, Willow was the talk of the floor. The nurses and assistants teased her and wanted to know who her secret admirer was. She smiled politely and said she had no idea. She could hear her heart pounding against her chest as she read the next note.

Dearest Willow,

> *I understand your fury. I myself have faced much anger and heartache and I'm still learning how to deal with it. I guess I'm not doing so great. If you'd like to have lunch, I am willing to tell you about it. I'll be at the café at 12 noon, if you'd care to join me.*

> *Your Friend*

Willow fumed. The more she thought about his behavior, the madder she became. She was well versed in this game – apologize until he wears you down, forgive until the behavior starts all over. This was turning out to be *exactly* like her last relationship and she wasn't going to let that happen again!

Chapter 123

Willow
Tuesday December 18th

Willow inhaled deeply and smiled. The research lab smelled like an outdoor field in the spring. While she hated to admit it, she loved the flowers. They brightened up the place and made the entire environment so peaceful. She was sitting at the large conference table with her staff when a clerk from the mailroom arrived holding a giant vase of white daisies. He didn't say a word.

"Just put them over there," she gestured toward the center of the table. "They add color to the room," she grinned as she grabbed the card and thrust it into her pocket.

The staff members laughed and said she was so lucky. "Tell us what's going on, Willow. Who's the mystery man?"

"Nobody I care to discuss. Now, let's finish the reports and get back to work."

Work was the furthest thing from her mind. The moment they were finished, she practically ran to the nearest storage closet and tore open the envelope.

Dearest Willow,

I deserve your wrath and can assure you I am suffering for it. I am deeply saddened that I hurt you. I miss you and our friendship. I know I have apologized many times, but I would like the opportunity to talk to you in person. I need to explain. I will be at the café on campus at 2:00 pm.

Your Friend

"Really? Well, it's way too late, mister."

She later handed the vase to one of the staff. "Distribute these to the patient's rooms."

Chapter 124

Willow
Wednesday December 19ᵗʰ

Willow received another mixed bouquet of colored roses during another staff meeting. She could feel the blood rushing to her face as the staff silently questioned and speculated about her secret admirer. She quickly grabbed the card before someone else had thoughts of taking it. It was burning a hole in the pocket of her suit jacket as she sat through the meeting not even paying attention as she was too distracted by the note.

"Distribute the flowers to the staff, patients, and to any common areas," she said to the nurse as she left the large vase at the nurse's station.

"But we have been doing that all week. The vases are full," the stunned nurse responded. "Then send them to another area of the hospital," she called. Back in her office she closed the door and tore open the note.

Dearest Willow,

I like what you've been doing with the flowers! They certainly brighten up the unit. The staff and families have commented on how nice they smell. I'll speak to the board

*about perhaps starting a floral program. I'll make sure to
tell them it was your idea!*

*I have become a fixture at the café during lunch. I am glad
you introduced me to the place, but it would be much more
enjoyable with you. I miss your company. Please join me
for lunch at 1:00 p.m. The fact that you will not respond is
a constant reminder of just how much I hurt you, which was
never my intention.*

Your Friend

Willow was tempted but instead scheduled a meeting. Having
an excuse not to meet him made her feel better. She spent the
afternoon trying to justify her thoughts and started wondering if
she was making a mistake. She questioned her level of maturity
and concluded that she didn't really care, or did she? Her own
self-assessment caused more pain reminding her this was not
how she should be feeling.

Chapter 125

Willow
Thursday December 20th

illow was seated in the lecture hall. It was the monthly meeting for the doctors to discuss the current treatments and cases. Physical, speech, and occupational therapy, cardio, neurology, pulmonology, social workers, and any department involved with treatment and recovery was present. It was one of the aspects that made the institute so spectacular. Not only did it focus on cutting edge research but on patient recovery as well. When a colleague told her about it, she became intrigued with the recovery rates of the patients and began doing a bit more research. If she wanted a change in her career this was going to be it. The monthly lecture was not only an update of the patients, but a discussion from each of the departments regarding why or why not a new type of therapy could begin or the current progress.

The meeting lasted most of the day. She had not spoken to Doctor Carter directly for a few weeks but did notice he was not in attendance. He had reassigned his cases and rounds to the other doctors due to personal reasons. A memo was eventually sent detailing a reorganization of his obligations. He would be more involved with surgery and would meet with the other neurosurgeons to discuss any pertinent issues. Jackson and Anna were the *only* cases he kept open. Lab research was delegated to another physician, who Willow now reported to. Willow had been fine with this restructuring. The less she had to see or talk with him the better. Still, she was surprised he was absent from the meeting.

The rest of the staff seemed fine with the changes. Like cars running around the racetrack at the Indy 500, the gossip loop was alive and active, despite warnings from the human resources department. There was talk that Doctor Carter may take on a different role, focus strictly on surgery or perhaps retire.

The director of cardiology, Doctor Lewis, was in the middle of speaking when someone from the mailroom walked directly out on stage. Doctor Lewis clearly was not pleased. He removed his glasses and glared at the mail clerk who whispered in his ear and handed him a note. He looked shocked as they heatedly continued to whisper back and forth. He then waved him off. He sighed heavily, and turned back toward the microphone and smirked, "It appears as if we have an important delivery, of which, I am told *must* be handed out *now*," he said bluntly. He motioned to the mail clerk, who quickly wheeled in a vase at least four feet high, filled with a large bouquet of colorful roses.

The gasps from the group echoed through the Anatomy Hall. Doctor Lewis spoke slowly as he emphasized each word and made eye contact with his audience. "It seems *someone* has an *admirer* and *I* apparently have been *designated* to *read* the card!" He was unmistakably annoyed that his report was interrupted, but forced a smile as he put his glasses back on, and said, "Who am I to stand in the way of *love*?"

The crowd laughed. Willow sank further into her seat. The nurse seated next to her said, "If these are for you, you should forgive him for whatever he did wrong. In all my life I have never seen such a beautiful arrangement. You're very lucky to have someone who would go to all this trouble."

Doctor Lewis opened the envelope and with raised eyebrows looked out at the audience and read, "*My Dearest Willow*," he stopped reading to search for her location and pointed, "there she is in the *fourth row*." People immediately stirred in their seats.

Willow could feel the eyes of the crowd shift in her direction. Doctor Lewis looked directly at her and read with the emotion of an actor on a Broadway stage.

My Dearest Willow,

> *I am sorry for being such a jerk!* Doctor Lewis put extra emphasis on the word "jerk" and everyone laughed.

> *I don't know what to say anymore. I hope that you take the flowers home with you to enjoy as the entire floor and patient rooms are already appreciating the previous ones. As I walk the halls, I see flowers everywhere and think of you. I am again so deeply sorry for my behavior.*

> *Your Friend*

Doctor Lewis paused, "Willow, please forgive the man. It is evident he has invested a small fortune on floral displays. I mean if he isn't a serial killer, in trouble with the law, or suffering from addiction, did I cover it all?" he said to the group.

"One of the nurses yelled out a few more problematic categories of men – "cheater, liar, or mama's boy."

"I thank you for your input, Nurse Yardley. I think that covers it. I believe it's fair to say there is still a *population of the male species that didn't turn out that bad*." Doctor Lewis was referring to himself. He was well respected in his profession and devoted to his family. He peered over his glasses. "Willow, please I implore you, just forgive the man so we can get on with the business of running our program!"

The delivery left the staff speculating who it could be. There were endless questions and assumptions. Willow was upset that her private life was on display. She thought back to the rigid privacy policy during her orientation and fully understood its value.

Chapter 126

Willow
Friday December 21st

*I*t was almost Christmas. Willow decided she would stay put and not fly back to the East Coast to visit her family and friends. She wanted to enjoy her first Christmas alone. She would continue exploring the area in her free time and planned on going skiing with some friends who would be flying out to one of the resorts. Her family planned to visit after the New Year.

She was finishing up reports when another delivery was sent to her office. She sighed heavily as she thanked the mail clerk and made room for the red holiday vase and arrangement on her desk. After the spectacle with Doctor Lewis, she had been sure that had been the last of the flowers. "Apparently not," she muttered as she reached for the card. She was tempted to put it through the shredder but human nature got the best of her and she opened it.

Dearest Willow,

There is nothing else I can say. Evidently I'm not great at apologizing. Perhaps I'm too old. But my attitude towards you and others was dreadful and inexplicable. I am certainly old enough to know the appropriate way to treat people.

I was married for a long time and when...well...when my wife died... I don't want you to feel bad or sorry for me. But it's just that...I wasn't expecting somebody to come and shake up my world the way you have. I'm not accustomed to feeling the way I feel when I'm with you. Let's just say I wasn't prepared for this.

This is confusing to me and I have much to learn when it comes to matters of the heart. I guess Doctor Lucardi was right – I'm not healed and need more therapy! The loss I suffered was so great, that I just didn't know what to do.

And then the patient in 524 had disclosed something during one of the sessions that rattled me to my core and I just couldn't deal with it. There are other things to be said, but I don't know what to tell you to make it right. I only know I need to speak with you in person, as you deserve a full explanation.

Coffee or lunch your choice. Just name the time and I'll be there.

Your Friend

Willow dropped the note. She was stunned. It was the first time he revealed personal information about himself. It was obvious the staff adhered to the strict non-disclosure policies as nobody ever talked about Doctor Carter's wife or family. She noticed photos in his office and knew she had passed away. Willow overheard the nurses talking one day in the cafeteria about Doctor Carter. One of the senior nurses was trying to tell one of the new younger female nurses not to ask anything about his family or wife; "The topic is off limits and he'll refuse to talk about it," she instructed. She also reminded her about the privacy policy. "So much for the policy," Willow thought to as she listened to the nurses' gossip.

While Willow was curious, she never asked. She just figured it would come up sooner or later.

At least she wasn't imagining things. She knew their relationship had changed –she couldn't recall when it happened, but instinctively she could feel it. She now understood why he struggled with asking her out for something as simple as dinner.

Did she want to risk more emotional turmoil? Was she willing to put herself out there again? Was this just another way to pull at her heart? She spent the day wondering and wrestling with question after question until she was mentally exhausted.

Chapter 127

Willow
Monday December 24th

Willow was in the middle of cleaning the lab when a small vase of mixed carnations was delivered.

Dearest Willow,

I received the letter from human resources. I am deeply saddened that you have decided to leave. It will be a great loss to the program and the patients. I am sorry that I have hurt you so much that you feel it necessary to take another job. I only wish you would give me the opportunity to explain, perhaps over a cup of coffee at the café? Please meet me at noon. I feel I owe you this.

Your friend

Willow sighed heavily. "I'm not leaving because of you," she whispered. "I'm leaving because I have to take care of myself for once."

***

Monday December 24th – Early Evening

Willow received a peace lily in a basket surrounded by other greenery. It arrived just as she was returning home from work. She went to tip the driver but he said it was already included. "At least he's not cheap," she mumbled as she opened the door. She made a cup of coffee, turned on the gas fireplace, and settled herself on the sofa before she pulled the card from the basket.

Willow,

So now I am bankrupt from what I've spent on flowers, only joking. ☺ I just wanted to say thank you for all your help. Wherever you're going, I know your work will be exceptional. I'm honored that you were part of our team!

I'm once again very sorry for my disruptive behavior and wish you would accept my apology. I know I deserve your silence for the way I treated you. I am totally responsible and feel horrible. I don't blame you for being angry. I believe I should have taken more time off to sort out my own issues. I let my private life get in the way of life – which I'm positive makes no sense to you.

I'm sorry if you're spending Christmas Eve by yourself. Nobody should be alone during the holidays. If you'd like to meet me at the Trattoria, I have reservations at 8:00 p.m. If not, I will understand. Merry Christmas.

Fondly,

Aaron

Willow sighed as she read the note over and over as she wrestled with the invitation. She had time to put something nice on and thought about the little black dress she had hanging in the back of the closet that highlighted her curves, just to make him feel worse. Afterward, she would give him a piece of her mind. Or she could just show up, enjoy the meal and leave. She could throw a glass of wine in his face or…ugh – this was all so petty! She knew if she went all it would take would be one look in his eyes and she'd forgive him. Her emotions were so erratic that they quickly turned to anger, and she cried out, "How dare he ask me to dinner in an apology note!"

Part of her wanted to go and the other part of her said to forget him. He had so much baggage and she didn't want to be his therapist or punching bag when something went wrong in life. She wanted a friend, a partner, someone she could lean on and trust. She didn't need someone lashing out at her every time something didn't go his way or when he got upset. She was tired of speculating, guessing, and wondering. She'd left a terrible relationship and didn't need to start another one. History wasn't going to repeat itself again, she vowed. She continued debating the positives and negatives and in the end grabbed a blanket and turned on the television. The tears fell like raindrops and she sobbed into a pillow until she had nothing left to cry about.

Chapter 128

Alastair

Alastair was on his knees in front of the Reflection Pond praying. "And because I forgot about my relationship with you…which I can't even understand how it happened… all I've been doing is *scheming* and *complaining*…I don't even know what road I've been traveling, so it's understandable that you're not listening." Cooper had followed him and was nudging him under his arm.

"So you see, God, first of all, I should have stayed and dealt with the situation. Just like Doctor Carter, I too, should have discussed and asked for help. I also should have reported to my supervisor immediately, conveyed what was taking place, and requested assistance…"

Cooper interrupted with a resounding *woof, woof,* and continued pawing at his shoulder.

"Cooper, what is it?" He turned and looked at the dog.

"So why did you leave?" the voice of Lucius echoed in the air.

Alastair didn't hesitate and answered immediately. "Shame, embarrassment, and my pride got in the way, for my supervisor is significantly *younger* than me. I shouldn't have questioned why he was sent to replace Giuseppe. I was very disappointed when my dear friend Giuseppe was transferred. After the change, I really lost *faith in the system*, the technological progress was encroaching and intimidating. I was not prepared to deal with the new ways; instead of embracing it all, I simply rejected EVERYTHING!" He paused, knowing it was only a matter of time before the great angel made an appearance.

Alastair bowed his head in shame before he looked up. As if on cue, there was Lucius calmly walking out of the surrounding forest, the forest that he'd plotted to escape into weeks earlier, the forest that immediately refused his entrance and zapped him back to the reflection pond. Alastair nodded acknowledging the great angel's presence.

"Please continue," Lucius said flatly.

"I admit this didn't happen overnight. I've been heading down the wrong path for centuries," he conceded gloomily. "I regret leaving my post and not speaking with the supervisor. I disobeyed protocol, brought disgrace to my family, and most importantly, disappointed the Lord and his wishes. He trusted me and I failed," Alastair said despondently. "I failed at the basics – following the established protocols. They're there for a reason. My decisions caused a domino effect on the lives of random people I watch and now pray for daily. I am deeply sorry I've caused so much hurt to the Lord and this group of people. In addition to figuring out how to help everyone, I understand I have much reflection and soul searching to work through."

Lucius regarded Alastair critically as he walked toward him. "You know Alastair, I'm surprised at you."

Alastair drew back nervously as the disapproving look on the formidable angel's face was distressing. He opened his mouth to speak but quickly closed it.

Lucius now stood in front of him. "And don't look at me like you don't know what I'm referring to." He paused as he drew his brows together and said, "forgive me, but first there was all this talk about veering off your path, and drifting aimlessly through the centuries, and now you're blaming a younger supervisor. You're lucky I have the *patience* that I have to listen to such *balderdash*!" Lucius leaned forward and looked him squarely in the eyes. "If you think for one minute that the senseless rhetoric you have been spouting is even deserving of an audience with the almighty then I fear I have made a mistake so huge that…that…" he took a deep breath as even he couldn't get the words out. "Let's just say that you will be sorry for what will come."

Alastair's muscles twitched as his eyes darted around the pond area. The water had stilled and the only sounds were from Cooper who was loudly licking his fur. His stomach lurched and he felt hollow inside.

Lucius slowly walked around him and said, "Why don't we get to the heart of the matter. Why don't you reach deep down to the core of your soul and tell me the root cause of why you drifted off course. Yes, I understand the pressure of your role and the challenges you faced century after century but what is the *real cause*!" His voice echoed through the pond.

Alastair could not only hear the menace in his voice but felt the great angel's frustration and anger pulsating through his body. He looked up as he understood the warning. He was so tired and knew he had finally reached rock bottom. Permission to speak freely sir?"

Lucius' nodded.

Alastair took a deep breath and blurted out, "*I should never have died*. I *resent* that I died young. I resent that I never had a chance to experience life like the others. I have been filled with *anger* - an *anger* so strong it turns into *rage*. How I've kept myself in check all these years, I don't know. Why me? I had so many plans, so much I want to accomplish. Why *take* my life? *It wasn't fair*!" He yelled.

Alastair trembled in fear as he waited for his punishment. Instead, the only thing he heard was the voice of Lucius who calmly said, "I'll leave you with your thoughts," Lucius' voice reverberated through the air as he quietly disappeared.

Alastair sat with his legs crossed and arms resting on his knees. "Perhaps I should be stripped of my rank," he muttered as he looked at Cooper, who was now sitting in front of him. Cooper drew his ears back as he turned his head to the side.

"If only you could talk, I wonder what advice you'd give me?"

A loud *woof* was how the canine answered.

Chapter 129

Noah

Noah's first semester had gone really well. He made new friends and they formed their own study group. He was so busy with his classes he barely had time to think about Gemma. Sometimes when he was in the library studying and came across a term or something Gemma had taught him, his attention wandered. He hoped she was okay. At night he included her in his prayers.

When he received his grades he made his mother open the envelope. She frowned. He saw the disappointment on her face as she shook her head from side to side.

"What, tell me; I can deal with it," he pleaded. "Did I fail a class?" His mind was racing as he tried to determine which course it was.

She screamed and gestured as she pointed to the paper. "Ha, ha! I gotcha! You earned all A's!" She smiled euphorically.

Noah exhaled deeply as he hadn't realized he was holding his breath. He joined in on the laughter. His eyes sparkled with delight. "Let me see that!" he yelled joyfully.

"I'm so proud of you," she beamed. "I'm going to frame it! Come, let's go downtown for dinner and we'll celebrate!"

Chapter 130

Jackson
January 2002

ackson was glad the holidays had passed quietly. While the Saviella incident was already old news, his father asked him to record exactly what happened in case there was a lawsuit.

He was sitting in his penthouse enjoying a cup of freshly brewed coffee as he opened his computer. What disturbed him the most was the deceit from his long-time friend Adam. He remembered exactly what happened that day. He unleashed his fury on the keyboard as he hit the keys hard, typing fast, as he recalled the incident in November.

After his fight with Adam, he immediately took a taxi to Saviella's agency and demanded the five-caret diamond ring back. She and her staff looked horrified when he barged into her office unannounced, disheveled and covered with blood. "Jackson, are you okay? What happened?" She looked genuinely concerned as she ran toward him.

"I'll just give you the cliff notes, Saviella. I woke up," he said angrily. "I remembered that night and what I saw!"

Saviella immediately dismissed the staff that sat around the conference table. She could feel the blood draining from her face. He jerked his arm away as she reached out for him. "Jackson, it's not what you think," she pleaded.

Jackson let out a sarcastic laugh. "Ironically, that's what Adam, you know my *best friend*, or I should say, *my former best friend*, said *that* night. I'm surprised you don't remember!"

She nervously pushed her hair behind her ear. "I'm not sure I follow," she said evenly.

Jackson chuckled at her attempt to stall; he knew her mind was racing. He smirked, "I'll make it really easy for you. This morning, during a conversation about nothing important, Adam said, 'It's not what you think!'" He spoke the phrase with such contempt, that his face-hardened, and his eyes followed her like a venomous snake waiting to pounce on his prey. "And *suddenly, just like that,*" he snapped his fingers, *"I remembered* what happened the night of my accident!" He coughed into his bloody handkerchief. "I want my ring back."

"Jackson, you can't do this," she cried.

His eyes blazed and his facial muscles tightened as he continued to stare at her. "It seems I already have. You see, as I recall it, I decided to take some more runs down the mountain with the others while you and Adam went back to the cabins. A storm was brewing and snow was beginning to fall. I was looking forward to a nice hot shower and quiet evening with my *fiancé* – perhaps a good meal and then you and I would snuggle in front of the fireplace. I remember thinking life was good. I had a great job, money, friends, and a beautiful fiancé who I loved." He took a breath before he continued, his eyes never leaving hers.

"I walked into the cabin and put my ski equipment in the mudroom. The fireplace already had a fire going and I noticed a bottle of opened wine on the table. One of the blankets was on the floor so I picked it up and threw it on the couch and called out for you.

"I heard water running so I figured you were in the hot tub. I headed back toward our bedroom and as I slid the door open – I remember the tightness in my stomach and chest," he sneered. "My throat constricted and I couldn't get the words out. I felt as if I was watching a bad porno movie as I observed *my best friend and fiancé naked in the throes of passion!"*

"Jackson, I can explain…"

"I *really* don't see the need for an explanation, Saviella. Like my father says, the *facts eventually reveal themselves,* and I think they are crystal clear. Another man might have charged forward and beat Adam, except in that split second," he snapped his fingers forcefully before he continued, "at that moment in time I knew it wasn't *worth it.* I even recall what I said to you both. I simply stated, "You can have her and left,'" his voice was cold as ice as he spoke.

"Jackson…"

He put up his hand to stop her from talking. "So you see, Saviella," he pointed toward her, "*I already broke up with you!* That's why you and Adam kept checking on me in the hospital and when I came home," he hissed. "You were both worried if I recalled anything about that night. Is there anything else I'm missing?"

Saviella knew this was her last chance to change his mind. "It was just wedding jitters, you know…"

"*No, I don't know,*" he shouted angrily interrupting her. "People who love one another don't cheat! I don't think you *ever* loved me," he sneered as he gestured angrily. "You *loved* the *money,* the *power* of our two families *merging* together, and the immense portfolio of wealth it would create," he said bitterly.

"Jackson," she said softly. "You have it all wrong. If you…"

He immediately cut her off. "Saviella, save the damage control for your clients. It's what you do best, right? I suggest you give me the ring on your finger now," he said evenly as he held out his hand.

The look on her face changed and she became the entertainment lawyer that she was best known for. "I think not; it was a gift and as a gift…"

Jackson was in no mood to listen. He had been there too long and could feel the pain mounting in his chest. He was positive his ribs were broken. "Save the bullshit for someone else," he snapped sharply. "If you don't return it, it's going to be all over the news about what you did with my best friend, how I walked in on the scene and that *you and Adam* were the cause of my accident! You probably continued the affair while I was in a coma. I'm sure if I ask around it will come out that your little fling persisted while I was recovering! Your career will be ruined!"

Saviella immediately pulled the stunning, sparkling diamond from her ring finger and dropped it into the palm of his waiting hand. "I'll have an agreement drawn up stating you will not discuss anything."

Jackson shrugged and said, "No problem. I'm sure you have a standard document on file. Print it out *now*; I'll sign it and give me a copy. I promise that *I* will not discuss this with anyone." He winced as the pain was now shooting down his arm.

She quickly moved to her computer and with a few clicks, the printer came to life and spit out the form.

"Just so you know," he said as he bent over the desk to sign, "I have no intention of getting involved in a lawsuit. I have enough of my own money and certainly don't need any of yours," he said bluntly.

After he left her office, he stood on the sidewalk and clutched his chest in agony. A police officer, concerned about his appearance, helped him hail a taxi. He called his mother and told her to meet him at the hospital.

Jackson chuckled to himself as he jotted more notes on his legal pad including a timeline of the events, before he resumed typing.

He soon burst into a fit of laughter, as he continued reminiscing about the incident. The following day the news media carried the story. Print, television, and social media had a field day with the account.

He recalled watching from his hospital bed, laughing as Saviella and her family tried to handle damage control. His arm was broken and in a cast and his face looked as if he had been in a boxing ring with a prizefighter. He had a few cracked ribs but that didn't keep him from laughing over the news stories that were circulating.

His father was appalled at what happened and assigned one of the associates, Bob Andrews, to handle the mess. Jackson was trying hard not to laugh as he watched Bob field questions from reporters, who accused Jackson of violating some confidentiality agreement. Bob confirmed that Jackson signed it; however, Jackson had been immediately hospitalized and in surgery when the story unfolded. His family and associates, who witnessed the altercation in the law firm, were doing all the talking. It was unavoidable when the police showed up with the ambulance. Statements were corroborated and taken from dozens of employees. As he watched, it occurred to him that Saviella never even asked him about Adam, and what happened to him. He wondered if she ever really cared about him or Adam at all.

Bob Andrews spoke evenly to the reporters. "The family is devastated. Can you imagine their son being injured in a terrible accident caused by the trauma of catching his best friend cheating with his fiancé while on vacation? It's an unfortunate tragedy for all and we only hope the best for Jackson and Ms. Saviella and their respective families during this difficult time. Please give everyone time to heal physically and emotionally," Bob said as he ended the interview.

Jackson smiled. Bob championed every woman who survived a bad relationship or had been cheated on. He also appealed to families whose loved ones suffered from injuries. And the list went on. The media was going crazy and news outlets wanted a comment from Jackson, who wanted to be left alone. He let the attorneys handle it all. Saviella and Adam would be lucky if they ever worked again. He was certain his father would make sure of it. Reporters worked overtime on the story and just as he predicted, it was soon discovered that Saviella was with Adam before, during, and after the accident.

"What a circus," he grabbed his chest as he tried not to laugh while recuperating in the hospital.

"Your ribs," his mother reminded him. "I'm sad that you had to go through this to discover the truth, but I guess God had another plan for you."

His father, not the most religious person, said, "*Plan! What plan could God have for him Stella!* Really? Why did he have to get into an accident? What kind of plan is that? God didn't have to put him in a coma to see his fiancé turn out to be a piece of trash. This is ridiculous!"

His mother placed her hand on her husband's arm, "Warren, can't you just stop questioning for once and be grateful."

"I am grateful, I just don't understand God," he muttered. "I don't understand his strategy. I mean he could have just…"

"Warren, we're *not* meant to understand," she interrupted him, smiling as she leaned over and kissed him on the cheek. "Just pray and be grateful."

"Well, at least he discovered this *before* he got married," his father grumbled.

"Perhaps that's what God's plan was all about," his mother said softly as they continued to converse about the inexplicable ways of the Lord and how the spiritual world operated.

"Do you think if God needed a lawyer, he'd call me?" His father smiled as he baited his wife.

"Think of all the people you've helped in the courtroom. God has called upon you many, many times, Warren, and you don't even realize it."

Chapter 131

Alastair

Upon hearing the words "Gods Plan," Alastair groaned with remorse. Just when he thought he was on the right track, he realized he was in deep, deep trouble. Anxiety was eating his skin like one of the many plagues he witnessed growing up. He oscillated back and forth between his desperation to speak with God to explain, how he was going to justify his actions, or pray. Nonetheless, he supposed after God was through with him *he* might be in need of legal representation.

Chapter 132

Chris and Doctor Aaron Carter

"*H*appy New Year!" Chris smiled as he and Doctor Carter shook hands and exchanged greetings. After he was reunited with Anna he had spent time helping her and Doctor Carter fill in some of the gaps regarding Anna's past. Most of it was about college, where they originally met. Chris departed to spend Christmas with his family and returned after New Year's to pick Anna up like he promised.

Aaron insisted they meet without Anna so he could review his notes. While Chris was warm hearted, confident, but aloof at times, Aaron like him and could see why he and Anna were friends. Chris got comfortable in one of the leather chairs and said, "So what else do you want to know, doc?"

"Did Anna like her work at the gallery?" he asked.

"Most definitely, doc," he nodded. "She liked being around the artists. In addition to planning exhibits, she learned from them too. She really wanted that experience. As time passed she also wanted to display her work," he said. His tone was serious and he leaned forward. "When she didn't even make the first round of cuts for another upcoming show, she gave her notice and decided to take my wife and I up on our offer and move west to try to sell her work in our gallery, *Starving Artists of Montana*.

Aaron leaned forward and folded his hands. "How long was she at the gallery on campus back East?"

Chris ran his hands through his thick, brown hair as he did the calculations. "She worked there part-time while she was finishing her MFA and then a full-time position opened. She was there for at least four or five years, but most of that was while she was in school. I'd say three years full-time," he nodded assuredly.

"Her entire life was spent on the East Coast, so this move was going to be a new adventure for her."

"Do you think it was *too* sudden a change?"

"No, definitely not. When Anna makes a decision she doesn't second-guess herself. We'd been discussing it for a while."

Aaron looked up from his note pad. "Are you positive she was ready to relocate?"

Christopher nodded. "Without a doubt. I'm telling you she was really looking forward to moving. She would fly to California, rent a car, visit some sites, and make her way to Montana. She had already shipped her art equipment ahead and was eager to get to Montana. Danella warned her that it gets dark quickly and she could run into snow and bad weather, and not to drive at night. If I know Anna, she probably wanted to surprise us and was trying to arrive before Christmas. She underestimated the power of the weather and got caught up in that storm and…" his voice trailed off as his eyes filled with tears. He didn't want to think about the accident.

"Chris, just inhale deeply," Aaron suggested understanding his pain. "Just remember that you are helping Anna."

Chris forced a smile, quickly wiped his eyes with the sleeve of his shirt and nodded knowingly.

"Do you know if she was travelling with anybody?"

"Not to my knowledge. But that doesn't mean she didn't meet someone along the way. But Anna really isn't the type to just pick someone up, if you know what I mean, doc."

"I understand," he nodded. "Do you know if she had a boyfriend?"

Chris shrugged. "I asked my wife who said she dated but there wasn't anybody serious." Chris shifted uncomfortably in the chair. He almost felt as if he was on trial with all the questions.

The doctor recognized his discomfort and offered him another bottle of water before he once again reminded Chris that this was about Anna and her condition.

"We thought she died in the accident when her rental car was discovered. It was difficult to get any information from the hospital, as we were not her immediate family. It was so chaotic. As I said before, my wife saw the painting posted in the brochure and was positive it was Anna's work. I tried calling this facility but they kept telling me there was nobody listed under the name of Anna Sinclair."

Aaron sighed heavily. "I apologize for that. It's an indication the phone staff need more training on how to field calls, especially when it comes to the trauma center. If I'd known someone was making inquiries, I would have responded." He took a sip of his coffee. "I was wondering if you know anything about her name."

Chris squinted his eyes and looked puzzled.

"Her birth certificate lists another name." He opened the file and shuffled through the papers. "Here it is, Folgier."

Chris stretched his back in the chair and sighed. "Oh, yeah. Sinclair is her mother's maiden name and Anna officially had it changed when she graduated. Her father was Ed Folgier. She hated what he did to her mother and wanted no part of his name. Her grandmother said she could change it when she became of age or was mature enough to decide if she was making the right decision."

"Did she change it immediately?"

Chris nodded to confirm. "As soon as she turned twenty-one she started the process, at least that is what she told Danella and I."

"Let's talk about Anna's financial situation. How did she afford school? Did her grandmother leave her any money?"

"Anna put herself through school by working and took out student loans. I don't exactly remember when, but her grandmother fell," he shook his head and took a gulp from the bottled water. "I think it was in Anna's freshman year of college. She broke her hip and couldn't take care of herself and eventually had to go into a nursing home. The senior community was close to the college and we all visited her. The money from the sale of her home went toward her care. When she passed, any money that was left, Anna used for school and her art supplies."

Chris scratched the back of his neck. "I remember helping Anna with the estate, but there wasn't much money. She must have all the paperwork inside one of her boxes that was shipped to us."

"Is there anything else you can think of regarding her parents?"

"I wish I could tell you more, doc. I already mentioned her father was an alcoholic and chain smoker. He was violently drunk one evening and he left a cigarette burning, the house caught fire, and well you know the rest."

"It's amazing she survived," the doctor said as he loosened his tie.

"Some neighbor awoke to his dog barking and alerted the fireman that Anna was probably inside the house. I think it happened when she was nine or ten. From what she tells me, she has no memory of the event, but that's what her grandmother told her."

Aaron rubbed his chin as he put the pieces of Anna's life together. "I'm sure being in the closet has something to do with her fear of the dark too. Was she afraid to go out at night while at school?"

"Not that I can recall, but then again the campus was *extremely* lit up at night. There were lights *everywhere*. We'd take the train to New York to visit museums, galleries, and shows, and she never showed any fear," he stated positively.

The doctor nodded. "It's not the same as being locked in a closet, inhaling smoke from a fire."

"How did you learn she was afraid of the dark and fire?"

Chris rested his chin in the palm of his hand before he spoke. "There was a time when we were at the Jersey Shore one summer and someone had a fire on the beach. She became pretty anxious and upset and said she was going to sit on the boardwalk. I could tell something was wrong. I walked with her and that's when she told me about the fire," he said as he recalled the memory. "I never understood why she kept nightlights around the apartment, until she told me that story," he mused.

"As I said earlier, being afraid of fire is an extreme trauma and I doubt it was ever addressed. Do you know if she ever had any therapy?"

Chris shook his head. "I have no idea. None that she ever spoke of."

"Can you tell me anything else about her parents?"

Chris shook his head again.

"Is there anything else you can tell me about Anna?"

"Anna is a really nice person. She's fun and full of life. She loves traveling and animals. She minored in English literature but loved art. We all met the first day of school. We were in the same dormitory then later moved into an apartment together. Anna is the one who suggested I ask Danella out. We've been together ever since. Anna is one of those people who'll be your friend for life. She doesn't need to be in the spotlight. She is competitive but not in an ugly way. She is down to earth and does not put on false pretenses; you know…she doesn't pretend to be something she's not. I hope that helps, doc."

Aaron nodded. "Chris, it does immensely, but I'm a bit concerned. You and your wife share experiences with Anna that she *may* or *may not recall* or *ever remember*. She may *not* be the same. Keeping a close eye on her could be difficult as you have a business and a new baby; however, it's going to be important. Anna is in a vulnerable state right now. I hate to see her leave, but she is insisting so I can't keep her here. You're going to have to help make sure she continues her outpatient calls."

"Don't worry, doc, Danella and I will take good care of her and make sure she follows up with you."

"It's important, especially if she starts to recall bits and pieces of her life. She is going to need help to work through any issues. I'll need to speak with your wife too, now that I have more information, just so she will know what to look for," he said, as he wrote down more notes.

Aaron struggled to maintain a calm composure, as he didn't want to alarm Chris. "You're from Montana and know what the nights are like – pitch black. This may frighten her. You have to pay attention to the signs. If you think there's something happening with her, anything, I want you to call me. No matter what she says, she is going to be dealing with a lot of stress and anxiety, *especially* if she recalls what happened when the accident occurred. She *will* need help."

Chris was anxious. "Can I see her now?"

"Of course. Let's go."

Chapter 133

Jackson

Jackson was in his office sorting through the mail. His father's was thrown in the right pile and his in the left. Normally the mailroom and the receptionists took care of this, but due to vacations the temporary clerk mixed some of it up. He turned the brown envelope over and his eyebrows shot up as he stared at the address before tearing it open.

"What the hell is this?" he muttered.

Chapter 134

Anna

Anna settled into the new apartment and quickly began sorting her belongings into the bedroom, bathroom, kitchen, and living room. She was so excited to have someplace to call home that she started unpacking everything at once. The space was just enough for her. It was cramped, but she didn't mind.

Christopher and his wife had converted a building into art studios so artists could come and work in the back. The front was the gallery and coffee bar, open to the public, which sold various coffee blends, cookies, and pastries. It also functioned as a beverage station for gallery openings.

Danella entered with some lunch and laughed at the mess. "Anna, why don't you take a break and have something to eat. I'll help you sort through the boxes," she said cheerfully as she put the tray down.

Anna hadn't realized how hungry she was until she drank some iced tea and took a bite out of the sandwich, while Danella began sorting through the mess. She held up items, of which Anna identified their location as she ate. Danella wanted her to feel at home. She noticed the strange look on Anna's face as she crushed an empty box. "Anna, what's wrong?"

Anna put her glass down. "I just don't know if I'm going to remember everything. I mean, I recognize both you and Chris and," she stopped talking as her eyes filled with tears.

Danella's hands flew to her face as she quickly made her way to Anna and knelt before her. "Anna," she said as she cupped her hands around Anna's cold fingers. "What's wrong?"

Anna's lips trembled. "Chris said we were all best friends and I don't remember all of it…and I'm so grateful for you taking me in and…and what if I don't recall any of it?"

Danella's heart was racing. She was grateful Doctor Carter had warned and prepared her for moments as such. "I hung some pictures of us on the walls from college and have a scrap book if you want to look through," she said nervously as she handed Anna a box of tissues.

Anna buried her face in her hands and cried.

Danella's mind was racing. She wasn't sure how to respond and didn't want to say something that would upset her. She pushed her long, black hair behind her ears and said, "Anna, look at me."

Anna raised her head revealing her now tear-stained cheeks.

Danella smiled confidently as she grasped her shoulders. "Chris and I will do our best to help you remember. And so what if you don't, we're going to make new memories together," she said positively, as she tried to make Anna feel more comfortable. "Now come on, let's get your stuff put away," she said as she hugged her tightly.

Anna nodded and wiped her eyes. They worked through the afternoon going through boxes, arranging some items and discarding others. A donate pile was also created for clothing she no longer wanted.

"I'm sorry, Anna, for the small space," Danella blurted as she stopped for a glass of tea. "Chris and I thought you were, well you know," she couldn't bring herself to say the word gone. "Complications from my pregnancy and the pressure of running the business prevented us from doing anything with your stuff…then we needed more space for the baby, so Chris knocked down a wall and made this into the smaller apartment."

Anna hugged her. "Don't worry. I love it here already. You were right. It's going to be okay. I'm so glad to be out of the hospital and be with people that I actually know, well that I sort of know," she half smiled and together they laughed like old friends.

Anna continued to arrange her paints, easel, and canvases. She made part of the living room her studio. She refused to take one of the open work areas in the back because she wanted to work in her room. "I just need time, Danella; besides I like the view and light coming in from the window up here."

Danella kept the studio space open for Anna and filled it with things she wanted to keep in case she decided to use the space later. She was nervous. She wasn't sure how Anna was going to react, especially after what Chris and Doctor Carter said regarding her mental health. She wasn't sure what she was going to remember, but Doctor Carter told them to take it one day at a time. "Are you sure you're going to be comfortable up here?" she asked hesitantly, as she pulled her long, silky hair into a ponytail.

Anna's eyes sparkled like her smile. "Don't worry about it. I'm so grateful to both of you for keeping my art supplies. I'll make do. Since I have no money, I can help out in the café and paint at night."

"Anna, you don't have to rush."

"I'll be fine. I know Doctor Carter told you to watch over me. I'm going to be okay. I just need to start painting. I don't want any special privileges either. If you don't want to hang my art or think it's worthy of your gallery, tell me. I won't be offended. Plus, as soon as I make some money, I'm going to pay you back."

Christopher walked in and kissed his wife. He was holding baby Cody and was grinning from ear to ear, laughing and repeating the sounds the baby was making while nuzzling his neck. They had their own private communication. He had overheard the end of their conversation and said sharply, "Absolutely not! You will not be working in the cafe until you create some paintings. It's not necessary. You're our best friend…"

"And you rescued me and I promised to help out," she interrupted, "and you two have your hands full with the baby. If you don't agree to it, I can't stay."

"Don't be absurd, Anna. Doctor Carter said you still have an adjustment period, so you need to take it easy," Danella stated firmly. "Besides, you have no place to go," she cried.

"Why do you have to be so stubborn?" Christopher laughed. "How about you start making some art *first* and when you sell *ten* paintings *then* you can work downstairs?"

At that moment the baby smiled and it looked as if he was nodding his head too. They all laughed. "See, Cody agrees," Chris said as he blew kisses on the baby's neck.

"Okay, deal!" Anna smiled jubilantly as she reached out and took the baby from Chris. "Perhaps I'll paint your portrait, you handsome little devil," she cooed in his ear.

Chapter 135

Willow

Willow was out enjoying a glass of wine with dinner after work. She and some of her colleagues wanted to try one of the new restaurants that had just opened downtown. "I just don't understand why you want to leave, Willow. The work you're doing for the department is phenomenal. I read the abstract you wrote and it's getting a lot of attention. I really think you should reconsider."

"Perhaps. I just need a change of scenery. This was temporary anyway."

"Liar! You love your work and what you do; besides, you just moved here. Is this talk because of *'flower man?'*"

"Flower Man," was the nickname that was given to the mysterious sender of the flowers. It spread throughout the floor and the hospital. Speculation intensified as to the identity of the 'flower-man.' She actually heard an office pool was started on the eighth floor.

"I hope you're not being chased off by *'flower man'* because if you are then…"

"It's nothing like that," Willow interrupted as she defended herself. "Forget I brought it up," she shrugged.

The women continued to stress her value and importance. Quitting was soon forgotten as the conversation changed to their vacation plans, families, and the usual girl chatter.

Chapter 136

Noah

Noah was anxious to start his second semester. He glanced at his schedule again to make sure he was heading to the correct lab. He was glad to be back in Montana. During the winter break he and his mother had taken a trip to visit family in California. She wanted to see her sister, so they decided this was the best time before his studies became more demanding.

It was a nice break and fun catching up with cousins he hadn't seen in a while. He also took time to reflect on his relationship with Gemma while sitting on the beach one evening. He missed her terribly and it still hurt as to why she left so abruptly. He replayed the last night he saw her over and over, and still did not understand the reason for her abrupt departure. Getting straight A's had boosted his confidence and he once again vowed he was going to focus on school and try not to think about Gemma so much.

Finding the class, he took a seat and opened up the textbook and began flipping through the pages while he waited for the professor.

"Hi," a cheerful voice announced. "I'm Crystal!"

Noah turned toward the soft voice. His jaw dropped as his mouth hung open.

"What? Do I smell or something?" she asked sharply, as if he offended her. The look of shock was apparent, as he said nothing and continued to stare at her. "Is there a problem? If there is I'll go right to the professor and…"

"Uh, n…no…no," he interrupted. "I mean…you…um…just…um…re…semble someone I once knew," he stammered. Noah stumbled over his words as he spoke. He was speechless as he looked into her eyes. They were deep blue like Gemma's, but her hair was a darker shade of blonde and longer. He could have sworn she had the same birthmark on the right side of her face, but she moved too quickly and her blond hair covered it. *What kind of cruel joke is this? Here I am trying to forget about Gemma and I get assigned a lab partner who looks exactly like her!*

Crystal still wasn't satisfied. "Well, get over it. You do realize we'll be lab partners for the entire year?" she asked tersely as she slammed her backpack on the table and took her seat.

Noah winced while others turned toward the loud whack. *The entire year!* He shook his head. He wasn't aware. Her complexion was clear and her teeth were perfectly white and straight, just like Gemma's! He groaned inwardly. To make matters worse, she had that million-dollar smile just like Gemma did. Only now, she wasn't smiling. He was too flabbergasted at the resemblance to speak.

"I'm planning on learning and I don't need a lab partner who is not going to work hard," she spat, clearly annoyed. "I certainly won't have someone impede my progress. I worked very diligently just to get into medical school," she stated crossly as she flipped her hair behind her ear. Her eyes narrowed like laser beams as she peered angrily at him. "And furthermore, I'll have you know I'm going to be a surgeon someday! If you're not going to talk or participate, I'll ask for someone else! And stop gawking at me like that. It's rude!"

Noah was mortified she was speaking to him like he was a child. *How dare she think I'm not going to work just as hard!* He swallowed hard. "I'm sorry. I didn't mean anything by it. My name is Noah. I apologize for staring, but you look like a friend of mine. I can assure you I'm not a slacker and plan on working just as hard as you!"

Crystal wasn't convinced. "We'll see about that," she countered curtly as she twisted in her seat, flipped her hair back, and opened her textbook to the first chapter.

Noah blinked with astonishment when she turned her head and tossed back her hair. He wasn't seeing things – the birthmark – it was exactly in the same spot as Gemma's; high on her right cheek. He had no idea how he was going to get through the semester.

Chapter 137

Jackson
February 2002

It was a week before Jackson was able to see his father after he had accidently opened mail addressed to him.

"What is it Jackson, what is it that can't possibly wait until the case we're working on is over? You know how much time this takes," his father indicated, clearly annoyed, as he dropped a handful of files on his desk and sat. He opened a bottle of water and took a sip.

"I'm sorry, sir, it's just that your mail was combined with mine and I found this letter from the hospital in Montana."

His father grabbed the letter Jackson laid on the desk and quickly glanced at it.

"So what? They're thanking me for the generous donation I made."

Jackson stood with his hands in his pockets. "I don't believe it," he said his voice filled with skepticism.

"Son, it's called philanthropy," his father retorted sarcastically. "As you are aware our foundation has been involved with many charitable organizations over the years. We made a donation to the hospital. Why wouldn't we after what you endured? What is the big deal? Why the third degree?" He was exhausted from the recent trial and the last thing he wanted to discuss was a monetary contribution.

"I just find it interesting that you somehow found the time to pay someone else's bill." Jackson handed him another piece of paper. "I just thought it would be something you would have mentioned."

His father snatched the paper from his son's hands. "Jackson, is it really that vital? Why would I burden you with this when you have been busy trying to get your life back together?"

"Well, Dad, I'm on the committee and I just wanted to know what this was all about."

His father shook his head annoyed and his facial muscles tightened, "It's called paying it forward and in case you have forgotten," his voice raised another octave, "and it's the mission of our foundation!"

His intercom hummed. "Mr. Wilson, your group is ready to meet in the conference room," his executive assistant announced. "They're all quiet and they don't look very happy. I think they're going to settle."

He slapped his hand on his desk and smiled slyly as he buzzed her back. "Good job, Sandy. Tell them I'm on my way." *Ha! I taught her well.* "Pay attention to people and gauge their emotions. You see, son, someone listens to me!"

Jackson rolled his eyes.

"Jackson, if you don't mind, I have work to do, as I'm sure you do as well," he said briskly, as he gathered his files and departed for the meeting.

Jackson jumped as the door slammed into the frame. He wasn't satisfied and vowed to look further into the matter.

Chapter 138

Anna

"**A**nna, a couple just purchased one of your paintings!" Chris said excitedly, as he burst into her apartment. He knocked but the words, "Come in," were barely out of Anna's mouth when the door flew open. "I think you should paint another one! I didn't know you painted landscapes. I don't ever recall seeing them with your work. Is this something new?"

Anna shrugged, "I don't know. You're right, it's a bit different from the portraits and abstracts I viewed in my portfolio; however, I keep seeing these images in my head and just paint them."

"Are they places you've been to before?"

Anna got up and grabbed another jar of azure paint off the shelf. "I'm not sure. It's like I've been dreaming of these locations, and I just start painting them," she said as she washed her brush and added more color to her palette. Splatters of paint and hues of color were splashed on her jeans and the old denim shirt she wore. Adjusting the stool she sat back down and continued with her work.

Curious, Chris walked over to the far wall where she had a few canvases, knelt down, and began flipping through the paintings. "Anna, these are really good. Are they finished?"

"Almost, I just need to add the final glaze. The one over there," she pointed toward the closet, "is completed."

"They really are stunning. Let me know when they're ready. In the meantime I'll display this one with the yellow lilies. I'm putting a huge price tag on it and we'll see what happens."

"Well, don't ask too much. Nobody around here will pay top dollar for that," she laughed. "What? What are you smirking about?"

"Anna," he grinned sheepishly, "that's why I came up here…to tell you the couple that just bought one of your landscape paintings; you know, the one with the green and white flowers by the cabin with the dog."

She nodded.

"They paid the *full* asking price of eight hundred dollars. You forget this is a tourist town with lots of art and culture. People who come here have money and they can afford it!"

"Here's your commission," he smiled as he held out the check. Danella will deposit it into the account we opened for you. You just need to sign the back."

Anna stopped painting as she turned toward Chris. Her mouth hung open. "Are you serious?" she gasped.

Chris nodded, unblinking. He was very serious. He was basically easygoing, and many perceived him as childlike, due to his carefree attitude, but when it came to business he was extremely determined and motivated to be successful. He thrust a pen toward her.

"Did you say eight hundred dollars?" It was her first sale. She jumped off the stool and hugged Chris tightly.

"Hey, watch that paint brush," he laughed. "We'll celebrate later. Just give me more paintings to display."

Chapter 139

Noah and Crystal

Noah and Crystal disagreed and argued about everything so much that their study group and classmates became displeased. Crystal demanded a new partner.

"Denied," Professor Toby exploded, as he slammed the textbook closed. "If you can't get along with each other, how are you going to deal with family members and patients? The next time you make an appointment to see me I hope it's regarding medical procedures," he spat irritably as he peered at her angrily over his bifocals.

Crystal left humiliated, but knew he was right.

Their competitive spirits were such that they debated like lawyers about medical techniques, anatomy, and procedures.

The professors took note of their unquestionable desire to learn and challenged them *and the entire freshman class more.* The anatomy lab became a bloodthirsty battle for who could answer the most questions. It was so exhausting that Doctor Dymond often lectured from a different textbook or made impromptu changes in the syllabus just to have some order in the class. When questioned, he fumed as his face-hardened and his eyes slowly scanned the lecture hall like radar from a ship. "If you think every surgery is going to be perfect, think again," he roared brusquely. "You need to be prepared for anything, so study harder," he spat, then added, "and next time come to class *prepared.* If that means reading more, then do it!"

Professor Bentley also took to giving spur-of-the-moment quizzes and increased the work in microbiology, while Doctor Potter added an additional lab when someone complained about the insurmountable workload. Everyone groaned.

She marched across the stage of the lecture hall, her high shoes clicking loudly on the hardwood floor, and snapped off the projector. Her eyes narrowed as she gazed out at the class. "This is real life people, not some entry-level sewing class! If you want to be the best doctors, you'll have to work harder," she exploded as she thrust her hands into her lab coat. "Besides, from what I've witnessed, the spirit of the group is copiously energized; therefore, we're going to kick it up a notch! Lab resumes after your last evening class." The class quietly packed up and waited until they were outside to protest, for fear more work would be assigned.

Noah and Crystal's arguments and aggressive nature pushed the other students to learn and participate, not sit back on the sidelines. The teaching staff agreed it was definitely going to be a great group of potential doctors and hoped the situation between Noah and Crystal would resolve itself soon.

Chapter 140

Alastair

As Alastair continued to watch the situation develop in the reflection pool, he felt more angst as he thought about the training class he had left behind. He had been so focused on what had happened, he had left his training group with Angel Trainer Guiscard.

Since Alastair had such a high rank, he had credentials to call upon a substitute. Guiscard was the only one available at the time. Not that Guiscard was an incapable trainer, it was just that he wasn't even in the top one hundred.

Alastair ran his hands nervously through his beard. He had been so distraught at what happened he hadn't been thinking clearly. He handed Guiscard his roster and simply told him, "Find them, and don't let them out of your sight. You must keep watch over them until I return."

There was one major problem with all of this – his class had fled when he entered the computer room. He never waited to see if Guiscard was able to track down all of them. Without his angel bracelet he couldn't dial in to see what the group was doing. If Guiscard was unable to locate them and keep them on track, they might be causing more damage than even he was aware of. He closed his eyes as his hands grabbed his head in despair. He looked up when he felt Cooper pawing at his shoulder. He huffed and peered up at the dog. "Perhaps the Lord will let me go and live with you Cooper. I don't know how much longer I can deal with the guilt and shame of my actions."

Chapter 141

Jackson

"Jackson, *what is the meaning of this*?" his father spat angrily as he stormed into his son's office waving an envelope in the air.

Jackson had been staring out the window at the city landscape. At one time he had loved this view but nowadays when he looked out the window, he instead saw snow covered mountains and panoramic views of the land out west.

He turned around to face his father. "Ah, I see you received a copy of my resignation letter."

"What the hell is this about?" his father said in a huff as he sat in one of the expensive leather chairs. His red face and the veins pulsing from his forehead indicated he was fuming.

Jackson shrugged and shook his head as he took a seat at his desk. "I just can't do this any longer, Dad. My life has changed since the accident. This just isn't working for me. I'm not happy and I just feel extremely empty inside, like something is missing and…"

"So take a fucking vacation!" his father interrupted irritated. "I blame this on your generation. Something isn't going right and you leave," he gestured angrily. His eyes narrowed as he peered at him hotly. "Your grandfather would never put up with this behavior; we worked and we worked hard," he waved his hand at his son to emphasize his disappointment.

Jackson ignored the statement and wasn't going to start a conversation about generational differences. "Did you ever think I tried to do too much too soon, Dad? I can't remember half of my life sometimes and I'm trying to work and…"

His father loosened his tie as his muscles on his face tightened. "Do you know what it was like for me to sit in that hospital day in and day out?" he interrupted bluntly. "Your mother and I sacrificed...how *could* you do such a thing?"

"This isn't about you, Dad!" Jackson shouted bitterly. As usual, his father was only hearing what suited him.

His father sighed heavily. "You need to be engaged in life. So what if you can't remember a few faces or facts from time to time?"

"You're not listening to me. I'm *not happy* and I've got to find what it is that…"

"*Not happy*? Is this about Saviella? If you want to be with her then go get her back. It was *your* choice to break it off."

Jackson looked at his father like he had turned into a horrific demon. "No, this has *NOTHING* to do with her!" He slammed his fist on the desk. He could feel the familiar tightening in his chest as his anxiety amplified.

"It's that *other* woman then," he pointed his finger in the air. "I knew it! It's always been about *that woman. You need to come clean. Who is she?*" his father demanded.

It was Jackson's turn to look surprised. "*What the hell are you talking about?*"

"The woman from Montana, the one you were *with* the night of the accident."

Jackson was still not clear what happened that night. Shadowy and blurry images of skiing, the cabin incident, snow, and driving flashed through his mind from time to time. He began to drum his fingers on the desk. "I have no idea what you're talking about."

"Oh, *spare* me the secrecy, Jackson!" he yelled as his fist hit the desk. "*You're not the first man to have an affair!*"

Jackson raised his eyebrows and wondered if his father was speaking about his own indiscretions. *That would be a shocker or would it?*

His father was exasperated. "*That woman*! The woman you arrived with and shared a room with at the trauma center. *It's all about her*! You lose your friendship with your best friend for cheating and *you're* the one that was having *an affair* as well! I assured your mother you were *not fooling around* with *that girl* and she believed me."

Jackson was speechless. "*I have absolutely no idea what you are talking about*," he shouted furiously.

His teeth clenched. "Then it's all still buried deep in your brain," he pointed to his head for emphasis. "I can't believe you're going to throw your entire career away; your mother will be heartbroken!" His eyebrows narrowed dramatically, like the thin lines on the eyes of an alligator, as his hands slashed through the air.

"Mom already knows and she just wants me to be happy. I never said I was going to stop practicing law. I'm just not going to do it here!"

His father rose and continued yelling. The veins protruded from his blood-red face and neck. His father was so angry that Jackson could feel the heat from the adrenaline coursing through his father's body across the desk. "Dad, your blood pressure," Jackson reminded him.

Facial muscles scrunched and contorted he continued, "You're going to regret this, Jackson," he gestured hotly. "You're throwing your career, this firm – this firm that your grandfather built from scratch, it's your legacy, and with one stroke of the pen," he threw the envelope containing the resignation letter on the desk, "you're throwing it all away, your entire career, down the drain over a woman. This is ludicrous! I'm not accepting this letter! You need to re-think what you're doing." he stormed out leaving Jackson to wonder what woman he meant.

Chapter 142

Willow
March 2002

illow was sitting in the indoor solarium with her morning coffee. She liked to come here early to watch the sun rise and get focused for the day ahead. "Is this seat taken?"

She turned to the familiar voice and her face lit up. "Jackson," she gasped, surprised, as she moved over and gestured for him to sit. "I almost didn't recognize you, clean-shaven and with such a flattering haircut. You look like you walked right out of the pages of *Vogue* magazine."

He gave her one of his best smiles and a side view of his face. "Thanks for the compliment."

"What are you doing here? I didn't know you were coming. How are you? Is everything all right?"

He limped over with his cane, gave her a quick hug, and sat. Her eyes danced with happiness and her face beamed with joy just as he had remembered. "I flew in last night. It was a last-minute decision. I need to see Doctor Carter."

She still couldn't get over how fantastic he looked. "You clean up nice," she nodded, gesturing to his face and hair.

"Only because it itched," he grinned.

Willow took a sip of her coffee before she spoke. "You could have called him on the phone. I'm sure he would have taken your call. Don't you have his cell phone number?"

"I do but it keeps going to voicemail," he said, dismayed.

Mmm, she thought. He must have really needed a vacation if he's not answering calls. I wonder if this has anything to do with what happened between us.

"Like I said, it was a last-minute decision."

"Well, unfortunately he's not on campus." She then noticed his hands. "I'm surprised. I thought you'd be married by now to that stunning woman."

"Let's just say it didn't work out."

Willow was bemused. Eyebrows raised she cocked her head to one side.

"Don't look *too* shocked," Jackson smirked. "Do you know how I can reach Doctor Carter? I really need to speak with him."

Willow could sense the agitation in his voice as he spoke. "He's on vacation. Apparently he needed some time off and won't be returning until April."

"An entire month?" Jackson exclaimed. "I can't wait that long!"

"Well, it's been a bit longer, since January."

It was Jacksons turn to look surprised. "I guess he really needed it."

Willow nodded. "He does work hard. It's been an exhausting year for him."

Jackson agreed. "No doubt."

"He deserved a break. His return date is April." She bit her lip and her tone of voice changed. She was all business. "Jackson, if there is something I can assist you with, I will try. I certainly don't want you flying back to New York without getting the help you seek," she said noticeably concerned.

Willow was taking a risk. He wasn't one of her patients and she knew the protocol. "I know you're not my patients, so how about we just talk like two friends who just met on the street and are catching up on life?"

Jackson smiled. He knew all about patient confidentiality, but at that moment, well, he wasn't interested in policy. "I just came by to see Doctor Carter and he wasn't available. I ran into you and I just felt like talking to someone. No harm in old acquaintances catching up. How about we grab some breakfast in the café downtown?"

"Excellent idea," she nodded smiling. "I could use more coffee."

***

"Sounds like you've been pretty busy," she said after Jackson gave her a detailed account of the past few months.

"My life felt as if it was spiraling out of control. The pace was grueling and," his voice cracked and lips twisted in anguish as he paused. He shook his head as if in doing so would erase his angst. "Let's just say it was too much for all the trauma I suffered."

Her heart ached for him, as she knew he was distressed. "So what brings you out here?"

"My father accused me of having an affair with someone I shared a room with. He said we arrived together? I don't recall someone sharing my room."

Her eyes widened in astonishment. "Is that all the facts your father has?" She questioned nonchalantly, as she pushed a lock of her hair behind her ear and sipped more coffee.

Jackson told her what happened. "We had the worst fight about a woman I don't even know and I believe he paid for her room. I almost think *he* was the one having the affair with *her*," he gestured as he spoke. "But that doesn't make any sense! It's all so frustrating! I just want answers," he said. Jackson touched his face. He could feel the blood rushing to his skin. "I'm getting hot and aggravated just talking about it!"

Willow observed his facial muscles tightening and contorting as he spoke and understood how agitated he was; however, this was serious and she wasn't about to risk patients' rights or confidentiality. Unblinking and very professional she stated, "Not much to tell but she is gone. She left with her family," she shrugged. "While I wasn't here when the incident occurred, you both were brought in together along with many others. From what I understand it was a full house. You weren't the only one sharing a room."

Jackson rubbed the back of his neck and let it drop. "Okay, well one mystery solved. My other issue is, I'm also starting to recall things that don't make sense and my family thinks I'm losing my mind because I handed in my resignation."

"Perhaps you're moving too fast and this is just a small set back?"

"Well, do setbacks include crazy dreams? That's the other reason why I came out here. Ever since the accident and even when I woke up, I'd have these dreams about people I don't know."

"Did you mention this to anyone?"

Jackson shrugged. "No, not really. I might have said something about the dreams but didn't disclose all the parts."

"I suppose you're trying to piece it together on your own?" she questioned knowingly.

Jackson nodded in agreement. "How'd you guess?"

She shook her head and smiled. "It's typical. Nobody wants assistance. What they don't realize is how important it is for them to *seek help*. You can benefit as the doctors comprehend and facilitate putting the puzzle together. Tell me about the dreams," she insisted.

"They came and went. Sort of fading in and out. After the office brawl, I began having them again. I don't know anyone or have any friends who go by the names of *Noah or Gemma*."

A shiver ran down Willow's back at the mention of the two names.

"You know something," Jackson accused her. "I saw that look of recognition on your face."

Willow adjusted her jacket and sighed heavily. "Jackson, I don't know, but I need to look at your chart, as you weren't my patient. She didn't reveal how Aaron cut the rest of the staff off from his file. Give me some time. Why don't we exchange phone numbers? Where will you be staying?"

"I thought about going back to the scene where it happened."

"Back to Hunters Glen?" Her eyes shot open in disbelief. "Are you ready for that?"

His lips pursed and he rubbed the back of his neck. He was so tense his muscles ached. "Doctor Carter suggested it months ago. I wasn't ready before, but I think I might be now. I don't really know," he scratched his head before he continued. "I was deliberating…like if I head to Hunters Glen and stay for a while it might help prepare me…"

She held up her hand gesturing for him to stop talking. "Jackson, before you do anything, I really suggest you speak with the doctor first. At least wait until he returns from vacation."

"Thanks for the advice, Willow. Don't think I'm going to do anything rash. I have a lot of time on my hands. I think I'm going to drive to Hunters Glen, get settled, and think about it a bit more. Call me if you find anything in my file that you think can help me. If you happen to hear from the doctor, let him know I'm in town and I really need to see him."

Chapter 143

Willow

Willow didn't care what happened, she needed answers. She went to Aaron's office and started going through her keys as she attempted to open the door. She tried key after key and pulling on the knob, but it wouldn't budge.

Roberto, the head of security, appeared instantly. "Do you need something?" he asked. His large size made him someone to reckon with. When he spoke, his soft voice maintained an even rhythm and when he smiled his eyes sparkled and you knew he had a heart of gold.

"I'm sorry, Roberto, I left the key for Doctor Carter's office at home and I need a file. It's in his office and he's on vacation." She smiled innocently, as she tried to sound convincing.

"I wasn't aware that he issued you a key?" he said suspiciously.

"Roberto, do you remember the male patient from New York that woke up from his coma?"

"Yeah, I remember, the guy with the crazy family; his father was a big-time lawyer and was always threatening the hospital with a lawsuit. How could I forget?"

"Exactly, that's the reason why I need the door opened now! The family is at it again," she lied easily. "If Doctor Carter has a problem with it, I promise I'll take all the blame."

"Okay, Miss Willow, I'll do it," he said a bit reluctantly for he wasn't going to argue with her. He, like the rest of the staff, loved Willow and he was sorry she would be leaving. He knew she was only looking out for the patients and hospital.

Willow scanned the file names and grabbed a stack off his desk. Roberto locked the door when she was done.

"Oh, Miss Willow, I almost forgot why I was up here. He handed her an envelope. I'm sorry it took so long, but I had a family emergency."

"What is this?"

"The transcription notes of the security tapes you requested."

"Did you find Noah?"

Roberto shook his head in disbelief. "You're not going to believe it; he was right under our noses all along."

"What do you mean?"

Roberto rolled his eyes and whispered. "He lives with his mother whose last name is Severini. After he graduated from his undergraduate program, he officially changed his name from Tremonte, his father's name, to Severini, his mother's maiden name. He now goes by Noah Severini."

"Did his parents' divorce?"

"Apparently. There was paperwork, birth certificates, and some passport issues for Noah, which started with the father, who ran off when the kid was just a baby, re-married then died. The kid must harbor some *real* resentment toward the man to change his name. He had to wait until he was of age to do it. It seems to be a big thing now. These kids today, they don't like their name and they just up and change it…what is wrong with them…why can't they just be happy…this generation is just lost I tell you…a generation lost...my father would not stand for some of the nonsense that takes place with today's youth," he rambled.

Willow had no time to listen to the challenges facing adolescent kids. "Roberto, you need to get to the point. I'm a bit pressed for time," she urged.

"Sorry, Miss Willow," he nodded apologetically. "Anyway, there were stacks of documents involved and I was waiting for my friend down at the courthouse to find some records, so I'm sorry this took so long. Then it looks like they moved sometime *after* he graduated. Anyhow, he is enrolled at the college next-door."

"You're kidding me! He's a medical student?" she asked. Dumbfounded, her mouth dropped open in amazement.

Chapter 144

Noah and Crystal

It took a while but Noah and Crystal eventually called a truce and became fast friends. It happened when Noah made a correction on their lab project and because of it they won the class challenge. "It seems there is more to you than you let on, Noah. Where did you learn that technique because it's clearly not first year material?"

Noah shrugged. "I read in my spare time."

Crystal looked at him suspiciously. "If you say so, but sometimes you seem to know a bit more than the rest of us first years."

Noah raised his eyebrows in surprise. It was a rare occasion that she acknowledged his astuteness. He wasn't going to argue with her. "If you want the truth, I worked in a hospital on the cleaning crew. I worked nights to help put myself through college. Let's just say, I saw a lot on the overnight shift." Noah said not caring that he admitted he was on the cleaning crew.

Crystal nodded. "A janitor?" She questioned with raised eyebrows, as if she wasn't sure she heard him correctly.

"Do you have a problem with that?" he asked, a bit defensively.

"Not really, Noah. It shows that you are dedicated to your goal. I also appreciate someone who is not afraid of hard work."

"Yeah, well, I've been at that hospital, since I obtained my working papers." He pointed in the direction of the building.

"I've worked on practically every floor and know my way around that building," he mused.

"Wow! Honesty. I like that. Always be honest. It will take you far." Crystal continued to ramble on about the importance of being truthful especially if you were going to be a doctor.

Noah stared at her as if he was seeing a ghost. *"Always be honest. It will take you far."* Gemma said that to him *all* the time. He smiled and thought, *What have I got to lose?*

"Noah," she scowled. "Are you listening to me? Have you heard anything I've said?"

He heard every word. But while she was talking he was thinking about a missed opportunity and he wasn't going to let it happen again.

"Crystal," he said firmly.

Her eyebrows shot up in disbelief at his tone of voice.

"I'm going to the café for coffee after class. Would you like to go with me? We can talk more about the upcoming assignment. Perhaps if we work together we could produce something that exceeds the expectations of the professors."

He extended the olive branch and it was the beginning of a solid friendship.

As Alastair watched Noah trying to work things out, he began to wonder where he went wrong with his training class. He understood the answer for he was too busy chasing, instead of providing instruction. He was reiterating what he had already revealed. He hadn't been paying attention and overlooked his own lessons, and education. He shook his head in misery. "I basically didn't care anymore. Yes, I showed up daily, but was going through the motions. I didn't care about that class because I felt they shouldn't be there. I lost my edge and was no longer concerned about the consequences."

Alastair leaned back on the cloud he was sitting on, closed his eyes and folded his hands across his chest. "I was too busy worrying about the younger supervisor, and the changing technology. I was consumed with my status and what others, espe-

cially my family, would think. If I wasn't so angry," he shook his head in shame. "I could have just asked for help," he said to Cooper, who was laying in the shade of some tree. "If only I had asked for help," he repeated, "maybe I wouldn't be in this mess," he contemplated. Alastair bowed his head, prayed, and began asking the Lord for help.

Chapter 145

Anna

"**A**nna? Are you okay?" Danella whispered as she knocked on the bedroom door. When there was no answer she opened it a crack and called her name again. She entered and peaked in the bedroom. "Anna!" She shouted as she ran over to the bed where she found her huddled under the covers and shaking.

"What's wrong? Are you sick? I thought I heard you crying."

"I don't know," she sobbed. "I keep having dreams about people that I don't know. It happens every night and I'm afraid to sleep."

"Perhaps I should call the doctor. Doctor Carter said you can call and talk with him anytime."

"It seems so silly," Anna sniffed as she took a tissue from the box Danella handed her. "I don't understand why I'm getting so emotional."

Danella tried to calm her down. "It's okay if you feel strange; we all do," she laughed. "Why don't you get up and I'll make some soup for you."

Danella was worried and would call Doctor Carter later. Anna still hadn't recalled much about her past or the accident. It was as if they were getting to know her all over again.

Alastair couldn't feel any worse. "And this is why I need to see the Lord," he shouted. "She's sick and in trouble no thanks to me. Lucius! I know you can hear me," he hollered, angrily. "I've been praying and nobody is listening to me."

He glanced at Cooper who was crouched with his head between his paws. The dog sighed heavily and closed his eyes. "I get it; you're tired of listening to me too. I'm sorry, but I don't know how far time was dialed back and...and...oh...the worry of it all," Alastair cried out, as he began pacing again.

Chapter 146

Jackson

After his meeting with Willow, Jackson had driven an hour south to Hunters Glen and rented a room in one of the local inns, *The Eagles Nest*. He told the young blond woman at the desk that his stay was indefinite and he'd tip well if she gave him the room with the best view.

The slender female smiled seductively and made comments alluding to her single status. He grinned and did his best to ignore her blatant flirting. The last thing he needed was to start a relationship. He wasn't sure what he was doing, but deep down he knew he needed to face his fears. He just didn't know if he'd ever be ready.

Days later he was having breakfast and enjoying a really good cup of coffee at one of the local cafes when he began thinking about what he started referring to as the "Lost Year."

Putting the pieces of that year back together had been difficult, but he was thankful he had his family. No matter how crazy they were, everyone had been there to help and support him. He found it ironic that he wanted to return back to where his "Lost Year" began. The highlight reel of events played over and over in his mind until he paused on the argument with his father. Was he running from something? If so, from what, he wondered. Perhaps his father was right; maybe he just needed a vacation. He closed his eyes and could feel an impending headache from thinking so hard. He reached into his pocket, pulled out the small container, and popped two aspirin. He later decided he wasn't going to dwell on anything and just enjoy life.

Over the next few weeks he simply spent time exploring Hunters Glen. He visited the local shops and restaurants.

Bear Run Ski Resort was nestled in the small town of Hunters Glen, Montana, population 35,000. The quaint town, known for its peaceful and scenic views, attracted cultural and outdoor enthusiasts year-round. Music, artistic festivals, and shows were plentiful. The culinary scene had evolved from casual to sophisticated dining. One of the biggest attractions was the ski resort on Cougar Mountain. It boasted a multitude of trails for all levels of skiing and offered a host of winter and summer activities for all. It was where he took his last ski run over a year ago. He wasn't sure if he'd be able to ski again. He thought about driving back to the resort but decided it wasn't the right time. Perhaps he would eventually. Maybe he'd stick to snowmobiling and forget about skiing.

The locals profited as the town grew into the popular tourist destination it became known for. Many people, who fell in love with the town, stayed and opened businesses. For those who preferred a more suburban and larger city life, the town of Seminole was an hour away. Seminole was home to colleges, research labs, large software companies, a medical school, and the hospital, where he was sent to recover.

One morning after breakfast, he headed out toward Main Street to continue investigating the town and try to figure out what he was going to do with the next chapter of his life.

Alastair stood and slowly walked around the Reflection Pond. "Perhaps I should've made an adjustment too," he said to Cooper who was following him. "I mean Angel Trainer of the Twelfth Order is remarkably impressive...but...this guy, who was in this horrible accident and is trying to recuperate and can't remember much of his life – no thanks to me, is attempting to make a change. He's adjusting to his situation and I'm just complaining. Why should anyone listen to me?" he muttered gloomily as his voice became a faint whisper. He continued walking around the reflection pond, praying for Jackson and his predicament.

Chapter 147

Doctor Aaron Carter
April 2002

Aaron was glad to be back at work. He spent the Christmas holiday alone and started cleaning the house. It was time to dispose of things that were keeping him from moving forward. He donated clothing, books, and other items he no longer had use for. It felt good to get rid of the clutter.

In February, he attended to some personal business and also scheduled a few visits with Doctor Lucardi, who told him to clear his mind a bit – so he went skiing and spent the remainder of the months at his other property in the mountains relaxing and enjoying nature. By April, he felt refreshed and was ready to return to work.

He entered his office, turned his computer monitor on, and began listening to his phone messages.

Doctor Roger Callahan was going to be in town and wanted to have lunch. Instead of writing the details down, his thoughts immediately drifted toward Willow. How she had enjoyed the lecture he had taken her too and the look of jubilation on her face when he introduced them. The crackling of the machine brought him back to the task at hand. There were families and staff who wanted to meet with him and other communications from hospital staff that could wait.

"Doctor Carter," his receptionist called. "I'm sorry to bother you since it's your first day back, but there is someone named Danella that keeps calling and I told her…"

"I'll take it. Put her through," he interrupted

"Hi Doctor Carter. This is Danella, you know, Anna's friend."

"Yes, Yes. I know who you are. Is Anna okay?"

"I've been trying to call you."

"I was on vacation and for the first time decided not to take my work phone. Is everything all right?"

"Anna is in trouble and she needs help. She keeps having dreams about people she doesn't know and it's scaring her. Chris and I are not sure what to do."

"Well, tell me what happened," he said, his voice filled with concern. He immediately reached for his notepad to record any pertinent notes.

"She calls out for someone in her sleep, but I can't make out the name. Other times she wakes up and says she needs to speak to her friends but can't find them."

"Did she tell you who?"

"She said she needs to give a message to Noah and she also mentioned someone named Gemma."

The silence on the other end of the phone was palpable. Aaron was stunned. He could feel the blood draining from his face. His palms grew sweaty and the back of his neck began to itch.

"Doctor Carter, are you still there?" Danella asked.

Aaron was shaken. He had taken four months off and just returned from weeks of intense therapy and did not expect this. He felt the familiar anxiety building inside him. The skin on the back of his neck was drenched with perspiration.

"Doctor Carter, are you there?"

He gulped for air. "Does she say what she wants to tell them?" he asked as his voice cracked.

"She said they can help her find someone and she also wants to thank them."

Chapter 148

Anna

"Anna, you look terrible. When is the last time you slept?" Danella whispered as she dropped off a tray of coffee and some light toast. She sat and waited for Anna to join her.

Anna left the easel and made her way to the small bistro table by the window. "I really appreciate it, but you didn't need to bring this for me. I can take care of myself."

"Really?" Danella questioned as her eyes scrutinized her friend. "Look at you, there are dark circles under your eyes, and you've lost a lot of weight. Chris and I are worried about you!"

Anna ate a piece of toast and took a sip of the coffee. "This is delicious. Thank you. I don't know what is going on. Ever since I left that clinic, I've been having crazy and vivid dreams, and I'm painting landscape themes, which as you know, wasn't really my thing. But I can't seem to stop." Anna walked back over to her canvas and picked up her brush.

Danella was nervous and worried. She didn't want anything to happen to her friend. She struggled to keep calm. "Did you have these dreams before?" Do you know the people in your dreams?" she probed a bit without arousing suspicion. The doctor said to ask questions calmly and report back to him within the week.

"Yes, the dreams were always there, but they were all so fuzzy. I was just trying to work on my physical therapy. I don't even know anybody named Noah or Gemma and I don't know why I would be calling for him or her."

"I'm sorry, I'm only telling you what I heard you say," Danella reminded her. "Perhaps they were childhood friends?"

Danella shrugged. "I never thought about that before." Danella wandered over to her canvas collection. "I can see why people like your work. These are very vivid and pull you into the landscape, as if you are there. Perhaps you should try to paint some animals and portraits so your portfolio isn't so limited?" Danella suggested as she pulled the colored band from her falling hair and redid her ponytail.

"Anna, Danella," Chris shouted, "Are you in there?"

"It's open," Anna called.

"Shh. You'll wake the baby," Danella whispered, as Chris burst into the room. He was out of breath and grinning like a Cheshire cat. "Anna, I just sold another one of your paintings. The yellow lilies, for one thousand dollars!"

Anna dropped her paintbrush on the table. "Are you serious?"

"Yes, totally. I'm going to increase the prices on your next pieces," he said adamantly.

"I don't know, Chris; don't you think that's pushing it a bit?" Danella asked, concerned.

"We're in the business to make money," he said confidently. "I have a wide range of prices on the other paintings and photographs and they are selling. If someone wants her work, they'll buy it. You'll see," he beamed as he hugged both of them. He grabbed a few more completed paintings and returned to the gallery below.

Danella smiled, "Perhaps I was wrong, and you should continue to paint flowers."

Anna picked up her brush and began cleaning it. "No. I think you're right. I should include animals. There is this image I have in my head of this dog. I see him so much that I'm going to add him into the next painting. People love animals right?"

"Well, come to think of it, you did paint one painting with a dog and cabin so do another," Danella urged her excitedly. "You can add birds, cats, rabbits, and more," she continued hoping it would take Anna's mind off her dreams.

Chapter 149

Willow and Doctor Aaron Carter

*A*aron had just hung up with Danella when his receptionist buzzed in to alert him to an emergency meeting in the boardroom. He reached for his pad and headed down the hall. As he rounded the corner he ran right into Willow.

His eyes widened in surprise as he took a step backwards. "Willow," he smiled. His heart was racing. She was the last person he expected to see. *I thought she had already left. Perhaps she changed her mind and decided to stay.* His heart began beating faster at the thought and he could feel the perspiration on his palms from his nervousness. "I thought you were leaving? Did you change your mind?"

Ugh? Was I too obvious?

She ignored the question. "I have some people you need to meet." She then decided she wasn't being fair and added, "I'll be leaving after this meeting."

He stood straighter and was all business "I'm sorry, Willow, it's my first day back and I have an emergency board meeting."

"Aaron, you need to watch the security tapes, which have been downloaded to your computer. You can view them later. Right now we have something more important to discuss."

It was one of the few times she addressed him by his first name instead of Doctor Carter. It sounded nice.

"Aaron. Are you listening to me? I've found Noah. We're meeting him now."

Chapter 150

Willow and Doctor Aaron Carter

"Noah?" he repeated.

"Yes, his name is Noah! He's the boy we have been searching for," she answered a bit annoyed. "The boy in the video tapes!"

Noah, the one Anna is dreaming about.

Willow was getting aggravated. She'd delayed her departure to help train her replacement. Apparently, she was required to give more notice before she left her job. Obviously, Aaron wasn't aware why she was still in town and she was fuming. Her anger was misplaced, as she knew it was her decision to stick around and help. It wasn't his fault he wasn't informed. She forced herself to focus on the matter at hand.

"We never really watched *all* the security tapes. You're going to be surprised at what you see." *I thought I'd be able to handle this but he is making me nervous. It's those eyes and muscular arms. Ugh! Just be calm and you're going to get through this.*

Aaron followed her into the boardroom. He was confused. "Willow, what is the meaning of this? It's my first day back and I have a board meeting and I can't be late."

"This *is your* meeting and it's *extremely* important that you hear what this young man has to say!" She ushered him into the conference room.

"How dare you interfere with my schedule," he spat tersely. *Why did I say that to her? She didn't deserve it.*

"I told you he was going to be testy. Just ignore him," she smiled as she addressed a young boy and girl seated across the table.

"Have a seat, Aaron, I think you're going to need it. This is Noah and his friend Crystal. They are medical students at the university next door," she said courteously.

"Med students," he repeated as he sat down. He stared at the two of them. He didn't know them but they both looked familiar. He finally blurted out, "I know you. You're that housekeeper!"

"Porter," Noah corrected.

Aaron's eyes narrowed as he studied him closer. "I questioned you once before."

"Yes, sir you are correct," Noah answered calmly. He was a bit nervous, but Willow had assured him nothing bad was going to happen and he wasn't going to get thrown out of school. He asked Crystal to accompany him for support, without telling her what the meeting entailed.

"What is this all about, Willow?"

"Noah, why don't you explain?"

Noah exhaled deeply. "I worked on the cleaning crew at the hospital for many years. My mother thought it would be a good idea to see what I'd be getting into if I really wanted to study medicine one day, so she helped me apply. I also worked to save money to put myself through college. I had been assigned to work on just about every floor and because of hiring issues I was sent to the basement or the morgue. I was irate but after a while it wasn't so bad. Then I was transferred…"

Aaron was fuming. "This is absurd," he interrupted. "What does this have to do with me or anything?"

"Aaron, can you just listen for another minute, please? I promise there is a point," Willow said softly.

She said my name again. I can't say no to her.

"Noah, please continue," Willow urged.

"In January of 2001, I was transferred to the fifth floor, which was the *last* place I wanted to be. I tried to get out of it; however, the supervisor said no. After the morgue I had seen enough or so I thought. That's when I met this nurse," he sighed heavily as he fidgeted nervously. "Her name was Gemma."

Chapter 151

Noah

Aaron sucked in his breath. The color drained from his face, which was now ashen.

Willow handed him a bottle of water. "Just let him finish."

"I eventually learned Gemma was a doctor. She introduced me to all the patients and told me everything about them. She divulged techniques she was using to try to help them recover." Aaron's eyes grew wider.

"She even let me assist her at night when I cleaned the rooms."

"Impossible," the doctor whispered as his heart beat faster.

Noah ignored him and rattled off techniques regarding neurotransmitters, magnets, massages, relaxation practices, and other things he helped her with. "She was *really smart* and I was learning a lot," he said proudly.

"Why don't you tell him about room 524?" Willow suggested.

"Oh, yeah. You see Gemma and I had an affinity for the patients in room 524. She told me they weren't ready to go and needed help getting better. At first I didn't believe her, but she convinced me to assist her, and she was right because eventually they both woke up!"

Willow could see the disbelief registered on Aaron's face. She thought his eyes were going to pop out of their sockets as Noah spoke.

Noah looked down at the table, took a deep breath as he looked up, and continued. "I fell in love with Gemma."

Doctor Carter's jaw dropped as he shook his head from side to side. "It's not possible," he muttered.

"The day that I was going to tell her how I felt, she *left* the hospital. The nurse said she was gone. I looked everywhere for her and had no idea why she left without even saying goodbye. I was heartbroken and miserable. When school began it was hard for me at first, as I kept hoping Gemma would come back. It was a very difficult time for me. I eventually met Crystal," he turned and smiled at the blond seated next to him. "She's my lab partner and my best friend." Noah reached for Crystal's hand and squeezed it hard.

Aaron sighed heavily. There were tears in his eyes. "I don't believe it. This has to be some kind of cruel joke."

"I can assure you, sir, I'm not lying!"

"Aaron, when you watch the security tapes, you'll see he's telling the truth."

"Tell me, what day did you meet Gemma?" Aaron demanded.

"It was January seventh," Noah said confidently.

Doctor Carter closed his eyes as he spoke. "How can you be so sure?"

"It was shortly after New Year's and the day I started working on the fifth floor.

Do you remember the day you had security bring me to your office?"

"Vaguely," Aaron muttered, as his mind was racing, as he tried to make sense of Noah's story.

Noah continued. "I asked you about the girl in the photo," he gestured. "She looked just like Gemma and you told me it wasn't Gemma, but I think you were lying!"

"*Noah!*" Crystal said aghast. "You can't be serious? How can you accuse the doctor of such a thing?"

Aaron held up his hand. "It's okay. This really is my fault. Perhaps I should have told *you* the truth when you picked up that photo, but I was still too distraught." He rubbed his forehead and his face was etched in pain.

Everyone in the room, held their breath as they waited in silence before the doctor spoke again.

"Gemma *was* my daughter. She was a brilliant neuroscientist and also studied chemistry. She ran the research lab here and was in the middle of some high-tech, cutting-edge research project." He put his head in his hands and rubbed the sides of his face. He wiped away the tears that were streaming down his cheeks when he looked up at everyone before he continued.

"She and my wife were in a car accident; they were hit by a drunk driver. They were both patients on the fifth floor."

Willow was stunned. She let out a gasp as her hand flew to her mouth in disbelief. She sucked in her breath and waited for him to finish. "There was no way my wife was going to survive, so I had to take her off life support months prior." He paused and rubbed his forehead. He didn't want to continue but knew he had to. Doctor Lucardi told him there would come a time to talk and this was it.

"But Gemma, she was so young. She was a gifted doctor and *way ahead* of others in the field. I thought she'd come back to me. I kept her alive far too long. The other doctors finally convinced me that the charts, scans, and data didn't lie. I was forced to take her off life support on *January seventh*. She never did come back like I hoped she would. She was only thirty-two years old, not even in the prime of her life. I still can't understand why…why take someone so intelligent and with a future so bright…she was so brilliant…so advanced…"

Willow squeezed his arm and handed him some tissues. The pain imprinted in his eyes was still so raw. Her heart ached for his misfortune and agony.

Noah gasped. "That was the day I met Gemma. She appeared out of nowhere! She said she worked on the floor."

"Then I was right, the picture in your office, it was her?"

Aaron shook his head. "No."

Noah's eyebrows furrowed. "I don't understand, sir. She looked exactly like Gemma."

"The photo you saw was of her *twin sister* Sophia. Her twin sister is out of the country and a physician in the Doctors Without Borders Program."

Crystal's eyes were wide open as she leaned forward and looked at everyone in the room, who were also clearly stunned by the entire story. "So are we to believe that Noah was talking to a ghost?" Crystal asked incredulously.

Alastair sat like a frozen statue as he listened to the tale. The earth-shattering revelation stunned him too. His mind raced as he tried to piece together the timeline of events and facts. He covered his face with both hands in despair, cringing in agony. He felt as if he had aged another century. "Just when I thought I was making progress, now this," he moaned.

Chapter 152

Doctor Aaron Carter and Noah

Aaron immediately began questioning Noah about Gemma. Noah told him everything he knew. He described her hair, eyes, marks, and scars on her skin, all of which the doctor confirmed. "She had a birth mark on her face; it was right here," he pointed to his face.

"You must have really loved her to notice all that about her. How do I know you are not making all of this up? You could have seen her photo somewhere," he accused.

"I'm telling you the truth sir. I'm not lying," he asserted. "I did love her. She was my friend and I miss her dearly; however, it took me a while to realize I was in love with the idea of being *in love* with someone like her, who was so beautiful and smart. "You see, Gemma talked to me and before that I really kept to myself. I was busy working and studying. I didn't know what it was like to have someone like Gemma in my life."

Noah paused before he continued. The pain of missing her was reflected in his eyes. "She inspired me to learn and look at the possibilities when healing people. I was really stuck, at a crossroads. I wasn't sure if I wanted to go to medical school. Then Gemma came, and she made me see and understand my potential. She would say, *'You have to put the time in for the reward and always be honest that it will take you far!'"* Noah had tears in his eyes as he spoke.

"I can't believe I'm going to say this, but that sounds just like my Gemma. She always *said* that to people."

"I was devastated when she left so suddenly. I didn't understand, but perhaps she was preparing me for something greater. Then I met Crystal and, well, my life really changed."

Crystal's smile broadened and her eyes sparkled as she glanced lovingly toward Noah. Noah reached over, tenderly squeezed her hand and kissed her on the cheek.

Aaron's face brightened at the affection. They reminded him of the love he shared with his wife when they first met; however, he still was skeptical about the entire story. *Gemma a ghost...could it be conceivable?*

"Noah, is it possible you can tell me more about what Gemma taught you?"

"Oh, that's easy. He spoke about her research and the treatments she did every night. She said doctors don't realize how *alive* the brain is in the evenings. Most of the treatments were done during the day, but at night the brain is active too. For example, the two patients in room 524, they reached out for one another, they held hands, and I saw her crying! It was fascinating. Gemma knew they were making progress. She changed the frequency of her treatment on the computer..."

"Impossible," interrupted the doctor.

Noah shook his head. "No, sir. Gemma...you see...she was positive they would wake up. She said it wasn't their time yet. She was quite adamant about it too."

"Not their time," Crystal said aghast. "How would she know that?"

"Gemma was intently working on some research study. She said she found a flaw in her formula and made some modifications and implemented it again. She bypassed the security codes..."

"Only I know the code," the doctor interrupted.

"No, sir, Gemma gave it to me. It was 0015-01.07.2001."

Willow scribbled the numbers on the yellow pad she had been writing her notes. She looked at Aaron and knew there is no way Noah could have gotten that code. He would have had to hack into the computer system. As she stared at the numbers, her hand flew to her mouth and she gasped, as she suddenly realized the significance – it was probably the time and date of Gemma's death.

"When the guy in 524 woke up, Gemma was elated. I was excited too and wanted to talk to him. Unfortunately, he was moved to a restricted area. Gemma made sure I wrote all the information down and told me to enter it on the monitor in room 524 for the girl."

"You did what?" The doctor shouted displeased.

Willow twisted in her seat, glared at the doctor angrily and said, "That explains why the scans showed more activity at night than in the day. It wasn't the equipment or one of us changing the dials, it was Gemma and Noah. I checked and compared the frequency changes and he's correct."

Doctor Carter was speechless and looked back at Noah. He didn't seem like he would be the type of person to hurt anyone or do something wrong; however, he had violated a host of policies. "Willow, he touched the equipment; he's not a doctor."

Willow glared at him fiercely and urged Noah to continue.

"At first I didn't believe Gemma, but I witnessed subtle miracles every night. Gemma said they were stuck and had followed the light and needed to come back and…and the female, well, she cried out at night and he would reach for her and…"

"I knew it!" Willow whispered. "Subconsciously they were somehow connected to one another. They were communicating!"

Aaron was astonished. It was all too much. While down deep in his heart he knew it was possible, he was not ready to accept it. The technique and processes Noah spoke of were written in Gemma's unpublished research. Ideas which even he didn't believe were conceivable. Ideas he refused to acknowledge.

"Noah, you do know the consequences for interfering in patient recovery when you're not even a doctor?"

The blood drained from Noah's face. He looked over at Willow. "I should never have come here. I told you he is going to kick me out of school."

"*Aaron*," Willow said sharply with the ferocity of a protective mother as she quickly turned in her chair to face him. "The boy is telling the truth. If you can't see that, I will never speak with you again!"

You're not speaking to me now, what does it matter?

Aaron threw up his hands in frustration. "Willow, do you know how preposterous this all sounds!"

Willow looked him straight in the eyes and yelled, "Why not, Aaron? What if we're pieces of matter just floating around and…"

Aaron shook his head vehemently. "I'm a scientist and I do not believe in the possibilities…"

"Gemma did," she countered. "And she wrote about her concepts. She believed! I doubt you ever read all of her notes." From the guilty look on his face, Willow immediately knew she was right.

"Doctor Carter, I'm telling you the truth," Noah interrupted. "Gemma inspired me so much that I took another class and read more to prepare for medical school. I wrote all her notes down and what we did in a journal. I'd be glad to share it with you if you'd like."

Aaron sighed heavily. He saw Willow glaring angrily at him from the corner of his eye. He knew that look. Like a caring mother, Willow wasn't going to let him do anything to ruin Noah's chances in medical school.

"Thank you, Noah, for sharing the story and, yes, I'd like to see the journal. I need some time to digest this information. You can imagine how hard it is for me to believe in *ghosts*, especially *ghosts* roaming about the fifth floor of this hospital, but you have definitely given me something to think about."

"Sir, you don't believe me? I didn't believe it either, but when I watched the tape with Willow, you don't see her, just voices…and people never question me because I'm always studying so they just thought I was talking to myself…but when I saw those tapes…and watched the dials on the equipment move…it was then I realized…"

"*If,* and I say this with great skepticism," he interrupted, "*if* Gemma did come back, why *didn't* she come and see me? *Why you?*"

Noah shrugged as he and Crystal stood to leave. "I have no idea, sir, but she must have had her reasons."

Chapter 153

Willow and Doctor Aaron Carter

"Aaron! That was rude of you. *Why* did you just dismiss him like that?" Her eyes blazed like daggers and her facial muscles were pinched tightly indicating just how incensed she was. "How could you *not* believe him?"

Aaron opened another bottle of water and took a long drink before answering. "It's simple. As a scientist, I believe in science. I *don't* believe in *ghosts*. Ghosts are characters in movies or decorations for Halloween," he replied evenly.

"Well, maybe when you watch the tapes you'll think differently," she countered cynically. "Don't you believe in *miracles*? I'm sure you *witnessed* enough of them being a doctor. You just had two miracles occur that *even you can't explain*," she reminded him as she slammed her hand on the table.

Aaron ran his fingers through his hair in frustration. As a scientist and doctor the concept was too abstract for him.

Her eyes narrowed as she continued glaring at him.

Aaron swallowed hard.

"He is telling the *truth* and do you know *how* I know this? Remember that box I found in the research lab? It belonged to Gemma, *didn't it*? And she worked with you and she was not on sabbatical, was she?" she demanded.

Aaron looked down and rubbed his forehead. He didn't want her to see any more of his pain, but knew it was unavoidable.

When he looked up and faced her, he did his best to keep his composure. But the tears in his eye told a different story. "Yes, you are correct," he answered quietly. "Her married name was Christo. Doctor Gemma Christo," he said proudly as he sighed heavily. "Someone must have written my name on the box with the intent of getting it back to me. "When Gemma passed, I was immediately sent on leave and forgot about collecting the box in the lab. Her personal things were packed up and delivered to her husband," he replied sadly.

Willow was confused. If Gemma was married, why didn't her husband pull the plug earlier?

As if reading her thoughts, Aaron said, "Her husband believed if anyone could bring her back, I could. He gave me power of attorney. After time passed, he and my children begged me, they didn't want to remember her like that…unfortunately, I refused…"

Willow handed him another bottle of water as his face paled. She saw pain – a deep torment – beyond the tears that were ready to burst from his eyes. Thin lines of his misery were etched on his face, forever reminding him of his personal tragedy – a tragedy he still hadn't come to terms with. Instead of offering thoughts of sympathy, she pressed on. "I read her work. Noah knew about it too. He could have only learned about it from Gemma. When I brought you that box, you already knew what was in it. Now I understand why you were mad at me, but that boy just told you things that a first year medical student – no, I'm sorry, he was just *finishing* his undergraduate degree at the time – and would not be familiar with her work."

Aaron was not prepared for her onslaught of the truth as he leaned back in the chair.

Eyes blazing she continued, "Furthermore, the medical techniques he shared were all in Gemma's *unpublished* notes!" She huffed, "Which you claimed you never read," she added heatedly. She threw the pen she had in her hands down on the table. "In addition, you ran around this hospital accusing us of tampering with the settings on the monitors. The equipment wasn't faulty, it *was* Gemma! I believe it!"

"Don't be ridiculous, Willow."

She ignored him and continued "Come to think of it, since the patients in 524 woke up, Gemma disappearing and Noah leaving to start school, there have been no more strange occurrences, misplaced files, issues with elevators, missing items from offices and labs that nobody could account for."

Aaron was incensed and ran his hands through his hair and across his chiseled jaw. "Willow, do you hear how insane this all sounds? Do you really expect me to believe any of this?"

Willow gasped and her jaw dropped. She pointed at him forcefully and said, "I asked you if there was anyone who would change those frequencies or the formula and you quickly said no, but you had the same strange, distant look on your face as you do now. You were thinking about Gemma and how she would be the only one who knew the formula. You already *knew* she was working on that project," she accused. "I bet you read her notes but disagreed with her, you probably thought her ideas were too outlandish or that it wasn't practical, until she became one of your patients. It wasn't until that time that you decided to perhaps consider her work." She paused, "unfortunately you couldn't figure out her formulas and it was too late. I think she came back to finish what she started."

There was a strange stillness in the room and the doctor cleared his throat and folded his hands. He was all business. "Do you know how ludicrous this sounds?" He gestured fanatically. "How did you even know about all of this? How did you put this all together?"

"I ran into Jackson, *your* patient. He came to see you while you were on vacation. He tried to reach you but you didn't return his calls. We started talking. He was having bad dreams and mentioned Noah and Gemma." She stopped and watched his facial expression change from curiosity to surprise. She knew what he was thinking. "Okay, who cares about the privacy policy, Aaron," she said reading his mind.

He shifted nervously in his chair.

"I'm leaving anyway. I started digging deeper and then the additional transcripts from the security camera arrived. I watched the tapes and saw Noah talking to someone he referred to as Gemma. You and I never watched *all* the tapes only a few of them! I also saw the notes from when you did hypnosis on Anna and she mentioned Noah and Gemma. Now I understand why you closed yourself off from the rest of us. That's why Jackson is dreaming about them. I bet it's happening to Anna too."

If it was true, he didn't want to admit it. He also didn't want to reveal the truth about what Danella had told him regarding Anna's dreams; instead, he reasoned differently.

"It's subconscious recall," he argued.

"Really? Then how do you explain why Noah was referring to someone named Gemma on the tapes while he was in the patient's rooms? Seriously Aaron, you heard what Noah said, 'They were reading to both of them.' Isn't it possible they were listening? It's not like it's a new technique."

Aaron said nothing. He had no answer.

His silence was enough evidence for Willow. She said, "If Anna is dreaming about Noah and Gemma she needs your help too."

"Willow, this is all too much," Aaron said wearily. "How am I to explain to Anna she was talking to a ghost!"

Willow ignored him. "At first I thought Noah was talking to himself, but then he started moving the patients and continued having conversations with nobody else in the room. I watched all the footage. After that, I had the security guard let me in your office and I found Anna and Jackson's files and began mapping out the commonalities. I hastily grabbed the files and in the process I found this." She bent over and pulled something out of her leather bag. "This was in one of the files," she pushed the worn journal toward him. "These are letters to Gemma aren't they?"

His journal. He'd been looking all over for it.

"You read this?" He asked, stunned that his private thoughts were no longer confidential.

She nodded. "I didn't mean to pry. It was just in the file and once I began reading, I couldn't put it down."

Aaron closed his eyes in embarrassment. *She read my intimate thoughts and about how I felt about her.* He rubbed the back of his neck and looked up at Willow, humiliated.

His face was colorless and his eyes were incredibly sad looking. "Gemma was my Sunshine; that was her nickname. She had the biggest and brightest smile that lit up the room when she walked in. She was always happy. Christmas was her favorite holiday. *Everyone loved her.* She and I worked side by side," his voice trailed off…

Willow could see how much discomfort he was in from the way his voice trembled and from the sorrowful reflection in his eyes. She said nothing as he struggled with every word. "I would…write to her…it was…my therapy…Doctor Lucardi, my therapist, suggested I write to help ease the pain…"

"You were hoping that she would return," Willow finished when she saw it was too excruciating for him to continue. "I think deep down you *believed* in Gemma's ideas – no matter how outlandish they seemed – you *believed* because in your letters to her you make reference to, 'her journey, what she saw, who she is visiting.' You believed or perhaps wanted to believe that when someone is in a coma the mind is traveling somewhere else…you asked Gemma who she saw… you were referring to your wife…you wrote to Gemma as if she was coming home or as if she was going to eventually wake up."

Aaron nodded in defeat. "It's all true, Willow, and I'm so sorry that…that…I…well, let's just say as a doctor, you think you can handle it because you give bad news to families more often than you'd like. But when it becomes your *own* family… the reality was *devastating* for me!"

"I'm sorry, Aaron. I am sorry for your loss. I am sorry all this happened," she said sadly. Her heart ached for him, his family, and his pain. She wanted to give him a hug, but knew it would only make things more confusing between them.

"Do you know that when my wife and daughter were brought in they were immediately admitted to the south wing? I knew the truth but didn't want to face it. My other children understood and urged me to end it, which I eventually did for my wife. But with Gemma, I refused to listen and today my children will not speak to me. I had such hope. I really thought Gemma would come back to me. She had always said when we were discussing other patients, *'If it was me I would find a way to come back, Dad.'*"

Willow swallowed hard. She felt heartbroken for his loss.

"I visited and read the doctor's notes daily. When she passed, I wanted no special treatment, no pity. I just wanted to work. I didn't want the staff talking about it or discussing my life. Maybe I should have spoken about it more," he said despondently. "I should have taken more time off. I thought if I worked, it would help ease my pain, but it didn't."

"I'm sorry. I understand you loved your wife and daughter and the way they died was so heartbreaking and tragic, but I'm sure they would want you to move on. This is so unhealthy for you."

Aaron didn't know if he was angry or relieved.

She caught the momentarily flash of fury in his eyes as he fidgeted uncomfortably in his chair.

Willow ignored any of his impending rage and continued. "This isn't about me or anyone else. *You're just pissed* that Gemma didn't come looking for *you*! I read your journal notes – you *wanted a sign from her*. You wanted *her* to let *you* know that *you* did the right thing. You wanted to stop feeling so *guilty* for ending her life. Ask yourself this, Aaron, is that how you wanted her to live the rest of her life in some comatose state? With you visiting daily hoping she was going to return?"

Aaron leaned back in the chair and rubbed his forehead. *He didn't want to admit she was right.*

Willow continued when he didn't respond. "Gemma found a flaw in her high-frequency brain study, but you didn't believe in her ideas or in her work. You were *never* going to entertain any of her theories and she knew it. So she found someone else who would not only believe but needed her too," she huffed as she gestured helplessly.

Aaron closed his eyes as anxiety filled him. He didn't want to admit the truth.

"Did you ever stop and think perhaps *you didn't need her and that someone else did?* You heard the boy; he was thinking of not going to medical school. I looked up his grades and spoke to some of his teachers. He studied and worked in *this* hospital to save money to go to college while he was in school. Apparently he is very intelligent and perhaps needed some guidance from up above! While this story seems impossible and I'm not sure what I believe, but I am certain *something happened*! Didn't you hear what he said - it was *Gemma* who helped him get *focused*! *Your Gemma, she helped someone who really needed it! Perhaps that's what her message to you was! Perhaps just this once, you'll have to take a leap of faith!*"

Chapter 154

Alastair

"A leap of faith," Alastair muttered. Once he heard those words he quickly realized he was in more trouble than he could imagine. His reactive behavior caused him to miss the basic fundamentals of life. It was simple – he needed to pray harder, which was difficult as he was desperate to speak with the Lord more than ever before, but the Lord was not answering, and he was beyond impatient. He stood and stretched as he decided what to do next.

"Okay, Lord, I guess I owe you an explanation." He noticed Cooper, who had been swimming in the Reflection Pond again, emerge and slowly walk in his direction. He stood in front of Alastair and rapidly shook his body. Water landed all over Alastair before he realized what the dog was going to do.

"Thanks a lot. If I wanted to cool off, I would have jumped in. Now sit still; I need to tell my story. It will make me feel like *someone* is listening to me," he said as he emphasized the word someone, making sure his voice was a bit louder.

Cooper immediately sat at his feet and cocked his head to the side as if waiting for him to talk while Alastair got comfortable.

"I should have mentioned Gemma the minute she went missing from the group."

"Why didn't you tell me what really happened, Alastair?" the voice of Lucius boomed.

Alastair shuddered, as he shot up from the rock he was sitting on, as he was still not accustomed to Lucius popping in and out. His head turned quickly as he looked for his presence. As his eyes scanned the area, he grabbed his chest, startled, as he discovered Lucius by his side. "You gave me a fright," he shouted as he tried to catch his breath. His breathing deepened as his body bent forward as if he was gasping for air. "Lucius, why must you sneak up on me? Can't you announce yourself like a normal person? My state of mind is too fragile for this. I feel like I'm dying another death each time you do this to me," he said as his body returned upright.

"If I remember correctly I did; unfortunately you looked the other way first," he stated calmly. "You really must compose yourself, Alastair, you're overreacting again," he said as he rubbed his hands together. "Why don't you continue your story?"

Alastair could have sworn he detected him smirking. There was an unmistakable glint of humor in his eyes as he watched him dust off his glimmering robes. Perhaps it was his imagination or just his nerves he thought. He certainly wasn't going to challenge the respectable angel over something so trivial.

"I have a full schedule today, Alastair," Lucius reminded him sharply.

Alastair immediately sat back down. "I lost the new arrival list and wasn't sure if she got processed. Because she did not get processed she never made it to…"

Lucius scratched the back of his neck as he sat down. His facial muscles were tightly crimped, and apprehension was etched, deep in each of the vertical lines stretching across his forehead. "I'm not sure I follow."

"Due to my technologically challenged, incompetent self, I accidently deleted the new arrival list on my angel bracelet."

"Mmmm, now we're getting somewhere. Go on," he urged.

"You know, everything would be so much simpler with a piece of parchment…the days of writing it down was so much easier!" Alastair said innocently.

The great angel raised his eyebrows in annoyance and looked as if he was losing his patience. "Alastair, if I wanted to discuss your opinions on the technical achievements of mankind I would have asked, but right now I suggest you get on with your story."

"I tried to retrieve the list but couldn't," he quickly added.

"Why didn't you tell one of the other angel supervisors?" Lucius interrupted.

Alastair was clearly distressed. "I was going to try again later, but I received an alert that the group had arrived early. Once in the training area, I noticed one empty cloudbank. "The class informed me she was called to another group at the check-in point. Since I didn't have anything to verify the statement, I believed them."

"As the days wore on the empty cloud-bank began to disturb me. In all my centuries as an Angel Trainer, I had never had an empty seat in my class. It seemed odd." He grimaced as his facial muscles tightened in annoyance. "If it wasn't for the group's incessant and disruptive behaviors, I wouldn't have forgotten about it," he said crossly as he shook his fist in the air.

"When did you realize there was a problem?"

Alastair groaned and realized his fate was clearly hanging by a thread. "Shortly after I discovered the miscreants hacked into the old database, my angel bracelet blazed with a 'White Alert.'" Alastair paused and took a deep breath. "I quickly scanned the notification and when I saw the female was assigned to me but never reported to my group, I was horrified. It was then I realized I was lied to. She never completed the check-in process and I had no idea where she could be. I lost a student," he whispered.

Lucius raised his eyebrows tentatively his expression was unreadable. They sat in awkward silence. Alastair had no idea what to say, but deep down in his heart he knew the truth.

Lucius cleared his throat before he spoke. "Alastair," he said sharply, as he looked him in the eyes. "What are the first three commandments for all new angel arrivals?"

Alastair sat straighter. "Well, there are ten specific commandments and...

Lucius cut him off. "There is no doubt in my mind that you can recite all the commandments and every rule in the Angel Code book, amongst others, but that was not the question," he bellowed vociferously. His voice echoed around them and his emerald green eyes glared like an impatient snake ready to seize on its prey.

Alastair fidgeted nervously and immediately stood up out of respect and began reciting the list. "Number one: Don't Ever Leave New Angels Alone. Number two: Don't Ever Bargain with New Arrivals - No Matter What the Circumstances. Number Three: Don't Ever Break Rules Number One and Two." Alastair stared wide-eyed in horror at the great angel. He had broken not just every rule, but the most important ones and more. "What's going to happen?" he muttered quietly.

Lucius stood and gave him an ominous, last warning. "I fear time is running out, Alastair. If you don't fix this, I shudder to think..." Lucius was gone before Alastair had the chance to ask any questions.

Alastair was shaking so much he slumped to the ground, paralyzed with fear and anxiety. As he lay there thinking how doomed he was, he heard Cooper splashing around in the pond again. The juxtaposition of his pain and the dog's happiness only made him gloomier.

Chapter 155

Willow and Doctor Aaron Carter

Willow was done talking. She got up and headed for the door.

"Willow, please wait," Aaron called after her.

She slowly turned and was startled to find him right in front of her.

He put his hand on the door and closed it. "Willow," he sighed as he breathed in her familiar, floral scent. "I don't want you to leave. I know I've made some mistakes."

"I'm sorry, Aaron," she interrupted. Her heart was racing at his proximity. She was sure he could hear it pounding against her chest. "I am flattered by what you wrote about me in the journal, and at least I know I wasn't crazy when I felt something going on with us. If only you had the courage to speak to me. At least now, I understand why you didn't ask me out," she said softly as she looked down at her shoes. Her stomach was in knots. If she didn't leave now…her thoughts trailed off.

"Willow?"

She swallowed hard and lifted her head, forcing herself to look at him. "You have nothing to feel guilty about, Aaron. Your wife has passed. Either you move forward or you don't."

"Sometimes it's just not that easy," he stated solemnly.

Willow nodded. "It must be extremely painful and I can't begin to understand your loss. I won't deny that I feel something for you, but the truth is - I just left a bad relationship and don't intend on starting another one! I think you need more help. Don't you see what the guilt you are carrying around is doing to you? It's not healthy. How can I possibly deal with that on a daily basis? Nobody should have to and I deserve more!"

"But that's what I'm trying to tell you; I just went back to therapy."

Willow smiled. She was happy for him. "One or two months of therapy *aren't* going to change things! You need time to heal and I need to figure out my own life!"

"Where will you go?"

"I'm taking some time off. I only agreed to stay and cover while you were on vacation and help train your new assistant," she said indifferently.

So she didn't stay for me, Aaron thought. He took a step away from her and the door.

"Aaron, the truth is I'm only recently divorced. My ex-husband is a cardiologist and he cheated on me with my best friend, who worked in the same hospital. The relationship was both physically and mentally abusive."

It was his turn to look shocked. "Willow, I'm so sorry," he shook his head sadly.

"I rushed out here thinking I could just start over, but I never healed, so I have some recovery of my own to do and need to tie up my own loose ends. I also want to travel a bit. I'm not sure what my next chapter is. Starting something with you right now isn't right. It will only end badly for both of us."

"I'm going to miss you," he whispered.

Willow did her best to hold back the tears that were ready to burst from her eyes. The best that she could do was nod. She forced herself to give him a half smile, said nothing and quickly departed. "And I'm going to miss you," she said once she was outside in her car. She rummaged in her purse for tissues as the tears streamed down her cheeks.

Chapter 156

Anna
Summer 2002

" Chris, I'm worried about Anna. She's becoming a recluse. All she does is paint and barely leaves that room!"

Chris kissed his wife lightly on the forehead and smiled as he proudly watched his son playing with blocks. He sat down next to her and the baby on the rug and started making funny faces and Cody laughed. Chris handed him another block.

Danella stretched while Chris played with Cody. "Perhaps he's going to be an architect someday the way he is stacking those," she laughed.

"Well, they are one of his favorite toys," he grinned as he handed his son another block. "Do you really think Anna is not doing well?"

"I'm not sure, Chris. Remember how outgoing and happy she used to be?"

"You have to remember that was the Anna we once knew."

"Okay, you're right. But now, it's like she has become a loner. It's not good. It's great she's painting all the time, but she rarely gets out of that room. I have to coax her to come outside for some air with me and the baby or even to eat with us."

Cody grabbed more blocks from his father's outstretched hand. "Is she speaking to the doctors on a regular basis? I thought she mentioned the doctor told her she was doing well."

Danella bit her lip. "Well she claims she is…but now that you mention it, perhaps she is *not* talking with him on a regular basis as you and I thought."

Chris ran his hands through the baby's hair and began tickling his neck. Cody laughed.

"Look, I remember one call we had and the doctor said painting is good therapy for her and her art is selling. People love the paintings she is doing. Danella, you worry too much. Let her paint. That's her therapy. At least she's not alone."

"I disagree. She barely eats and is losing too much weight. Then there are those strange dreams she has. Something is terribly wrong. I think we should call Doctor Carter again. Something isn't right."

Chapter 157

Jackson and Doctor Aaron Carter

"It's good to see you, Jackson," Doctor Carter said surprised as they shook hands. "I'm so sorry I didn't get your messages, but I was on vacation and when I returned in April, I had so much to catch up on. Then I was making a lot of changes in the department. One of them was my calendar, of which. I have asked my executive assistant to start keeping. Things were just getting too hectic and I had to make some modifications. Anyway, Willow did tell me you came by and I did tell my assistant to call and put you on my schedule for an appointment."

"No problem, doc," he smiled brightly. "No explanation needed. She did call but I've been busy. I'll follow up with her next week and make an official appointment."

Jackson was dressed in a gray suit and tie. "You look like you're on your way to the courtroom. What are you doing here? You're not going to sue the hospital for something," he joked as they stood in the lobby.

"I was just coming to see if you have time for coffee with an old friend."

"Absolutely, I know a great café on the campus. We can grab some lunch too."

Once they were settled the doctor asked, "So tell me, what brings you to the hospital? I know it wasn't to see me," he laughed.

"I don't know. I guess I missed you and the landscape," he chuckled as he rubbed his chin. "I did call to make sure you were here today."

Doctor Carter chuckled. "Really, what are you up to?"

Jackson took a sip of his coffee and gave him a brief rundown. "I left my father's firm, moved out here, and decided to set up my own practice. I'm actually going to be doing some work for the foundation and just finished meeting with the hospital attorneys."

Doctor Carter raised his eyebrows in surprise. "I can't imagine what your father said after that announcement. It's pretty drastic."

Jackson chuckled as he described the incident. "In the end we came to a compromise. After I took some time off, I decided to set up shop out here. I'm going to take the state bar exam and do what I need to become official. I'd like to help out at the hospital."

"Well, it sounds as if you are happy."

"I am. But I do have some questions to ask you and want to discuss some things that are troubling…"

"Jackson, this is really not the place to talk about your recovery." He interrupted. We can schedule time for that."

Jackson flashed him a half smile. "Look we are just two friends who are having lunch. We did run into one another in the lobby, didn't we?"

Aaron nodded.

"Besides, I did make an appointment and your staff input the time incorrectly so we are having my appointment during lunch at *my* request and not in your stuffy office."

The corners of Aaron's mouth curved into a grin as he nodded. "Nice attempt at avoiding the policy. Also, I didn't realize you considered my office stuffy."

"Well, today I do," he laughed.

"Okay, but next time in my office."

Jackson got the message and didn't want to overstep the patient-friendship boundary. He nodded knowingly.

Doctor Carter leaned forward. "How is your health overall?"

"I don't feel as anxious. Living out here is growing on me. I like the slower pace of life. It suits me. I feel relaxed and much calmer. Don't get me wrong, I have my days and still have crazy dreams, but I'm working on it. I'll schedule an appointment with you."

Aaron was surprised and glad for him. "Willow mentioned you two spoke."

"Willow, what a beautiful and helpful person she is," Jackson's smile widened when he said her name. "I was surprised and sorry to hear she was leaving and that the job didn't work out. She seemed like she had it together. I told her to keep in touch."

"Yeah, well people come and go. Sometimes it's just not the right fit," Aaron added solemnly. "Did she by chance tell you where she was going? You're not going to be chasing after her, now that you're single?" *Aaron was horrified at the thought.*

Jackson eyed him suspiciously. He saw that look of pain in the doctor's eyes. "For someone who doesn't seem to care you seem *too* interested. I told you to send flowers; didn't you listen to me?" he laughed.

Aaron rolled his eyes and gave him the highlights of his flower caper.

Jackson burst into a fit of laughter and said, "Well at least you gave it one hundred percent effort!"

Aaron rested his chin in the palm of his hand and said, "I don't think I'll ever send a woman flowers again."

"If she loves you, she'll be back! And if she comes back you better make it right!" He smiled. "Hey, speaking of women, I wanted to ask you if you could tell me anything about the girl that I apparently shared the room with while I was in the hospital?"

Aaron took another sip of his coffee before answering. "How did you hear about that?"

"I received my father's mail by mistake and noticed he paid her hospital bill.

To make a long story short, he accused me of having an affair with her!"

Aaron had heard the bill was paid and was surprised Jackson's father followed through with the suggestion. He probably felt guilty. Although the senior Wilson believed his son and the girl had no relationship to one another, Aaron had convinced him to pay just in case it turned out his son did know her; besides, it would make a nice donation, which was to be anonymous. He would be violating the agreement if he said anything.

"Nothing really to tell. She already returned to her family. You two just happened to be in the same room as there were not enough beds at the time. You do know that your father did make a generous contribution to the hospital, perhaps that was part of his donation?"

Jackson shrugged. "I guess you're right. Okay, mystery solved."

Chapter 158

Anna and Doctor Aaron Carter

"**A**nna, it's good to hear your voice. How are you?"

Anna didn't want to take the call, but Danella insisted. "I'm fine, Doctor Carter," she answered. Her voice was a soft whisper.

"So I was thinking we could talk a bit about Noah and Gemma, Danella told me you have dreams about them and…"

Anna was mortified. "Danella had no right to tell you about my dreams, she interjected."

"Anna please calm down. She is your friend and just wants to help you. She and Chris are worried about your health. So please don't be mad at them."

An uncomfortable silence lingered before she blurted, "there is nothing wrong with me. I'm fine," she eventually said.

"Anna, I know you are having difficulty; it's to be expected considering what you have gone through. I need you to start thinking how to face your fears. I promise it will help you. We could talk by phone and you may want to start by going…"

"Face my fears? I'm not sure what you mean?" she interrupted. "I'm not afraid of anything!" she said adamantly. The tension in her voice did not go unnoticed.

"Anna," the doctor said firmly. "We know your history; your father, the fire, and the loss. I know you're afraid…"

"I'm afraid of nothing," she shouted a bit too loudly into the phone. "Thank you for calling Doctor Carter, but I have to get back to my work!" She hung up before he could say another word.

Anna was sorry she spoke to the doctor so rudely, but she really didn't think there was anything wrong with her. *I just want to paint and make up for lost time,* she justified.

Chapter 159

Chris

"I would like to meet the artist who painted the paintings I've purchased."

Christopher was busy making coffee and handed the gentleman his cup. "I'm sorry, sir, the artist doesn't meet with patrons. Can I ask what you're doing with the artist's work?"

"They're hanging in my office, and I'd like to commission some additional pieces for gifts."

"Like I said, it's impossible. The artist works off site. The art is sent by courier and I never know when the next shipment will arrive."

"Ok, I'll stop by again, and maybe I'll see something else. The coffee is excellent. Thanks for your help."

Chapter 160

Jackson and Doctor Aaron Carter

Aaron met with Jackson at least once if not twice a month. While their friendship had grown beyond the doctor-patient relationship he still made sure to keep it professional when it came to Jackson's care. He did give Jackson the option of seeing another physician, but Jackson wasn't interested. They mostly talked about hospital business and his life in Hunters Glen. "Are you going to look for a place to live anytime soon?"

Jackson chuckled at the thought. "Why should I? I like the inn and the people; besides, I don't have to worry about taking care of all the problems that come with owning a home. Furthermore, the food is delicious!"

"Have you considered moving to Seminole?"

Jackson shrugged nonchalantly. "I just left a big city and I'm not sure if I want to move back into another."

"You don't have to live *in* the city. You can live on the outskirts of it. There are a multitude of quiet neighborhoods nearby."

"I don't know, doc, for the first time in my life I am feeling really relaxed in a smaller town. Hunters Glen has a special character to it; besides, the women in the shops and restaurants all know and love me," he said as he smiled roguishly.

"They are only gossiping and just wondering who is going to get the first date with the rich attorney," he laughed spiritedly.

"Well, that's the last thing on my mind right now. I just like the small-town vibe. In the big city, I was always moving, there was always a schedule – I was just rushing to get from one place to the next. Half the time, I didn't know what I did all day. The pace and the constant noise – it was just too much. My mother told me I never had the anxiety I've been suffering until after the accident. In Hunters Glen, it's quiet and peaceful. The air is clean, and I know someone everywhere I go. It's kind of nice," he gestured indifferently.

"Have you made a decision about what I recommended for your therapy?" He knew Jackson was still on edge and having difficulty sleeping.

Jackson rested his chin in the palm of his hand. His facial muscles contorted and he shook his head. "I think about it and when I contemplate driving in that direction, I have heart palpitations and begin sweating profusely," he answered honestly.

"I could give you a sedative," the doctor offered.

"No, absolutely no prescriptions. If I'm going to do this, it will be without medication."

The doctor scratched his neck and said, "When the time is right, you'll know. Not to change the subject, but just remember I will be out of town for the next few months. You can reach me by phone if you need me. My book is coming out and I'm committed to some lectures. I may not be available but you can leave a message. I promise I'll call you back. Is there anything on your mind today regarding your recovery?"

Jackson looked the doctor in the eyes and got right to the point. "Noah and Gemma. That's what's on my mind. I want to know more about these people who haunt my dreams."

"Jackson, we've already discussed this," he said as he removed his glasses and rubbed his eyes, as he was not sure he was up to conversing about either of them.

Jackson ran his hands through his hair. "I'm sorry, doc, I just find it hard to believe, and I keep having dreams about them."

Doctor Carter looked down at Jackson's file and shuffled some papers around, "Unfortunately the dreams are the same.

You haven't disclosed anything different," he said as he looked up and stared pensively at his troubled friend.

Jackson put his head between his hands and ran his hand through his sandy blond hair. "Ugh," he shouted looking up. "It's bothering me and I think about them more than I care to admit."

Doctor Carter shook his head, sighed, and gave him a short version of the story again. "Look," he said firmly, "I don't know if I believe it myself, but I think perhaps your subconscious mind heard them or just Noah talking and reading to you."

"A housekeeper and a ghost? They aided in my recovery?" he asked with skepticism.

Doctor Carter shrugged, "Noah was a porter who *insisted* he saw the ghost of my daughter and he was helping patients wake up. Is it conceivable? I still have no answer."

Jackson burst out laughing. "I still don't believe it. Can't you do better?"

"Jackson, we have already been over this," he said as he scratched his neck and sighed exasperated. "I previously told you the story and also about my personal loss and grief. You must know how difficult this is for me as well," he said as he glanced down. He didn't want Jackson to see him get upset.

Jackson could see he was getting agitated. "I'm sorry, doc," his eyes and brows scrunched, as he had momentarily forgotten about the doctor's personal tragedy. "I hate that you're in pain too," he whispered sincerely. "I just have difficulty believing the rest of it. Did you add this in your book?"

"Absolutely not! My credibility as a physician would be ruined!"

Hearty laughter resounded in the office from both of them.

"Seriously, Jackson, you need to think about the implications if this really reached the ears of the public."

Jackson searched his face before speaking. "I understand why you're keeping this quiet. It has to do with my father?"

Aaron nodded. "Yes, *and* people *like* him."

Jackson huffed. "Yeah, I get it, he would love to sue the hospital for anything and something like a housekeeper, who wasn't a doctor, helping a patient, who was his son…it would be scandalous," he whispered knowingly as his eyes widened.

"Exactly," the doctor interrupted as he threw up his hands. "And then there is the trauma center that I worked hard to help build for sick people. In addition, the reputation of the medical school needs to be considered as well."

Jackson nodded. "I see your point."

Aaron fidgeted with the coffee cup. "Besides, I promised Willow – she was the one who put the pieces together. She's like a detective and wouldn't give up."

Jackson noticed how his eyes brightened when he spoke of her, but he also saw something else. It was a faint, glimmer of pain and the forced smile when her name was mentioned. "You miss her, don't you? Why don't you just call her?"

He couldn't bring himself to tell Jackson she didn't leave her number; instead, he ignored the question. "I just promised her I wouldn't do anything to ruin the boy's medical career."

Jackson leaned forward. "Can't you tell me about *the girl*?"

Doctor Carter hadn't spoken much to Anna. She didn't want to talk to anyone. As long as she was painting, she believed she was doing well. His attempts to speak to her about Noah and Gemma failed. He planned to give her some space before he'd make another attempt to talk with her, even if he had to drive to Hunters Glen.

Aaron peered at Jackson over his glasses that had fallen halfway down his nose. "Friendship or not, we have been over this before. Unfortunately, I can't. It's a violation of a host of hospital privacy policies, not to mention I could lose my license and…"

"Come on, doc," Jackson pleaded. "You know my father accused me of having an affair with her and…"

"Look, Jackson," the doctor interrupted as he rubbed his forehead. "You need to let it go and concentrate on yourself. Perhaps there will come a time when you two can meet. She is not in a good place right now so it could set her own recovery back and I don't think you want to be responsible for that! I've said too much already," he stated, as he finished his coffee.

"I want you to think about what I said earlier – perhaps you should drive out to where the accident happened. We can do it together. It might bring you some clarity or even peace."

"Truthfully, doc, I don't think I can handle it."

"What are you afraid of?" the doctor challenged.

"I considered it at one time, but I like the way my life is going. I don't want to do anything to jeopardize a relapse of any sort. Going to the scene of the crime, so to speak, could produce something that I'm not willing to address."

Chapter 161

Noah and Crystal
Fall 2002

Noah and Crystal grabbed seats up front in the packed lecture hall. The fall semester had just started and they were excited about their new courses. They spent the summer taking classes and had talked about moving in together as their relationship, to the surprise of their classmates, had changed from adversaries, to friendship to official couple.

It made sense as they had become inseparable. While both their families disapproved, feeling they were rushing things, they also knew there was nothing that was going to keep them apart. Noah's mother believed he was too young to get serious and was afraid he was heading down the same path she had taken with his father. While she knew Noah wasn't like his father and had better morals and values, she was a mother and still worried.

"Trust me, Mom, and have faith," he said to her one day over dinner. As she studied him she was amazed at how much he had change in the last year. He even decided to cut his hair, and no longer had those scruffy locks flying in his face. He was beginning to look professional. In the end, she helped them get settled in their new apartment.

Weeks prior, they wouldn't have thought about moving in together because they hadn't yet worked out how they were going to *even* pay for an apartment. This all changed one afternoon before the semester began when they were both summoned to the Office of Dean Edwards.

"Did we do something wrong, sir?" Noah questioned; his voice strained as he was a bit nervous.

Dean Edwards peered at the two of them over his bifocals. His cheeks were beet red and the veins on his neck protruded angrily. It was clear he wasn't happy. "No!" He spat annoyed. "Have a seat," he gestured toward the two chairs in front of his desk. His lips were pursed as if he was getting ready to announce he was going to expel them immediately.

Noah and Crystal looked at one another in horror and thought perhaps the Gemma incident had been exposed.

"I'll get right to the point," he said firmly, as he opened the file forcefully. "A mysterious donor has awarded you both full scholarships!"

Noah almost fell off the chair. He gripped the arms tightly, "Did you say *full scholarships*?"

The dean's paunchy neck hung over his tight-fitting shirt, looking as if it was going to choke him. His facial muscles contorted and his eyes tightened as he peered furiously over his glasses again. "*What* is there something wrong with your hearing? If there is, I suggest you get it checked by the school nurse. *I said full scholarships for you both*!"

Noah and Crystal gasped in unison. "*A full scholarship for both of us!*" Crystal shouted.

"Do you have any idea who would award *both* of you scholarships?" the dean growled as he slammed the paperwork on the desk furiously. The blood flowed back and forth from his baldhead to his flushed face. Noah thought his tiny capillaries were going to explode.

Crystal and Noah jumped in their chairs.

Dean Edwards regarded them suspiciously as he watched their faces for any signs of recognition. He was puzzled, and it seemed they were just as stunned.

"Is that it, sir? Can you tell us anything else?" Noah whispered.

Dean Edwards ran his hand over his head a habit from when he used to have hair. He was now completely bald and blamed his hair loss on the students and the stress of the job. "No!" he hissed. "There is nothing more to divulge. You both have *full scholarships*. And *if* for some reason you *have no culinary skills*, your benefactor has included meal passes as well!" He picked up the paperwork and smirked, "Oh and I almost forgot, there is one stipulation," he gestured with his extravagant, school-issued fountain pen.

Crystal and Noah held their breath as they waited for the dean to speak.

"You both need to maintain *your* grades!"

"Sir, does it say anything at all? *Who* could it be from?" Crystal inquired excitedly.

"No!" He barked crossly as he thrust the papers into a file folder and slammed it shut. "*That's the problem*! The donor wishes to remain *anonymous*," he gestured frantically.

Noah and Crystal looked at each other, bewildered.

The dean removed his glasses and leaned forward. His eyes blazed as he glared at the two of them like a wolf stalking his prey. It was evident he was just as confused and agitated, as his hands continued to slice madly through the air as he spoke. "Do you *two* realize *I* know *every* endowment, scholarship, and award that is distributed? I have spent *years* cultivating relationships with people and *now* some *mysterious donor* comes along and *awards* not *one* but *two full scholarships, mid semester* and *I* don't have a *clue* who it is!" he stated bitterly before he took a sip of his cold coffee.

Noah and Crystal sat unmoving as Dean Edwards continued his rant. "Now I must spend time adjusting the budget and report to the board, that *I* have *no* idea *who* this person is and they will want to know *how and why* I missed developing a relationship with some potential benefactor who apparently has lots of money…"

"Sir," Noah interrupted boldly. "When does it start?"

The dean shook his head and handed them some paperwork. "*Now!*" he answered sharply and dismissed them with a wave of his hand.

Noah and Crystal were overwhelmed as they quickly stood to leave.

"There is one more item," Dean Edwards said, as his lips curled and eyebrows furrowed in annoyance at the arrangement he knew nothing about. "Apparently your benefactor wants to make sure that all you do is study, so your apartment is paid for as well!"

They both shuddered and their shoulders jolted when he put extra emphasis on the word benefactor.

"My executive assistant will give you keys and the rest of the financial details." He shook his finger at both of them, "I'll be monitoring your grades and if I see one B minus, I'll be forced to report it to the board immediately!"

Noah and Crystal practically ran out of the office and could hear Dean Edwards bellowing into the phone, as he tried to uncover more information about the mysterious patron. They laughed and hugged one another tightly once outside. There was much speculating about the donor. "My mother doesn't have that kind of money," Noah claimed.

"Neither does my family," added Crystal. "Who else do we know who would do something like this? Two full scholarships is extremely monumental. Besides the professors, the only people we know are Doctor Carter…"

"No way," Noah immediately interrupted. "He doesn't think too highly of me after the story I told him, and what I was doing on the fifth floor in his section of the hospital. I'm the *last* person he'd give a scholarship to. I'm lucky he allowed me to remain in school – and that's only because of Willow."

"Perhaps she had something to do with it," Crystal deliberated. "We really don't know too much about her."

Noah shook his head. "It's possible, but I heard she quit. I have no idea where she went; besides, she was renting an apartment, so I doubt she had this type of money. If she did, she probably wouldn't have to work."

Once inside, they grabbed lunch and sat next to each other in one of the corner benches to continue their conversation as they scanned the contents of the envelope. "Noah, what's wrong? Your face it's as white as a ghost!"

Noah looked around to make sure nobody was listening. His voice was barely a whisper as he leaned closer toward Crystal. "I know this sounds weird, but do you think Gemma had something to do with this?" he asked in disbelief.

They looked at one another strangely. "Is it possible?" Crystal wondered out loud.

Noah didn't know what to think. "I don't know. I'm dumfounded. Should we say something?" he wondered.

"Noah, you heard the dean; the donor wishes to remain anonymous. So we'll be grateful, study hard, and create scholarships of our own when we become doctors someday."

Noah nodded. "That's a fantastic idea!" Crystal was right. There was no reason to speculate. They would just be thankful and simply pay it forward. Together they began writing down their ideas for future scholarships in a special notebook.

They were so busy with school, studying, and planning their life together that the entire Gemma episode was forgotten. Well almost.

Noah eventually told his mom about Gemma one evening over dinner. Her only comment was, "The Lord moves in mysterious ways." If it was true, she was thankful that divine intervention helped guide her son.

When Noah was alone, he prayed and thanked Gemma for everything.

Chapter 162

Alastair

Alastair was pacing frantically, after he admitted to Lucius how he broke the most important rules for new arrivals. Clouds of dust followed as he kicked stones and dirt in his frustration. He was trying to decide if it was considered a lie or if he just omitted the truth. Was it on purpose or did he do it unconsciously? Was it possible for an angel to veer so far off the path that reality and fantasy become intertwined and distorted? The clarity of messages becomes ambiguous? What about his knowledge regarding Gemma?" he deliberated.

While he wasn't sure about Gemma or what her role was, it was apparent something occurred – and that something happened on his watch. He had become careless.

"Cooper, I don't even know why you hang with a miserable, old angel like me?" Cooper sighed as Alastair walked by. "Why do you bother? I'm sure you're sick of listening to me and…and…oh my…you stay because…"

Alastair's stopped speaking mid-sentence and his frown turned into the biggest grin. He began laughing and shook his head and shouted, "The answer has been in front of me the entire time – I was so caught up in my own misery…how could I have been so foolish?"

Alastair immediately dropped to his knees and began praying. He bent forward with hands folded and head down and prayed harder. Tears flowed from his face as he finally realized he'd been praying in desperation only because he was attempting to get out of his own mess. I created more of a mess by leaving out the facts. "I am sorry, Lord," he cried. "I twisted and manipulated what occurred to try to justify my actions. You may have heard me but had every right *not* to listen. I never really asked for help… I am lost and I should have trusted you and for that I am deeply sorry."

Alastair's knees dug deeper into the ground as he bent further toward the earth. "I forgot about my relationship with you and I understand why you don't answer me. I know I have failed you. Lord, forgive me for losing my faith."

Alastair lost track of time as the days passed but he continued praying and asking forgiveness and, eventually, he felt a warm light on his back. He immediately looked up. His eyes were transfixed on the sky above. His eyes sparkled and he grinned as he sought out Cooper, who was seated across the Reflection Pond. For the first time since their arrival, they were bathed in brilliant beams of sunlight, which was now shining down upon the entire area.

Chapter 163

Willow

Willow was excited and nervous. She was starting her new job today. There were too many *what ifs*, and she didn't know how she was going to deal with deciding which one of the *what ifs* could actually come to fruition.

Chapter 164

Jackson and Doctor Aaron Carter

"So how's our *ghost whisperer*?" Jackson chuckled as he spoke.

Doctor Carter ignored the question. "Jackson we need to talk about *you* and what is going on in *your* mind," he illustrated as he pointed to his head.

"Do you want to know what I think about a lot lately, doc? *Noah and Gemma.*"

The doctor sighed as he leaned back in his chair and closed his eyes.

"You know I've finally realized this is just as difficult for me as it is for you to talk about. So how about we try to get through it together?" Jackson suggested.

The doctor leaned forward and stretched. They were meeting in his office today. He wasn't surprised at this reasoning. "Always pragmatic and to the point! I bet you graduated at the top of your class."

Jackson beamed proudly. "Naturally, my father wouldn't have it any other way! I could have worked anywhere. But I don't really want to talk about him today. I want to know more about *The Ghost Whisperer.*"

"He's currently at the top of *his* class. He's smart and works hard. He has a serious girlfriend, who studies just as hard and has perfect grades too."

Jackson's eyebrows creased and he frowned suspiciously. "How do they afford school? I thought you told me Noah was very poor? Furthermore, for someone who isn't interested, you seem to know a lot about them."

The doctor shrugged as if he didn't care. "It's not uncommon for doctors to follow the new students. We need to know who is excelling…what fields they may be leaning toward… who they may be interested in training with…we hear things. As far as the money, I have no idea. Do I look like the financial aid department?"

"Really, doc, I think you can do better than that," he grinned.

He discovered the truth. "I feel like I'm on trial today. You must have been phenomenal in the court room."

"From what I've been told, one of the best, especially in research and that's one of the reasons why my father is so angry at me." He leaned forward in his chair, "So let's get back to the *Ghost Whisperer*," he smiled warmly.

Aaron wasn't going to hide anything. It was just a matter of time before Jackson discovered the facts especially since he was working with the hospital board and their lucrative foundation.

"Well, I understand they took out student loans. Noah had a small, partial scholarship and was working in one of the labs. It was hard not to hear about Dean Edwards and his ongoing investigation. The man really should retire. He is so focused on finding some donor who gave Noah and Crystal both full scholarships along with an apartment."

"Ahhh, it all makes sense now," Jackson said knowingly. "The mysterious donor. I found the paperwork in the files when I was sitting with some of the board members discussing fundraising. Apparently Dean Edwards is in the hot seat about some monies that appeared at the last minute. The board members claim it's scholarship money and wouldn't provide any more information. Naturally, I became suspicious and they explained about some fund that was recently set up. I just started putting the pieces together. Do you really believe Noah's story, doc? I mean, two full scholarships to medical school? Is it worth the risk? What if it's all some sort of hoax?"

Doctor Carter debated what to say next. He eventually said, "after viewing the security tapes, I'm not sure if I believe it either. Perhaps Noah is a really good magician," he grinned. "All I know is that Noah and someone he claimed to be Gemma, talked to patients, including *you,* every night. Somehow it aided in your recovery. If his story were true, Gemma would have wanted it that way. Let's just say I'm taking a leap of faith!"

"A leap of faith? Why I'm a bit shocked," he smiled cheerfully. "The great Dr. Aaron Carter who is rooted in scientific methods and needs to prove…"

"A good friend suggested I try it," he interrupted as he held up his hand indicating the conversation had ended.

Chapter 165

Anna
December 2002

Danella already had her white hat and furry boots on and was excited about the trip. "Don't forget we're going to get a Christmas tree and we'd like you to come with us today," she reminded Anna, as she popped her head in her apartment and dropped off extra gloves.

"Uh, I don't know. I told you I don't think it's a good idea," she said as she turned away from the window where she had been enjoying her morning coffee.

Danella had been arguing with Anna since yesterday about going out and she had enough.

"Anna, you haven't been out of this room in months!"

"I go outside," she argued

"Sitting out back doesn't qualify. You need to do this for Cody. It will be fun and you are Cody's godmother after all. I want to take some pictures of you and the baby. It's his first Christmas and you need to do this for him!" she finished sharply.

Anna sighed reluctantly. She owed Danella and Chris her life. Perhaps if she went, they wouldn't bother her again about going out. She took a deep breath. "Okay, what time are we leaving?"

Chapter 166

Anna

"**W**hy are we stopping?"

"There's traffic and some congestion ahead," Chris said nonchalantly. He smiled as he checked on Anna and his child in the rear view mirror. He was amazed at how fast Cody was growing. They had just celebrated his first birthday in November.

The pickup truck crawled along the highway. There were vehicles parked along the sides of the road.

"Chris, can you park? The baby is fussing. I'd like to walk a bit."

Anna's heart started racing at the thought of getting out of the truck. People were walking everywhere.

"Um, I'm not sure about this," Anna said. Her voice was a bit raspy and she clasped her hands nervously as Chris parked and got out.

Danella was sitting in the front and twisted in her seat to face Anna in the back. *"Anna, I've had just about enough of you, your sullen emotions and attitude. Your behavior isn't healthy for you, Chris, me, or Cody. You need to get on with life! It's Christmas. Cody has needs and all you can think about is yourself! Can't you find something to be happy about?"* she snapped as she exited the vehicle.

Anna flinched nervously as the door slammed.

Danella came around to the other side of the truck and said nothing as she unbuckled the baby from the car seat and met Chris as he had already retrieved the stroller from the truck bed. *She was sorry she was so rude but enough was enough!*

Anna sighed heavily. She wanted to cry, but quickly brushed the tears away from the corner of her eyes, opened the car door, and followed. She hadn't realized what she had been doing to her friends. Danella and Chris had been nothing but kind and generous. She needed to get herself together. The fresh mountain air stung her face the moment her feet touched the ground. It was not only refreshing but reminded her immediately of the haze of pollution she had left behind on the East Coast. Why she thought about that, she had no idea. She hadn't left the safety of the studio since her arrival and wasn't paying attention as Chris drove because she was sitting in the back seat entertaining the baby, so she had no idea where she was. Chris, the baby, and Danella were already out of her sight.

She stopped walking to let people pass. She was on some scenic path that overlooked the stunning, snow-covered mountains. The view was breathtaking only she couldn't understand why there were so many people lingering. As she followed the path, hoping to catch up with her friends, she caught bits and pieces of conversations. "Tragic…too bad…what an unfortunate way to pass…the poor soul…do you think…I didn't know him…she was my neighbor for twenty years…they had gone skiing…"

Anna could feel her heart start beating faster. A wave of fear and anxiety filled her as she began to understand where she was – the crash site. Her eyes filled with tears again as she scanned the crowd looking for Chris, Danella, and the baby. There were too many people. She started walking backward. She was shaking.

"Are you all right, miss?" a woman stopped to ask her. She nodded and mumbled she was okay. She turned and kept going down the path. The anxiety and fear were strangling her as she wondered why Danella and Chris – her best friends could bring her here. She was shaking and sweating and felt lost as she stumbled through the crowd of people, frantic to return to the safety of the vehicle. She looked for the truck but there were cars and people everywhere. Anna felt as if she was carrying hundreds of pounds on her back as she trudged forward. "Hey miss," someone called. "Be careful! You're too clos…"

At that moment Anna felt her shoe catch on something and in the next instant she was tumbling in dirt and gravel…

Chapter 167

Jackson

Jackson had arrived and was walking along the footpath. He found a picnic table and sat gazing out at the ground below. People were dropping off flowers and other mementos and leaving them in specified locations. There were markers below and signs posted around the crash site with a list of the people who passed. It was a miracle he had survived.

He had finally read the articles in the local library one afternoon after he observed a plaque on the wall that spoke of the tragedy. The librarian pulled the information and one by one, he scanned through them all. His heart raced as he read about his reality – how buses had collided due to a storm, falling snow, and rocks – construction should have been diverted and halted that night but wasn't.

Since the incident, highway traffic had been routed away from the edge of the mountain, the scenic look out points had been relocated, and sturdy guard rails were installed. There were still some incomplete construction areas but they were roped off.

Jackson looked at the drop below. His heart was racing and he could feel his blood pressure rising as beads of moisture dripped down his back. He wasn't sure how long he would stay or how being here was going to help him. "This is ridiculous," he muttered. He didn't know why he decided to come. The receptionist at the inn told him to avoid the highway due to the traffic for the special ceremony. It was a last-minute decision and he didn't even tell Doctor Carter his plans. His apprehension was building and he could feel the familiar, tight knot in his chest. "When are you going to help me?" he asked, as he looked toward the sky.

Shouting from a crowd interrupted his thoughts. Jackson turned his head. "What the…" he muttered as he squinted at a faint image that flashed to his right.

"Someone help!"

"Holy shit," he screamed as he jumped off the bench and started running as best he could with his bad leg.

Chapter 168

Anna

Anna could feel herself tumbling down the mountain. She was begging for God to help her while her arms thrashed at dirt and rocks as she tried to grab on to something. The snow and ice made it worse. "Noooo," she called as she continued to slip. Her foot suddenly got caught on some rocks and roots, which stopped her from falling further. She was shaking and breathing heavily as the tears began streaming down her face.

"Why!" she shouted as she looked toward the sky. "Why are you doing this to me?"

Chapter 169

An Unexpected Meeting

"*O*ver there," a man shouted. "She's down there! I think she jumped over the side of the mountain!"

Jackson limped forward and from the corner of his eye he thought he saw someone fall over. It had happened a few feet away from where he had been sitting. He stopped dead in his tracks when he heard the voice calling out for help. "Shit," he muttered. He reacted immediately and peered over the side. "Answer me if you can hear me…are you okay?"

"I don't know," the voice cried out anxiously.

"Call for help," he said firmly to the crowd that was growing around him. He then turned and yelled over the edge, "Don't move; I'm coming for you." And without thinking, Jackson slid down the side of the mountain, using his cane to help guide him from slipping too fast, as he tried to get close to the female.

"It's going to be okay. What's your name?" He called.

"Anna," she whispered, in between sobs of terror.

Jackson's adrenaline had peaked so much that he didn't have time to be terrified. He kept his voice calm and steady, as not to make her nervous, so she wouldn't slip further. "Can you reach for my cane, Anna? Grab on to it. I promise you I will not let you go."

Anna looked up and tried to focus but was afraid to move her hands to wipe the tears streaming from her eyes. She squinted and it appeared a man was sliding down the mountain, with what appeared to be a disability, as he was holding out his cane. It was too surreal. "I can't. You're too far," she shouted.

"Give me a minute. I'll try to come closer." Dust swirled around them as he slipped further down. "Keep talking to me. Take deep breaths. I'll be there in a moment."

There was something about his voice, it was soothing, and the more he spoke, the more she began to focus. While her heart was still racing, the river of tears had temporarily stopped.

"Your voice. It sounds familiar. Do I know you?" She moaned as the pain on her side pulsated.

Jackson smiled. "I doubt it, I can assure you I don't usually make it a habit of bringing any of my dates this far down the side of a mountain. I prefer a quiet evening at a restaurant."

Anna was breathing heavily and was silent for a minute before her lips curled into a half smile. "Oh, you're joking, right?"

He grinned. The distraction was all Jackson needed. He was close enough and slowly inched forward. "Just reach for my cane," he called again.

He felt the tug, as she grabbed on to the end.

Jackson had slid halfway down a dangerous mountain – a mountain that had almost killed him – and even he wasn't sure if he was going to be all right. He was positive he'd need intense therapy after this. There was something about the girl who was clearly paralyzed with fear that was spellbinding. "Just sit tight, and I'll come to you."

Jackson slithered in the mixture of ice, dirt, and snow, towards her and held out his hand. "Take my hand; it's okay," he called.

She tentatively reached for his hand and when their fingers touched something happened. It was as if lightening had struck them simultaneously and a galvanizing charge of energy coursed through their veins. They both stared at one another wide eyed as it occurred within a split second. Jackson saw the distress in her eyes as she quickly released her hand from his.

Not wanting to drop her, he instantly grabbed her hand again and held it tightly. In that moment, his head immediately felt as if it was going explode as image upon image flashed within. It was so fast, he felt as if he was on a ride that was spinning out of control. He had no idea what happened. Upon opening his eyes, he saw her face twisted in anguish.

Her eyes widened instantly as she gripped his hand tighter in terror as everything around her was spinning. He released his hand and swiftly inched closer and dragged her toward his body and wrapped his arms tightly around her shoulders as she passed out. He yelled to the bystanders at the top of the mountain, "She's in shock. We need help now!"

The rescue team was already on their way and as he waited he felt the strangest sense of peace fall over him as he held her tightly in his arms.

"Oh no," Alastair muttered as he dropped to his knees, bowed, and began praying again. "Lord, I have faith that you will help these two; they do not deserve such pain due to my own impetuous behavior. I know I am repeating myself and I will continue to admit to you that I have lost my way and desperately need your help...the answer was in front of me the entire time and I was too blind to see it...I was not listening to everyone who I have encountered on this journey. I am ashamed at myself for my feeble attempt to negotiate my way out...ugh...the magnitude of my desperation reached is inexcusable! I can't blame you for not listening to me," he cried out. "Save them Lord, please, I accept my punishment, but save these people. Do what you will with me, but these people deserve to live! I take full responsibility for my actions and the entire escapade and for my lack of faith."

Alastair continued as he summoned all the strength and willpower he could muster as he repeated his prayer over and over again...and continued asking for forgiveness.

Chapter 170

Jackson

"*I*'m okay!" he stated curtly to the medic's as he began dusting himself off. "Just help her; she needs assistance now!" Jackson stepped aside while they tended to the girl. As they worked on her, he moved quietly away from the scene and headed toward his car.

"Not so fast, buddy."

Jackson turned and found himself face to face with more paramedics and a few police officers.

"This is not necessary," he said as they led him back to another ambulance.

"Sorry, sir, you need to answer a few questions and must be checked out at the hospital," the officer replied sternly. "You could have a concussion and we don't need you driving around these treacherous mountain roads if you're not feeling well."

Jackson wasn't going to fight it. While the paramedics took his vitals in the ambulance he described what occurred.

From the emergency room he made a phone call from his cell phone.

"It's Jackson. I need to see you. It's important."

"Well, hello to you too, Jackson," Doctor Carter answered a bit sarcastically. "Unfortunately, it will have to wait. I have an emergency with a patient and can't talk with you right now. I will call you when I'm available."

The resounding click annoyed Jackson. "But I had a break-through," he whispered.

The blond-haired nurse adjusting his IV heard him. She smiled and flirted. "Is there something I can help you with?"

"No, I'm fine. I just need to check out," he said impatiently.

She got the message. He barely looked at her and she wasn't going to waste her time. Turning quickly, she made some notes on his chart and checked the vitals on the monitors. "Not until the doctor clears you. He'll be in shortly," she said sternly.

Chapter 171

Chris and Danella

"She'll be okay," Chris assured Danella as he sat with her in the waiting area. Baby Cody quietly entertained himself with toys attached to his stroller parked on the other side of her.

"No, it's all my fault. We shouldn't have agreed to this intervention with Doctor Carter. We shouldn't have left her alone – this was a stupid idea," she cried as the tears rolled down her already red cheeks.

Chris put his arm around her tenderly and wiped her swollen face gently with his thumb. He looked her squarely in the eyes and said, "Danella, you need to stop. After speaking with Doctor Carter, we all agreed her health was in jeopardy. Anna needs *serious help*. She would never have consented to a trip to the crash site. She requires more assistance than we can provide for her. This was part of the plan, take her to the crash site, and meet up with Doctor Carter. We never anticipated the crowd or that the doctor would be stuck in traffic."

"The plan didn't include her falling down the mountain!" she interrupted. "We shouldn't have left her alone," she repeated. "If I hadn't pressed her, this wouldn't have happened," she sobbed. "I just don't understand; she was there one minute and…and what do you think made her get so close to the edge?"

Chris pushed Danella's soft hair away from her face. "It's not your fault. The witnesses said she tripped. She is going to be all right."

"I heard people say she was crying and confused," Danella interrupted sharply. *"I will never forgive myself if something happens to her!"*

Chris exhaled deeply, held her hand and rubbed his wife's back as he continued to comfort her. "Danella," he said firmly, "Doctor Carter said Anna was already in a fragile state and should have sought more treatment; instead, she refused to face what had happened. She was becoming a recluse and her health was suffering. She needs more care than we can provide. Don't worry. I'm confident the good doctor will know what to do. Let's just pray he can help her."

Alastair prayed harder than he had ever prayed in his entire life. He asked the Lord to give them the strength and fortitude to get through. "Have faith everybody," he whispered.

Chapter 172

Anna and Doctor Aaron Carter

*H*er eyes fluttered open as she tried to focus on her surroundings.

"Well hello, young lady. How are you feeling?" Her eyes were sunken and she looked terribly pale. Scratches covered her face and she had some contusions and a broken arm. He read the rest of the chart and while her bones would heal he was worried about her mind and the lack of progress she had made.

"Doctor Carter?" she asked, unsure why he was in her room.

"Do you remember what happened?"

Anna blinked and gasped. "I fell…and…it...was…terrible…I fell down the mountain," she began sobbing as her hand flew to her face.

"Shh…you're fine," he said confidently as he handed her some tissues.

"What are you doing here? How did you know I was here?" Anna whispered, still confused.

"Well, I received a call from your friends, who I understand are very worried about you. You weren't trying to hurt yourself were you?"

Anna shook her head.

Doctor Carter shifted in his chair; he was extremely concerned about her state of mind. He could see how exhausted she looked by the dark circles under her eyes. Even the red scratches couldn't hide her pale skin. He needed to try a different approach. "Anna, I'm going to be completely honest with you. Your health has declined considerably. You need to focus on getting better – this includes trying to recall what you have been blocking out. You are *never* going to be able to go forward unless some progress is made. The stress isn't good for your well-being. But if you want to spend the rest of your life locked in a room painting, that is your choice," he said nonchalantly.

The doctor ignored the tears that were streaming down her pale face and continued speaking.

"But you can't do it at Chris and Danella's. They have a family and a life and can't spend it worrying about you; it's not healthy. So you need to decide if you want to get better. Your friends are suffering because of your lack of participation and, quite frankly, I can no longer treat you in this manner. Again, it's your choice," he said firmly as he folded his hands.

Anna was blindsided. Doctor Carter had never spoken so harshly to her before.

"I didn't try to kill myself if that is what you think," she cried.

He handed her some more tissues.

"Then how did you end up falling?"

"I did something terrible," she stated.

"Anna, I need the truth, the entire truth. If you don't tell me, I can't help you." He stated firmly.

The tears continued streaming down her cheeks. "I remembered something, fragments of what I have been seeing in my dreams and I was so frightened…and confused…there were so many people and I was lost…I tried to get away and I looked over to the side and I slipped on the gravel and simply fell."

Doctor Carter breathed a sigh of relief. She confirmed what he already knew…that she wasn't suicidal. "I think you've known for a long time what happened and have chosen to ignore it all. Again are you going to tell me the truth and why you refuse to discuss anything?"

When she didn't respond he repeated the question. *"I need the truth, Anna. It's time,"* he said briskly.

Anna began sobbing uncontrollably before she finally blurted out her crime. *"I killed a man!"*

Doctor Carter's eyes opened wide and his jaw dropped, astonished at the revelation. This was certainly a new development. He couldn't see someone like Anna involved in a killing. "Why don't we start at the beginning and you tell me what exactly happened?"

Chapter 173

Jackson

"**N**urse," the emergency room doctor bellowed, "where is the patient who was in here?"

The nurse came running in as soon as she heard Doctor Chase yelling. She scratched her head as she stared at the empty bed and tubes hanging from the disconnected equipment. "He was here a minute ago," she answered a bit nervously as she ran and checked the closest bathroom. "Oh my," she gasped as her hands flew to her face. "His clothes are gone!"

"Alert security," the doctor shouted, as he thrust the chart into her hands, clearly annoyed that this had happened on his shift. There would be more paperwork and reports to fill out and he wouldn't be leaving on time.

Chapter 174

Jackson

Jackson had quickly dressed and was in the parking lot waiting for the taxi he had called. He felt fine and the last place he wanted to be was in the hospital. He tried to call Doctor Carter twice but it went directly to voicemail. He didn't bother leaving a message. He needed to talk with him immediately and his anxiety level was intensifying. It was so bad he could hear his heart beating against his chest.

"Are you Jackson Wilson?" a voice called to him.

Jackson nodded and slowly made his way to the black Chevy Blazer, which had pulled to the curb. As he grabbed the door handle, his eye caught sight of an attendant getting into a black Mercedes from the valet area. He watched as the man drove the vehicle toward the parking lot.

"Are you coming? I have two more rides to pick up after you," the young driver said a bit impatiently.

Jackson reached into his wallet and grabbed a fifty-dollar bill and thrust it toward the kid. "Sorry, I've changed my mind as I've forgotten something in my room."

The taxi driver took the cash, shook his head, and sped off.

Chapter 175

Jackson

"Who are you here to visit, sir?"

Jackson gave the receptionist his nicest smile. "Hello, I am Doctor Aaron Carter's assistant and it seems he left his wallet in my car. Can you tell me what room he is in?" He grinned and winked as he waved the leather wallet in front of her.

The girl blushed and grinned seductively. "You can leave it here and we can get it to him."

Jackson leaned forward and made sure he looked deep into her eyes and smiled brightly. "I can see why the hospital has you working at the reception area. You aren't only beautiful but also smart," he said cheerfully.

She blushed again and Jackson beamed, as he continued to compliment her hair and clothing.

His stomach lurched. Flirting like this was beneath him, as he hated to resort to such trickery. He made a note to apologize later. "I'm his assistant and he would never forgive me if I let his *personal information* out of my sight. He is very particular about things like this. I should only be a minute. You wouldn't want me to get fired, would you?"

"Well, I guess it will be okay. I'll look up his location." She typed into the computer and grabbed a pass. "He's in room 212.

Take the elevator to the second floor, make a right and follow the signs."

Jackson took the pass, thanked her, and winked as he headed for the elevators.

Chapter 176

Danella and Chris

Chris and Danella had moved to another waiting area and were expecting to see Anna at any moment. Chris had just returned with coffee and some snacks for Danella and the baby. Danella continued talking about how worried she was about Anna when she noticed Chris twisting in his seat. She followed his gaze to the elevators. "Chris? Are you listening to me? What's wrong?"

Her husband was frowning and his brows were furrowed. His face hardened as he scrutinized the visitor. "What the hell is he doing here?" he asked, as he jumped up and chased after the man. Danella stared open mouthed. She had never witnessed her husband projecting such fury. The hairs on the back of her neck stood and she shivered as she wondered what was going on.

Chapter 177

Anna and Doctor Aaron Carter

"So that's what happened," Doctor Carter. "*That's how I killed him!*"

"Anna, how can you be so sure?"

"I see him every day. I see him in my dreams, at the bottom of the mountain, just lying there face down. He *died* because I couldn't help him. I'm telling you he *died* because of me! I just don't know how I can live with myself knowing this!"

Before he could respond the door flew open and hit the back of the wall with such force that the room shook. "There you are," the voice spat accusingly.

Doctor Carter stared in disbelief. "Jackson," he said firmly, "I don't know *what* you're doing here, but this isn't the time, I can assure you," he gestured. "How did you know I was even here?" he asked, bewildered.

"I saw your car. You're the only doctor I know who drives a luxury vehicle in the snow!"

"Seriously, Jackson," he said miffed. "I'll have you know it's not snowing and I checked the weather, so I'll drive the car of my choice," he shook his head exasperated. "Furthermore, I told you, I had an appointment and was not able to speak with you when you phoned. You're not my only patient. Now what are you doing here?"

"That's what I'd like to know," announced Chris, who entered the room next. "What are *you* doing here? Why are *you* stalking her?" He pointed to Anna.

"*Stalking*," Jackson answered, stunned at the accusation, as he turned and looked at Chris. "I admit I have my faults, but don't be ridiculous. *Never* in my life have I stalked someone and I don't intend to start now!"

"Then why are you here? What do you want? I already told you *no*," Chris spat clearly annoyed.

"Chris, what is this about? How do you know this man?" Danella demanded as she had grabbed the baby and followed her husband down the hall and into Anna's room.

"This is the man," he pointed at Jackson. "This is the man who bought some of Anna's art and wants to commission more. He's the guy I told you about who keeps coming to the gallery to buy coffee. He wants to meet the artist and I told him *no*. He is getting *obsessed* and Anna doesn't need that right now!"

"This is the gentleman who bought one of the lily paintings?" Danella gawked as she scrutinized him. Instinctively she somehow knew this handsome man, who clearly had some disability or injury as was evident by his cane, was not a stalker. "You actually think he's a stalker?" She asked her husband incredulously. She continued to glare at him and her tone suggested it was highly doubtful.

Chris nodded. "That's what I'm trying to tell you," he said impatiently. Hand gestures cut through the air as he continued to explain who the man was to his wife.

Jackson was barely listening. His gaze wandered to the girl in the bed and back at Doctor Carter, as he limped further into the room with his cane. He turned toward Doctor Carter and said suspiciously, "Something is wrong and I think you have the answers," he said pointedly.

Just then two large hospital security guards entered the room. "Doctor Carter, are you okay? We have a missing patient who appears to be *pretending to be your assistant*. We saw him on the security camera, tracked him here, and he fits the description of this man," the head guard pointed at Jackson.

"See…he's a stalker and a liar," Chris confirmed.

Like an owl, Danella's head whipped around and she glared at her husband. "Chris," she spat, "you can't go around accusing people like that!"

"Okay, everyone calm down," Doctor Carter laughed. "First, my last assistant was female and she recently quit. I can assure you I came out here alone. But not to worry, I know him," he pointed to Jackson. "While he has his faults, I can assure you stalking is not one of them. He can stay. I'll call you if I need help."

Jackson limped over to get a closer look at the female in the bed as the guards departed. "You're the woman from the mountain," he stated. "You're the woman that I helped rescue."

"Do I know you?" Anna whispered. *His voice, she thought she recognized it.*

Jackson looked over at Doctor Carter again. "I think there is more to this story. This is the patient you needed to see?"

Doctor Carter nodded. He smiled inwardly. He was going to let the truth come out and see what happened. The original intervention involved Anna, Chris, and Danella. Unbeknownst to Jackson, the doctor was going to call him to meet only after his assessment of Anna, but this was turning out to be even better. "Jackson, stop hovering over her. Sit down, you're scaring her," Doctor Carter said sharply as he watched Anna's facial expression.

Jackson moved slowly around to the side of the bed away from everyone. "I'm right, aren't I, doc?"

"Why don't you tell me, Jackson," the doctor said confidently.

"I've been trying to put the pieces together for so long. I started thinking about the events…"

"I'm sorry, I'm confused," Danella blurted. "This is the man buying the 'Lily' paintings, so what?"

Doctor Carter held up his hand, toward Chris and Danella, nodded and mouthed that it was okay.

Jackson pulled a chair toward the bed and sat. "I didn't mean to scare you; it's just that I think you and I have met before. He held out his hand, "May I?"

She nodded.

He slowly reached for her hand and she met him halfway. He closed his eyes when they touched. "Lily," he whispered ever so softly that nobody could hear him. Minutes later she dropped his hand as if it were on fire.

"Anna," Doctor Carter called. "It's okay. Tell me what you see. Is everything all right?"

Anna smiled as her hands flew to her cheeks. "*He's alive. I didn't kill him.* I didn't kill him," she cried. "It's him, the images were all so blurry before, but now…its him…it's really him and he's alive," she shouted jubilantly.

There was a brief moment of silence in the room, before Chris and Danella began yelling, "Killed someone? Who? Anna killed someone? What's going on? Who did she kill?"

"Him," Doctor Carter pointed toward Jackson, smiling.

Chapter 178

Anna

"Anna, you don't even know this man." Danella cried. "How could you possibly think you killed him?"

Anna stared straight ahead as if in a trance. "I wanted to surprise you. I wanted to make it before Christmas. The weather…I was rushing…there was an unexpected storm…the visibility was so bad… …there was more snow…falling rock…and then deer ran out in the road…then the crash…there were buses and cars …they tumbled down the hill. It all happened so fast," she whispered as tears began rolling down her face.

Doctor Carter looked around the room for another box of tissues but saw she had already wiped her tears away with the back of her hand.

"I somehow managed to get out of my vehicle and then I heard someone calling… the fire…it was all around me," she gasped as she could barely get the words out. Her mouth was dry and she reached for her water. Jackson quickly passed the cup to her.

"Fire, but you're afraid of fire," Chris said. "Or, let me re-phrase that, you're terrified of it!"

"I know," she mumbled. "I heard him calling out for help… the car, it was on its side…he was half in and half out…I couldn't let him die and I just went to help. I crawled across the snow and rocks…I kept telling him to hang on and that he had to live…somehow I pulled him out…it was so dark and there was so much smoke and flames and then…"

She paused and her heart was racing as she continued recalling the events of the accident.

"It's okay, Anna," Doctor Carter said reassuringly, as he leaned forward and rubbed her arm. "Just continue slowly."

"There…there was an…an explosion and I don't know what happened next."

Danella and Chris gasped.

Anna took another sip of water before she continued. "During my recovery, I started to remember bits and pieces of things. At first it didn't make sense. Then when I realized the truth, I thought it was my fault…that I killed him. First my parents and then this! I was so distraught."

"Anna, your father was an alcoholic and fell asleep with cigarettes burning. That's what started that fire that killed your parents," Chris reminded her. "It's not the same."

Jackson's eyes grew wider at the revelation.

"But it is," Dr. Carter corrected. "Anna is afraid of fire and the dark and has been most of her life. She risked her life to help someone in a fire, she told him to hang on because she didn't want him to die. She didn't want him to die as her parents did. As some of her memory started to return, she assumed she killed him."

"Oh, Anna, is this what's been haunting you?" Danella cried.

She nodded. "Yes, I was so afraid to say something, and when the dreams were getting worse, I was ever so certain that his death was my fault. I felt so guilty. But I could never see his face…just his body laying there as I tried to help…until our hands touched," her voice trailed off into a whisper that nobody heard the last few words.

"Is this why you were calling for Noah and Gemma?" Who are they to you?" Danella questioned.

Anna's face twisted in agony. "Noah and Gemma were the only ones who knew me and my pain. They came to see me.

They were with me…they helped me wake up. I dream about them and I wanted desperately to talk with them. I didn't think anybody would believe me and…and then Gemma…she told me it was okay, but I really believed I killed him," she pointed toward Jackson.

Doctor Carter beamed. "Anna, you didn't kill him, rather you saved his life! I'm sure if you continued with your therapy, we would have discovered this sooner."

He looked at Jackson, "Wait until your father hears about this."

"Her voice… She's the one," he whispered. "This is the woman, I shared the room with, isn't it, doc? This is the woman that my father thinks I had…um…had…and…knew prior?"

Doctor Carter nodded. He made a mental note to review his notes on voice recognition and talk more about it with Jackson and Anna at a later time. Perhaps if he had introduced them sooner… *Willow was right all along,* he thought to himself. "You both arrived together so everyone assumed you were a couple when they found you at the crash site! Your car probably was on fire and burst into flames after Anna pulled you out. You were found holding on to one another. People presumed you were together. Anna's car or what was left of it was found further down the mountain. I'm sure with all the confusion and chaos the details and correct facts were never pieced together."

"So you're not stalking Anna," Chris demanded while still glaring at Jackson, unsure if he could be trusted.

"I was out walking one day and was intrigued by the painting in the window. It called to me, and I had to have it. I can't explain why…there was just something about it…I felt as if I knew the place…like I'd been there before. As I told you, I only wanted to meet the artist and commission more work." As Jackson spoke he never stopped looking into Anna's eyes. His father was right the truth always reveals itself, sometimes in the strangest ways.

Chapter 179

Doctor Aaron Carter
February 2003

"$\mathcal{E}$xcuse me, Professor, I was wondering if you had a moment?"

Willow recognized the voice immediately and looked up from the table where she had been stuffing papers in her leather briefcase. It was inevitable. She rehearsed over and over what she might say, but everything she thought she'd say, she had immediately forgotten the moment she looked into his blue eyes. The only thing she was able to mutter was, "Hello."

There was an awkward moment of silence as they both gazed openly at one another. For some reason her eyes glanced at his hands. She immediately noticed he was no longer wearing his wedding ring. She put her head down to hide her smile and continued stuffing her tablet and cords into her bag.

He walked closer to the table and grinned. "Glad you decided to stick around."

He wasn't going to ask why she didn't call him; instead he said, "What made you come back?"

I missed you. You look handsome in that blue shirt. It brings out the blue in your eyes.

She looked up and beamed. She could have told him the truth; instead, she said a bit nonchalantly, "I missed the mountain air."

"Well then, I hope the mountain air has been good for you."
Did you miss me?

There was another awkward moment of silence as she latched the satchel shut.

"I hope everything is going well for you." *Translation…did you get help.*

"If you want to know how I've really been doing the answer is extremely well. I'm in a much better place than I was when we first met."

She looked stunning. Her hair was cut shorter and styled in loose waves, which framed her face and fell just below her shoulders. The soft highlights and bangs gave her a youthful glow.

"I like your hair cut."

"Thanks. It was time. I needed a change." There was more uncomfortable silence before she spoke. "I know you didn't come by to sign up for my class," she joked. "It's entry level and I'm sure you could recite the course in your sleep; after all you did write the textbook."

She could have used many textbooks, but she chose one of his.

Eyebrows rose in question as he peered over his glasses and said, "Interesting selection?"

She grinned. "Don't think I had much of a choice, since you're the head of the department at the adjoining hospital and have made a bit of a name for yourself in trauma recovery… the university thought it was best. Oh, but don't be too full of yourself, as they did allow me to add other reading materials to the syllabus, which *I thought would be important*," she made it a point to emphasize the last few words. "After all, it is *my course*," she said warmly.

"Ah, the politics of it all," he nodded. "Actually I came to ask you something."

Finally? She looked at him anticipating the big question.

"Okay."

He held up an envelope which he had pulled from the inside pocket of his jacket. "It seems I was invited to a wedding. I was wondering if you would like to accompany me? No, what I meant to say was, I was wondering if you would be my *date* for the evening?" He made a point to emphasize the word date.

Willow's heart was racing. She took a deep breath. Did she hear him correctly? Did he just ask her out on a date? She looked quickly away from his face.

"Who's getting married?"

Aaron held the invitation towards her.

She took it and read aloud, "*Jackson Thomas Wilson and Anna Lily Sinclair.*" Willow blinked with surprise as she looked up. She read the names again and immediately knew the implications of the nuptials. *The coma patients?* Her head shot up quickly and her eyes twinkled. "Hmm. Well, this *is* an interesting twist. I was right all along," she smirked knowingly. "Something happened in that room with those two. They were communicating, the possibilities," she laughed.

"I would love to tell you all about it over dinner. You see I know this *fantastic* restaurant in town – that is, if you're not busy?" he asked with confidence.

Willow's heart was beating so fast she wondered if he could hear it pounding. She grinned, "Well, Aaron, you have perfect timing, as I have an opening in my schedule. I'd love to have dinner with you. It seems as if you have a most unusual story to tell me."

"Fantastic! Then it will be our official *first* date," he grinned as he grabbed her briefcase and they left the lecture hall together.

Chapter 180

Anna and Jackson
October 2003

Jackson and Anna had been inseparable after they learned about the circumstances that brought them together. Their courtship was quick and they were married in a small ceremony on the ten acres of property they purchased in May. Their immediate friends and family attended. Jackson's family welcomed her with open arms. They flew to New York to meet his family prior to the wedding who were astounded when they heard the entire story and how she was responsible for rescuing their son.

His father did his best to try to convince them to move back to New York on many occasions, including at the wedding. The conversation ended when he caught his wife glaring at him. "Warren, I think it's time we go outside and enjoy the fresh air," she said as she politely grabbed his arm and steered him toward the door. "Enough talk of work; this is a day for celebration," she reminded him.

Their log cabin was on a secluded area just on the outskirts of Hunters Glen. When they had both walked in, they looked at one another and told the real estate agent they would take it.

"But you haven't seen the entire home or property yet," she cried.

Lily laughed. "Let's just say, we've been dreaming about something like this for a long time. It's perfect!"

"Just draw up the contract and get it to me. Here's my business card," Jackson thrust it toward her.

Jackson, with the help of his father, had set up a small office for his law firm in town, which would be an extension of the New York office. His father made sure it was staffed appropriately and hired a partner in New York to assist his son, as his memory was still fuzzy.

Jackson agreed for he knew he would need support. He was in a much better place with his father, who visited monthly along with other family members. While he was no longer, nor would ever be the sharp, accomplished attorney he was in New York before the accident, he was okay with the entire situation. He enjoyed the slower pace of life and was able to manage with the help of his family.

While his father still hoped he would return to New York, he was glad he was still practicing law. Together they also helped Anna, Danella, and Chris manage the art studio and gallery. Jackson had passed the bar, was part of the legal team for the hospital in Seminole, and occasionally did some consulting work for the hospital in Hunters Glen.

Jackson kissed Anna deeply and pulled her close as they snuggled in front of the large, outdoor fireplace. While she still wasn't over her fear of fire, she was working hard to overcome it. "I love you, Lily," he whispered in her ear as they watched Bear and Bella, two large mix breed rescue dogs they had adopted, run around the property chasing one another.

Anna sighed deeply. She couldn't get enough of him. She wasn't surprised to hear him call her by her middle name. She wiggled in his arms so she was facing him. His eyes were magnetic and she could never get enough of staring into them. "When did you know, J.T.?"

Jackson Thomas or J.T., as his closest friends called him, didn't hesitate to answer. "Your voice…it sounded *so familiar* when I heard you calling out, but I couldn't place it. But the moment our fingers touched on that mountain, I saw images and the images came more and more, but it was like a movie on fast forward. When I touched your hands at the hospital, it all started coming back to me."

She giggled. "Is that why you loved to hold my hand so much when we were dating?"

Jackson gently caressed her arm. "Not really, I just wanted to be close to you. It felt right, and well…the images just helped me put the pieces together. To be honest, it wasn't until we kissed that I saw it all. Was it the same for you?"

Anna's breath caught in her throat. "Remember in the hospital when you whispered, 'Lily,' I was confused, but like you said…the moment our fingers touched – well, I started seeing the images too, and like you when we eventually kissed, I saw it all."

"Why didn't you say something?" he asked.

"Probably for the same reason you didn't. Plus I didn't want you to think I was crazy. Jackson, I keep thinking about it. Do you really think it all happened? Do you really think we both followed the light? Do you believe it was real?"

Jackson nuzzled her neck. "Lily, I totally believe it! I'm telling you I heard you calling for me."

"I was probably calling out to you because I was sick of hearing your family yelling when they came to visit!"

They both burst out laughing.

Anna Lily Sinclair Wilson smiled contentedly, as she absently ran her hands over the carved initials, J.T., in the worn picnic table. It was something they found on the property and kept it.

"Do you think we should say something?" She said after she told him how she came up with his name J.T.

Jackson turned and looked deep into her eyes. "Why? Nobody would believe us."

"I agree," she answered and kissed him lovingly on the forehead.

"Tell me something, how did you find your way back to me? You never really told me," he questioned.

"Let's just say I had some celestial help."

Jackson nodded. "Gemma?"

"Yes," she whispered.

"Are you going to tell Doctor Carter?"

Anna shrugged. "Perhaps at a later date. I think he's had enough heartache; besides, Gemma probably has her own way of communicating if she felt it necessary."

"What about Noah? Are you going to say something to him?"

Anna smiled. "At the wedding, when we danced, I simply told him Gemma would be so proud of him. He smiled and said it was enough for him. Noah is going to be all right."

"I think everyone is going to be fine," Jackson said as he rubbed her shoulders.

"Isn't it strange how *you* think you're traveling on the right path and then something happens that connects the *oddest* group of people and changes their lives and the road they had been traveling?" Anna wondered aloud.

Jackson nodded as he snuggled closer to her. "I know. When I look back I can't even imagine my life and where I was going. Then I wonder how I ever wound up with Saviella and didn't even know my best friend was sleeping with her. They left ahead of me that night and I stayed to ski more," he recalled. "I remember walking in on them. And my best friend or whom I thought was my best friend had the nerve to say when I caught them, 'It's not what you think!' Ironically those were the magic words that helped me recall the reason I had the accident."

"Isn't it weird we had to go through all of this to get here?" Anna whispered in his ear. "Why do you think something like this had to happen?"

"I don't know. It's like, you, me, Noah, Doctor Carter, Willow, Gemma, Danella, Chris...we're all part of some bigger story. A story *so immense* we can't even begin to conceive how it could possibly end. If you think about it, we're just a small chapter in a much, much, much larger book."

"Can you imagine what our lives would have been like if the accident didn't happen?" Anna questioned.

"I would have married Saviella, eventually discovered her cheating, there would be a messy and *very costly divorce*. I'd be miserable and perhaps my view of the world would have become jaded. I think my anger would have turned me into a bitter person. What about you, Anna?"

"I probably would have never sought help about my childhood trauma and at some point, would suffer a nervous breakdown."

Together they laughed as they continued to exchange possible scenarios for their lives if they had not met.

"You know, it took me a while to get over what Saviella and Adam did, only because their deceit hurt terribly. I think I was more troubled because I trusted them and *thought* they were my friends. When I first discovered them together, the shock of it all was too much, and I jumped in the car and just started driving, never knowing that I was driving toward something better!"

"Hmm. That's certainly an interesting way to look at things."

They hugged one another tightly and kissed.

"How do you think you missed what was going on?" Anna asked.

Jackson shrugged indifferently. "Probably because I was so caught up in my career, money, and what my father wanted for my life, I just missed all the signs and forgot about myself. I believe divine intervention or perhaps someone from above was just looking out for us and stepped in."

"Jackson," Anna said absently. "Do you think we will ever recall everything about our past? I know you've remembered a lot more than me."

"Considering what we've been through, does it really matter? I mean we have each other and, it's like my mother said, we'll make new memories together; besides, you have Chris and Danella, and Doctor Carter to help fill in the gaps, and I have my crazy family. Don't worry so much. I think we're doing extremely well so far."

The dogs wandered over and plopped down at their feet. "I guess they've had enough fun for the evening and are ready to go inside." Anna smiled as she bent down and hugged their furry pets. "I think angels are everywhere, and they're here for us when we don't realize we need them. Do you think Bear was an angel?"

"I don't know, but he certainly provided comfort and looked out for us."

"You know Jackson, dog spelled backward is *GOD*."

Jackson laughed. "You're not saying…"

Anna smiled merrily. "No, but it's something to think about."

"Enough talk for one evening. Let's go inside. It's getting chilly."

Hearing the word *inside*, the dogs immediately got up and ran for the front door.

Jackson doused the fire and they walked hand in hand ready to celebrate and face life together.

Chapter 181

Alastair and Lucius
October 2003

Lucius appeared behind Alastair, "So do you still think you need to see the Lord?"

Alastair's hand flew to his chest as he gasped and twirled around to face him. "If I wasn't already dead, you would have given me a heart attack and surely sent me to my grave. Why must you sneak up and startle me like that? Why can't you just announce yourself?" he asked exasperatedly. "I'm feverish with anxiety from the turmoil I have endured…the apprehension that courses through my body of the punishment awaiting me afflicts me like a pestilence…"

"Enough with the melodramatic monologue," Lucius interrupted. "I'm once again going to ignore your theatrics and repeat the question, do you still think you need to see the Lord?"

"No," Alastair said confidently. "I never made a mistake; it was all predetermined. I should have found a better way to deal with the group and not leave my post, but you knew I was going to do that. If I hadn't panicked and followed procedures, I would have figured it out. Again, you knew I was going to panic. You could have put a stop to all of this."

"Perhaps. But that was not for me to decide."

"Will I be released from the Reflection Pond?"

Lucius shrugged. "I think it is safe to say that you are ready to go; however, there is still one final part of your assignment that you must finish."

Alastair was confused. "I wasn't aware that I had an assignment, and what about Cooper? I've grown quite fond of him. We just can't leave him here. What if he can't find his way to the Rainbow Bridge?"

Lucius glanced at Cooper who was already heading down the rocky path. "What makes you think he doesn't know his way around?"

"I don't know; it's just that he was here with me the entire time…and…if he is lost, I'd feel really bad just leaving him…"

"Come Alastair, I have something to show you."

Chapter 182

Doctor Carter
December 2003

Aaron Carter picked up the worn journal. He had since sold his home and purchased a beautiful log cabin with Willow in Hunters Glen. He'd taken a page out of his friend Jackson's playbook and decided to slow down and enjoy life. He did some consulting for the trauma center in Seminole and would work at the local hospital in Hunters Glen to help improve the current trauma ward. Willow would teach some classes at the hospital and in Seminole. There was also a plan to merge Franklin Memorial with the program in Seminole.

As for Willow, he eventually disclosed more about his past, including what led up to the death of his wife and daughter in that tragic accident. When the time was right he'd tell her the rest of the story. Doctor Lucardi assured him it would be okay. If they were going to have a life together they both needed to share and would make new memories. They'd been busy unpacking when he came across the journal. He smiled as he flipped through the pages for the last time.

Willow came up behind him and rubbed his shoulders as they sat down on the sofa. "Doctor Lucardi told me to write my thoughts as part of my therapy. At the time I didn't realize how much it was helping me. As I look through this, I recognized at some point I had started writing more about *you* than *Gemma*.

In August I stopped writing letters completely and didn't even realize it!"

Willow kissed him on the cheek and gazed into his deep blue eyes. She was glad he finally sought the help he needed and was now in a much better place as was she, and knew he needed a moment. "I'll get us some more coffee."

The journal, once therapy to help him cope with the pain over the loss of his wife and daughter, was now, well, he wasn't sure. He was flipping through the pages when something caught his eye. "Incredible," he whispered. He did a double take as he looked at the unmistakable handwriting.

Dad –

I'm sorry I could not come back but it seems I was needed elsewhere. Don't worry you did the right thing. No regrets. My love for you is eternal. I'm glad you're happy.

All my love -

Gemma

Willow entered the room and saw him holding the journal with tears in his eyes. "Are you okay?" She asked as she sat down next to him on the couch.

"Yeah, take a look at this."

Willow grabbed the book and stared at the page. "What? I'm looking at a blank page. Is there something else you wanted me to see?"

Aaron scratched his head and looked over her shoulder and saw the words Gemma had written as clear as day. He smiled. "No, I guess what I meant to say, was this is going to be my last entry and I was showing you the page I was going to write on."

Willow looked at him a bit strangely and smiled. She knew how much the journal helped him get through the tragedy. She stood up and said, "Okay, I'll leave you to it and go finish up in the kitchen. Let me know when you're ready for dinner. There's a new restaurant in town I'd like to try or we can just stay home, and I'm looking forward to visiting Anna, Jackson, Danella and Chris for dinner tomorrow. It will be nice to see the baby and do some shopping…and those dogs, remind me to bring them some treats."

Aaron wrote a quick note, closed the journal, and put it in the box marked attic, as he absently listened to Willow talking about their plans. Life was too short to live in the past and he really wanted to begin enjoying life. He rose and went to tell his future wife just how much he loved her.

Afterward

Within a blink of an eye Alastair and Lucius had arrived at a large field. The grass was vibrant green, which was surrounded by trees and mountains as far as the eye could see. The brilliant sunlight shown through the trees creating the most picturesque of any landscape he'd ever seen. It was as if an explosion of light had just materialized and the rays filtered through every element in the spectacular landscape.

Like an Impressionist painting, light bounced off tree leaves and limbs, creating a brilliant, rainbow pallet of colors. Flowers of all varieties propagated throughout. It was as if the sun had burst into infinite rays and blanketed the earth with the most amazing floral display he'd ever seen.

Alastair was speechless as he observed the beauty around him. Lucius steered him to a bench and they sat. "What is this place?" he whispered.

"One of the most sacred areas of Gods celestial realm. Only a *few* have had the privilege to view this area," he answered proudly.

Alastair was still trying to take it all in when a movement in the distance caught his eye. He leaned forward and squinted as he tried to make out the object. It looked as if…no it couldn't be…or could it? His eyes grew wider as he tried to get a closer glimpse of what looked like a dog, but it was too far away. "That almost looks like...Coo…per," he stammered as he observed him running freely across the field. Alastair lifted his arm and hand to shield his eyes from the dazzling sunlight and thought the dog disappeared into the dense forest. Suddenly a huge, beautiful eagle emerged from the trees and flew majestically across the sky.

"God is with us all the time," Alastair stated smiling confidently. "Guardian angels are with us too, and we just never know what form they may take. I was *so lost* that I missed *all* the signs. *Finally, there's a reason for everything.*"

Alastair looked up at Lucius and quietly said, "Are you mad, sir?"

Lucius laughed and answered, "Young Alastair, why would you think that?"

"Well, thank you for the complement, but I don't know if I should be considered young, since I'm a few thousand years old," Alastair stated matter-of-factly.

Lucius smiled. "Believe me, Alastair, after all the things I have witnessed, to me you are young. So tell me, why do you believe I'm angry?"

"I should have known the answers all along. But I was so focused on the problem of time being altered, lives were changed, it shouldn't have happened...and the peer pressure from the group...my anger about my early death..."

Lucius nodded pensively. "Yes," he interrupted. "Anger is one emotion that can eat at one like a maggot and cause us to lose focus. I understand your pain, but you will need to come to terms with it."

"I know. But I can still be disappointed."

"Just because we have passed into another realm, doesn't mean we stop having emotions," Lucius smiled. As for our group..."

"Miracles did occur, and everything turned out for the better, don't you think?" Alastair interrupted. However, it just seemed so unnecessary. What I mean is why? Why?" Alastair questioned.

"I think you already know the answer to that. But before you reply, I should tell you that I'm impressed by you."

"Impressed?" Alastair repeated, not understanding.

"Alastair, only a *few* have made a journey as such solo. Especially, the passage through the *Twelve Realms*! I am awestruck by your determination. But being strong-minded or determined is only part of it. I want you to tell me in *one* word, what do you think enabled you to travel so far into the realm?"

Alastair looked off into the distance at the beautiful rays of sun shining through the trees. After a few moments of deep thought, his lips slowly curled, as a big angelic smile formed on his face. He turned and looked into the eyes of the great angel and uttered, "*Faith,*" Alastair said confidently, grinning as if he had just solved the theory of relativity. "I never needed my wings or angel bracelet to solve problems. As your *faith* gets stronger and grows...you don't need these things or magic. If you live your life through *faith and prayer*…if you pray more and leave it in God's hands, he will help you."

Alastair stopped and took a deep breath before he continued. "Not only did I forget about praying, but I lost faith. I can't imagine what the Lord must think of me. Ugh! I'm doomed. How could I have possibly forgotten my upbringing, which was rooted in faith and prayer? I spent my life, as short as it was, building houses of worship…and...I've disappointed the Lord, my family, and myself."

Lucius nodded, "And…"

"God wasn't going to answer me. He knew what was going on the entire time. He gave me what I believe that training group referred to as a 'time out.'" He laughed. "But seriously, I lost my way and lost faith. I was *so lost* that I forgot about the power of prayer. Instead of listening, I pleaded, bargained, and schemed. I was no better than those trainees. When I started praying I wasn't sincere because I was desperate. So desperate, that I even started negotiating with God," he shook his head in disbelief. "And for that, I'm truly sorry. If you have and stay in faith, God will guide you through."

Lucius' eyes beamed brightly as he nodded and whispered, "Alastair, you have passed your test."

Alastair nodded and immediately understood. *"That unruly group was purposely sent to me. I shouldn't have been so impatient. I should have followed the guidelines, if only…if only I prayed and stayed in faith. If only I had trusted in the Lord. Trusted my own relationship with him as he was with me the entire time. I was asking for help and it was there all the time.* You, Raphael, and Thelonious, *told me to pray and I didn't listen.* I was told to go back, but you and everyone let me continue on my path because we have free will, and nobody can mess with free will."

Lucius nodded and urged Alastair to continue. "And…"

"And God lines things up to steer us back to him. He has it all under control. I should have prayed *more* and prayed because I meant it, and not just to get out of the mess I made. I never really asked God for help or to guide me. I also forgot that prayers might not be answered in *my* time frame. God gives us what we need and not what we want."

Alastair looked upward and then back at Lucius. "We go to God because he can fix it and we want to put it behind us. I was so stressed that I forgot there was a process and sometimes the process has consequences.

Alastair glanced at Lucius who was nodding and added, "But you already knew that."

Lucius smiled reflectively. "Alastair, there is a very respectable and extremely gifted female pastor, Pastor Marcia Stanford, perhaps you've heard of her?"

Alastair shook his head.

"Anyway, she is someone I follow in the earthly realm. She said in a sermon once, "God tests and stretches you…God stands still until you understand it…sometimes he uses circumstances to get our attention because we're not listening. God is not going to jump up and fix the mess until we fully comprehend what we've done. He stands still until we're ready to get it and only then will he listen," Lucius finished. After a brief pause he added, "Did you ever stop and think that perhaps *all the people involved* were not listening either or needed help too?"

Alastair looked bewildered as to how this could apply to him when he was already dead. As if reading his mind, Lucius said, "And yes, Alastair, even in death…"

"…We continue to be tested," Alastair finished; his face brightened as if suddenly someone hit him over the head with the answers. "All those people I watched were being tested too. I am utterly ashamed of my behavior, even with *all my knowledge* and training, after thousands of years, I grew stale," he said regretfully.

"It was *I* who needed to make some major changes. *I* should have embraced the young angel supervisor who was put in place to deal with the new technology. I should have asked for more help; instead, I was too busy trying to live up to the expectation of my level of achievement, *Angel of the Twelfth Order,*" he emphasized sourly. "I had forgotten the basic, fundamentals of all our angel training and spiritual life. When I tried to handle the situation on my own, I only made things worse."

"Nobody is perfect, Alastair. And yes, we all are tested daily even after death."

Alastair looked pensive. "Gemma, she had her own assignment and test too, I gather?"

Lucius nodded. "In many ways, everything, including people, is all connected. There is always a *reason* for everything."

"Unfortunately, I'd forgotten all of it," Alastair said sadly. "But how did you know I would make it through the Twelve Realms?"

"It's simple. You were resolute! You didn't look back. Your determination, your fortitude, and dedication is why *you* were chosen."

Alastair beamed, understanding, when a familiar loud beeping interrupted his thoughts. He quickly looked about then immediately lifted the sleeve of his cloak and noticed his angel device had returned. His smile turned to a frown as he read the message, "This is absurd," he shouted. "My bracelet returns and the first thing I receive is a meaningless advertisement reminding me about an extended warranty on my wings. Do you know how many times I've already listened to this? My fragile nerves can't take it," he cried.

Non-pulsed, Lucius shrugged, "I suggest you get accustomed to it. I agree it's a nuisance of the utmost proportions that unfortunately has followed us into the heavenly realm. Technology, it's such an intriguing part of man's progress, but at the same time, frustrating and challenging. Nonetheless, when you entered your angel code into the device, you activated and prompted the re-occurring message."

Alastair's jaw dropped at the revelation. His eyes widened in disbelief as he recalled the incident, and how he tried to trick the talking machine at the information pole by pushing zero. "Alastair, you should have remembered whether in the earthly or heavenly realm, there *are no shortcuts.*"

"But, but can't the Lord fix it?" he asked, aghast.

Lucius shrugged unflappably. "I'd like to think *we* are possibly being tested or maybe the Lord has a sense of humor, as it seems no matter what the remedy, it has continued to cause great stress to *both* the earthly and celestial population. It's out of my control. Perhaps if you just sign up for the extended warranty, it will stop," he said cheerfully.

"Don't be ridiculous. My wings are in perfect condition. I wouldn't waste my money," he spat irritably.

"Well, I'm confident you will find a way to deal with the technological nuisance, which I can assure you will not go away!"

Alastair's eyes grew wider. He frowned, disappointed.

Lucius shrugged, "Now is there anything else before we move on?"

Alastair nodded. "Yes," he said as he ran his hand through his beard. "There is a part of the story that was never resolved. It has gaps."

"Really?" Lucius asked as he turned toward Alastair and looked at him strangely. "Such as?"

"Well, I sense something else is going on with Doctor Carter…his guilt was so…I don't know…it was so overwhelming…I feel there is something missing."

Lucius chuckled knowingly. The pupils in his eyes gleamed like perfect diamonds. "I knew I was right," he smirked. "I knew you were the right choice."

Alastair looked bewildered.

"Alastair, you were right when you said you were guilty of not evolving with the times and it is partially our fault. You see the Twelve Realms is such an ancient order and because it did not adapt and change, well, you see what happened to you."

Alastair was still confused. "Are you dissolving the group? What about my rank and my family…"

Lucius folded his hands. "Not in the least. We are, however, going to make some changes."

Alastair's brow arched in question.

Lucius continued smiling and rose. "We have a new challenge for you. A new division has been established. In order to evolve with the changes in humanity we have learned we must advance further," he stated. "Come," he gestured assuredly. "We'll discuss the details of your new assignment. But before we do anything, we must make one more stop."

Alastair's face dropped.

"After several years at the Reflection Pond, you my friend, have the stench of a garbage heap in an alley way, and are in need of a bath," he laughed heartedly. "And some new robes," he added while smirking.

Alastair breathed a sigh of relief and silently prayed they were heading toward the thermal gardens he had once heard about.

As they walked toward an unknown destination Alastair moved with a newfound confidence and was excited about his next journey. He didn't have to look over his shoulder as he could already feel his angel wings had returned.

Echoing through the atmosphere was the now recognizable beeping pattern signaling another incoming notification for the extended warranty for his wings. "Really Lucius…how do you possibly expect me to…"

The beeping and voices faded into the distant heavenly realm as they disappeared from the quadrant.

THE END

From the Authors Desk

s I stated in my introduction the Twelve Realms was conceived as I observed the changing landscape on my commute to and from work.

Commuting, especially in New Jersey, is always fraught with perils and challenges. Most days just trying to get to work tests every nerve and muscle in your body! There are construction, traffic delays, detours, tolls, missed signs, dodging debris from items not secured properly, the occasional oddities like the plane that landed on the Ninth Street bridge in Ocean City, speeding, there is always someone getting pulled over and, finally, whether or not my coins would be accepted when thrown in the basket at the toll plaza. An ongoing battle with my husband rages on as to why I refuse to get EZ Pass!

In addition, there is the *weather*. The weather often changes from exit to exit. Going from a light drizzle to fog, to torrential downpours, back to fog, and sun all in one hour is not uncommon in the direction I travel.

But through it all I couldn't help but notice views of the bay, smells of the marsh, and salt water from the ocean or intra-coastal waterways. Or the brilliant sun as it shines through the Pine Barrens and other dense foliage. Eagles, hawks, and other bird species of the Jersey Shore fly freely in the dazzling blue and colorful skies of the rising and setting sun, as it cast strong reflections on the water and landscape.

As the seasons changed so do the animals. Herds of deer, fawns, turkeys, are out and about. If you're lucky, you might catch a piebald deer or see a hawk with his wings extended, drying his feathers in a tree in the morning. And just before exit 48 for Port Republic and Smithville, there is a stretch of road that curves, twists, rising and extending over a body of water. As you go over the small bridge, and on a clear day when the weather is perfect, looming in the distance is the Atlantic City casinos. Through sun and fog, rising like Gods, or false gods, beacons for the promise of monetary or financial fortune, only for those who dare to take a chance.

This *view* was my inspiration for the gleaming, white tower that Alastair *is trying to and believes he needs to reach for help and answers*. Perhaps if Alastair just, "stayed in faith," as my mother likes to remind me, things might have turned out differently for him.

My goal was *NOT* to write a book about religion, but to tell an interesting story, which somewhere along the way included how we move about dealing with the obstacles thrown at us daily and how *difficult* it can be to practice faith; how hard it can be to forget the basics when we're frazzled and anxious. I had already finished the manuscript and was in the process of editing when I started feeling anxious. Did I capture Alastair and his dilemma? Did I get it right?

On July 7, 2021, I stopped by to see Pastor Marcia at work. I *hadn't* told her anything about my latest book. I just started asking about the difference between praying just to pray and other hypothetical questions. *She looked at me as if I was the most troubled soul in the world.* I voraciously took notes as she spoke, came home that evening, printed out the *entire manuscript* for fact checking. Unbeknownst to her she had validated all my thoughts, and I knew I was on the right track with Alastair.

I ran into Marcia two days later said she was going to send me something she read pertaining to *our conversation*, hoping she would be able to help whatever was plaguing me. I hope she has a sense of humor and will be laughing hilariously as she reads the story!

My mother, suspicious about all my questions about the saints, wanted to know what I was up to. I explained it was research for a story idea I was working on. As a child she would have told me to get the Bible or encyclopedia and *look it up*; instead, she now told me to Google it! Days later, I received a package in the mail from my mother – a calendar featuring saints with the Blessed Virgin Mary – straight from the Basilica of the National Shrine of the Immaculate Conception! Just in case I need a refresher course!

Santiago de Compostela and Ste-Foy are actual pilgrimage road churches constructed during the Middle Ages. These were churches people journeyed to for the purpose of hoping to see or touch a famous relic that they believed had special powers – perhaps to restore illness or perform some other miracle. Ste-Foy was in Conques, France. Foy, meaning Faith, was named for a nine-year-old girl, Foy, who in the fourth century was killed for her Christian philosophies.

Another famous pilgrimage was to the place where the apostle Saint James may have been buried – at Santiago de Compostela, in Spain. Alastair equates his journey to see God, like that of a pilgrimage he took to these places as a boy. This was just to give an idea of his age. Alastair lived sometime in the Middle Ages and worked on the cathedrals as I alluded to in the story.

The Twelfth Order was created for him.

The fictitious town of Hunters Glen, Seminole Montana, and other names of hospitals, and schools are also made up – along with the angels and characters of the celestial realm.

The answer to Alastair's troubles can be found in a code in the Twelve Realms in the beginning of the story. Were you able to locate it?

About the Author

Michele A. Fabiano was born and raised in New Jersey. She earned a bachelor's degree in Art History from Rutgers University and master's degree in Art History from The City College of New York. She is the author of *The Agony Continues: Michelangelo's Search for Art in 20th Century NYC*, *You're Not a Fucking Bachelor Anymore* and *The Donation*.

Michele has taught art history courses at the City College of New York, The University of North Alabama, Brookdale Community College in Northern New Jersey, and Ocean County Community College in central New Jersey.

She has worked as a freelance writer and photographer for Riverview's and Neighbor's Magazine. She also authored the college textbook *From Cubs to Lions Your Guide to Success at the University of North Alabama*.

Michele resides in New Jersey with her husband Joe and two dogs.

Author's Note

Dear Reader,

I hope you enjoyed reading *Alastair's Dilemma* as much as I enjoyed writing it. Please do me a favor and write a review on Amazon. The reviews are important, and your support is greatly appreciated.

Thank you,

Michele A. Fabiano

The Agony Continues

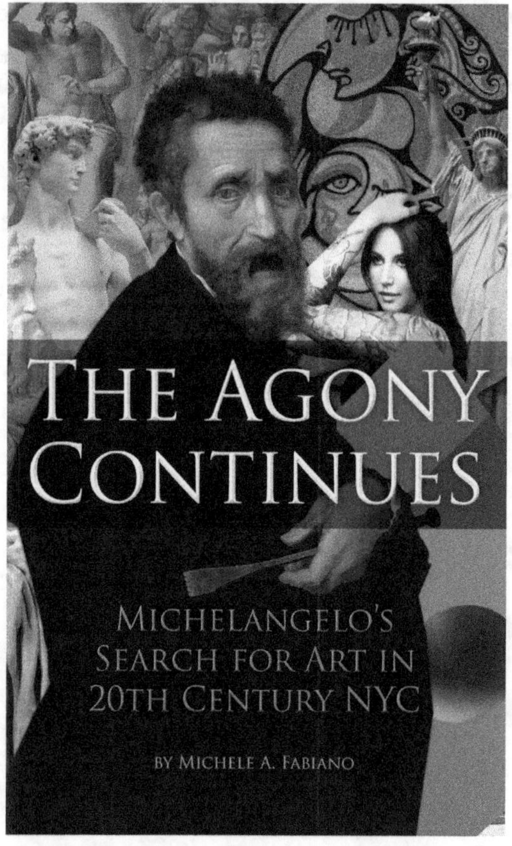

St. Peter grants Michelangelo a vacation request, allowing him to travel to the twentieth century to view art. Not only does Michelangelo want to see what artists have been creating after his death but he also desires confirmation that his own work is remembered.

As Michelangelo roams about New York City he meets a variety of people who attempt to help him make sense of modern sculpture, painting, and architecture.

Michelangelo compares everything he sees to specific works he created throughout his life. He finally meets Vinnie, a tough city boy, who agrees to help with his journey.

Trying to convince contemporary society what 'real art' is becomes infuriating as Michelangelo holds amusing discussions about enlarged, abstract geometric shapes, gigantic statues rising out of the river, graffiti, tattoos, and more which he vehemently contends cannot be art.

His conversations reflect his historical interactions with political figures who commissioned art, his family, and other noteworthy artists.

Time is running out as St. Peter has allowed Michelangelo to spend only three weeks in the twentieth century. Michelangelo's frustration mounts as he struggles to comprehend the modern world and educate people on the art of the past.

You're Not a F*cking Bachelor Anymore

What happens after you get married? After the wedding, after the honeymoon, and you move in together? What happens when you combine assets, share space, need to make decisions together, and regard one another?

My breaking point came when I ran out of the bathroom, naked, enraged and screaming nonsensically at my husband as to why he couldn't put a roll of toilet paper on the toilet paper holder! I am an educated person with a master's degree trying to debate logically about the function of a plastic roller and toilet paper! Like a lawyer I'd provide endless, rational arguments for this simple task to no avail.

In addition to toilet paper, we fought over mundane objects including lint traps, the TV remote, coffee, money, and other routine responsibilities of daily living. The quarreling and disputes became ridiculous. When had we become so unreasonable? When had I become so irrational?

This book is for anyone in a relationship or contemplating getting involved in one.

The Donation

A strange donation of Egyptian jars to a museum leaves celebrity museum director John Pierre Boudreau and the museum board at odds. The shady board members have their own secrets as they debate on the validity of the gift.

Are these artifacts fake?
How can they be verified?

When their secret is unlocked a now rapidly aging John Pierre must race against time as they try to discover the truth before the jars get into the wrong hands, those of the great God Anubis.

Surprises emerge for everyone as the portal of the past is unlocked and the race through ancient Egypt begins.

Coming Soon

Matchmakers From Heaven

The renowned Doctor Aaron Carter has recently passed away and to his surprise can't get into Heaven; instead, he is sent to spend eternity with his deceased first wife. In order to get through the pearly gates he *and* his first wife must right a wrong that involves their oldest son Logan.

They have one year to complete their task, which begins when Logan receives a note from his estrange, dead father that to his consternation brings him back to Montana, where he was born and now must live for one year in order to inherit his father's estate *and* money he desperately needs.

Logan is not exactly ready for a trip down memory lane as he attempts to solve his father's cryptic letter. While he searches for the truth, he meets Samantha, a woman working at a dog park. Logan inadvertently feels he is the cause of her injury and gets more than he bargained for when he decides to nurse her back to health along with her three dogs. In return, Samantha agrees to try and help him solve his mystery in the upcoming *Matchmakers from Heaven*.

KCM Publishing
a division of KCM Digital Media, LLC

www.ingramcontent.com/pod-product-compliance
Lightning Source LLC
Chambersburg PA
CBHW071957190726
48293CB00001B/63